CURTAIN
&
THE MYSTERIOUS
AFFAIR AT STYLES

AGATHA CHRISTIE

CURTAIN

&

The Mysterious
Affair at Styles

INTERNATIONAL COLLECTORS LIBRARY
GARDEN CITY, NEW YORK

CURTAIN

1

Who is there who has not felt a sudden startled pang at reliving an old experience or feeling an old emotion?

"*I have done this before . . .*"

Why do those words always move one so profoundly?

That was the question I asked myself as I sat in the train watching the flat Essex landscape outside.

How long ago was it that I had taken this selfsame journey? Had felt (ridiculously) that the best of life was over for me! Wounded in that war that for me would always be *the* war—the war that was wiped out now by a second and a more desperate war.

It had seemed in 1916 to young Arthur Hastings that he was already old and mature. How little had I realized that, for me, life was only then beginning.

I had been journeying, though I did not know it, to meet the man whose influence over me was to shape and mould my life. Actually I had been going to stay with my old friend John Cavendish, whose mother, recently remarried, had a country house named "Styles." A pleasant renewing of old acquaintanceships, that was all I had thought it, not foreseeing that I was shortly to plunge into all the dark embroilments of a mysterious murder.

It was at Styles that I had met again that strange little man, Hercule Poirot, whom I had first come across in Belgium.

How well I remembered my amazement when I had seen the limping figure with the large moustache coming up the village street.

Hercule Poirot! Since those days he had been my dearest friend; his influence had moulded my life. In company with him, in the hunting down of yet another murderer, I had met my wife, the truest and sweetest companion any man could have had.

She lay now in Argentine soil, dying as she would have wished, with no long-drawn-out suffering or feebleness of old age. But she had left a very lonely and unhappy man behind her.

Ah! If I could go back—live life all over again. If this could have been that day in 1916 when I first travelled to Styles . . . What changes had taken place since then! What gaps among the familiar faces. Styles itself had been sold by the Cavendishes. John Cavendish was dead, though his wife Mary (that fascinating, enigmatical creature) was still alive, living in Devonshire. Lawrence was living with his wife and children in South Africa. Changes—changes everywhere.

But one thing, strangely enough, was the same. I was going to Styles to meet Hercule Poirot.

How stupefied I had been to receive his letter, with its heading Styles Court, Styles, Essex.

I had not seen my old friend for nearly a year. The last time I had seen him I had been shocked and saddened. He was now a very old man, and almost crippled with arthritis. He had gone to Egypt in the hopes of improving his health, but had returned, so his letter told me, rather worse than better. Nevertheless, he wrote cheerfully . . .

"And does it not intrigue you, my friend, to see the address from which I write? It recalls old memories, does it not? Yes, I am here, at Styles. Figure to yourself, it is now what they call a guest house. Run by one of your so British old colonels—very 'old school tie' and 'Poona.' It is his wife, *bien entendu,* who makes it pay. She is a good manager, that one, but the tongue like vinegar, and the poor Colonel, he suffers much from it. If it were me, I would take a hatchet to her!

"I saw their advertisement in the paper, and the fancy took me to go once again to the place which first was my home in this country. At my age one enjoys reliving the past.

"Then, figure to yourself, I find here a gentleman, a baronet who is a friend of the employer of your daughter. (That phrase, it sounds a little like the French exercise, does it not?)

"Immediately I conceive a plan. He wishes to induce the Franklins to come here for the summer. I in my turn will persuade you, and we shall be all together, *en famille*. It will be most agreeable. Therefore, mon cher Hastings, *dépêchez vous*, arrive with the utmost celerity. I have commanded for you a room with bath (it is modernized now, you comprehend, the dear old 'Styles') and disputed the price with Mrs. Colonel Luttrell until I have made an arrangement *très bon marche*.

"The Franklins and your charming Judith have been here for some days. It is all arranged, so make no histories. *A bientôt*. Yours always, Hercule Poirot."

The propsect was alluring, and I fell in with my old friend's wishes without demur. I had no ties and no settled home. Of my children, one boy was in the Navy, the other married and running the ranch in the Argentine. My daughter Grace was married to a soldier and was at present in India. My remaining child, Judith, was the one whom secretly I had always loved best, although I had never for one moment understood her. A queer, dark, secretive child, with a passion for keeping her own counsel, which had sometimes affronted and distressed me. My wife had been more understanding. It was, she assured me, no lack of trust or confidence on Judith's part, but a kind of fierce compulsion. But she, like myself, was sometimes worried about the child. Judith's feelings, she said, were too intense, too concentrated, and her instinctive reserve deprived her of any safety valve. She had queer fits of brooding silence and a fierce, almost bitter power of partisanship. Her brains were the best of the family and we gladly fell in with her wish for a university education. She had taken her B.Sc. about a year ago, and had then taken the post of secretary to a doctor who was engaged in research work connected with tropical disease. His wife was somewhat of an invalid.

I had occasionally had qualms as to whether Judith's absorption in her work and devotion to her employer were not signs that she might be losing her heart, but the businesslike footing of their relationship assured me.

Judith was, I believed, fond of me, but she was very undemonstrative by nature, and she was often scornful and impatient of what she called my sentimental and outworn ideas. I was, frankly, a little nervous of my daughter!

At this point my meditations were interrupted by the train drawing up at the station of Styles St. Mary. That at least had not changed. Time had passed it by. It was still perched up in the midst of fields, with apparently no reason for existence.

As my taxi passed through the village, though, I realized the passage of years. Styles St. Mary was altered out of all recognition. Petrol stations, a cinema, two more inns and rows of council houses.

Presently we turned in at the gate of the Styles. Here we seemed to recede again from modern times. The park was much as I remembered it, but the drive was badly kept and much overgrown with weeds—growing up over the gravel. We turned a corner and came in view of the house. It was unaltered from the outside and badly needed a coat of paint.

As on my arrival all those years ago, there was a woman's figure stooping over one of the garden beds. My heart missed a beat. Then the figure straightened up and came towards me, and I laughed at myself. No greater contrast to the robust Evelyn Howard could have been imagined.

This was a frail elderly lady with an abundance of curly white hair, pink cheeks, and a pair of cold pale blue eyes that were widely at variance with the easy geniality of her manner, which was frankly a shade too gushing for my taste.

"It'll be Captain Hastings now, won't it?" she demanded. "And me with my hands all over dirt and not able to shake hands. We're delighted to see you here—the amount we've heard about you! I must introduce myself. I'm Mrs. Luttrell. My husband and I bought this place in a fit of madness and have been trying to make a paying concern of it. I never thought the day would come when I'd be a hotelkeeper! But I'll warn you, Captain Hastings, I'm a very businesslike woman. I pile up the extras all I know how."

We both laughed as though at an excellent joke, but it occurred to me that what Mrs. Luttrell had just said was in all probability the literal truth. Behind the veneer of her charming old-lady manner, I caught a glimpse of flintlike hardness.

Although Mrs. Luttrell occasionally affected a faint brogue, she had no Irish blood. It was a mere affectation.

I inquired after my friend.

"Ah, poor little M. Poirot. The way he's been looking forward to your coming. It would melt a heart of stone. Terribly sorry I am for him, suffering the way he does."

We were walking towards the house and she was peeling off her gardening gloves.

"And your pretty daughter, too," she went on. "What a lovely girl she is. We all admire her tremendously. But I'm old-fashioned, you know, and it seems to me a shame and a sin that a girl like that, that ought to be going to parties and dancing with young men, should spend her time cutting up rabbits and bending over a microscope all day. Leave that sort of thing to the frumps, I say."

"Where is Judith?" I asked. "Is she somewhere about?"

Mrs. Luttrell made what children call "a face."

"Ah, the poor girl! She's cooped up in that studio place down at the bottom of the garden. Dr. Franklin rents it from me and he's had it all fitted up. Hutches of guinea pigs he's got there, the poor creatures, and mice and rabbits. I'm not sure that I like all this science, Captain Hastings. Ah, here's my husband."

Colonel Luttrell had just come round the corner of the house. He was a very tall, attenuated old man with a cadaverous face, mild blue eyes and a habit of irresolutely tugging at his little white moustache.

He had a vague, rather nervous manner.

"Ah, George, here's Captain Hastings arrived."

Colonel Luttrell shook hands. "You came by the five—er—forty, eh?"

"What else should he have come by?" said Mrs. Luttrell sharply. "And what does it matter anyway? Take him up and show him his room, George. And then maybe he'd like to go straight to M. Poirot—or would you rather have tea first?"

I assured her that I did not want tea and would prefer to go and greet my friend.

Colonel Luttrell said, "Right. Come along. I expect—er— they'll have taken your things up already—eh, Daisy?"

Mrs. Luttrell said tartly, "That's your business, George. I've been gardening. I can't see to everything."

"No, no, of course not. I—I'll see to it, my dear."

I followed him up the front steps. In the doorway we encountered a grey-haired man, slightly built, who was hurrying out with a pair of field glasses. He limped, and had a boyish, eager face. He said, stammering slightly, "There's a pair of n-nesting birds down by the sycamore."

As we went into the hall, Luttrell said, "That's Stephen Norton. Nice fellow. Crazy about birds."

In the hall itself, a very big man was standing by the table. He had obviously just finished telephoning. Looking up, he said, "I'd like to hang, draw and quarter all contractors and builders. Never get anything done right, curse 'em."

His wrath was so comical and so rueful that we both laughed. I felt attracted at once towards the man. He was very good-looking, though a man well over fifty, with a deeply tanned face. He looked as though he had led an out-of-door life, and he looked, too, the type of man that is becoming more and more rare—an Englishman of the old school, straightforward, fond of out-of-door life, and the kind of man who can command.

I was hardly surprised when Colonel Luttrell introduced him as Sir William Boyd Carrington. He had been, I knew, governor of a province in India, where he had been a signal success. He was also renowned as a first-class shot and big game hunter. The sort of man, I reflected sadly, that we no longer seemed to breed in these degenerate days.

"Aha," he said. "I'm glad to meet in the flesh that famous personage *mon ami* Hastings." He laughed. "The dear old Belgian fellow talks about you a lot, you know. And then, of course, we've got your daughter here. She's a fine girl."

"I don't suppose Judith talks about me much," I said, smiling.

"No, no, far too modern. These girls nowadays always seem embarrassed at having to admit to a father or mother at all."

"Parents," I said, "are practically a disgrace."

He laughed. "Oh, well—I don't suffer that way. I've no children, worse luck. Your Judith is a very good-looking wench, but terribly highbrow. I find it rather alarming." He picked up the telephone receiver again. "Hope you don't mind, Luttrell, if I start damning your exchange to hell. I'm not a patient man."

"Do 'em good," said Luttrell.

He led the way upstairs and I followed him. He took me along the left wing of the house to a door at the end, and I realized that Poirot had chosen for me the room I had occupied before.

There were changes here. As I walked along the corridor, some of the doors were open and I saw that the old-fashioned large bedrooms had been partitioned off so as to make several smaller ones.

My own room, which had not been large, was unaltered save for the installation of hot and cold water, and part of it had been partitioned off to make a small bathroom. It was furnished in a cheap modern style which rather disappointed me. I should have preferred a style more nearly approximating the architecture of the house itself.

My luggage was in my room and the Colonel explained that Poirot's room was exactly opposite. He was about to take me there when a sharp cry of "George" echoed up from the hall below.

Colonel Luttrell started like a nervous horse. His hand went to his lips.

"I—I—sure you're all right? Ring for what you want—"

"*George.*"

"Coming, my dear, coming."

He hurried off down the corridor. I stood for a moment looking after him. Then, with my heart beating slightly faster, I crossed the corridor and rapped on the door of Poirot's room.

2

Nothing is so sad, in my opinion, as the devastation wrought by age.

My poor friend. I have described him many times. Now to convey to you the difference. Crippled with arthritis, he propelled himself about in a wheelchair. His once plump frame had fallen in. He was a thin little man now. His face was lined and wrinkled. His moustache and hair, it is true, were still of a jet-black colour, but candidly, though I would not for the world have hurt his feelings by saying so to him, this was a mistake. There comes a moment when hair dye is only too painfully obvious. There had been a time when I had been surprised to learn that the blackness of Poirot's hair came out of a bottle. But now the theatricality was apparent and merely created the impression that he wore a wig and had adorned his upper lip to amuse the children!

Only his eyes were the same as ever, shrewd and twinkling, and now—yes, undoubtedly—softened with emotion:

"Ah, *mon ami* Hastings—*mon ami* Hastings . . ."

I bent my head and, as was his custom, he embraced me warmly.

"*Mon ami* Hastings!"

He leaned back, surveying me with his head a little on one side.

"Yes, just the same—the straight back, the broad shoulders, the grey of the hair—*très distingué*. You know, my friend, you have worn well. *Les femmes,* they still take an interest in you? Yes?"

"Really, Poirot," I protested. "Must you—"

"But I assure you, my friend, it is a test—it is the test. When the very young girls come and talk to you kindly, oh, so kindly—it is the end! 'The poor old man,' they say; 'we must be nice to him. It must be so awful to be like that.' But you, Hastings—*vous êtes encore jeune.* For you there are still possibilities. That is right, twist your moustache, hunch your shoulders—I see it is as I say— you would not look so self-conscious otherwise."

I burst out laughing.

"You really are the limit, Poirot. And how are you yourself?"

"Me," said Poirot with a grimace. "I am a wreck. I am a ruin. I cannot walk. I am crippled and twisted. Mercifully I can still feed myself, but otherwise I have to be attended to like a baby. Put to bed, washed and dressed. *Enfin,* it is not amusing, that. Mercifully, though the outside decays, the core is still sound."

"Yes, indeed. The best heart in the world."

"The heart? Perhaps. I was not referring to the heart. The brain, *mon cher,* is what I mean by the core. My brain, it still functions magnificently."

I could at least perceive clearly that no deterioration of the brain in the direction of modesty had taken place.

"And you like it here?" I asked.

Poirot shrugged his shoulders.

"It suffices. It is not, you comprehend, the Ritz. No, indeed. The room I was in when I first came here was both small and in-adequately furnished. I moved to this one with no increase of price. Then, the cooking, it is English at its worst. Those Brussels sprouts so enormous, so hard, that the English like so much. The potatoes boiled and either hard or falling to pieces. The vegeta-bles that taste of water, water, and again water. The complete ab-sence of the salt and pepper in any dish—" He paused expres-sively.

"It sounds terrible," I said.

"I do not complain," said Poirot, and proceeded to do so. "And there is also the modernization, so called. The bathrooms, the taps everywhere, and what comes out of them? Lukewarm water, *mon ami*, at most hours of the day. And the towels, so thin, so meagre!"

"There is something to be said for the old days," I said thoughtfully. I remembered the clouds of steam which had gushed from the hot tap of the one bathroom Styles had originally possessed, one of those bathrooms in which an immense bath with mahogany sides had reposed proudly in the middle of the bathroom floor. Remembered, too, the immense bath towels, and the frequent shining brass cans of boiling hot water that stood in one's old-fashioned basin.

"But one must not complain," said Poirot again. "I am content to suffer—for a good cause."

A sudden thought struck me.

"I say, Poirot, you're not—er—hard up, are you? I know the war hit investments very badly—"

Poirot reassured me quickly.

"No, no, my friend. I am in most comfortable circumstances. Indeed, I am rich. It is not the economy that brings me here."

"Then that's all right," I said.

I went on:

"I think I can understand your feeling. As one gets on, one tends more and more to revert to the old days. One tries to recapture old emotions. I find it painful to be here, in a way, and yet it brings back to me a hundred old thoughts and emotions that I'd quite forgotten I ever felt. I daresay you feel the same."

"Not in the least. I do not feel like that at all."

"They were good days," I said sadly.

"You may speak for yourself, Hastings. For me, my arrival at Styles St. Mary was a sad and painful time. I was a refugee, wounded, exiled from home and country, existing by charity in a foreign land. No, it was not gay. I did not know then that England would come to be my home and that I should find happiness here."

"I had forgotten that," I admitted.

"Precisely. You attribute always to others the sentiments that you yourself experience. Hastings was happy—everybody was happy!"

"No, no," I protested, laughing.

"And in any case it is not true," continued Poirot; "you look back, you say, the tears rising in your eyes, 'Oh, the happy days. Then I was young.' But indeed, my friend, you were not so happy as you think. You had recently been severely wounded, you were fretting at being no longer fit for active service, you had just been depressed beyond words by your sojourn in a dreary convalescent home, and as far as I remember, you proceeded to complicate matters by falling in love with two women at the same time."

I laughed and flushed.

"What a memory you have, Poirot."

"Ta ta ta—I remember now the melancholy sigh you heaved as you murmured fatuities about two lovely women."

"Do you remember what you said? You said, 'And neither of them is for you! Never mind. Console yourself, *mon ami*. We may hunt together again and then—'"

I stopped. For Poirot and I had gone hunting again to France and it was there that I had met the one woman . . .

Gently my friend patted my arm.

"I know, Hastings, I know. The wound is still fresh. But do not dwell on it, do not look back. Instead look forward."

I made a gesture of disgust.

"Look forward? What is there to look forward to?"

"*Eh bien*, my friend, there is work to be done."

"Work? Where?"

"Here."

I stared at him.

"Just now," said Poirot, "you asked me why I had come here. You may not have observed that I gave you no answer. I will give you the answer now. I am here to hunt down a murderer."

I stared at him with even more astonishment. For a moment I thought he was rambling.

"You really mean that?"

"But certainly I mean it. For what other reason did I urge you to join me? My limbs, they are no longer active, but my brain, as I told you, is unimpaired. My rule, remember, has been always the same—sit back and think. That I still can do. In fact, it is the only thing possible to me. For the more active side of the campaign I shall have with me my invaluable Hastings."

"You really mean it?" I gasped.

"Of course I mean it. You and I, Hastings, *are going hunting once again.*"

It took me some minutes to grasp that Poirot was really in earnest.

Fantastic though his statement sounded, I had no reason to doubt his judgment.

With a slight smile he said, "At last you are convinced. At first you imagined, did you not, that I had the softening of the brain?"

"No, no," I said hastily. "Only this seems such an unlikely place."

"Ah, you think so?"

"Of course I haven't seen all the people yet—"

"Whom have you seen?"

"Just the Luttrells, and a man called Norton, seems an inoffensive chap, and Boyd Carrington—I must say I took the greatest fancy to him."

Poirot nodded.

"Well, Hastings, I will tell you this. When you have seen the rest of the household, my statement will seem to you just as impossible as it is now."

"Who else is there?"

"The Franklins—Doctor and Mrs.—the hospital nurse who attends to Mrs. Franklin, your daughter Judith. Then there is a man called Allerton, something of a lady-killer, and a Miss Cole, a woman of about thirty-five. They are all, let me tell you, very nice people."

"And one of them is a murderer?"

"And one of them is a murderer."

"But why—how—why should you think—?"

I found it hard to frame my questions; they tumbled over each other.

"Calm yourself, Hastings. Let us begin from the beginning. Reach me, I pray you, that small box from the bureau. *Bien*. And now the key—so—"

Unlocking the dispatch case, he took from it a mass of typescript and newspaper clippings.

"You can study these at your leisure, Hastings. For the moment I should not bother with the newspaper cuttings. They are merely the press accounts of various tragedies, occasionally inaccurate, sometimes suggestive. To give you an idea of the cases, I suggest that you should read through the précis I have made."

Deeply interested, I started reading.

Case A. Etherington

Leonard Etherington. Unpleasant habits—took drugs and also drank. A peculiar and sadistic character. Wife young and attractive. Desperately unhappy with him. Etherington died, apparently of food poisoning. Doctor not satisfied. As a result of autopsy, death discovered to be due to arsenical poisoning. Supply of weed killer in the house, but ordered a long time previously. Mrs. Etherington arrested and charged with murder. She had recently been friends with a man in Civil Service returning to India. No suggestion of actual infidelity, but evidence of deep sympathy between them. Young man had since become engaged to be married to girl he met 'on voyage out. Some doubt as to whether letter telling Mrs. Etherington of this fact was received by her after or before her husband's death. She herself says before. Evidence against her mainly circumstantial, absence of another likely suspect and accident highly unlikely. Great sympathy felt with her at trial owing to husband's character and the bad treatment she had received from him. Judge's summing up was in her favour, stressing that verdict must be beyond any reasonable doubt.

Mrs. Etherington was acquitted. General opinion, however, was that she was guilty. Her life afterwards very difficult owing to friends, etc., cold-shouldering her. She died as a result of taking an overdose of sleeping draught two years after the trial. Verdict of accidental death returned at inquest.

Case B. Sharples

Elderly spinster. An invalid. Difficult, suffering much pain. She was looked after by her niece, Freda Clay. Miss Sharples died as a result of an overdose of morphia. Freda Clay admitted an error, saying that her aunt's sufferings were so bad that she could not stand it and gave her more morphia to ease the pain. Opinion of police that act was deliberate, not a mistake, but they considered evidence insufficient on which to prosecute.

Case C. Riggs

Edward Riggs, agricultural labourer. Suspected his wife of infidelity with their lodger, Ben Craig. Craig and Mrs. Riggs found shot. Shots proved to be from Riggs's gun. Riggs gave himself up to the police, said he supposed he must have done it, but couldn't remember. His mind went blank, he said. Riggs sentenced to death, sentence afterwards commuted to penal servitude for life.

Case D. Bradley

Derek Bradley. Was carrying on an intrigue with a girl. His wife discovered this; she threatened to kill him. Bradley died of potassium cyanide administered in his beer. Mrs. Bradley arrested and tried for murder. Broke down under cross-examination. Convicted and hanged.

Case E. Litchfield

Elderly tyrant, Matthew Litchfield. Four daughters at home, not allowed any pleasures or money to spend. One evening on returning home, he was attacked outside his side door and killed by a blow on the head. Later, after police investigation, his eldest daughter, Margaret, walked into the police station and gave herself up for her father's murder. She did it, she said, in order that her younger sisters might be able to have a life of their own before it was too late. Litchfield left a large fortune. Margaret Litchfield was adjudged insane and committed to Broadmoor, but died shortly afterwards.

I read carefully, but with a growing bewilderment. Finally I put the paper down and looked inquiringly at Poirot.

"Well, *mon ami?*"

"I remember the Bradley case," I said slowly. "I read about it at the time. She was a very good-looking woman."

Poirot nodded.

"But you must enlighten me. What is all this about?"

"Tell me first what it amounts to in your eyes."

I was rather puzzled.

"What you gave me was an account of five different murders. They all occurred in different places and amongst different classes of people. Moreover, there seems no superficial resemblance between them. That is to say, one was a case of jealousy, one was an unhappy wife seeking to get rid of her husband, another had money for a motive, another was, you might say, unselfish in aim since the murderer did not try to escape punishment, and the fifth was frankly brutal, probably committed under the influence of drink.

I paused and said doubtfully:

"Is there something in common between them all that I have missed?"

"No, no, you have been very accurate in your summing up. The only point that you might have mentioned but did not, was the fact that in none of those cases did any real *doubt* exist."

"I don't think I understand?"

"Mrs. Etherington, for instance, was acquitted. But everybody, nevertheless, was quite certain that she did it. Freda Clay was not openly accused, but no one thought of any alternative solution of the crime. Riggs stated that he did not remember killing his wife and her lover, but there was never any question of anybody else having done so. Margaret Litchfield confessed. In each case, you see, Hastings, there was one clear suspect and no other."

I wrinkled my brow.

"Yes, that is true—but I don't see what particular inferences you draw from that."

"Ah, but you see, I am coming to a fact that you do not know as yet. Supposing, Hastings, that in each of these cases that I have outlined, there was one alien note common to them all?"

"What do you mean?"

Poirot said slowly:

"I intend, Hastings, to be very careful in what I say. Let me put it this way. There is a certain person—X. In none of these cases did X (apparently) have any motive in doing away with the victim. In one case, as far as I have been able to find out, X was actually two hundred miles away when the crime was committed. Nevertheless, I will tell you this. X was on intimate terms with Etherington, X lived for a time in the same village as Riggs, X was acquainted with Mrs. Bradley. I have a snap of X and Freda Clay walking together in the street, and X was near the house when old Matthew Litchfield died. What do you say to that?"

I stared at him. I said slowly:

"Yes, it's a bit too much. Coincidence might account for two cases, or even three, but five is a bit too thick. There must, unlikely as it seems, be some connection between these different murders."

"You assume, then, what I have assumed?"

"That X is the murderer? Yes."

"In that case, Hastings, you will be willing to go with me one step further. Let me tell you this. *X is in this house.*"

"Here? At Styles?"

"At Styles. What is the logical inference to be drawn from that?"

I knew what was coming as I said:

"Go on—say it."

Hercule Poirot said gravely:

"A murder will shortly be committed here—*here.*"

3

For a moment or two I stared at Poirot in dismay, then I reacted.

"No, it won't," I said. "You'll prevent that."

Poirot threw me an affectionate glance.

"My loyal friend. How much I appreciate your faith in me. *Tout de même*, I am not sure if it is justified in this case."

"Nonsense. Of course you can stop it."

Poirot's voice was grave as he said:

"Reflect a minute, Hastings. One can catch a murderer, yes. But how does one proceed to stop a murder?"

"Well, you—you—well, I mean—if you know beforehand—"

I paused rather feebly—for suddenly I saw the difficulties.

Poirot said:

"You see? It is not so simple. There are, in fact, only three methods. The first is to warn the victim. To put the victim on his or her guard. That does not always succeed, for it is unbelievably difficult to convince some people that they are in grave danger—possibly from someone near and dear to them. They are indignant and refuse to believe. The second course is to warn the murderer. To say, in language that is only slightly veiled: '*I know your intentions*. If so-and-so dies, my friend, *you* will most surely hang.' That succeeds more often than the first method, but even there it is likely to fail. For a murderer, my friend, is more conceited than any creature on this earth. A murderer is always more clever than anyone else—no one will ever suspect him or her—the police will be utterly baffled, et cetera. Therefore he (or she) goes ahead just the same, and all you can have is the satisfaction of hanging them afterwards." He paused and said thoughtfully:

"Twice in my life I have warned a murderer—once in Egypt, once elsewhere. In each case, the criminal was determined to kill . . . It may be so here."

"You said there was a third method," I reminded him.

"Ah yes. For that one needs the utmost ingenuity. You have to guess exactly how and when the blow is timed to fall and you have to be ready to step in at the exact psychological moment. You have to catch the murderer, if not quite red-handed, then guilty of the intention beyond any possible doubt.

"And that, my friend," went on Poirot, "is, I can assure you, a matter of great difficulty and delicacy, and I would not for a moment guarantee its success! I may be conceited, but I am not so conceited as *that*."

"Which method do you propose to try here?"

"Possibly all three. The first is the most difficult."

"Why? I should have thought it the easiest."

"Yes, if you know the intended victim. But do you not realize, Hastings, that here I do not know the victim?"

"What?"

I gave vent to the exclamation without reflecting. Then the difficulties of the position began to dawn on me. There was, there must be, some link connecting this series of crimes, but we did not know what that link was. The motive, the vitally important motive, was missing. And without knowing that, we could not tell who was threatened.

Poirot nodded as he saw by my face that I was realizing the difficulties of the situation.

"You see, my friend, it is not so easy."

"No," I said. "I see that. You have so far been able to find no connection between these varying cases?"

Poirot shook his head.

"Nothing."

I reflected again. In the A.B.C. crimes, we had to deal with what purported to be an alphabetical series, though in actuality it had turned out to be something very different.

I asked:

"There is, you are quite sure, no far-fetched financial motive— nothing, for instance, like you found in the case of Evelyn Carlisle?"

"No. You may be quite sure, my dear Hastings, that financial gain is the first thing for which I look."

That was true enough. Poirot has always been completely cynical about money.

I thought again. A vendetta of some kind? That was more in accordance with the facts. But even there, there seemed a lack of any connecting link. I recalled a story I had read of a series of purposeless murders—the clue being that the victims had happened to serve as members of a jury, and the crimes had been committed by a man whom they had condemned. It struck me that something of that kind would meet this case. I am ashamed to say that I kept the idea to myself. It would have been such a feather in my cap if I could go to Poirot with the solution.

Instead I asked:

"And now tell me, who is X?"

To my intense annoyance Poirot shook his head very decidedly.

"That, my friend, I do not tell."

"Nonsense. Why not?"

Poirot's eyes twinkled.

"Because, *mon cher*, you are still the same old Hastings. You have still the speaking countenance. I do not wish, you see, that you should sit staring at X with your mouth hanging open, your face saying plainly: 'This—this that I am looking at is a murderer.'"

"You might give me credit for a little dissimulation at need."

"When you try to dissimulate, it is worse. No, no, *mon ami*, we must be very incognito, you and I. Then, when we pounce, we pounce."

"You obstinate old devil," I said. "I've a good mind to—"

I broke off as there was a tap on the door. Poirot called, "Come in," and my daughter Judith entered.

I should like to describe Judith, but I've always been a poor hand at descriptions.

Judith is tall, she holds her head high, she has level dark brows and a very lovely line of cheek and jaw—severe in its austerity. She is grave and slightly scornful, and to my mind there has always hung about her a suggestion of tragedy.

Judith didn't come and kiss me—she is not that kind. She just smiled at me and said, "Hullo, Father."

Her smile was shy and a little embarrassed, but it made me feel that in spite of her undemonstrativeness she was pleased to see me.

"Well," I said, feeling foolish as I so often do with the younger generation, "I've got here."

"Very clever of you, darling," said Judith.

"I describe to him," said Poirot, "the cooking."

"Is it very bad?" asked Judith.

"You should not have to ask that, my child. Is it that you think of nothing but the test tubes and the microscopes? Your middle finger, it is stained with methylene blue. It is not a good thing for your husband if you take no interest in his stomach."

"I daresay I shan't have a husband."

"Certainly you will have a husband. What did the *bon Dieu* create you for?"

"Many things, I hope," said Judith.

"*Le mariage* first of all."

"Very well," said Judith. "You shall find me a nice husband and I will look after his stomach very carefully."

"She laughs at me," said Poirot. "Someday she will know how wise old men are."

There was another tap on the door and Dr. Franklin entered. He was a tall, angular young man of thirty-five, with a decided jaw, reddish hair, and bright blue eyes. He was the most ungainly man I had ever known, and was always knocking into things in an absent-minded way.

He cannoned into the screen round Poirot's chair and half

turning his head murmured "I beg your pardon" to it automatically.

I wanted to laugh, but Judith, I noted, remained quite grave. I suppose she was quite used to that sort of thing.

"You remember my father," said Judith.

Dr. Franklin started, shied nervously, screwed up his eyes and peered at me, then stuck out a hand, saying awkwardly:

"Of course, of course, how are you? I heard you were coming down."

He turned to Judith.

"I say, do you think we need change? If not, we might go on a bit after dinner. If we got a few more of those slides prepared—"

"No," said Judith. "I want to talk to my father."

"Oh yes. Oh, of course." Suddenly he smiled, an apologetic boyish smile. "I am sorry—I get so awfully wrapped up in a thing. It's quite unpardonable—makes me so selfish. Do forgive me."

The clock struck and Franklin glanced at it hurriedly.

"Good Lord, is it as late as that? I shall get into trouble. Promised Barbara I'd read to her before dinner."

He grinned at us both and hurried out, colliding with the doorpost as he went out.

"How is Mrs. Franklin?" I asked.

"The same and rather more so," said Judith.

"It's very sad her being such an invalid," I said.

"It's maddening for a doctor," said Judith. "Doctors like healthy people."

"How hard you young people are!" I exclaimed.

Judith said coldly:

"I was just stating a fact."

"Nevertheless," said Poirot, "the good doctor hurries to read to her."

"Very stupid," said Judith. "That nurse of hers can read to her perfectly well if she wants to be read to. Personally I should loathe anyone reading aloud to *me*."

"Well, well, tastes differ," I said.

"She's a very stupid woman," said Judith.

"Now there, *mon enfant,*" said Poirot, "I do not agree with you."

"She never reads anything but the cheapest kind of novel. She takes no interest in his work. She doesn't keep abreast of current thought. She just talks about her health to everyone who will listen."

"I still maintain," said Poirot, "that she uses her grey cells in ways that you, my child, know nothing about."

"She's a very feminine sort of woman," said Judith. "She coos and purrs. I expect you like 'em like that, Uncle Hercule."

"Not at all," I said. "He likes them large and flamboyant and Russian for choice."

"So that is how you give me away, Hastings? Your father, Judith, has always had a penchant for auburn hair. It has landed him in trouble many a time."

Judith smiled at us both indulgently. She said:

"What a funny couple you are."

She turned away and I rose.

"I must get unpacked, and I might have a bath before dinner."

Poirot pressed a little bell within reach of his hand and a minute or two later his valet attendant entered. I was surprised to find that the man was a stranger.

"Why! Where's Georges?"

Poirot's valet, Georges, had been with him for many years.

"Georges has returned to his family. His father is ill. I hope he will come back to me sometime. In the meantime," he smiled at the new valet, "Curtiss looks after me."

Curtiss smiled back respectfully. He was a big man with a bovine rather stupid face.

As I went out of the door, I noted that Poirot was carefully locking up the dispatch case with the papers inside it.

My mind in a whirl, I crossed the passage to my own room.

4

I went down to dinner that night feeling that the whole of life had become suddenly unreal.

Once or twice, while dressing, I had asked myself if possibly Poirot had imagined the whole thing. After all, the dear old chap was an old man now and sadly broken in health. He himself might declare his brain was as sound as ever—but in point of fact, was it? His whole life had been spent in tracking down crime. Would it really be surprising if, in the end, he was to fancy crimes where no crimes were? His enforced inaction must have fretted him sorely. What more likely than that he should invent for himself a new manhunt? Wishful thinking—a perfectly reasonable neurosis. He had selected a number of publicly reported happenings, and had read into them something that was not there—a shadowy figure behind them—a mad mass murderer. In all probability Mrs. Etherington had really killed her husband, the labourer had shot his wife, a young woman had given her old aunt an overdose of morphia, a jealous wife had polished off her husband as she had threatened to do, and a crazy spinster had really committed the murder for which she had subsequently given herself up. In fact these crimes were exactly what they seemed!

Against that view (surely the common-sense one) I could only set my own inherent belief in Poirot's acumen.

Poirot said that a murder had been arranged. For the second time Styles was to house a crime.

Time would prove or disprove that assertion, but if it were true, it behooved us to forestall that happening.

And Poirot knew the identity of the murderer, which I did not.

The more I thought about that, the more annoyed I became! Really, frankly, it was damned cheek of Poirot! He wanted my cooperation and yet he refused to take me into his confidence!

Why? There was the reason he gave—surely a most inadequate one! I was tired of this silly joking about my "speaking countenance." I could keep a secret as well as anyone. Poirot has always persisted in the humiliating belief that I am a transparent character and that anyone can read what is passing in my mind. He tries to soften the blow sometimes by attributing it to my beautiful and honest character, which abhors all form of deceit!

Of course, I reflected, if the whole thing was a chimera of Poirot's imagination, his reticence was easily explained.

I had come to no conclusion by the time the gong sounded, and I went down to dinner with an open mind, but with an alert eye, for the detection of Poirot's mythical X.

For the moment I would accept everything that Poirot had said as gospel truth. There was a person under this roof who had already killed five times and who was preparing to kill again. *Who was it?*

In the drawing room before we went in to dinner I was introduced to Miss Cole and Major Allerton. The former was a tall, still handsome woman of thirty-three or -four. Major Allerton I instinctively disliked. He was a good-looking man in the early forties, broad-shouldered, bronzed of face, with an easy way of talking, most of what he said holding a double implication. He had the pouches under his eyes that come with a dissipated way of life. I suspected him of racketing around, of gambling, of drinking hard, and of being first and last a womanizer.

Old Colonel Luttrell, I saw, did not much like him either, and Boyd Carrington was also rather stiff in his manner towards him. Allerton's success was with the women of the party. Mrs. Luttrell twittered to him delightedly, while he flattered her lazily and with a hardly concealed impertinence. I was also annoyed to see that Judith, too, seemed to enjoy his company and was exerting herself far more than usual to talk to him. Why the worst type of man can always be relied upon to please and interest the nicest of women has long been a problem beyond me. I knew instinctively that Allerton was a rotter—and nine men out of ten would have agreed with me. Whereas nine women or possibly the whole ten would have fallen for him immediately.

As we sat down at the dinner table and plates of white gluey liquid were set before us, I let my eyes rove round the table while I summed up the possibilities.

If Poirot were right and retained his clearness of brain unimpaired, one of these people was a dangerous murderer—and probably a lunatic as well.

Poirot had not actually said so, but I presumed that X was probably a man. Which of these men was it likely to be?

Surely not old Colonel Luttrell, with his indecision and his general air of feebleness. Norton, the man whom I had met rushing out of the house with field glasses? It seemed unlikely. He appeared to be a pleasant fellow, rather ineffective and lacking in vitality. Of course, I told myself, many murderers have been small insignificant men—driven to assert themselves by crime for that very reason. They resented being passed over and ignored. Norton might be a murderer of this type. But there was his fondness for birds. I have always believed that a love of nature was essentially a healthy sign in a man.

Boyd Carrington? Out of the question. A man with a name known all over the world. A fine sportsman, an administrator, a man universally liked and looked up to. Franklin I also dismissed. I knew how Judith respected and admired him.

Major Allerton now. I dwelt on him appraisingly. A nasty fellow if I ever saw one! The sort of fellow who would skin his grandmother. And all glossed over with this superficial charm of manner. He was talking now—telling a story of his own discomfiture and making everybody laugh with his rueful appreciation of a joke at his expense.

If Allerton was X, I decided, his crimes had been committed for profit in some way.

It was true that Poirot had not definitely said that X was a man. I considered Miss Cole as a possibility. Her movements were restless and jerky—obviously a woman of nerves. Handsome in a hag-ridden kind of way. Still, she looked normal enough. She, Mrs. Luttrell and Judith were the only women at the dinner table. Mrs. Franklin was having dinner upstairs in her room, and the nurse who attended to her had her meals after us.

After dinner I was standing by the drawing-room window looking out into the garden and thinking back to the time when I had seen Cynthia Murdoch, a young girl with auburn hair, run across that lawn. How charming she had looked in her white overall . . .

Lost in thoughts of the past, I started when Judith passed her arm through mine and impelled me with her out of the window onto the terrace.

She said abruptly, "What's the matter?"

I was startled. "The matter? What do you mean?"

"You've been so queer all through the evening. Why were you staring at everyone at dinner?"

I was annoyed. I had had no idea I had allowed my thoughts so much sway over me.

"Was I? I suppose I was thinking of the past. Seeing ghosts perhaps."

"Oh yes, of course you stayed here, didn't you, when you were a young man? An old lady was murdered here, or something?"

"Poisoned with strychnine."

"What was she like? Nice or nasty?"

I considered the question.

"She was a very kind woman," I said slowly. "Generous. Gave a lot to charity."

"Oh, *that* kind of generosity."

Judith's voice sounded faintly scornful. Then she asked a curious question:

"Were people—happy here?"

No, they had not been happy. That, at least I knew. I said slowly:

"No."

"Why not?"

"Because they felt like prisoners. Mrs. Inglethorp, you see, had all the money—and—and doled it out. Her stepchildren could have no life of their own."

I heard Judith take a sharp breath. The hand on my arm tightened.

"That's wicked—wicked. An abuse of power. It shouldn't be allowed. Old people, sick people, they shouldn't have the power to hold up the lives of the young and strong. To keep them tied down, fretting, wasting their power and energy that could be used—that's *needed*. It's just selfishness."

"The old," I said drily, "have not got a monopoly of that quality."

"Oh, I know, Father, you think the young are selfish. So we are, perhaps, but it's a *clean* selfishness. At least we only want to do what we want ourselves, we don't want everybody else to do what we want, we don't want to make slaves of other people."

"No, you just trample them down if they happen to be in your way."

Judith squeezed my arm. She said:

"Don't be so bitter! I don't really do much trampling—and you've never tried to dictate our lives to any of us. We are grateful for that."

"I'm afraid," I said honestly, "that I'd have liked to, though. It was your mother who insisted you should be allowed to make your own mistakes."

Judith gave my arm another quick squeeze. She said:

"I know. You'd have liked to fuss over us like a hen! I do hate fuss. I won't stand it. But you do agree with me, don't you, about useful lives being sacrificed to useless ones?"

"It does sometimes happen," I admitted. "But there's no need for drastic measures . . . It's up to anybody just to walk out, you know."

"Yes, but is it? *Is* it?"

Her tone was so vehement that I looked at her in some astonishment. It was too dark to see her face clearly. She went on, her voice low and troubled.

"There's so much—it's so difficult—financial considerations, a sense of responsibility, reluctance to hurt someone you've been fond of—all those things, and some people are so unscrupulous—they know just how to play on all those feelings. Some people—some people are like *leeches!*"

"My dear Judith," I exclaimed, taken aback by the positive fury of her tone.

She seemed to realize that she had been overvehement, for she laughed and withdrew her arm from mine.

"Was I sounding very intense? It's a matter I feel rather hotly about. You see, I've known a case . . . An old brute. And when someone was brave enough to—to cut the knot and set the people she loved free, they called her mad. Mad? It was the sanest thing anyone could do—and the bravest!"

A horrible qualm passed over me. Where, not long ago, had I heard something like that?

"Judith," I said sharply. "Of what case are you talking?"

"Oh, nobody you know. Some friends of the Franklins. Old man called Litchfield. He was quite rich and practically starved his wretched daughters—never let them see anyone, or go out. He was mad, really, but not sufficiently so in the medical sense."

"And the eldest daughter murdered him," I said.

"Oh, I expect you read about it? I suppose you would call it murder—but it wasn't done from personal motives. Margaret Litchfield went straight to the police and gave herself up. I think she was very brave. I wouldn't have had the courage."

"The courage to give yourself up or the courage to commit murder?"

"Both."

"I'm very glad to hear it," I said severely, "and I don't like to hear you talking of murder as justified in certain cases." I paused and added: "What did Dr. Franklin think?"

"Thought it served him right," said Judith. "You know, Father, some people really ask to be murdered."

"I won't have you talking like this, Judith. Who's been putting these ideas into your head?"

"Nobody."

"Well, let me tell you that it's all pernicious nonsense."

"I see. We'll leave it at that." She paused. "I came really to give you a message from Mrs. Franklin. She'd like to see you if you don't mind coming up to her bedroom."

"I shall be delighted. I'm so sorry she was feeling too ill to come down to dinner."

"She's all right," said Judith unfeelingly. "She just likes making a fuss."

The young are very unsympathetic.

5

I had only met Mrs. Franklin once before. She was a woman about thirty—of what I should describe as the Madonna type. Big brown eyes, hair parted in the centre, and a long gentle face. She was very slender and her skin had a transparent fragility.

She was lying on a day bed, propped up with pillows, and wearing a very dainty negligee of white and pale blue.

Franklin and Boyd Carrington were there drinking coffee. Mrs. Franklin welcomed me with an outstretched hand and a smile.

"How glad I am you've come, Captain Hastings. It will be so nice for Judith. The child has really been working far too hard."

"She looks very well on it," I said as I took the fragile little hand in mine.

Barbara Franklin sighed.

"Yes, she's lucky. How I envy her. I don't believe really that she knows what ill health is. What do you think, Nurse? Oh! Let me introduce you. This is Nurse Craven, who's so terribly, terribly good to me. I don't know what I should do without her. She treats me just like a baby."

Nurse Craven was a tall good-looking young woman with a fine colour and a handsome head of auburn hair. I noticed her hands, which were long and white—very different from the hands of so many hospital nurses. She was in some respects a taciturn girl, and sometimes did not answer. She did not now, merely inclined her head.

"But really," went on Mrs. Franklin, "John has been working that wretched girl of yours too hard. He's such a slave driver. You are a slave driver, aren't you, John?"

Her husband was standing looking out of the window. He was whistling to himself and jingling some loose change in his pocket. He started slightly at his wife's question.

"What's that, Barbara?"

"I was saying that you overwork poor Judith Hastings shamefully. Now Captain Hastings is here, he and I are going to put out heads together and we're not going to allow it."

Persiflage was not Dr. Franklin's strong point. He looked vaguely worried and turned to Judith inquiringly. He mumbled:

"You must let me know if I overdo it."

Judith said:

"They're just trying to be funny. Talking of work, I wanted to ask you about that stain for the second slide—you know, the one that—"

He turned to her eagerly and broke in.

"Yes, yes. I say, if you don't mind, let's go down to the lab. I'd like to be quite sure—"

Still talking, they went out of the room together.

Barbara Franklin lay back on her pillows. She sighed. Nurse Craven said suddenly and rather disagreeably:

"It's Miss Hastings who's the slave driver, I think!"

Again Mrs. Franklin sighed. She murmured:

"I feel so *inadequate*. I ought, I know, to take more interest in John's work, but I just can't do it. I daresay it's something wrong in me, but—"

She was interrupted by a snort from Boyd Carrington, who was standing by the fireplace.

"Nonsense, Babs," he said. "*You're* all right. Don't worry yourself."

"Oh, but, Bill dear, I *do* worry. I get so discouraged about myself. It's all—I can't help feeling it—it's all so *nasty*. The guinea pigs and the rats and everything. Ugh!" She shuddered. "I know it's stupid, but I'm such a fool. It makes me feel quite sick. I just want to think of all the lovely happy things—birds and flowers, and children playing. *You* know, Bill."

He came over and took the hand she held out to him so pleadingly. His face as he looked down at her was changed, as gentle as any woman's. It was, somehow, impressive—for Boyd Carrington was so essentially a manly man.

"You've not changed much since you were seventeen, Babs," he said. "Do you remember that garden house of yours and the bird bath, and the cocoanuts?"

He turned his head to me.

"Barbara and I are old playmates," he said.

"Oh! Playmates!" she protested.

"Oh, I'm not denying that you're over fifteen years younger than I am. But I played with you as a tiny tot when I was a young man. Gave you pickabacks, my dear. And then later, I came home to find you a beautiful young lady—just on the point of making your debut in the world—and I did my share by taking you out on the golf links and teaching you to play golf. Do you remember?"

"Oh, Bill, do you think I'd forget?"

"My people used to live in this part of the world," she explained to me. "And Bill used to come and stay with his old uncle, Sir Everard, at Knatton."

"And what a mausoleum it was—and is," said Boyd Carrington. "Sometimes I despair of getting the place livable."

"Oh, Bill, it could be made marvellous—quite marvellous!"

"Yes, Babs, but the trouble is I've got no ideas. Baths and some really comfortable chairs—that's all I can think of. It needs a woman."

"I've told you I'll come and help. I mean it. Really."

Sir William looked doubtfully towards Nurse Craven.

"If you're strong enough, I could drive you over. What do you think, Nurse?"

"Oh yes, Sir William. I really think it would do Mrs. Franklin good—if she's careful not to overtire herself, of course."

"That's a date, then," said Boyd Carrington. "And now you have a good night's sleep. Get into good fettle for tomorrow."

We both wished Mrs. Franklin "Good night" and went out together. As we went down the stairs, Boyd Carrington said gruffly:

"You've no idea what a lovely creature she was at seventeen. I was home from Burma—my wife died out there, you know. Don't mind telling you I completely lost my heart to her. She married Franklin three or four years afterwards. Don't think it's been a happy marriage. It's my idea that that's what lies at the bottom of her ill health. Fellow doesn't understand her or appreciate her. And she's the sensitive kind. I've an idea that this delicacy of hers is partly nervous. Take her out of herself, amuse her, interest her, and she looks a different creature! But that damned sawbones only takes an interest in test tubes and West African natives and cultures."

He snorted angrily.

I thought that there was, perhaps, something in what he said. Yet it surprised me that Boyd Carrington should be attracted by Mrs. Franklin who, when all was said and done, was a sickly creature though pretty in a frail chocolate box way. But Boyd Carrington himself was so full of vitality and life that I should have thought he would merely have been impatient with the neurotic type of invalid. However, Barbara Franklin must have been quite lovely as a girl, and with many men, especially those of the idealistic type such as I judged Boyd Carrington to be, early impressions die hard.

Downstairs Mrs. Luttrell pounced upon us and suggested bridge. I excused myself on the plea of wanting to join Poirot.

I found my friend in bed. Curtiss was moving around the room tidying up, but he presently went out, shutting the door behind him.

"Confound you, Poirot," I said. "You and your infernal habit of keeping things up your sleeve. I've spent the whole evening trying to spot X."

"That must have made you somewhat distrait," observed my

friend. "Did nobody comment on your abstraction and ask you what was the matter?"

I reddened slightly, remembering Judith's questions. Poirot, I think, observed my discomfiture. I noticed a small malicious smile on his lips. He merely said, however:

"And what conclusion have you come to on that point?"

"Would you tell me if I was right?"

"Certainly not."

I watched his face closely.

"I had considered Norton—"

Poirot's face did not change.

"Not," I said, "that I've anything to go upon. He just struck me as perhaps less unlikely than anyone else. And then he's—well —inconspicuous. I should imagine the kind of murderer we're after would have to be inconspicuous."

"That is true. But there are more ways than you think of being inconspicuous."

"What do you mean?"

"Supposing, to take a hypothetical case, that if a sinister stranger arrives there some weeks before the murder, for no apparent reason, he will be noticeable. It would be better, would it not, if the stranger were to be a negligible personality, engaged in some harmless sport like fishing?"

"Or watching birds," I agreed. "Yes, but that's just what I was saying."

"On the other hand," said Poirot, "it might be better still if the murderer were already a prominent personality—that is to say, he might be the butcher. That would have the further advantage that no one notices bloodstains on a butcher!"

"You're just being ridiculous. Everyone would know if the butcher had quarrelled with the baker."

"Not if the butcher had become a butcher *simply in order to have a chance of murdering the baker*. One must always look one step behind, my friend."

I looked at him closely, trying to decide if a hint lay concealed in those words. If they meant anything definite, they would seem to point to Colonel Luttrell. Had he deliberately opened a guest house in order to have an opportunity of murdering one of the guests?

Poirot very gently shook his head. He said:

"It is not from my face that you will get the answer."

"You really are a maddening fellow, Poirot," I said with a sigh. "Anyway, Norton isn't my only suspect. What about this fellow Allerton?"

Poirot, his face still impassive, inquired:

"You do not like him?"

"No, I don't."

"Ah. What you call the nasty bit of goods. That is right, is it not?"

"Definitely. Don't you think so?"

"Certainly. He is a man," said Poirot slowly, "very attractive to women."

I made an exclamation of contempt.

"How women can be so foolish. What do they see in a fellow like that?"

"Who can say? But it is always so. The *mauvais sujet*—always women are attracted to him."

"But why?"

Poirot shrugged his shoulders.

"They see something, perhaps, that we do not."

"But what?"

"Danger, possibly . . . Everyone, my friend, demands a spice of danger in their lives. Some get it vicariously—as in bullfights. Some read about it. Some find it at the cinema. But I am sure of this—too much safety is abhorrent to the nature of a human being. Men find danger in many ways—women are reduced to finding their danger mostly in affairs of sex. That is why, perhaps, they welcome the hint of the tiger—the sheathed claws—the treacherous spring. The excellent fellow who will make a good and kind husband—they pass him by."

I considered this gloomily in silence for some minutes. Then I reverted to the previous theme.

"You know, Poirot," I said. "It will be easy enough really for me to find out who X is. I've only got to poke about and find who was acquainted with all the people. I mean the people of your five cases."

I brought this out triumphantly, but Poirot merely gave me a look of scorn.

"I have not demanded your presence here, Hastings, in order to watch you clumsily and laboriously following the way I have already trodden. And let me tell you it is not quite so simple as you think. Four of those cases took place in this county. The people assembled under this roof are not a collection of strangers who have arrived here independently. This is not a hotel in the usual sense of the word. The Luttrells come from this part of the world; they were badly off and bought this place and started it as a venture. The people who come here are their friends, or friends recommended by their friends. Sir William persuaded the Franklins to come. They in turn suggested it to Norton, and, I believe, to Miss Cole—and so on. Which is to say that there is a very fair chance of a certain person who is known to one of these people being known to all of these people. It is also open to X to lure wherever the facts are best known. Take the case of the labourer Riggs. The village where that tragedy occurred is not far from the house of Boyd Carrington's uncle. Mrs. Franklin's people, also, lived near. The inn in the village is much frequented by tourists. Some of Mrs. Franklin's family's friends used to put up there. Franklin himself has stayed there. Norton and Miss Cole may have stayed there and probably have.

"No, no, my friend. I beg that you will not make these clumsy attempts to unravel a secret that I refuse to reveal to you."

"It's so damned silly. As though I should be likely to give it away. I tell you, Poirot, I'm tired of these jokes about my speaking countenance. It's not funny."

Poirot said quietly:

"Are you so sure that is the only reason? Do you not realize, my friend, that such knowledge may be dangerous? Do you not see that I concern myself with your safety?"

I stared at him open-mouthed. Up till that minute I had not appreciated that aspect of the matter. But it was, of course, true enough. If a clever and resourceful murderer who had already got away with five crimes—unsuspected, as he thought—once awoke to the fact that someone was on his trail, then indeed there was danger for those on his track.

I said sharply:

"But then you—you yourself are in danger, Poirot?"

Poirot, as far as he was able to in his crippled state, made a gesture of supreme disdain.

"I am accustomed to that; I can protect myself. And see, have I not here my faithful dog to protect me also? My excellent and loyal Hastings!"

6

Poirot was supposed to keep early hours. I left him therefore to go to sleep and went downstairs, pausing to have a few words with the attendant Curtiss on the way.

I found him a stolid individual, slow in the uptake, but trustworthy and competent. He had been with Poirot since the latter's return from Egypt. His master's health, he told me, was fairly good, but he occasionally had alarming heart attacks, and his heart was much weakened in the last few months. It was a case of the engine slowly failing.

Oh, well, it had been a good life! Nevertheless my heart was wrung for my old friend who was fighting so gallantly every step of the downward way. Even now, crippled and weak, his indomitable spirit was still leading him to ply the craft at which he was so expert.

I went downstairs sad at heart. I could hardly imagine life without Poirot . . .

A rubber was just finishing in the drawing room, and I was invited to cut in. I thought it might serve to distract my mind and I accepted. Boyd Carrington was the one to cut out, and I sat down with Norton and Colonel and Mrs. Luttrell.

"What do you say now, Mr. Norton," said Mrs. Luttrell. "Shall you and I take the other two on? Our late partnership's been very successful."

Norton smiled pleasantly, but murmured "that perhaps, really, they ought to cut—what?"

Mrs. Luttrell assented, but with rather an ill grace, I thought.

Norton and I cut together against the Luttrells. I noticed that Mrs. Luttrell was definitely displeased by this. She bit her lip, and her charm and Irish brogue disappeared completely for the moment.

I soon found out why. I played on many future occasions with Colonel Luttrell, and he was not really such a very bad player. He was what I should describe as a moderate player, but inclined to be forgetful. Every now and then he would make some really bad mistake owing to this. But playing with his wife, he made mistake after mistake without ceasing. He was obviously nervous of her, and this caused him to play about three times as badly as was normal. Mrs. Luttrell herself was a very good player indeed, though a rather unpleasant one to play with. She snatched every conceivable advantage, ignored the rules if her adversary was unaware of them, and enforced them immediately when they served her. She was also extremely adept at a quick sideways glance into her opponent's hand. In other words, she played to win.

And I understood soon enough what Poirot had meant by vinegar. At cards her self-restraint failed, and her tongue lashed every mistake her wretched husband made. It was really most uncomfortable for both Norton and myself, and I was thankful when the rubber came to an end.

We both excused ourselves from playing another on the score of the lateness of the hour.

As we moved away, Norton rather incautiously gave way to his feelings.

"I say, Hastings, that was pretty ghastly. It gets my back up to see that poor old boy bullied like that. And the meek way he takes it! Poor chap. Not much of the peppery-tongued Indian colonel about him."

"Ssh," I warned, for Norton's voice had been raised and I was afraid old Colonel Luttrell would overhear.

"No, but it is too bad."

I said with feeling:

"I shall understand it if he ever takes a hatchet to her."

Norton shook his head.

"He won't. The iron's entered into his soul. He'll go on: 'Yes, m'dear, no, m'dear, sorry, m'dear,' pulling at his moustache and bleating meekly until he's put in his coffin. He couldn't assert himself if he tried!"

I shook my head sadly, for I was afraid Norton was right.

We paused in the hall and I noticed that the side door to the garden was open and the wind blowing in.

"Ought we to shut that?" I asked.

Norton hesitated a minute before saying:

"Well—er—I don't think everybody's in yet."

A sudden suspicion darted through my mind.

"Who's out?"

"Your daughter, I think—and—er—Allerton."

He tried to make his voice extra casual, but the information coming on top of my conversation with Poirot made me feel suddenly uneasy.

Judith—and Allerton. Surely Judith, my clever, cool Judith, would not be taken in by a man of that type? Surely she would see through him?

I told myself that repeatedly as I undressed, but the vague uneasiness persisted. I could not sleep and lay tossing from side to side.

As is the way with night worries, everything gets exaggerated. A fresh sense of despair and loss swept over me. If only my dear wife were alive. She on whose wise judgment I had relied for so many years. She had always been wise and understanding about the children.

Without her, I felt miserably inadequate. The responsibility for their safety and happiness was mine. Would I be equal to that task? I was not, Heaven help me, a clever man. I blundered—made mistakes. If Judith was to ruin her chances of happiness, if she were to suffer—

Desperately I switched the light on and sat up.

It was no good going on like this. I must get some sleep. Getting out of bed, I walked over to the washbasin and looked doubt-fully at a bottle of aspirin tablets.

No, I needed something stronger than aspirin. I reflected that Poirot, probably, would have some sleeping stuff of some kind. I crossed the passage to his room and stood hesitating a minute out-side the door. Rather a shame to wake the old boy up.

As I hesitated, I heard a footfall and looked round. Allerton was coming along the corridor towards me. It was dimly lit and until he came near I could not see his face, and wondered for a minute who it was. Then I saw, and stiffened all over. For the man was smiling to himself, and I disliked that smile very much.

He looked up and raised his eyebrows.

"Hullo, Hastings, still about?"

"I couldn't sleep," I said shortly.

"Is that all? I'll soon fix you up. Come with me."

I followed him into his room, which was the next one to mine. A strange fascination drove me to study this man as closely as I could.

"You keep late hours yourself," I remarked.

"I've never been an early bed-goer. Not when there's sport abroad. These fine evenings aren't made to be wasted."

He laughed—and I disliked the laugh.

I followed him into the bathroom. He opened a little cupboard and took out a bottle of tablets.

"Here you are. This is the real dope. You'll sleep like a log—and have pleasant dreams, too. Wonderful stuff Slumberyl—that's the patent name for it."

The enthusiasm in his voice gave me a slight shock. Was he a drug taker as well? I said doubtfully:

"It isn't—dangerous?"

"It is if you take too much of it. It's one of the barbiturates—whose toxic dose is very near the effective one." He smiled, the corners of his mouth sliding up his face in an unpleasant way.

"I shouldn't have thought you could get it without a doctor's prescription," I said.

"You can't, old boy. Anyway, quite literally, *you* can't. I've got a pull in that line."

I suppose it was foolish of me, but I get these impulses. I said: "You knew Etherington, I think?"

At once I knew that I had struck a note of some kind. His eyes grew hard and wary. He said—and his voice had changed—it was light and artificial:

"Oh yes—I knew Etherington. Poor chap." Then, as I did not speak, he went on: "Etherington took drugs, of course—but he overdid it. One's got to know when to stop. He didn't. Bad business. That wife of his was lucky. If the sympathy of the jury hadn't been with her, she'd have hanged."

He passed me over a couple of the tablets. Then he said casually:

"Did you know Etherington well?"

I answered with the truth.

"No."

He seemed for a moment at a loss how to proceed. Then he turned it off with a light laugh:

"Funny chap. Not exactly a Sunday school character, but he was good company sometimes."

I thanked him for the tablets and went back to my room.

As I lay down again and turned off the lights, I wondered if I had been foolish.

For it came to me very strongly that Allerton was almost certainly X. And I had let him see that I suspected the fact.

7

My narrative of the days spent at Styles must necessarily be somewhat rambling. In my recollection of it, it presents itself to me as a series of conversations—of suggestive words and phrases that etched themselves into my consciousness.

First of all, and very early on, there came the realization of Hercule Poirot's infirmity and helplessness. I did believe, as he had said, that his brain still functioned with all its old keenness, but the physical envelope had worn so thin that I realized at once that my part was destined to be a far more active one than usual. I had to be, as it were, Poirot's eyes and ears.

True, every fine day Curtiss would pick up his master and carry him carefully downstairs to where his chair had been carried down beforehand and was awaiting him. Then he would wheel Poirot out into the garden and select a spot that was free from draughts. On other days, when the weather was not propitious, he would be carried to the drawing room.

Wherever he might be, someone or other was sure to come and sit with him and talk, but this was not the same thing as if Poirot could have selected for himself his partner in the tête-à-tête. He could no longer single out the person he wanted to talk to.

On the day after my arrival I was taken by Franklin to an old studio in the garden which had been fitted up in a rough-and-ready fashion for scientific purposes.

Let me make clear here and now that I myself have not got the scientific mind. In my account of Dr. Franklin's work I shall probably use all the wrong terms and arouse the scorn of those properly instructed in such matters.

As far as I, a mere layman, could make out, Franklin was experimenting with various alkaloids derived from the Calabar bean, Physostigma venenosum. I understood more after a conversation which took place one day between Franklin and Poirot. Judith, who tried to instruct me, was, as is customary with the earnest young, almost impossibly technical. She referred learnedly to the alkaloids physostigmine, eserine, physovenine, and geneserine, and then proceeded to a most impossible-sounding substance, prostigmin or the demethylcarbonic ester of 3-hydroxyphenyl trimethyl lammonum, etc., etc., and a good deal more which, it appeared, was the same thing, only differently arrived at! It was all, at any rate, double Dutch to me, and I aroused Judith's contempt by asking what good all this was likely to do to mankind? There is no question that annoys your true scientist more. Judith at once threw me a scornful glance and embarked on another lengthy and learned explanation. The upshot of it was, so I gathered, that certain obscure tribes of West African natives had shown a remarkable immunity to an equally obscure, though deadly disease called, as far as I remember, Jordanitis—a certain enthusiastic Dr. Jordan having originally tracked it down. It was an extremely rare tropical ailment, which had been, on one or two occasions, contracted by white people, with fatal results.

I risked inflaming Judith's rage by remarking that it would be more sensible to find some drug that would counteract the aftereffects of measles!

With pity and scorn Judith made it clear to me that it was not the benefaction of the human race, but the enlargement of human knowledge, that was the only goal worthy of attainment.

I looked at some slides through the microscope, studied some photographs of West African natives (really quite entertaining!), caught the eye of a soporific rat in a cage and hurried out again into the air.

As I say, any interest I could feel was kindled by Franklin's conversation with Poirot.

He said:

"You know, Poirot, the stuff's really more up your street than mine. It's the ordeal bean—supposed to prove innocence or guilt. These West African tribes believe it implicitly—or did do so— they're getting sophisticated nowadays. They'll solemnly chew it up quite confident that it will kill them if they're guilty and not harm them if they're innocent."

"And so, alas, they die?"

"No, they don't all die. That's what has always been over- looked up to now. There's a lot behind the whole thing—a medicine man ramp, I rather fancy. There are two distinct species of this bean—only they look so much alike that you can hardly spot the difference. But there *is* a difference. They both contain physostigmine and geneserine and the rest of it, but in the second species you can isolate, or I think I can, yet another alkaloid—and the action of that alkaloid neutralizes the effect of the others. What's more, that second species is regularly eaten by a kind of inner ring in a secret ritual—and the people who eat it never go down with Jordanitis. This third substance has a re- markable effect on the muscular system—without deleterious effects. It's damned interesting. Unfortunately the pure alkaloid is very unstable. Still, I'm getting results. But what's wanted is a lot more research out there on the spot. It's work that ought to be done! Yes, by heck, it is . . . I'd sell my soul to—"

He broke off abruptly. The grin came again.

"Forgive the shop. I get too het up over these things!"

"As you say," said Poirot placidly, "it would certainly make my profession much easier if I could test guilt and innocence so eas- ily. Ah, if there were a substance that could do what is claimed for the Calabar bean!"

Franklin said:

"Ah, but your troubles wouldn't end there! After all, what *is* guilt or innocence?"

"I shouldn't think there could be any doubt about *that,*" I remarked.

He turned to me.

"What is evil? What is good? Ideas on them vary from century to century. What you would be testing would probably be a *sense* of guilt or a sense of innocence. In fact no value as a test at all."

"I don't see how you make that out."

"My dear fellow, suppose a man thinks he has a divine right to kill a dictator or a moneylender or a pimp or whatever arouses his moral indignation. He commits what *you* consider a guilty deed— but what *he* considers is an innocent one? What is your poor ordeal bean to do about it?"

"Surely," I said, "there must always be a feeling of guilt with murder?"

"Lots of people *I'd* like to kill," said Dr. Franklin cheerfully. "Don't believe my conscience would keep me awake at night afterwards. It's an idea of mine, you know, that about eighty per cent of the human race ought to be eliminated. We'd get on much better without them."

He got up and strolled away, whistling cheerfully to himself.

I looked after him doubtfully. A low chuckle from Poirot recalled me.

"You look, my friend, like one who has envisaged a nest of serpents. Let us hope that our friend the doctor does not practice what he preaches."

"Ah," I said. "But supposing he does?"

II

After some hesitations I decided that I ought to sound Judith on the subject of Allerton. I felt that I must know what her reactions were. She was, I knew, a level-headed girl, well able to take care of herself, and I did not think that she would really be taken in by the cheap attraction of a man like Allerton. I suppose, actually, that I tackled her on the subject because I wanted to be reassured on that point.

Unfortunately I did not get what I wanted . . . I went about it clumsily, I daresay. There is nothing that young people resent so much as advice from their elders. I tried to make my words quite careless and debonair. I suppose that I failed.

Judith bristled at once.

"What's this?" she said. "A parental warning against the big bad wolf?"

"No, no, Judith, of course not."

"I gather you don't like Major Allerton?"

"Frankly, I don't. Actually I don't suppose you do either."

"Why not?"

"Well—er—he isn't your type, is he?"

"What do you consider is my type, Father?"

Judith can always flurry me. I boggled rather badly. She stood looking at me, her mouth curving upwards in a slightly scornful smile.

"Of course *you* don't like him," she said. "I do. I think he's very amusing."

"Oh, amusing—perhaps." I endeavoured to pass it off.

Judith said deliberately:

"He's very attractive. Any woman would think so. Men, of course, wouldn't see it."

"They certainly wouldn't." I went on, rather clumsily: "You were out with him very late the other night—"

I was not allowed to finish. The storm broke.

"Really, Father, you're being too idiotic. Don't you realize that at my age I'm capable of managing my own affairs. You've no earthly right to control what I do or whom I choose to make a friend of. It's this senseless interference in their children's lives that is so infuriating about fathers and mothers. I'm very fond of you—but I'm an adult woman and my life is my own. Don't start making a Mr. Barrett of yourself."

I was so hurt by this extremely unkind remark that I was quite incapable of replying and Judith went quickly away.

I was left with the dismayed feeling that I had done more harm than good.

I was standing lost in my thoughts when I was roused by the voice of Mrs. Franklin's nurse exclaiming archly:

"A penny for your thoughts, Captain Hastings!"

I turned gladly to welcome the interruption.

Nurse Craven was really a very good-looking young woman.

Her manner was perhaps a little on the arch and sprightly side, but she was pleasant and intelligent.

She had just come from establishing her patient in a sunny spot not far from the improvised laboratory.

"Is Mrs. Franklin interested in her husband's work?" I asked.

Nurse Craven tossed her head contemptuously.

"Oh, it's a good deal too technical for *her*. She's not at all a clever woman, you know, Captain Hastings."

"No, I suppose not."

"Dr. Franklin's work, of course, can only be appreciated by someone who knows something about medicine. He's a very clever man indeed, you know. Brilliant. Poor man, I feel so sorry for him."

"Sorry for him?"

"Yes. I've seen it happen so often. Marrying the wrong type of woman, I mean."

"You think she's the wrong type for him?"

"Well, don't you? They've nothing at all in common."

"He seems very fond of her," I said. "Very attentive to her wishes and all that."

Nurse Craven laughed rather disagreeably.

"She sees to that, all right!"

"You think she trades on her—on her ill health?" I asked doubtfully.

Nurse Craven laughed.

"There isn't much you could teach her about getting her own way. Whatever her ladyship wants happens. Some women are like that—clever as a barrel full of monkeys. If anyone opposes them, they just lie back and shut their eyes and look ill and pathetic, or else they have a nerve storm—but Mrs. Franklin's the pathetic type. Doesn't sleep all night and is all white and exhausted in the morning."

"But she is really an invalid, isn't she?" I asked, rather startled.

Nurse Craven gave me a rather peculiar glance. She said drily:

"Oh, of course," and then turned the subject rather abruptly.

She asked me if it was true that I had been here long ago, in the first war.

"Yes, that's quite true."

She lowered her voice.

"There was a murder here, wasn't there? So one of the maids was telling me. An old lady?"

"Yes."

"And you were there at the time?"

"I was."

She gave a slight shiver. She said:

"That explains it, doesn't it?"

"Explains what?"

She gave me a quick sideways glance.

"The—the atmosphere of the place. Don't you feel it? I do. Something *wrong,* if you know what I mean?"

I was silent a moment considering. Was it true what she had just said? Did the fact that death by violence—by malice aforethought—had taken place in a certain spot leave its impression on that spot so strongly that it was perceptible after many years? Psychic people said so. Did Styles definitely bear traces of that event that had occurred so long ago? Here, within these walls, in these gardens, thoughts of murder had lingered and grown stronger and had at last come to fruition in the final act. Did they still taint the air?

Nurse Craven broke in on my thoughts by saying abruptly:

"I was in a house where there was a murder case once. I've never forgotten it. One doesn't, you know. One of my patients. I had to give evidence and everything. Made me feel quite queer. It's a nasty experience for a girl."

"It must be. I know myself—"

I broke off as Boyd Carrington came striding round the corner of the house.

As usual, his big buoyant personality seemed to sweep away shadows and intangible worries. He was so large, so sane, so out of doors—one of those lovable, forceful personalities that radiate cheerfulness and common sense.

"Morning, Hastings; morning, Nurse. Where's Mrs. Franklin?"

"Good morning, Sir William. Mrs. Franklin's down at the bottom of the garden under the beech tree near the laboratory."

"And Franklin, I suppose, is *inside* the laboratory?"

"Yes, Sir William—with Miss Hastings."

"Wretched girl. Fancy being cooped up doing stinks on a morning like this! You ought to protest, Hastings."

Nurse Craven said quickly:

"Oh, Miss Hastings is *quite* happy. She likes it, you know, and the doctor couldn't do without her, I'm sure."

"Miserable fellow," said Boyd Carrington. "If I had a pretty girl like your Judith as a secretary, I'd be looking at *her* instead of at guinea pigs, eh what?"

It was the kind of joke that Judith would particularly have disliked, but it went down quite well with Nurse Craven, who laughed a good deal.

"Oh, Sir William," she exclaimed. "You really mustn't say things like that. I'm sure we all know what *you'd* be like! But poor Dr. Franklin is so serious—quite wrapped up in his work."

Boyd Carrington said cheerfully:

"Well, his wife seems to have taken up her position where she can keep her eye on her husband. I believe she's jealous."

"You know far too much, Sir William!"

Nurse Craven seemed delighted with this badinage. She said reluctantly:

"Well, I suppose I ought to be going to see about Mrs. Franklin's malted milk."

She moved away slowly and Boyd Carrington stood looking after her.

"Good-looking girl," he remarked. "Lovely hair and teeth. Fine specimen of womanhood. Must be a dull life on the whole always looking after sick people. A girl like that deserves a better fate."

"Oh, well," I said. "I suppose she'll marry one day."

"I expect so."

He sighed—and it occurred to me that he was thinking of his dead wife. Then he said:

"Like to come over with me to Knatton and see the place?"

"Rather. I'd like to. I'll just see first if Poirot needs me."

I found Poirot sitting on the verandah, well muffled up. He encouraged me to go.

"But certainly go, Hastings, go. It is, I believe, a most handsome property. You should certainly see it."

"I'd like to. But I didn't want to desert you."

"My faithful friend! No, no, go with Sir William. A charming man, is he not?"

"First class," I said with enthusiasm.

Poirot smiled.

"Ah yes. I thought he was your type."

III

I enjoyed my expedition enormously.

Not only was the weather fine—a really lovely summer's day—but I enjoyed the companionship of the man.

Boyd Carrington had that personal magnetism, that wide experience of life and of places that made him excellent company. He told me stories of his administrative days in India, some intriguing details of East African tribal lore and was altogether so interesting that I was quite taken out of myself and forgot my worries about Judith and the deep anxieties that Poirot's revelations had given me.

I liked, too, the way Boyd Carrington spoke of my friend. He had a deep respect for him—both for his work and his character. Sad though Poirot's present condition of ill health was, Boyd Carrington uttered no facile words of pity. He seemed to think that a lifetime spent as Poirot's had been was in itself a rich reward and that in his memories my friend could find satisfaction and self-respect.

"Moreover," he said, "I'd wager his brain is as keen as ever it was."

"It is; indeed it is," I assented eagerly.

"No greater mistake than to think that because a man's tied by the leg it affects his brain pan. Not a bit of it. Anno Domini affects headwork much less than you'd think. By Jove, I wouldn't care to undertake to commit a murder under Hercule Poirot's nose—even at this time of day."

"He'd get you if you did," I said, grinning.

"I bet he would. Not," he added ruefully, "that I should be much good at doing a murder anyway. I can't plan things, you know. Too impatient. If I did a murder, it would be done on the spur of the moment."

"That might be the most difficult crime to spot."

"I hardly think so. I'd probably leave clues trailing along behind me in every direction. Well, it's lucky I haven't got a criminal mind. Only kind of man I can imagine myself killing is a blackmailer. That is a foul thing, if you like. I've always thought a blackmailer ought to be shot. What do you say?"

I confessed to some sympathy with his point of view.

Then we passed on to an examination of the work done on the house as a young architect came forward to meet us.

Knatton was mainly of Tudor date with a wing added later. It had not been modernized or altered since the installation of two primitive bathrooms in the eighteen-forties or thereabouts.

Boyd Carrington explained that his uncle had been more or less of a hermit, disliking people and living in a corner of the vast house. Boyd Carrington and his brother had been tolerated, and had spent their holidays there as schoolboys before Sir Everard had become as much of a recluse as he afterwards became.

The old man had never married, and had spent only a tenth of his large income, so that even after death duties had been paid, the present baronet had found himself a very rich man.

"But a very lonely one," he said, sighing.

I was silent. My sympathy was too acute to be put into words. For I, too, was a lonely man. Since Cinders had died, I felt myself to be only half a human being.

Presently, a little haltingly, I expressed a little of what I felt.

"Ah yes, Hastings, but you've had something I never had."

He paused a moment and then—rather jerkily he gave me an outline of his own tragedy.

Of the beautiful young wife, a lovely creature full of charm and accomplishments but with a tainted heritage. Her family had nearly all died of drink, and she herself fell a victim to the same curse. Barely a year after their marriage she had succumbed and had died a dipsomaniac's death. He did not blame her. He realized that heredity had been too strong for her.

After her death he had settled down to lead a lonely life. He had determined, saddened by his experience, not to marry again.

"One feels," he said simply, "safer alone."

"Yes, I can understand your feeling like that—at any rate at first."

"The whole thing was such a tragedy. It left me prematurely aged and embittered." He paused. "It's true—I was once very much tempted. But she was so young—I didn't feel it would be fair to tie her to a disillusioned man. I was too old for her—she was such a child—so pretty—so completely untouched."

He broke off, shaking his head.

"Wasn't that for her to judge?"

"I don't know, Hastings. I thought not. She—she seemed to like me. But then, as I say, she was so young. I shall always remember her as I saw her the last day of that leave. Her head a little on one side—that slightly bewildered look—her little hand—"

He stopped. The words conjured up a picture that seemed vaguely familiar, though I could not think why.

Boyd Carrington's voice, suddenly harsh, broke into my thoughts.

"I was a fool," he said. "Any man is a fool who lets opportunity slip by him. Anyway, here I am, with a great mansion of a house far too big for me, and no gracious presence to sit at the head of my table."

To me there was a charm in his slightly old-fashioned way of putting things. It conjured up a picture of old-world charm and ease.

"Where is the lady now?" I asked.

"Oh—married." He turned it off briefly. "Fact is, Hastings, I'm cut out now for a bachelor existence. I've got my little ways. Come and look at the gardens. They've been badly neglected, but they're very fine in their way."

We walked round the place and I was much impressed with all

I saw. Knatton was undoubtedly a very fine estate and I did not wonder that Boyd Carrington was proud of it. He knew the neighbourhood well and most of the people roundabout, though of course there had been newcomers since his time.

He had known Colonel Luttrell in the old days and expressed his earnest hope that the Styles venture was going to pay.

"Poor old Toby Luttrell's very hard up, you know," he said. "Nice fellow. Good soldier, too, and a very fine shot. Went on safari with him in Africa once. Ah, those were the days! He was married then, of course, but his missus didn't come along, thank goodness. Pretty woman she was—but always a bit of a Tartar. Funny the things a man will stand from a woman. Old Toby Luttrell who used to make subalterns shake in their shoes, he was such a stern martinet! And there he is, henpecked and bullied and meek as they make 'em! No doubt about it, that woman's got a tongue like vinegar. Still, she's got a head on her. If anyone can make the place pay, she will. Luttrell never had much of a head for business—but Mrs. Toby would skin her grandmother!"

"She's so gushing with it all," I complained.

Boyd Carrington looked amused.

"I know. All sweetness. But have you played bridge with them?"

I replied feelingly that I had.

"On the whole I steer clear of women bridge players," said Boyd Carrington. "And if you take my tip, you'll do the same."

I told him how uncomfortable Norton and myself had felt on the first evening of my arrival.

"Exactly. One doesn't know where to look!"

He added:

"Nice fellow, Norton. Very quiet though. Always looking at birds and things. Doesn't care for shooting them, he told me. Extraordinary! No feeling for sport. I told him he missed a lot. Can't see myself what excitement there can be stalking about through cold woods peering at birds through glasses."

How little we realized then that Norton's hobby might have an important part to play in the events that were to come.

8

The days passed. It was an unsatisfactory time—with its uneasy feeling of waiting for something.

Nothing, if I may put it in such a way, actually *happened*. Yet there were incidents, scraps of odd conversations, sidelights upon the various inmates of Styles, elucidating remarks. They all mounted up and, if properly pieced together, could have done a lot towards enlightening me.

It was Poirot who, with a few forceful words, showed me something to which I had been criminally blind.

I was complaining, for the umpteenth time, of his wilful refusal to admit me to his confidence. It was not fair, I told him. Always he and I had had equal knowledge—even if I had been dense and he had been astute in drawing the right conclusions from that knowledge.

He waved an impatient hand.

"Quite so, my friend. It is not fair! It is not sporting! It is not playing the game! Admit all that and pass from it. This is *not* a game—it is not *le sport*. For you, you occupy yourself in guessing wildly at the identity of X. It is not for that that I asked you to come here. Unnecessary for you to occupy yourself with that. *I* know the answer to that question. But what I do not know and what I must know is this: 'Who is going to die—very soon?' It is a question, *mon vieux*, not of you playing a guessing game, but of preventing a human being from dying."

I was startled.

"Of course," I said slowly. "I—well, I did know that you practically said so once, but I haven't quite realized it."

"Then realize it now—immediately."

"Yes, yes, I will—I mean, I do."

"*Bien!* Then tell me, Hastings, who is it who is going to die?"

I stared at him blankly.

"I have really no idea!"

"Then you should have an idea! What else are you here for?"

"Surely," I said, going back over my meditations on the subject, "there must be a connection between the victim and X so that if you told me who X was—"

Poirot shook his head with so much vigour that it was quite painful to watch.

"Have I not told you that that is the essence of X's technique? There will be nothing connecting X with the death. That is certain."

"The connection will be hidden, you mean?"

"It will be so well hidden that neither you nor I will find it."

"But surely by studying X's past—"

"I tell you, no. Certainly not in the *time*. Murder may happen any moment, you comprehend?"

"To someone in this house?"

"To someone in this house."

"And you really do not know who, or how?"

"Ah, if I did, I should not be urging you to find out for me!"

"You simply base your assumption on the presence of X?"

I sounded a little doubtful. Poirot, whose self-control had lessened as his limbs were perforce immobile, fairly howled at me.

"Ah, *ma foi*, how many times am I to go over all this? If a lot of war correspondents arrive suddenly in a certain spot of Europe, it means what? It means war! If doctors come from all over the world to a certain city—it shows what? That there is to be a medical conference. Where you see a vulture hovering, there will be a carcass. If you see beaters walking up a moor, there will be a shoot. If you see a man stop suddenly, tear off his coat and plunge into the sea, it means that there, there will be a rescue from drowning.

"If you see ladies of middle age and respectable appearance peering through a hedge, you may deduce that there is there an impropriety of some kind! And finally, if you smell a succulent smell and observe several people all walking along a corridor in the same direction, you may safely assume that a meal is about to be served!"

I considered these analogies for a minute or two, then I said, taking the first one:

"All the same, one war correspondent does not make a war!"

"Certainly not. And one swallow does not make a summer. But one murderer, Hastings, does make a murder."

That, of course, was undeniable. But it still occurred to me, as it did not seem to have occurred to Poirot, that even a murderer has his off times. X might be at Styles simply for a holiday with no lethal intent. Poirot was so worked up, however, that I dared not propound this suggestion. I merely said that the whole thing seemed to me hopeless. We must wait—

"And see," finished Poirot. "Like your Mr. Asquith in the last war. That, *mon cher*, is just what we must not do. I do not say, mark you, that we shall succeed, for as I have told you before, when a killer has determined to kill, it is not easy to circumvent him. But we can at least try. Figure to yourself, Hastings, that you have here the bridge problem in the paper. You can see all the cards. What you are asked to do is 'Forecast the result of the deal.'"

I shook my head.

"It's no good, Poirot. I haven't the least idea. If I knew who X was—"

Poirot howled at me again. He howled so loud that Curtiss came running in from the next room looking quite frightened. Poirot waved him away and when he had gone out again, my friend spoke in a more controlled manner.

"Come, Hastings, you are not so stupid as you like to pretend. You have studied those cases I gave you to read. You may not know who X is, but you know X's technique for committing a crime."

"Oh," I said. "I see."

"Of course you see. The trouble with you is that you are mentally lazy. You like to play games and guess. You do not like to work with your head. What is the essential element of X's technique? Is it not that the crime, when committed, is complete? That is to say, there is a motive for the crime, there is an opportunity, there is means and there is, last and most important, the guilty person all ready for the dock."

At once I grasped the essential point and realized what a fool I had been not to see it sooner.

"I see," I said. "I've got to look round for somebody who—who answers to those requirements—the potential victim."

Poirot leaned back with a sigh.

"Enfin! I am very tired. Send Curtiss to me. You understand your job now. You are active, you can get about, you can follow people about, talk to them, spy upon them unobserved—" (I nearly uttered an indignant protest, but quelled it. It was too old an argument.) "You can listen to conversations, you have knees that will still bend and permit you to kneel and look through keyholes—"

"I will not look through keyholes," I interrupted hotly.

Poirot closed his eyes.

"Very well, then. You will not look through keyholes. You will remain the English gentleman and someone will be killed. It does not matter, that. Honour comes first with an Englishman. Your honour is more important than somebody else's life. Bien! It is understood."

"No, but dash it all, Poirot—"

Poirot said coldly:

"Send Curtiss to me. Go away. You are obstinate and extremely stupid and I wish that there were someone else whom I could trust, but I suppose I shall have to put up with you and your absurd ideas of fair play. Since you cannot use your grey cells as you do not possess them, at any rate use your eyes, your ears and your nose if need be in so far as the dictates of honour allow."

II

It was on the following day that I ventured to broach an idea which had come into my mind more than once. I did so a little dubiously, for one never knows how Poirot may react!

I said:

"I've been thinking, Poirot. I know I'm not much of a fellow. You've said I'm stupid. Well, in a way it's true. And I'm only half the man I was. Since Cinders' death—"

I stopped. Poirot made a gruff noise indicative of sympathy.

I went on:

"But there is a man here who could help us—just the kind of man we need. Brains, imagination, resource—used to making decisions and a man of wide experience. I'm talking of Boyd Carrington. He's the man we want, Poirot. Take him into your confidence. Put the whole thing before him."

Poirot opened his eyes and said with immense decision:

"Certainly not."

"But why not? You can't deny that he's clever—a good deal cleverer than I am."

"That," said Poirot with biting sarcasm, "would be easy. But dismiss the idea from your mind, Hastings. We take *no one* into our confidence. That is understood—*hein?* You comprehend, I forbid you to speak of this matter."

"All right, if you say so, but really Boyd Carrington—"

"Ah ta ta! Boyd Carrington. Why are you so obsessed with Boyd Carrington? What is he, after all? A big man who is pompous and pleased with himself because people have called him 'Your Excellency.' A man with—yes, a certain amount of tact and charm of manner. But he is not so wonderful, your Boyd Carrington. He repeats himself, he tells the same story twice—and what is more, his memory is so bad that he tells back to you the story

that you have told to him! A man of outstanding ability? Not at
all. An old bore—a windbag—*enfin*—the stuffed shirt!"

"Oh," I said as enlightenment came to me.

It was quite true that Boyd Carrington's memory was not good.
And he had actually been guilty of a *gaffe* which I now saw had
annoyed Poirot a good deal. Poirot had told him a story of his
police days in Belgium, and only a couple of days afterwards,
when several of us were assembled in the garden, Boyd Carrington had in bland forgetfulness told the same story back again to
Poirot, prefacing it with the remark: "I remember the Chef de la
Sûrété in Paris telling me—"

I now perceived that this had rankled!

Tactfully, I said no more and withdrew.

III

I wandered downstairs and out into the garden. There was no
one about and I strolled through a grove of trees and up to a
grassy knoll which was surmounted by a somewhat earwiggy
summerhouse in an advanced stage of decrepitude. Here I sat
down, lit my pipe, and settled down to think things out.

Who was there at Styles who had a fairly definite motive for
murdering somebody else—or who might be made out to have
one?

Putting aside the somewhat obvious case of Colonel Luttrell
who, I was afraid, was hardly likely to take a hatchet to his wife
in the middle of a rubber, justifiable though that course might be,
I could not at first think of anyone.

The trouble was that I did not really know enough about these
people. Norton, for instance, and Miss Cole? What were the
usual motives for murder? Money? Boyd Carrington was, I
fancied, the only rich man of the party. If he died, who would inherit that money? Anyone at present in the house? I hardly
thought so, but it was a point that might bear inquiry. He might,
for instance, have left his money to research, making Franklin a
trustee. That, with the doctor's rather injudicious remarks on the
subject of eliminating 80 per cent of the human race, might make

out a fairly damning case against the red-haired doctor. Or possibly Norton or Miss Cole might be a distant relative and would inherit automatically. Far-fetched but possible. Would Colonel Luttrell, who was an old friend, benefit under Boyd Carrington's will? These possibilities seemed to exhaust the money angle. I turned to more romantic possibilities. The Franklins. Mrs. Franklin was an invalid. Was it possible that she was being slowly poisoned—and would the responsibility for her death be laid at her husband's door? He was a doctor; he had opportunity and means, no doubt. What about motive? An unpleasant qualm shot across my mind as it occurred to me that Judith might be involved. I had good reason to know how businesslike their relations were—but would the general public believe that? Would a cynical police officer believe it? Judith was a very beautiful young woman. An attractive secretary or assistant had been the motive for many crimes. The possibility dismayed me.

I considered Allerton next. Could there be any reason for doing away with Allerton? If we had to have a murder, I would prefer to see Allerton the victim! One ought to be able to find motives easily for doing away with him. Miss Cole, though not young, was still a good-looking woman. She might, conceivably, be actuated by jealousy if she and Allerton had ever been on intimate terms, though I had no reason to believe that that was the case. Besides, if Allerton was X—

I shook my head impatiently. All this was getting me nowhere. A footstep on the gravel below attracted my attention. It was Franklin walking rapidly towards the house, his hands in his pockets, his head thrust forward. His whole attitude was one of dejection. Seeing him thus, off guard, I was struck by the fact that he looked a thoroughly unhappy man.

I was so busy staring at him that I did not hear a footfall nearer at hand and turned with a start when Miss Cole spoke to me.

"I didn't hear you coming," I explained apologetically as I sprang up.

She was examining the summerhouse.

"What a Victorian relic!"

"Isn't it? It's rather spidery, I'm afraid. Do sit down. I'll dust the seat for you."

For it occurred to me that here was a chance to get to know one of my fellow guests a little better. I studied Miss Cole covertly as I brushed away cobwebs.

She was a woman of between thirty and forty, slightly haggard, with a clear-cut profile and really very beautiful eyes. There was about her an air of reserve, more—of suspicion. It came to me suddenly that this was a woman who had suffered and who was, in consequence, deeply distrustful of life. I felt that I would like to know more about Elizabeth Cole.

"There," I said with a final flick of the handkerchief, "that's the best I can do."

"Thank you." She smiled and sat down. I sat down beside her. The seat creaked ominously, but no catastrophe occurred.

Miss Cole said:

"Do tell me, what were you thinking about when I came up to you? You seemed quite sunk in thought."

I said slowly:

"I was watching Dr. Franklin."

"Yes?"

I saw no reason for not repeating what had been in my mind.

"It struck me that he looked a very unhappy man."

The woman beside me said quietly:

"But of course he is. You must have realized that."

I think I showed my surprise. I said, stammering slightly:

"No—no—I haven't. I've always thought of him as absolutely wrapped up in his work."

"So he is."

"Do you call that unhappiness? I should have said it was the happiest state imaginable."

"Oh yes, I'm not disputing it—but not if you're hampered from doing what you feel it's in it to do. If you can't, that is to say, produce your best."

I looked at her, feeling rather puzzled. She went on to explain.

"Last autumn, Dr. Franklin was offered the chance of going out to Africa and continuing his research work there. He's tremendously keen, as you know, and has really done first-class work already in the realm of tropical medicine."

"And he didn't go?"

"No. His wife protested. She herself wasn't well enough to stand the climate and she kicked against the idea of being left behind, especially as it would have meant very economical living for her. The pay offered was not high."

"Oh," I said. I went on slowly: "I suppose he felt that in her state of health he couldn't leave her."

"Do you know much about her state of health, Captain Hastings?"

"Well, I—no— But she is an invalid, isn't she?"

"She certainly enjoys bad health," said Miss Cole drily. I looked at her doubtfully. It was easy to see that her sympathies were entirely with the husband.

"I suppose," I said slowly, "that women who are—delicate are apt to be selfish?"

"Yes, I think invalids—chronic invalids—usually are very selfish. One can't blame them perhaps. It's so easy."

"You don't think that there's really very much the matter with Mrs. Franklin?"

"Oh, I shouldn't like to say that. It's just a suspicion. She always seems able to do anything she wants to do."

I reflected in silence for a minute or two. It struck me that Miss Cole seemed very well acquainted with the ramifications of the Franklin ménage. I asked with some curiosity:

"You know Dr. Franklin well, I suppose?"

She shook her head.

"Oh no. I had only met them once or twice before we met here."

"But he has talked to you about himself, I suppose?"

Again she shook her head.

"No, what I have just told you I learnt from your daughter Judith."

Judith, I reflected with a moment's bitterness, talked to everyone except me.

Miss Cole went on:

"Judith is terrifically loyal to her employer and very much up in arms on his behalf. Her condemnation of Mrs. Franklin's selfishness is sweeping."

"You, too, think she is selfish?"

"Yes, but I can see her point of view. I—I—understand invalids. I can understand, too, Dr. Franklin's giving way to her. Judith, of course, thinks he should park his wife anywhere and get on with the job. Your daughter's a very enthusiastic scientific worker."

"I know," I said rather disconsolately. "It worries me sometimes. It doesn't seem natural, if you know what I mean. I feel she ought to be—more human—more keen on having a good time. Amuse herself—fall in love with a nice boy or two. After all, youth is the time to have one's fling—not to sit poring over test tubes. It isn't natural. In our young days we were having fun—flirting—enjoying ourselves—*you* know."

There was a moment's silence. Then Miss Cole said in a queer cold voice:

"I don't know."

I was instantly horrified. Unconsciously I had spoken as though she and I were contemporaries—but I realized suddenly that she was well over ten years my junior and that I had been unwittingly extremely tactless.

I apologized as best I could. She cut into my stammering phrases.

"No, no, I didn't mean that. Please don't apologize. I meant just simply what I said. *I don't know.* I was never what you mean by 'young.' I never had what is called 'a good time.'"

Something in her voice, a bitterness, a deep resentment, left me at a loss. I said rather lamely but with sincerity:

"I'm sorry."

She smiled.

"Oh, well, it doesn't matter. Don't look so upset. Let's talk about something else."

I obeyed.

"Tell me something about the other people here," I said. "Unless they're all strangers to you."

"I've known the Luttrells all my life. It's rather sad that they should have to do this—especially for him. He's rather a dear. And she's nicer than you'd think. It's having had to pinch and scrape all her life that has made her rather—well—predatory. If you're always on the make, it does tell in the end. The only thing I do rather dislike about her is that gushing manner."

"Tell me something about Mr. Norton."

"There isn't really much to tell. He's very nice—rather shy— just a little stupid, perhaps. He's always been rather delicate. He's lived with his mother—rather a peevish, stupid woman. She bossed him a good deal, I think. She died a few years ago. He's keen on birds and flowers and things like that. He's a very kind person—and he's the sort of person who sees a lot."

"Through his glasses, you mean?"

Miss Cole smiled.

"Well, I wasn't meaning it quite so literally as that. I meant more that he *notices* a good deal. Those quiet people often do. He's unselfish—and very considerate for a man, but he's rather— ineffectual, if you know what I mean."

I nodded.

"Oh yes, I know."

Elizabeth Cole said suddenly, and once more the deep bitter note was in her voice:

"That's the depressing part of places like this. Guest houses run by broken-down gentlepeople. They're full of failures—of people who have never got anywhere and never will get any- where, of people who—who have been defeated and broken by life, of people who are old and tired and finished."

Her voice died away. A deep and spreading sadness permeated me. How true it was! Here we were, a collection of twilit people. *Grey heads, grey hearts, grey dreams.* Myself, sad and lonely, the woman beside me also a bitter and disillusioned creature. Dr. Franklin, his ambitions curbed and thwarted, his wife a prey to ill health. Quiet little Norton limping about looking at birds. Even Poirot, the once brilliant Poirot, now a broken, crippled old man.

How different it had been in the old days—the days when I had first come to Styles. The thought was too much for me—a stifled exclamation of pain and regret came to my lips.

My companion said quickly:

"What is it?"

"Nothing. I was just struck by the contrast—I was here, you know, many years ago, as a young man. I was thinking of the difference between then and now."

"I see. It was a happy house then? Everyone was happy here?"

Curious, sometimes, how one's thoughts seemed to swing in a kaleidoscope. It happened to me now. A bewildering shuffling and reshuffling of memories, of events. Then the mosaic settled into its true pattern.

My regret had been for the past as the past, not for the reality. For even then, in that far-off time, there had been no happiness at Styles. I remembered dispassionately the real facts. My friend John and his wife, both unhappy and chafing at the life they were forced to lead. Lawrence Cavendish, sunk in melancholy. Cynthia, her girlish brightness damped by her dependent position. Inglethorp married to a rich woman for her money. No, none of them had been happy. And now, again, no one here was happy. Styles was not a lucky house.

I said to Miss Cole:

"I've been indulging in false sentiment. This was never a happy house. It isn't now. Everyone here is unhappy."

"No, no. Your daughter—"

"Judith's not happy."

I said it with the certainty of sudden knowledge. No, Judith wasn't happy.

"Boyd Carrington," I said doubtfully. "He was saying the other day that he was lonely—but for all that I think he's enjoying himself quite a good deal—what with his house and one thing and another."

Miss Cole said sharply:

"Oh yes, but then Sir William is different. He doesn't belong here like the rest of us do. He's from the outside world—the world of success and independence. He's made a success of his life and he knows it. He's not one of—of the maimed."

It was a curious word to choose. I turned and stared at her.

"Will you tell me," I asked, "why you used that particular expression?"

"Because," she said with a sudden fierce energy, "it's the truth. The truth about me, at any rate. I am maimed."

"I can see," I said gently, "that you have been very unhappy."

She said quietly:

"You don't know who I am, do you?"

"Er—I know your name—"

"Cole isn't my name—that is to say, it was my mother's name. I took it—afterwards."

"After?"

"My real name is Litchfield."

For a minute or two it didn't sink in—it was just a name vaguely familiar. Then I remembered.

"Matthew Litchfield."

She nodded.

"I see you know about it. That was what I meant just now. My father was an invalid and a tyrant. He forbade us any kind of normal life. We couldn't ask friends to the house. He kept us short of money. We were—in prison."

She paused, her eyes, those beautiful eyes, wide and dark.

"And then my sister—my sister—"

She stopped.

"Please don't—don't go on. It is too painful for you. I know about it. There is no need to tell me."

"But you don't know. You can't. Maggie. It's inconceivable—unbelievable. I know that she went to the police, that she gave herself up, that she confessed. But I still sometimes can't believe it! I feel somehow that it wasn't true—that it didn't—that it couldn't have happened like she said it did."

"You mean"—I hesitated—"that the facts were at—at variance—"

She cut me short.

"No, no. Not that. No, it's Maggie herself. It wasn't *like* her. It wasn't—it wasn't *Maggie!*"

Words trembled on my lips, but I did not say them. The time had not yet come when I could say to her:

"You are right. *It wasn't Maggie . . .*"

9

It must have been about six o'clock when Colonel Luttrell came along the path. He had a rook rifle with him and was carrying a couple of dead wood pigeons.

He started when I hailed him and seemed surprised to see us.

"Hullo, what are you two doing there? That tumble-down old place isn't very safe, you know. It's falling to pieces. Probably break up about your ears. Afraid you'll get dirty there, Elizabeth."

"Oh, that's all right. Captain Hastings has sacrificed a pocket handkerchief in the good cause of keeping my dress clean."

The Colonel murmured vaguely:

"Oh, really? Oh well, that's all right."

He stood there pulling at his lip and we got up and joined him.

His mind seemed far away this evening. He roused himself to say:

"Been trying to get some of these cursed wood pigeons. Do a lot of damage, you know."

"You're a very fine shot, I hear," I told him.

"Eh? Who told you that? Oh, Boyd Carrington. Used to be— used to be. Bit rusty nowadays. Age will tell."

"Eyesight," I suggested.

He negatived the suggestion immediately.

"Nonsense. Eyesight's as good as ever it was. That is—have to wear glasses for reading, of course. But far sight's all right."

He repeated a minute or two later:

"Yes—all right. Not that it matters . . ."

His voice tailed off into an absent-minded mutter.

Miss Cole said, looking round:

"What a beautiful evening it is."

She was quite right. The sun was drawing to the west and the light was a rich golden, bringing out the deeper shades of green in the trees in a deep, glowing effect. It was an evening, still and calm, and very English, such as one remembers when in far-off tropical countries. I said as much.

Colonel Luttrell agreed eagerly.

"Yes, yes, often used to think of evenings like this—out in India, you know. Makes you look forward to retiring and settling down—what?"

I nodded. He went on, his voice changing:

"Yes, settling down—coming home—nothing's ever quite what you picture it—no—no."

I thought that that was probably particularly true in his case. He had not pictured himself running a guest house, trying to make it pay, with a nagging wife forever snapping at him and complaining.

We walked slowly towards the house. Norton and Boyd Carrington were sitting on the verandah and the Colonel and I joined them while Miss Cole went on into the house.

We chatted for a few minutes. Colonel Luttrell seemed to have brightened up. He made a joke or two and seemed far more cheerful and wide-awake than usual.

"Been a hot day," said Norton. "I'm thirsty."

"Have a drink, you fellows. On the house, what?" The Colonel sounded eager and happy.

We thanked him and accepted. He got up and went in.

The part of the terrace where we were sitting was just outside the dining-room window, and that window was open.

We heard the Colonel inside—opening a cupboard, then heard the squeak of a corkscrew and the subdued pop as the cork of the bottle came out.

And then, sharp and high came the unofficial voice of Mrs. Colonel Luttrell!

"What are you doing, George?"

The Colonel's voice was subdued to a mutter. We only heard a mumbled word here and there—fellows outside—drink—

The sharp, irritating voice burst out indignantly:

"You'll do no such thing, George. The idea now. How do you think we'll ever make this place pay if you go round standing everybody drinks? Drinks here will be paid for. *I've* got a business head if you haven't. Why, you'd be bankrupt tomorrow if it wasn't for me! I've got to look after you like a child. Yes, just like a child. You've got no sense at all. Give me that bottle. Give it me, I say."

Again there was an agonized low protesting mumble.

Mrs. Luttrell answered snappishly:

"I don't care whether they do or they don't. The bottle's going back in the cupboard, and I'm going to lock the cupboard too."

There was the sound of a key being turned in the lock.

"There now. That's the way of it."

This time the Colonel's voice came more clearly:

"You're going too far, Daisy. I won't have it."

"*You* won't have it? And who are you, I'd like to know? Who runs this house? I do. And don't you forget it."

There was a faint swish of draperies and Mrs. Luttrell evidently flounced out of the room.

It was some few moments before the Colonel reappeared. He looked in those few moments to have grown much older and feebler.

There was not one of us who did not feel deeply sorry for him and who would not willingly have murdered Mrs. Luttrell.

"Awfully sorry, you chaps," he said, his voice sounding stiff and unnatural. "Seem to have run out of whisky."

He must have realized that we could not have helped overhearing what had passed. If he had not realized it, our manner would soon have told him. We were all miserably uncomfortable, and Norton quite lost his head, hurriedly saying first that he didn't really want a drink—too near dinner, wasn't it, and then elaborately changing the subject and making a series of the most unconnected remarks. It was indeed a bad moment. I myself felt paralyzed and Boyd Carrington, who was the only one of us who might conceivably have managed to pass it off, got no opportunity with Norton's babble.

Out of the tail of my eye I saw Mrs. Luttrell stalking away down one of the paths equipped with gardening gloves and a dandelion weeder. She was certainly an efficient woman, but I felt bitterly towards her just then. No human being has a right to humiliate another human being.

Norton was still talking feverishly. He had picked up a wood pigeon and from first telling us how he had been laughed at at his prep school for being sick when he saw a rabbit killed, had gone on to the subject of grouse moors, telling a long and rather pointless story of an accident that had occurred in Scotland when a beater had been shot. We talked of various shooting accidents we had known, and then Boyd Carrington cleared his throat and said:

"Rather an amusing thing happened once with a batman of mine. Irish chap. He had a holiday and went off to Ireland for it. When he came back, I asked him if he had had a good holiday.

"'Ah shure, your Honour, best holiday I've ever had in my life!'

"'I'm glad of that,' I said, rather surprised at his enthusiasm.

"'Ah yes, shure, it was a grand holiday! I shot my brother.'

"'You shot your brother!' I exclaimed.

"'Ah yes, indade. It's years now that I've been wanting to do it. And there I was on a roof in Dublin and who should I see coming down the street but my brother and I there with a rifle in my hand. A lovely shot it was, though I say it myself. Picked him off as clean as a bird. Ah! It was a foine moment, that, and I'll never forget it!'"

Boyd Carrington told a story well, with exaggerated dramatic emphasis, and we all laughed and felt easier. When he got up and strolled off saying he must get a bath before dinner, Norton voiced our feeling by saying with enthusiasm:

"What a splendid chap he is!"

I agreed, and Luttrell said: "Yes, yes, a good fellow."

"Always been a success everywhere, so I understand," said

Norton. "Everything he's turned his hand to has succeeded. Clear-headed, knows his own mind—essentially a man of action. The true successful man."

Luttrell said slowly:

"Some men are like that. Everything they turn their hand to succeeds. They can't go wrong. Some people—have all the luck."

Norton gave a quick shake of the head.

"No, no, sir. Not luck." He quoted with meaning. "Not in our stars, dear Brutus—but in ourselves."

Luttrell said: "Perhaps you're right."

I said quickly:

"At any rate he's lucky to have inherited Knatton. What a place! But he certainly ought to marry. He'll be lonely there by himself."

Norton laughed. "Marry and settle down? And suppose his wife bullies him—"

It was the purest bad luck. The sort of remark that anyone could make. But it was unfortunate in the circumstances, and Norton realized it just at the moment that the words came out. He tried to catch them back, hesitated, stammered, and stopped awkwardly. It made the whole thing worse.

Both he and I began to speak at once. I made some idiotic remark about the evening light. Norton said something about having some bridge after dinner.

Colonel Luttrell took no notice of either of us. He said in a queer, inexpressive voice:

"No, Boyd Carrington won't get bullied by his wife. He's not the sort of man who *lets* himself get bullied. *He's* all right. He's a *man!*"

It was very awkward. Norton began babbling about bridge again. In the middle of it a large wood pigeon came flapping over our heads and settled on the branch of a tree not far away.

Colonel Luttrell picked up his gun.

"There's one of the blighters," he said.

But before he could take aim the bird had flown off again through the trees where it was impossible to get a shot at it.

At the same moment, however, the Colonel's attention was diverted by a movement on the far slope.

"Damme, there's a rabbit nibbling the bark of those young fruit trees. Thought I'd wired the place."

He raised the rifle and fired, and as I saw—

There came a scream in a woman's voice. It died in a kind of horrible gurgle.

The rifle fell from the Colonel's hand, his body sagged—he caught his lip.

"My God—it's Daisy."

I was already running across the lawn. Norton came behind me. I reached the spot and knelt down. It was Mrs. Luttrell. She had been kneeling, tying a stake against one of the small fruit trees. The grass was long there so that I realized how it was that the Colonel had not seen her clearly and had only distinguished movement in the grass. The light, too, was confusing. She had been shot through the shoulder and the blood was gushing out.

I bent to examine the wound and looked up at Norton. He was leaning against a tree and was looking green and as though he were going to be sick. He said apologetically:

"I can't stand blood."

I said sharply:

"Get hold of Franklin—at once. Or the nurse."

He nodded and ran off.

It was Nurse Craven who appeared first upon the scene. She was there in an incredibly short time and at once set about in a businesslike way to stop the bleeding. Franklin arrived at a run soon afterwards. Between them they got Mrs. Luttrell into the house and to bed. Franklin dressed and bandaged the wound and sent for her own doctor and Nurse Craven stayed with her.

I ran across Franklin just as he left the telephone.

"How is she?"

"Oh! She'll pull through all right. It missed any vital spot luckily. How did it happen?"

I told him. He said:

"I see. Where's the old boy? He'll be feeling knocked out, I shouldn't wonder. Probably needs attention more than she does. I shouldn't say his heart is any too good."

We found Colonel Luttrell in the smoking room. He was a blue colour round the mouth and looked completely dazed. He said brokenly:

"Daisy? Is she—how is she?"

Franklin said quickly:

"She'll be all right, sir. You needn't worry."

"I thought—rabbit—nibbling the bark—don't know how I came to make such a mistake. Light in my eyes."

"These things happen," said Franklin drily. "I've seen one or two of them in my time. Look here, sir, you'd better let me give you a pick-me-up. You're not feeling too good."

"I'm all right. Can I—can I go to her?"

"Not just now. Nurse Craven is with her. But you don't need to worry. She's all right. Dr. Oliver will be here presently and he'll tell you the same."

I left the two of them together and went out into the evening sunshine. Judith and Allerton were coming along the path towards me. His head was bent to hers and they were both laughing.

Coming on top of the tragedy that had just happened, it made me feel very angry. I called sharply to Judith and she looked up surprised. In a few words I told them what had occurred.

"What an extraordinary thing to happen," was my daughter's comment.

She did not seem nearly as perturbed as she should have done, I thought.

Allerton's manner was outrageous. He seemed to take the whole thing as a good joke.

"Serves the old harridan damn well right," he observed. "Think the old boy did it on purpose."

"Certainly not," I said sharply. "It was an accident."

"Yes, but I know these accidents. Damned convenient sometimes. My word, if the old boy shot her deliberately, I take off my hat to him."

"It was nothing of the kind," I said angrily.

"Don't be too sure. I've known two men who shot their wives. Cleaning his revolver one was. The other fired point-blank at her as a joke, he said. Didn't know the thing was loaded. Got away with it, both of them. Damned good release, I should say myself."

"Colonel Luttrell," I said coldly, "isn't that type of man."

"Well, you couldn't say it wouldn't be a blessed release, could you?" demanded Allerton pertinently. "They hadn't just had a row or anything, had they?"

I turned away angrily, at the same time trying to hide a certain perturbation. Allerton had come a little too near the mark. For the first time a doubt crept into my mind.

It was not bettered by meeting Boyd Carrington. He had been for a stroll down towards the lake, he explained. When I told him the news, he said at once:

"You don't think he meant to shoot her, do you, Hastings?"

"My dear man."

"Sorry, sorry. I shouldn't have said that. It was only, for the moment, one wondered . . . She—she gave him a bit of provocation, you know."

We were both silent for a moment as we remembered the scene we had so unwillingly overheard.

I went upstairs feeling unhappy and worried and rapped on Poirot's door.

He had already heard through Curtiss of what had occurred, but he was eager for full details. Since my arrival at Styles I had got into the way of reporting most of my daily encounters and conversations in full detail. In this way I felt that the dear old fellow felt less cut off. It gave him the illusion of actually participating in everything that went on. I have always had a good and accurate memory and found it a simple matter to repeat conversations verbatim.

Poirot listened very attentively. I was hoping that he would be able definitely to pooh-pooh the dreadful suggestion that had by now taken uneasy control of my mind, but before he had a chance of telling me what he thought, there came a light tap on the door.

It was Nurse Craven. She apologized for disturbing us.

"I'm so sorry, but I thought Doctor was here. The old lady is conscious now and she's worrying about her husband. She'd like to see him. Do you know where he is, Captain Hastings? I don't want to leave my patient."

I volunteered to go and look for him. Poirot nodded approval and Nurse Craven thanked me warmly.

I found Colonel Luttrell in a little morning room that was seldom used. He was standing by the window looking out.

He turned sharply as I came in. His eyes asked a question. He looked, I thought, afraid.

"Your wife is conscious, Colonel Luttrell, and is asking for you."

"Oh." The colour surged up in his cheeks and I realized then how very white he had been before. He said slowly, fumblingly, like an old, old man:

"She—she—is asking for me? I'll—I'll come—at once."

He was so unsteady as he began shuffling towards the door that I came and helped him. He leaned on me heavily as we went up the stairs. His breathing was coming with difficulty. The shock, as Franklin had prophesied, was severe.

We came to the door of the sickroom. I tapped and Nurse Craven's brisk, efficient voice called "Come in."

Still supporting the old man, I went with him into the room. There was a screen round the bed. We came round the corner of it.

Mrs. Luttrell was looking very ill—white and frail, her eyes closed. She opened them as we came round the corner of the screen.

She said in a small breathless voice:

"George—George—"

"Daisy—my dear . . ."

One of her arms was bandaged and supported. The other, the free one, moved unsteadily towards him. He took a step forward and clasped her frail little hand in his. He said again:

"Daisy . . ." And then, gruffly, "Thank God, you're all right."

And looking up at him, seeing his eyes slightly misty, and the deep love and anxiety in them, I felt bitterly ashamed of all our ghoulish imaginings.

I crept quietly out of the room. Camouflaged accident indeed! There was no disguising that heartfelt note of thankfulness. I felt immeasurably relieved.

The sound of the gong startled me as I went along the passage. I had completely forgotten the passage of time. The accident had upset everything. Only the cook had gone on as usual and produced dinner at the usual time.

Most of us had not changed and Colonel Luttrell did not appear. But Mrs. Franklin, looking quite attractive in a pale pink evening dress, was downstairs for once and seemed in good health and spirits. Franklin, I thought, was moody and absorbed.

After dinner, to my annoyance, Allerton and Judith disappeared into the garden together. I sat around a while, listening to Franklin and Norton discussing tropical diseases. Norton was a sympathetic and interested listener, even if he knew little of the subject under discussion.

Mrs. Franklin and Boyd Carrington were talking at the other end of the room. He was showing her some patterns of curtains or cretonnes.

Elizabeth Cole had a book and seemed deeply absorbed in it. I fancied that she was slightly embarrassed and ill at ease with me. Perhaps not unnaturally so after her confidences of the afternoon. I was sorry about it, all the same, and hoped she did not regret all she had told me. I should have liked to have made it clear to her that I should respect her confidence and not repeat it. However, she gave me no chance.

After a while I went up to Poirot.

I found Colonel Luttrell sitting in the circle of light thrown by the one small electric lamp that was turned on.

He was talking and Poirot was listening. I think the Colonel was speaking to himself rather than to his listener.

"I remember so well—yes, it was at a hunt ball. She wore white stuff, called tulle, I think it was. Floated all round her. Such a pretty girl—bowled me over then and there. I said to myself, 'That's the girl I'm going to marry.' And by Jove, I brought it off.

Awfully pretty way she had with her—saucy, you know, plenty of back chat. Always gave as good as she got, bless her."

He chuckled.

I saw the scene in my mind's eye. I could imagine Daisy Luttrell with a young saucy face and that smart tongue—so charming then, so apt to turn shrewish with the years.

But it was as that young girl, his first real love, that Colonel Luttrell was thinking of her tonight. His Daisy.

And again I felt ashamed of what we had said such a few hours previously.

Of course, when Colonel Luttrell had at last taken himself off to bed, I blurted out the whole thing to Poirot.

He listened very quietly. I could make nothing of the expression on his face.

"So that is what you thought, Hastings—that the shot was fired on purpose?"

"Yes. I feel ashamed now—"

Poirot waved aside my present feelings.

"Did the thought occur to you of your own accord, or did someone else suggest it to you?"

"Allerton said something of the kind," I said resentfully. "He would, of course."

"Anyone else?"

"Boyd Carrington suggested it."

"Ah! Boyd Carrington."

"And after all, he's a man of the world and has experience of these things."

"Oh, quite so, quite so. He did not see the thing happen, though?"

"No, he'd gone for a walk. Bit of exercise before changing for dinner."

"I see."

I said uneasily:

"I don't think I really believed that theory. It was only—"

Poirot interrupted me.

"You need not be so remorseful about your suspicions, Hastings. It was an idea quite likely to occur to anyone given the circumstances. Oh yes, it was all quite natural."

There was something in Poirot's manner I did not quite understand. A reserve. His eyes were watching me with a curious expression.

I said slowly:

"Perhaps. But seeing now how devoted he really is to her—"

Poirot nodded.

"Exactly. That is often the case, remember. Underneath the quarrels, the misunderstandings, the apparent hostility of everyday life, a real and true affection can exist."

I agreed. I remembered the gentle, affectionate look in little Mrs. Luttrell's eyes as she looked up at her husband stooping over her bed. No more vinegar, no impatience, no ill temper.

Married life, I mused, as I went to bed, was a curious thing.

That something in Poirot's manner still worried me. That curious watchful look—as though he were waiting for me to see—what?

I was just getting into bed when it came to me. Hit me bang between the eyes.

If Mrs. Luttrell had been killed, it would have been a case like those other cases. Colonel Luttrell would, apparently, have killed his wife. It would have been accounted an accident, yet at the same time nobody would have been sure that it was an accident, or whether it had been done on purpose. Insufficient evidence to show it as murder, but quite enough evidence for murder to be suspected.

But that meant—that meant—

What did it mean?

It meant—if anything at all was to make sense—that it was *not* Colonel Luttrell who shot Mrs. Luttrell, but X.

And that was clearly impossible. I had seen the whole thing. It was Colonel Luttrell who had fired the shot. No other shot had been fired.

Unless— But surely that would be impossible. No, perhaps not impossible—merely highly improbable. But possible, yes . . . Supposing that someone else had waited his moment and, at the exact instant when Colonel Luttrell had fired (at a rabbit), this other person had fired at Mrs. Luttrell. Then only the one shot would have been heard. Or, even with a slight discrepancy, it would have been put down as an echo. (Now I come to think of it, there had been an echo, surely.)

But no, that was absurd. There were ways of deciding exactly what weapon a bullet had been fired from. The marks on the bullet must agree with the rifling of the barrel.

But that, I remembered, was only when the police were anxious to establish what weapon had fired the shot. There would have been no enquiry in this business. For Colonel Luttrell would have been quite as certain as everyone else that it was he who had fired the fatal shot. That fact would have been admitted, accepted without question, there would have been no question of tests. The only doubt would have been whether the shot was fired accidentally or with criminal intent—a question that could never be resolved.

And therefore the case fell into line exactly with those other cases—with the case of the labourer Riggs, who didn't remember but supposed he must have done it; with Maggie Litchfield, who went out of her mind and gave herself up—for a crime she had not committed.

Yes, this case fell into line with the rest and I knew now the meaning of Poirot's manner. He was waiting for me to appreciate the fact.

10

I opened the subject with Poirot the following morning. His face lighted up and he wagged his head appreciatively.

"Excellent, Hastings. I wondered if you would see the similarity. I did not want to prompt you, you understand."

"Then I am right. This is another X case?"

"Undeniably."

"But *why*, Poirot? What is the motive?"

Poirot shook his head.

"Don't you know? Haven't you any idea?"

Poirot said slowly:

"I have an idea, yes."

"You've got the connection between all these different cases?"

"I think so."

"Well, then."

I could hardly restrain my impatience.

"No, Hastings."

"But I've got to know."

"It is much better that you should not."

"Why?"

"You must take it from me that it is so."

"You are incorrigible," I said. "Twisted up with arthritis. Sitting here helpless. And still trying to play a 'lone hand.'"

"Do not figure to yourself that I am playing a lone hand. Not at all. You are, on the contrary, very much in the picture, Hastings. You are my eyes and my ears. I only refuse to give you information that might be dangerous."

"To me?"

"To the murderer."

"You want him," I said slowly, "not to suspect that you are on his track? That is it, I suppose. Or else you think that I cannot take care of myself."

"You should at least know one thing, Hastings. A man who has killed once will kill again—and again and again and again."

"At any rate," I said grimly, "there hasn't been another murder this time. One bullet at least has gone wide."

"Yes, that was very fortunate—very fortunate indeed. As I told you, these things are difficult to foresee."

He sighed. His face took on a worried expression.

I went away quietly, realizing sadly how unfit Poirot was now for any sustained effort. His brain was still keen, but he was a sick and tired man.

Poirot had warned me not to try to penetrate the personality of X. In my own mind I still clung to my belief that I had penetrated that personality. There was only one person at Styles who struck me as definitely evil. By a simple question, however, I could make sure of one thing. The test would be a negative one, but would nevertheless have a certain value.

I tackled Judith after breakfast.

"Where had you been yesterday evening when I met you, you and Major Allerton?"

The trouble is that when you are intent on one aspect of a thing, you tend to ignore all other aspects. I was quite startled when Judith flared out at me.

"Really, Father, I don't see what business it is of yours."

I stared at her, rather taken aback.

"I—I only asked."

"Yes, but *why*? Why do you have to be continually asking questions? What was I doing? Where did I go? Who was I with? It's really intolerable!"

The funny part of it was, of course, that this time I was not really asking at all where Judith was. It was Allerton I was interested in.

I tried to pacify her.

"Really, Judith, I don't see why I can't ask a simple question."

"I don't see why you want to know."

"I don't particularly. I mean, I just wondered why neither of you—er—seemed to know what had happened."

"About the accident, do you mean? I'd been down to the village, if you must know, to get some stamps."

I pounced on the personal pronoun.

"Allerton wasn't with you then?"

Judith gave an exasperated gasp.

"No, he was not," she said in tones of cold fury. "Actually we'd met just near the house and only about two minutes before we met you. I hope you're satisfied now. But I'd just like to say that if I'd spent the whole day walking around with Major Allerton, it's really not your business. I'm twenty-one and earning my own living and how I spend my time is entirely my own business."

"Entirely," I said quickly, trying to stem the tide.

"I'm glad you agree." Judith looked mollified. She gave a rueful half smile. "Oh, dearest, do try and not come the heavy father quite so much. You don't know how maddening it is. If you just wouldn't *fuss* so."

"I won't—I really won't in future," I promised her.

Franklin came striding along at this minute.

"Hullo, Judith. Come along. We're later than usual."

His manner was curt and really hardly polite. In spite of myself I felt annoyed. I knew that Franklin was Judith's employer, that he had a call upon her time and that, since he paid for it, he was entitled to give her orders. Nevertheless I did not see why he could not behave with common courtesy. His manners were not what one would call polished to anyone, but he did at least behave to most people with a certain amount of everyday politeness. But to Judith, especially of late, his manner was always curt and dictatorial in the extreme. He hardly looked at her when he spoke and merely barked out orders. Judith never appeared to resent this, but I did on her behalf. It crossed my mind that it was especially unfortunate since it contrasted in such a very marked way with Allerton's exaggerated attention. No doubt John Franklin was a ten times better man than Allerton, but he compared very badly with him from the point of view of attraction.

I watched Franklin as he strode along the path towards the laboratory, his ungainly walk, his angular build, the jutting bones of his face and head, his red hair and his freckles. An ugly man and an ungainly man. None of the more obvious qualities. A good brain, yes, but women seldom fall for brains alone. I reflected with dismay that Judith, owing to the circumstances of her job, practically never came into contact with other men. She had no opportunity of sizing up various attractive men. Compared with the gruff and unattractive Franklin, Allerton's meretricious charms stood out with all the force of contrast. My poor girl had no chance of appraising him at his true worth.

Supposing that she should come seriously to lose her heart to him? The irritability she had shown just now was a disquieting sign. Allerton, I knew, was a real bad lot. He was possibly something more. If Allerton were X—?

He could be. At the time that the shot was fired, he had not been with Judith.

But what was the motive of all these seemingly purposeless crimes? There was, I felt sure, nothing of the madman about Allerton. He was sane—altogether sane—and utterly unprincipled.

And Judith—my Judith—was seeing altogether too much of him.

II

Up to this time, though I had been faintly worried about my daughter, my preoccupation over X and the possibility of a crime occurring at any moment had successfully driven more personal problems to the back of my mind.

Now that the blow had fallen, that a crime had been attempted and had mercifully failed, I was free to reflect on these things. And the more I did so, the more anxious I became. A chance word spoken one day revealed to me the fact that Allerton was a married man.

Boyd Carrington, who knew all about everyone, enlightened me further. Allerton's wife was a devout Roman Catholic. She had left him a short time after their marriage. Owing to her religion there had never been any question of divorce.

"And if you ask me," said Boyd Carrington frankly, "it suits the blighter down to the ground. His intentions are always dishonourable, and a wife in the background suits the book very well."

Pleasant hearing for a father!

The days after the shooting accident passed uneventfully enough on the surface, but they accompanied a growing undercurrent of unrest on my part.

Colonel Luttrell spent much time in his wife's bedroom. A nurse had arrived to take charge of the patient and Nurse Craven was able to resume her ministrations to Mrs. Franklin.

Without wishing to be ill-natured, I must admit that I had observed signs on Mrs. Franklin's part of irritation at not being the invalid *en chef*. The fuss and attention that centred round Mrs. Luttrell was clearly very displeasing to the little lady who was accustomed to her own health being the main topic of the day.

She lay about in a hammock chair, her hand to her side, complaining of palpitations. No food that was served was suitable for her, and all her exactions were masked by a veneer of patient endurance.

"I do so hate making a fuss," she murmured plaintively to Poirot. "I feel so ashamed of my wretched health. It's so—so *humiliating* always to have to ask people to be doing things for me. I sometimes think ill health is really a crime. If one isn't healthy and insensitive, one isn't fit for this world and one should just be put quietly away."

"Ah no, madame." Poirot, as always, was gallant. "The delicate exotic flower has to have the shelter of the greenhouse—it cannot endure the cold winds. It is the common weed that thrives in the wintry air—but it is not to be prized higher on that account. Consider my case—cramped, twisted, unable to move, but I—I do not think of quitting life. I enjoy still what I can—the food, the drink, the pleasures of the intellect."

Mrs. Franklin sighed and murmured:

"Ah, but it's different for you. You have no one but yourself to consider. In my case, there is my poor John. I feel acutely what a burden I am to him. A sickly useless wife. A millstone hung round his neck."

"He has never said that you are that, I am sure."

"Oh, not *said* so. Of course not. But men are so transparent, poor dears. And John isn't any good at concealing his feelings. He doesn't mean, of course, to be unkind, but he's—well, mercifully for himself he's a very insensitive sort of person. He's no feelings and so he doesn't expect anyone else to have them. It's so terribly lucky to be born thick-skinned."

"I should not describe Dr. Franklin as thick-skinned."

"Wouldn't you? Oh, but you don't know him as well as I do. Of course I know that if it wasn't for me, he would be much freer. Sometimes, you know, I get so terribly depressed that I think what a relief it would be to end it all."

"Oh, come, madame."

"After all, what use am I to anybody? To go out of it all into the Great Unknown—" She shook her head. "And then John would be free."

"Great fiddlesticks," said Nurse Craven when I repeated this conversation to her. "She won't do anything of the kind. Don't you worry, Captain Hastings. These ones that talk about 'ending it all' in a dying duck voice haven't the faintest intention of doing anything of the kind."

And I must say that once the excitement aroused by Mrs. Luttrell's injury had died down and Nurse Craven was once more in attendance, Mrs. Franklin's spirits improved very much.

On a particularly fine morning Curtiss had taken Poirot down to the corner below the beech trees near the laboratory. This was a favourite spot of his. It was sheltered from any east wind and in fact hardly any breeze could ever be felt there. This suited Poirot, who abhorred draughts and was always suspicious of the fresh air.

Actually, I think, he much preferred to be indoors but had grown to tolerate the outer air when muffled in rugs.

I strolled down to join him there, and just as I got there, Mrs. Franklin came out of the laboratory.

She was most becomingly dressed and looked remarkably cheerful. She explained that she was driving over with Boyd Carrington to see the house and to give expert advice in choosing cretonnes.

"I left my handbag in the lab yesterday when I was talking to John," she explained. "Poor John, he and Judith have driven into Tadcaster—they were short of some chemical reagent or other."

She sank down on a seat near Poirot and shook her head with a comical expression. "Poor dears—I'm so glad I haven't got the scientific mind. On a lovely day like this—it—all seems so puerile."

"You must not let scientists hear you say that, madame."

"No, of course not." Her face changed. It grew serious. She said quietly:

"You mustn't think, M. Poirot, that I don't admire my husband. I do. I think the way he just lives for his work is really—tremendous."

There was a little tremor in her voice.

A suspicion crossed my mind that Mrs. Franklin rather liked playing different roles. At this moment she was being the loyal and hero-worshipping wife.

She leaned forward, placing an earnest hand on Poirot's knee.

"John," she said, "is really a—a kind of *saint*. It makes me quite frightened sometimes."

To call Franklin a saint was somewhat overstating the case, I thought, but Barbara Franklin went on, her eyes shining:

"He'll do anything—take any risk—just to advance the sum of human knowledge. That is pretty fine, don't you think?"

"Assuredly, assuredly," said Poirot quickly.

"But sometimes, you know," went on Mrs. Franklin, "I'm really nervous about him. The lengths to which he'll go, I mean. This horrid bean thing he's experimenting with now. I'm so afraid that he'll start experimenting on himself."

"He'd take every precaution, surely," I said.

She shook her head with a slight, rueful smile.

"You don't know John. Did you never hear about what he did with that new gas?"

I shook my head.

"It was some new gas they wanted to find out about. John volunteered to test it. He was shut up in a tank for something like thirty-six hours—taking his pulse and temperature and respiration—to see what the aftereffects were and if they were the same for men as for animals. It was a frightful risk, so one of the professors told me afterwards. He might easily have passed out altogether. But that's the sort of person John is—absolutely oblivious of his own safety. I think it's rather wonderful, don't you, to be like that? *I* should never be brave enough."

"It needs, indeed, high courage," said Poirot, "to do these things in cold blood."

Barbara Franklin said:

"Yes, it does. I'm awfully proud of him, you know, but at the same time it makes me rather nervous, too. Because, you see, guinea pigs and frogs are no good after a certain point. You want the human reaction. That's why I feel so terrified that John will go and dose himself with this nasty ordeal bean and that something awful might happen." She sighed and shook her head. "But he only laughs at my fears. He really *is* a sort of saint, you know."

At this moment Boyd Carrington came towards us.

"Hullo, Babs, ready?"

"Yes, Bill, waiting for you."

"I do hope it won't tire you too much."

"Of course it won't. I feel better today than I have for ages."

She got up, smiled prettily at us both, and walked up the lawn with her tall escort.

"Dr. Franklin—the modern saint—h'm," said Poirot.

"Rather a change of attitude," I said. "But I think the lady is like that."

"Like what?"

"Given to dramatizing herself in various roles. One day the

misunderstood neglected wife, then the self-sacrificing suffering woman who hates to be a burden on the man she loves. Today it's the hero-worshipping helpmate. The trouble is that all the roles are slightly overdone."

Poirot said thoughtfully:

"You think Mrs. Franklin, do you not, rather a fool?"

"Well, I wouldn't say that—yes, perhaps not a very brilliant intellect."

"Ah, she is not your type."

"Who is my type?" I snapped.

Poirot replied unexpectedly:

"Open your mouth and shut your eyes and see what the fairies will send you—"

I was prevented from replying because Nurse Craven came tripping hastily across the grass. She gave us a smile with a brilliant flash of teeth, unlocked the door of the lab, passed inside and reappeared with a pair of gloves.

"First a hanky and now gloves, always something left behind," she observed as she sped back with them to where Barbara Franklin and Boyd Carrington were waiting.

Mrs. Franklin, I reflected, was that rather feckless type of woman who always did leave things behind, shedding her possessions and expecting everybody to retrieve them as a matter of course, and even, I fancied, was rather proud of herself for so doing. I had heard her more than once murmur complacently:

"Of course I've got a head like a *sieve*."

I sat looking after Nurse Craven as she ran across the lawn and out of sight. She ran well, her body was vigorous and well balanced. I said impulsively:

"I should think a girl must get fed up with that sort of life. I mean when there isn't much nursing to be done—when it's just fetch and carry. I don't suppose Mrs. Franklin is particularly considerate or kindly."

Poirot's response was distinctly annoying. For no reason whatever, he closed his eyes and murmured:

"Auburn hair."

Undoubtedly Nurse Craven had auburn hair—but I did not see why Poirot should choose just this minute to comment upon it.

I made no reply.

11

It was, I think, on the following morning before lunch that a conversation took place which left me vaguely disquieted.

There were four of us—Judith, myself, Boyd Carrington and Norton.

Exactly how the subject started, I am not sure, but we were talking of euthanasia—the case for and against it.

Boyd Carrington, as was natural, did most of the talking, Norton putting in a word or two here and there, and Judith sitting silent but closely attentive.

I myself had confessed that though there seemed, on the face of it, every reason to support the practice, yet in actuality I felt a sentimental shrinking from it. Besides, I said, I thought it would put too much power in the hands of relatives.

Norton agreed with me. He added that he thought it should only be done by the wish and consent of the patient himself where death after prolonged suffering was certain.

Boyd Carrington said:

"Ah, but that's the curious thing. Does the person most concerned ever wish to 'put himself out of his misery,' as we say?"

He then told a story, which he said was authentic, of a man in terrible pain from inoperable cancer. This man had begged the doctor in attendance to "give him something that would finish it all." The doctor had replied: "I can't do that, old man." Later, on leaving, he had placed by the patient some morphia tablets, telling him carefully how many he could safely take and what dose would be dangerous. Although these were left in the patient's charge and he could easily have taken a fatal quantity, he did not do so, "thus proving," said Boyd Carrington, "that, in spite of his words, the man preferred his suffering to a swift and merciful release."

It was then that Judith spoke for the first time, spoke with vigour and abruptly:

"Of course he would," she said. "It shouldn't have been left to him to decide."

Boyd Carrington asked what she meant.

"I mean that anyone who's weak—in pain and ill—hasn't got the strength to make a decision. They can't. It must be done for them. It's the duty of someone who loves them to make the decision."

"Duty?" I queried dubiously.

Judith turned on me.

"Yes, *duty*. Someone whose mind is clear and who will take the responsibility."

Boyd Carrington shook his head.

"And end up in the dock charged with murder?"

"Not necessarily. Anyway, if you love someone, you would take the risk."

"But look here, Judith," said Norton. "What you're suggesting is simply a terrific responsibility to take."

"I don't think it is. People are too afraid of responsibility. They'll take responsibility where a dog is concerned—why not with a human being?"

"Well—it's rather different, isn't it?"

Judith said:

"Yes, it's more important."

Norton murmured:

"You take my breath away."

Boyd Carrington asked curiously:

"So *you'd* take the risk, would you?"

"I think so," said Judith. "I'm not afraid of taking risks."

Boyd Carrington shook his head.

"It wouldn't do, you know. You can't have people here, there, and everywhere taking the law into their own hands. Deciding matters of life and death."

Norton said:

"Actually, you know, Boyd Carrington, most people wouldn't have the nerve to take the responsibility."

He smiled faintly as he looked at Judith.

"Don't believe you would if it came to the point."

Judith said composedly:

"One can't be sure, of course. I think I should."

Norton said with a slight twinkle:

"Not unless you had an axe of your own to grind."

Judith flushed hotly. She said sharply:

"That just shows you don't understand at all. If I had a—a personal motive, I couldn't do anything. Don't you see?" she appealed to us all. "It's got to be absolutely impersonal. You could only take the responsibility of—of ending a life if you were quite sure of your motive. It must be absolutely selfless."

"All the same," said Norton, "you wouldn't do it."

Judith insisted:

"I would. To begin with I don't hold life as sacred as all you people do. Unfit lives, useless lives—they should be got out of the way. There's so much *mess* about. Only people who can make a decent contribution to the community ought to be allowed to live. The others ought to be put painlessly away."

She appealed suddenly to Boyd Carrington.

"You agree with me, don't you?"

He said slowly:

"In principle, yes. Only the worthwhile should survive."

"Wouldn't you take the law into your own hands if it was necessary?"

Boyd Carrington said slowly:

"Perhaps. I don't know . . ."

Norton said quietly:

"A lot of people would agree with you in theory. But practice is a different matter."

"That's not logical."

Norton said impatiently:

"Of course it's not. It's really a question of *courage*. One just hasn't got the *guts*—to put it vulgarly."

Judith was silent. Norton went on.

"Frankly, you know, Judith, you'd be just the same yourself. You wouldn't have the courage when it came to it."

"Don't you think so?"

"I'm sure of it."

"I think you're wrong, Norton," said Boyd Carrington. "I think Judith has any amount of courage. Fortunately the issue doesn't often present itself."

The gong sounded from the house.

Judith got up.

She said very distinctly to Norton:

"You're wrong, you know. I've got more—more guts than you think."

She went swiftly towards the house. Boyd Carrington followed her, saying:

"Hey, wait for me, Judith."

I followed, feeling for some reason rather dismayed. Norton, who was always quick to sense a mood, endeavoured to console me.

"She doesn't mean it, you know," he said. "It's the sort of half-baked idea one has when one is young—but fortunately one doesn't carry it out. It remains just talk."

I think Judith overheard, for she cast a furious glance over her shoulder.

Norton dropped his voice.

"Theories needn't worry anybody," he said. "But look here, Hastings—"

"Yes?"

Norton seemed rather embarrassed. He said:

"I don't want to butt in, but what do you know of Allerton?"

"Of Allerton?"

"Yes, sorry if I'm being a Nosy Parker, but frankly—if I were you, I shouldn't let that girl of yours see too much of him. He's—well, his reputation isn't very good."

"I can see for myself the sort of rotter he is," I said bitterly. "But it's not so easy in these days."

"Oh, I know. Girls can look after themselves, as the saying goes. Most of them can, too. But—well—Allerton has rather a special technique in that line."

He hesitated, then said:

"Look here, I feel I ought to tell you. Don't let it go further, of course—but I do happen to know something pretty foul about him."

He told it me then and there—and I was able to verify it in every detail later. It was a revolting tale. The story of a girl, sure of herself, modern, independent. Allerton had brought all his "technique" to bear upon her. Later had come the other side of the picture—the story ended with a desperate girl taking her own life with an overdose of Veronal.

And the horrible part was that the girl in question had been of much the same type as Judith—the independent highbrow kind. The kind of girl who when she does lose her heart, loses it with a desperation and an abandonment that the silly little fluffy type can never know.

I went in to lunch with a horrible sense of foreboding.

12

"Is anything worrying you, *mon ami?*" asked Poirot that afternoon.

I did not answer, merely shook my head. I felt that I had no right to burden Poirot with this, my purely personal problem. It was not as though he could help in any way.

Judith would have treated any remonstrances on his part with the smiling detachment of the young towards the boring counsels of the old.

Judith, my Judith . . .

It is hard now to describe just what I went through that day. Afterwards, thinking it over, I am inclined to put something down to the atmosphere of Styles itself. Evil imaginings came easily to the mind there. There was, too, not only the past, but a sinister present. The shadow of murder and a murderer haunted the house.

And to the best of my belief the murderer was Allerton, and Judith was losing her heart to him! It was all unbelievable—monstrous—and I didn't know what to do.

It was after lunch that Boyd Carrington drew me aside. He hemmed and hawed a bit before coming to the point. At last he said rather jerkily:

"Don't think I'm interfering, but I think you ought to speak to that girl of yours. Give her a word of warning—eh? You know this fellow Allerton—reputation's pretty bad, and she—well, it looks rather like a case."

So easy for these men without children to speak like that! Give her a word of warning?

Would it be any use? Would it make things worse?

If only Cinders were here. She would know what to do—what to say.

I was tempted, I admit, to hold my peace and say nothing. But I reflected after a while that this was really only cowardice. I shrank from the unpleasantness of having things out with Judith. I was, you see, afraid of my tall, beautiful daughter.

I paced up and down the gardens in increasing agitation of mind. My footsteps led me at last to the rose garden, and there, as it were, the decision was taken out of my hands, for Judith was sitting on a seat alone, and in all my life I have never seen an expression of greater unhappiness on any woman's face.

The mask was off. Indecision and deep unhappiness showed only too plainly.

I took my courage in my hands. I went to her. She did not hear me until I was beside her.

"Judith," I said. "For God's sake, Judith, don't mind so much."

She turned on me, startled.

"Father? I didn't hear you."

I went on, knowing that it would be fatal if she managed to turn me back to normal everyday conversation.

"Oh, my dearest child, don't think I don't know, that I can't see. He isn't worth it—oh, do believe me, he isn't worth it."

Her face, troubled, alarmed, was turned towards me. She said quietly:

"Do you think you really know what you are talking about?"

"I do know. You care about this man. But, my dear, it's no good."

She smiled sombrely. A heartbreaking smile.

"Perhaps I know that as well as you do."

"You don't. You can't. Oh, Judith, what can come of it all? He's a married man. There can be no future there for you—only sorrow and shame—and all ending in bitter self-loathing."

Her smile grew wider—even more sorrowful.

"How fluently you talk, don't you?"

"Give it up, Judith—give it all up."

"No!"

"He's not worth it, my dear."

She said very quietly and slowly:

"He's worth everything in the world to me."

"No, no. Judith, I beg of you—"

The smile vanished. She turned on me like an avenging fury.

"How dare you? How dare you interfere? I won't stand it. You are never to speak to me of this again. I hate you—I hate you. It's no business of yours. It's *my* life—my own secret inside life!"

She got up. With one firm hand she pushed me aside and went past me. Like an avenging fury. I stared after her—dismayed.

II

I was still there, dazed and helpless, unable to think out my next course of action, some quarter of an hour later.

I was there when Elizabeth Cole and Norton found me.

They were, I realized later, very kind to me. They saw, they must have seen, that I was in a state of great mental perturbation. But tactfully enough they made no slightest allusion to my state of mind. Instead they took me with them on a rambling walk. They were both nature lovers. Elizabeth Cole pointed out wild flowers to me, Norton showed me birds through his field glasses.

Their talk was gentle, soothing, concerned only with feathered beings and with woodland flora. Little by little I came back to normal although underneath I was still in a state of the utmost perturbation.

Moreover I was, as people are, convinced that any happening that occurred was connected with my own particular perplexity.

So, therefore, when Norton, his glasses to his eyes, exclaimed: "Hullo, if that isn't a speckled woodpecker. I never—" and then broke off suddenly, I immediately leapt to suspicion. I held out my hand for the glasses.

"Let me see."

My voice was peremptory.

Norton fumbled with the glasses. He said in a curious, hesitating voice:

"I—I—made a mistake—it's flown away—at least, as a matter of fact, it was quite a common bird."

His face was white and troubled. He avoided looking at us. He seemed both bewildered and distressed.

Even now I cannot think I was altogether unreasonable in jumping to the conclusion that he had seen through those glasses of his something that he was determined to prevent my seeing.

Whatever it was that he had seen, he was so thoroughly taken aback by it that it was noticeable to both of us.

His glasses had been trained on a distant belt of woodland. What had he seen there?

I said peremptorily:

"Let me look."

I snatched at the glasses. I remember he tried to defend them from me, but he did it clumsily. I seized them roughly.

Norton said weakly:

"It wasn't really— I mean, the bird's gone . . . I wish—"

My hands shaking a little, I adjusted the glasses to my eyes. They were powerful glasses. I trained them as nearly as I could on the spot where I thought Norton had been looking.

But I saw nothing—nothing but a gleam of white (a girl's white dress?) disappearing into the trees.

I lowered the glasses. Without a word I handed them back to Norton. He did not meet my eyes. He was looking worried and perplexed.

We walked back to the house in silence and I remember that Norton was very silent all the way.

III

Mrs. Franklin and Boyd Carrington came in shortly after we got back to the house. He had taken her in his car to Tadminster because she wanted to do some shopping.

She had done it, I gather, pretty thoroughly. Lots of parcels came out of the car and she was looking quite animated, talking and laughing and with quite a colour in her cheeks.

She sent Boyd Carrington up with a particularly fragile purchase and I gallantly received a further consignment.

Her talk was quicker and more nervous than usual.

"Frightfully hot, isn't it? I think there's going to be a storm. This weather must break soon. They say, you know, there's quite a water shortage. The worst drought there's been for years."

She went on, turning to Elizabeth Cole:

"What have you all been doing with yourselves? Where's John? He said he'd got a headache and was going to walk it off. Very unlike him to have a headache. I think, you know, he's worried about his experiments. They aren't going right or something. I wish he'd talk more about things."

She paused and then addressed Norton:

"You're very silent, Mr. Norton. Is anything the matter? You look—you look scared. You haven't seen the ghost of old Mrs. Whoever-it-was?"

Norton started.

"No, no. I haven't seen any ghosts. I—I was just thinking of something."

It was at that moment that Curtiss came through the doorway wheeling Poirot in his invalid chair.

He stopped with it in the hall, preparatory to taking his master out and carrying him up the stairs.

Poirot, his eyes suddenly alert, looked from one to the other of us.

He said sharply:

"What is it? Is anything the matter?"

None of us answered for a minute, then Barbara Franklin said with a little artificial laugh:

"No, of course not. What should be the matter? It's just—perhaps thunder coming? I—oh, dear—I'm terribly tired. Bring those things up, will you, Captain Hastings. Thank you so much."

I followed her up the stairs and along the east wing. Her room was the end one on that side.

Mrs. Franklin opened the door. I was behind her, my arms full of parcels.

She stopped abruptly in the doorway. By the window Boyd Carrington was having his palm examined by Nurse Craven.

He looked up and laughed a little sheepishly.

"Hullo, I'm having my fortune told. Nurse is no end of a hand reader."

"Really? I had no idea of that." Barbara Franklin's voice was sharp. I had an idea that she was annoyed with Nurse Craven. "Please take these things, Nurse, will you? And you might mix me an egg flip. I feel very tired. A hot water bottle, too, please. I'll get to bed as soon as possible."

"Certainly, Mrs. Franklin."

Nurse Craven moved forward. She showed no signs of anything but professional concern.

Mrs. Franklin said:

"Please go, Bill, I'm terribly tired."

Boyd Carrington looked very concerned.

"Oh, I say, Babs, has it been too much for you? I *am* sorry. What a thoughtless fool I am. I shouldn't have let you overtire yourself."

Mrs. Franklin gave him her angelic martyr's smile.

"I didn't want to say anything. I do hate being *tiresome*."

We two men went out of the room somewhat abashed and left the two women together.

Boyd Carrington said contritely:

"What a damned fool I am. Barbara seemed so bright and gay I forgot all about tiring her. Hope she's not knocked herself out."

I said mechanically:

"Oh, I expect she'll be all right after a night's rest."

He went down the stairs. I hesitated and then went along the other wing towards my own room, and Poirot's. The little man would be expecting me. For the first time I was reluctant to go to him. I had so much to occupy my thoughts, and I still had that dull sick feeling at the pit of my stomach.

I went slowly along the corridor.

From inside Allerton's room I heard voices. I don't think I meant consciously to listen, though I stopped for a minute automatically outside his door. Then, suddenly, the door opened and my daughter Judith came out.

She stopped dead when she saw me. I caught her by the arm and hustled her along into my room. I was suddenly intensely angry.

"What do you mean by going to that fellow's room?"

She looked at me steadily. She showed no anger now, only complete coldness. For some few seconds she did not reply.

I shook her by the arm.

"I won't have it, I tell you. You don't know what you are doing."

She said then in a low, biting voice:

"I think you have a perfectly filthy mind."

I said:

"I daresay I have. It's a reproach your generation is fond of levelling at mine. We have, at least, certain standards. Understand this, Judith, I forbid you absolutely to have anything more to do with that man."

She looked at me steadily. Then she said quietly:

"I see. So that's it."

"Do you deny that you're in love with him?"

"No."

"But you don't know what he is. You can't know."

Deliberately, without mincing my language, I repeated to her the story I had heard about Allerton.

"You see," I said when I had finished. "That's the kind of foul brute he is."

She seemed quite unmoved. Her lip curled upwards scornfully.

"I never thought he was a saint, I can assure you."

"Doesn't this make any difference to you? Judith, you can't be utterly depraved."

"Call it that if you like."

"Judith, you haven't—you aren't—"

I could not put my meaning into words. She shook her arm free from my detaining hand.

"Now, listen, Father. I do what I choose. You can't bully me.

And it's no good ranting. I shall do exactly as I please with my life, and you can't stop me."

In another instant she was out of the room.

I found my knees trembling.

I sank down onto a chair. It was worse—much worse than I thought. The child was utterly infatuated. There was no one to whom I could appeal. Her mother, the only person she might have listened to, was dead. It all depended on me.

I do not think that either before or since I have ever suffered as I suffered then . . .

IV

Presently I roused myself. I washed and shaved and changed. I went down to dinner. I behaved, I fancy, in quite a normal manner. Nobody seemed to notice anything amiss.

Once or twice I saw Judith flash a curious glance at me. She must have been puzzled, I think, by the way I was able to appear quite like my usual self.

And all the time, underneath, I was growing more and more determined.

All that I needed was courage—courage and brains.

After dinner we went outside, looked up at the sky, commented on the closeness of the atmosphere, prophesied rain—thunder—a storm.

Out of the tail of my eye I saw Judith disappear round the corner of the house. Presently Allerton strolled in the same direction.

I finished what I was saying to Boyd Carrington and wandered that way myself.

Norton, I think, tried to stop me. He took my arm. He tried, I think, to suggest walking up to the rose garden. I took no notice.

He was still with me as I turned the corner of the house.

They were there. I saw Judith's upturned face, saw Allerton's bent down over it—saw how he took her in his arms and the kiss that followed.

Then they broke away quickly. I took a step forward. Almost

by main force, Norton hauled me back and round the corner. He said:

"Look here, you can't—"

I interrupted him. I said forcefully:

"I can. And I will."

"It's no *good*, my dear fellow. It's all very distressing, but all it comes to is that there's nothing you *can* do."

I was silent. He might think that that was so, but I knew better.

Norton went on:

"I know how ineffectual and maddened one feels, but the only thing to do is to admit defeat. *Accept* it, man!"

I didn't contradict him. I waited, allowing him to talk. Then I went firmly round the corner of the house again.

The two of them had disappeared now, but I had a shrewd idea of where they might be. There was a summerhouse concealed in a grove of lilac trees not far away.

I went towards it. I think Norton was still with me, but I'm not sure.

As I got nearer, I heard voices and stopped. It was Allerton's voice I heard.

"Well, then, my dear girl, that's settled. Don't make any more objections. You go up to town tomorrow. I'll say I'm running over to Ipswich to stay with a pal for a night or two. You wire from London that you can't get back. And who's to know of that charming little dinner at my flat? You won't regret it, I can promise you."

I felt Norton tugging at me, and suddenly, meekly, I turned. I almost laughed at the sight of his worried, anxious face. I let him drag me back to the house. I pretended to give in because I knew, at that moment, exactly what I was going to do . . .

I said to him clearly and distinctly:

"Don't worry, old chap. It's all no good—I see that now. You can't control your children's lives. I'm through."

He was ridiculously relieved.

Shortly afterwards, I told him I was going to bed early. I'd got a bit of a headache, I said.

He had no suspicions at all of what I was going to do.

V

I paused for a moment in the corridor. It was quite quiet.
There was no one about. The beds had been all turned down
ready for the night. Norton, who had a room on this side, I had
left downstairs. Elizabeth Cole was playing bridge. Curtiss, I
knew, would be downstairs having his supper. I had the place to
myself.

I flatter myself that I have not worked with Poirot for so many
years in vain. I knew just what precautions to take.

Allerton was *not* going to meet Judith in London tomorrow.

Allerton was not going anywhere tomorrow . . .

The whole thing was really so ridiculously simple.

I went to my own room and picked up my bottle of aspirins.
Then I went into Allerton's room and into the bathroom. The
tablets of Slumberyl were in the cupboard. Eight, I considered,
ought to do the trick. One or two was the stated dose. Eight,
therefore, ought to be ample. Allerton himself had said the toxic
dose was not high. I read the label: "It is dangerous to exceed the
prescribed dose."

I smiled to myself.

I wrapped a silk handkerchief round my hand and unscrewed
the bottle carefully. There must be no fingerprints on it.

I emptied out the tablets. Yes, they were almost exactly the
same size as the aspirins. I put eight aspirins in the bottle, then
filled up with the Slumberyls, leaving out eight of them. The bottle now looked exactly as it had before. Allerton would notice no
difference.

I went back to my room. I had a bottle of whisky there—most
of us had at Styles. I got out two glasses and a siphon. I'd never
known Allerton refuse a drink yet. When he came up, I'd ask
him in for a nightcap.

I tried the tablets in a little of the spirit. They dissolved easily
enough. I tasted the mixture gingerly. A shade bitter perhaps, but
hardly noticeable. I had my plan. I should be just pouring myself
out a drink when Allerton came up. I would hand that to him
and pour myself out another. All quite easy and natural.

He could have no idea of my feelings—unless of course Judith had told him. I considered this for a moment, but decided that I was quite safe here. Judith never told anyone anything.

He would probably believe me to be quite unsuspicious of their plans.

I had nothing to do but to wait. It would be a long time, probably an hour or two before Allerton came up to bed. He was always a late bird.

I sat there quietly waiting.

A sudden knock on the door made me start. It was only Curtiss, however. Poirot was asking for me.

I came to myself with a shock. Poirot! I had never once thought of him all evening. He must have wondered what had become of me. It worried me a little. First of all because I was ashamed of never having been near him, and secondly I did not want him to suspect that anything out of the way had happened.

I followed Curtiss across the passage.

"*Eh bien,*" exclaimed Poirot. "So you desert me, *hein?*"

I forced a yawn and an apologetic smile.

"Awfully sorry, old boy," I said. "But to tell the truth, I've got such a blinding headache I can hardly see out of my eyes. It's the thunder in the air, I suppose. I really have been feeling quite muzzy with it—in fact so much so, I entirely forgot I hadn't been in to say good night to you."

As I had hoped, Poirot was immediately solicitous. He offered remedies. He fussed. He accused me of having sat about in the open air in a draught. (On the hottest day of the summer!) I refused aspirin on the grounds that I had already taken some, but I was not able to avoid being given a cup of sweet and wholly disgusting chocolate!

"It nourishes the nerves, you comprehend," Poirot explained.

I drank it to avoid argument and then, with Poirot's anxious and affectionate exclamations still ringing in my ears, I bade him good night.

I returned to my own room and shut the door ostentatiously. Later, I opened it a crack with the utmost caution. I could not fail now to hear Allerton when he came. But it would be some time yet.

I sat there waiting. I thought of my dead wife. Once, under my breath, I murmured:

"You understand, darling, I'm going to save her."

She had left Judith in my care. I was not going to fail her.

In the quiet and the stillness I suddenly felt that Cinders was very near to me.

I felt almost as though she were in the room.

And still I sat on, grimly waiting.

13

There is something about writing down an anticlimax in cold blood that is somewhat shattering to one's self-esteem.

For the truth of the matter is, you see, that I sat there waiting for Allerton and that I fell asleep!

Not so surprising, really, I suppose. I had slept very badly the night before. I had been out in the air the whole day. I was worn out with worry and the strain of nerving myself for doing what I had decided to do. On top of all that was the heavy thundery weather. Possibly even the fierce effort of concentration I was making helped.

Anyway, it happened. I fell asleep there in my chair, and when I woke, birds were twittering outside, the sun was up and there was I cramped and uncomfortable, slipped down in my chair in my evening dress, with a foul taste in the mouth and a splitting head.

I was bewildered, incredulous, disgusted, and finally immeasurably and overwhelmingly relieved.

Who was it who wrote: "The darkest day (Live till tomorrow) will have pass'd away"? And how true it is. I saw now, clearly and sanely, how overwrought and wrong-headed I had been. Melodramatic, lost to all sense of proportion. I had actually made up my mind to kill another human being.

At this moment my eyes fell on the glass of whisky in front of me. With a shudder I got up, drew the curtains and poured it out of the window. I must have been mad last night!

I shaved, had a bath and dressed. Then, feeling very much better, I went across to Poirot. He always woke very early, I knew. I sat down and made a clean breast of the whole thing to him.

I may say it was a great relief.

He shook his head gently at me.

"Ah, but what follies it is you contemplate. I am glad you came to confess your sins to me. But why, my dear friend, did you not come to me last night and tell me what was in your mind?"

I said shamefacedly:

"I was afraid, I suppose, that you would have tried to stop me."

"Assuredly I would have stopped you. Ah, that, certainly. Do you think I want to see you hanged by the neck, all on account of a very unpleasant scoundrel called Major Allerton?"

"I shouldn't have been caught," I said. "I'd taken every precaution."

"That is what all murderers think. You had the true mentality! But let me tell you, *mon ami*, you were not as clever as you thought yourself."

"I took every precaution. I wiped my fingerprints off the bottle."

"Exactly. You also wiped Allerton's fingerprints off. And when he is found dead—what happens? They perform the autopsy and it is established that he died of an overdose of Slumberyl. Did he take it by accident or intention? *Tiens*, his fingerprints are not on the bottle. But why not? Whether accident or suicide, he would have no reason to wipe them off. And then they analyze the remaining tablets and find nearly half of them have been replaced by aspirin."

"Well, practically everyone has aspirin tablets," I murmured weakly.

"Yes, but it is not everyone who has a daughter whom Allerton is pursuing with dishonourable intentions—to use an old-fashioned melodramatic phrase. And you have had a quarrel with your daughter on the subject the day before. Two people, Boyd Carrington and Norton, can swear to your violent feeling against the man. No, Hastings, it would not have looked too good. Attention would immediately have been focussed upon you, and by that time you would probably have been in such a state of fear—or even remorse, that some good solid inspector of police would have made up his mind quite definitely that you were the guilty party. It is quite possible, even, that someone may have seen you tampering with the tablets."

"They couldn't. There was no one about."

"There is a balcony outside the window. Somebody might have been there, peeping in. Or, who knows, someone might have been looking through the keyhole."

"You've got keyholes on the brain, Poirot. People don't really spend their time looking through keyholes as much as you seem to think."

Poirot half closed his eyes and remarked that I had always had too trusting a nature.

"And let me tell you, very funny things happen with keys in this house. Me, I like to feel that my door is locked on the inside, even if the good Curtiss is in the adjoining room. Soon after I am here, my key disappears—but entirely! I have to have another one made."

"Well, anyway," I said with a deep breath of relief, my mind still laden up with my own troubles, "it didn't come off. It's awful to think one can get worked up like that." I lowered my voice. "Poirot, you don't think that because—because of that murder long ago there's a sort of infection in the air?"

"A virus of murder, you mean? Well, it is an interesting suggestion."

"Houses do have an atmosphere," I said thoughtfully. "This house has a bad history."

Poirot nodded.

"Yes. There have been people here—several of them—who desired deeply that someone else should die. That is true enough."

"I believe it gets hold of one in some way. But now, Poirot, tell me, what am I to do about all this—Judith and Allerton, I mean? It's got to be stopped somehow. What do you think I'd better do?"

"Do nothing," said Poirot with emphasis.

"Oh, but—"

"Believe me, you will do least harm by not interfering."

"If I were to tackle Allerton—"

"What can you say or do? Judith is twenty-one and her own mistress."

"But I feel I ought to be able—"

Poirot interrupted me.

"No, Hastings. Do not imagine that you are clever enough, forceful enough, or even cunning enough to impose your personality on either of those two people. Allerton is accustomed to dealing with angry and impotent fathers, and probably enjoys it as a good joke. Judith is not the sort of creature who can be browbeaten. I would advise you—if I advised you at all—to do something very different. I would trust her, if I were you."

I stared at him.

"Judith," said Hercule Poirot, "is made of very fine stuff. I admire her very much."

I said, my voice unsteady:

"I admire her, too. But I'm afraid for her."

Poirot nodded his head with sudden energy.

"I, too, am afraid for her," he said. "But not in the way you are. I am terribly afraid. And I am powerless—or nearly so. And the days go by. There is danger, Hastings, and it is very close."

II

I knew as well as Poirot that the danger was very close. I had more reason to know it than he had, because of what I had actually overheard the previous night.

Nevertheless I pondered on that phrase of Poirot's as I went down to breakfast. "I would trust her if I were you."

It had come unexpectedly—but it had given me an odd sense of comfort. And almost immediately, the truth of it was justified. For Judith had obviously changed her mind about going up to London that day.

Instead she went off with Franklin to the lab as usual directly after breakfast, and it was clear that they were to have an arduous and busy day there.

A feeling of intense thanksgiving rushed over me. How mad, how despairing I had been last night. I had assumed—assumed quite certainly that Judith had yielded to Allerton's specious proposals. But it was true, I reflected now, that I had never heard her actually assent. No, she was too fine, too essentially good and true, to give in. She had refused the rendezvous.

Allerton had breakfast early, I found, and gone off to Ipswich. He, then, had kept to the plan and must assume that Judith was going up to London as arranged.

Well, I thought grimly, he would get a disappointment.

Boyd Carrington came along and remarked rather grumpily that I looked very cheerful this morning.

"Yes," I said. "I've had some good news."

He said that it was more than he had. He'd had a tiresome telephone call from the architect, some building difficulty—a local surveyor cutting up rough. Also worrying letters. And he was afraid he'd let Mrs. Franklin overdo herself the day before.

Mrs. Franklin was certainly making up for her recent bout of good health and spirits. She was, so I gathered from Nurse Craven, making herself quite impossible.

Nurse Craven had had to give up her day off which had been promised her to go and meet some friends, and she was decidedly sour about it. Since early morning Mrs. Franklin had been calling for sal volatile, hot water bottles, various patent foods and drinks, and was unwilling to let Nurse leave the room. She had neuralgia, a pain round the heart, cramps in her feet and legs, cold shivers and I don't know what else.

I may say here and now that neither I nor anyone else was inclined to be really alarmed. We all put it down as part of Mrs. Franklin's hypochondriacal tendencies.

This was true of Nurse Craven and Dr. Franklin as well.

The latter was fetched from the laboratory, he listened to his wife's complaints, asked her if she would like the local doctor called in (violently negatived by Mrs. Franklin), he then mixed her a sedative, soothed her as best he could and went off back to work again.

Nurse Craven said to me:

"He knows, of course, she's just playing up."

"You don't really think there's anything much the matter?"

"Her temperature is normal, and her pulse is perfectly good. Just fuss, if you ask me."

She was annoyed and spoke out more imprudently than usual.

"She likes to interfere with anyone else enjoying themselves. She'd like her husband all worked up, and me running round after her, and even Sir William has got to be made to feel a brute because he 'overtired her yesterday.' She's one of that kind."

Nurse Craven was clearly finding her patient almost impossible today. I gathered that Mrs. Franklin had been really extremely rude to her. She was the kind of woman whom nurses and servants instinctively disliked—not only because of the trouble she gave, but because of her manner of doing so.

So, as I say, none of us took her indisposition seriously.

The only exception was Boyd Carrington, who wandered round looking rather pathetically like a small boy who has been scolded.

How many times since then have I not gone over and over the events of that day, trying to remember something so far unheeded—some tiny forgotten incident, striving to remember exactly the manner of everybody. How far they were normal, or showed excitement.

Let me, once more, put down exactly what I remember of everybody.

Boyd Carrington, as I have said, looked uncomfortable and rather guilty. He seemed to think that he had been rather overexuberant the day before and had been selfish in not thinking more of the frail health of his companion. He had been up once or twice to inquire about Barbara Franklin, and Nurse Craven, herself not in the best of tempers, had been tart and snappish with him. He had even been to the village and purchased a box of chocolates. This had been sent down. "Mrs. Franklin couldn't bear chocolates."

Rather disconsolately, he opened the box in the smoking room and Norton and I and he all solemnly helped ourselves.

Norton, I now think, had definitely something on his mind that morning. He was abstracted; once or twice his brows drew together as though he were puzzling over something.

He was fond of chocolates, and ate a good many in an abstracted fashion.

Outside the weather had broken. Since ten o'clock the rain had been pouring down.

It had not the melancholy that sometimes accompanies a wet day. Actually it was a relief to us all.

Poirot had been brought down by Curtiss about midday and ensconced in the drawing room. Here Elizabeth Cole had joined him and was playing the piano to him. She had a pleasant touch, and played Bach and Mozart—both favourite composers of my friend.

Franklin and Judith came up from the garden about a quarter to one. Judith looked white and strained. She was very silent, looked vaguely about her as though lost in a dream, and then went away. Franklin sat down with us. He, too, looked tired and absorbed, and he had, too, the air of a man very much on edge.

I said, I remember, something about the rain being a relief, and he said quickly:

"Yes. There are times—when *something's* got to break—"

And somehow—I got the impression that it was not merely of the weather that he spoke. Awkward as always in his movements, he jerked against the table and upset half the chocolates. With his usual startled air, he apologized—apparently to the box.

"Oh, sorry."

It ought to have been funny, but somehow it wasn't. He bent quickly and picked up the spilt chocolates.

Norton asked him if he had had a tiring morning.

His smile flashed out then—eager, boyish, very much alive.

"No—no—just realized, suddenly, I've been on the wrong track. Much simpler process altogether is what's needed. Can take a short cut now."

He stood swaying slightly to and fro on his feet, his eyes absent yet resolved.

"Yes, short cut. Much the best way."

III

If we were all nervy and aimless in the morning, the afternoon was unexpectedly pleasant. The sun came out, the temperature was cool and fresh. Mrs. Luttrell was brought down and sat on the verandah. She was in excellent form—exercising her charm and manner with less gush than usual, and with no latent hint of vinegar in reserve. She chaffed her husband, but gently and with a kind of affection, and he beamed at her. It was really delightful to see them on such good terms.

Poirot permitted himself to be wheeled out also, and he was in good spirits too. I think he liked seeing the Luttrells on such a friendly footing with each other. The Colonel was looking years younger. His manner seemed less vacillating, he tugged less at his moustache. He even suggested that there might be some bridge that evening.

"Daisy here misses her bridge."

"Indeed I do," said Mrs. Luttrell.

Norton suggested it would be tiring for her.

"I'll play one rubber," said Mrs. Luttrell, and added with a twinkle: "And I'll behave myself and not bite poor George's head off."

"My dear," protested her husband, "I know I'm a shocking player."

"And what of that?" said Mrs. Luttrell. "Doesn't it give me grand pleasure badgering and bullying you about it?"

It made us all laugh. Mrs. Luttrell went on:

"Oh, I know my faults, but I'm not going to give them up at my time of life. George has just got to put up with me."

Colonel Luttrell looked at her quite fatuously.

I think it was seeing them both on such good terms that led to a discussion on marriage and divorce that took place later in the day.

Were men and women actually happier by reason of the

greater facilities afforded for divorce, or was it often the case that a temporary period of irritation and estrangement—or trouble over a third person—gave way after a while to a resumption of affection and friendliness?

It is odd sometimes to see how much at variance people's ideas are with their own personal experiences.

My own marriage had been unbelievably happy and successful, and I am essentially an old-fashioned person, yet I was on the side of divorce—of cutting one's losses and starting afresh. Boyd Carrington, whose marriage had been unhappy, yet held for an indissoluble marriage bond. He had, he said, the utmost reverence for the institution of marriage. It was the foundation of the state.

Norton, with no ties and no personal angle, was of my way of thinking. Franklin, the modern scientific thinker, was, strangely enough, resolutely opposed to divorce. It offended, apparently, his ideal of clear-cut thinking and action. One assumed certain responsibilities. Those must be carried through and not shirked or set aside. A contract, he said, is a contract. One enters upon it of one's own free will, and must abide by it. Anything else resulted in what he called a mess. Loose ends, half-dissolved ties.

Leaning back in his chair, his long legs kicking vaguely at a table, he said:

"A man chooses his wife. She's his responsibility until she dies —or he does."

Norton said rather comically:

"And sometimes—oh, blessed death, eh?"

We laughed, and Boyd Carrington said:

"You needn't talk, my lad; you've never been married."

Shaking his head, Norton said:

"And now I've left it too late."

"Have you?" Boyd Carrington's glance was quizzical. "Sure of that?"

It was just at that moment that Elizabeth Cole joined us. She had been up with Mrs. Franklin.

I wondered if it was my fancy, or did Boyd Carrington look

meaningly from her to Norton, and was it possible that Norton blushed?

It put a new idea into my head and I looked searchingly at Elizabeth Cole. It was true that she was still a comparatively young woman. Moreover, she was quite a handsome one. In fact a very charming and sympathetic person who was capable of making any man happy. And she and Norton had spent a good deal of time together of late. In their hunts for wild flowers and birds, they had become friends; I remembered how she had spoken of Norton being such a kind person.

Well, if so, I was glad for her sake. Her starved and barren girlhood would not stand in the way of her ultimate happiness. The tragedy that had shattered her life would not have been enacted in vain. I thought, looking at her, that she certainly looked much happier and—yes, gayer, than when I had first come to Styles.

Elizabeth Cole and Norton—yes, it might be.

And suddenly, from nowhere, a vague feeling of uneasiness and disquiet assailed me. It was not safe—it was not right—to plan happiness here. There was something malignant about the air of Styles. I felt it now—this minute. Felt suddenly old and tired—yes, and afraid.

A minute later the feeling had passed. Nobody had noticed it, I think, except Boyd Carrington. He said to me in an undertone a few minutes later:

"Anything the matter, Hastings?"

"No, why?"

"Well—you looked—I can't quite explain it."

"Just a feeling—apprehension."

"A premonition of evil?"

"Yes, if you like to put it that way. A feeling that—that something was going to happen."

"Funny. I've felt that once or twice. Any idea what?"

He was watching me narrowly.

I shook my head. For indeed I had had no definite apprehension of any particular thing. It had only been a wave of deep depression and fear.

Then Judith had come out of the house. She had come slowly, her head held high, her lips pressed together, her face grave and beautiful.

I thought how unlike she was to either me or Cinders. She looked like some young priestess. Norton felt something of that too. He said to her:

"You look like your namesake might have looked before she cut off the head of Holofernes."

Judith smiled and raised her eyebrows a little.

"I can't remember now why she wanted to."

"Oh, strictly on the highest moral grounds for the good of the community!"

The light banter in his tones annoyed Judith. She flushed and went past him to sit by Franklin. She said:

"Mrs. Franklin is feeling much better. She wants us all to come up and have coffee with her this evening."

IV

Mrs. Franklin was certainly a creature of moods I thought as we trooped upstairs after dinner. Having made everyone's life unbearable all day, she was now sweetness itself to everybody.

She was dressed in a negligee of pale eau-de-Nil and was lying on her chaise longue. Beside her was a small revolving bookcase-table with the coffee apparatus set out. Her fingers, deft and white, dealt with the ritual of coffee making with some slight aid from Nurse Craven. We were all there with the exception of Poirot, who always retired before dinner; Allerton, who had not returned from Ipswich; and Mrs. and Colonel Luttrell, who had remained downstairs.

The aroma of coffee came to our noses—a delicious smell. The coffee at Styles was an uninteresting muddy fluid, so we all looked forward to Mrs. Franklin's brew with freshly ground berries.

Franklin sat on the other side of the table handing the cups as she filled them. Boyd Carrington stood by the foot of the sofa. Elizabeth Cole and Norton were by the window. Nurse Craven had retired to the background by the head of the bed. I was sit-

ting in an armchair wrestling with the *Times* crossword and reading out the clues.

"Even love—or third party risk?" I read out. "Eight letters."

"Probably an anagram," said Franklin.

We thought for a minute. I went on:

"The chaps between the hills are unkind."

"Tormentor," said Boyd Carrington quickly.

"Quotation: '*And Echo whate'er is asked her answers*'—blank.
Tennyson. Five letters."

"Where," suggested Mrs. Franklin. "Surely that's right. 'And
Echo answers where'?"

I was doubtful.

"It would make a word end in 'w.'"

"Well, lots of words end in 'w.' *How* and *now* and *snow*."
Elizabeth Cole said from the window:

"The Tennyson quotation is: '*And Echo whate'er is asked her
answers Death.*'"

I heard a quick sharp intake of breath behind me. I looked up.
It was Judith. She went past us to the window and out upon the
balcony.

I said, as I wrote the last clue in: "Even love can't be an anagram. The second letter now is 'A.'"

"What's the clue again?"

"Even love or third party risk. Blank A and six blanks."

"Paramour," said Boyd Carrington.

I heard the teaspoon rattle on Barbara Franklin's saucer. I went
on to the next clue.

"'Jealousy is a green-eyed monster,' this person said."

"Shakespeare," said Boyd Carrington.

"Was it Othello or Emilia?" said Mrs. Franklin.

"All too long. The clue is only five letters."

"Iago."

"I'm *sure* it was Othello."

"It wasn't in *Othello* at all. Romeo said it to Juliet."

We all voiced our opinions. Suddenly from the balcony Judith
cried out:

"Look, a shooting star. Oh, there's another."

Boyd Carrington said: "Where? We must wish." He went out on the balcony, joining Elizabeth Cole, Norton and Judith. Nurse Craven went out too. Franklin got up and joined them. They stood there exclaiming, gazing out into the night.

I remained with my head bent over the crossword. Why should I wish to see a falling star? I had nothing to wish for . . .

Suddenly Boyd Carrington wheeled back into the room.

"Barbara, you must come out."

Mrs. Franklin said sharply:

"No, I can't. I'm too tired."

"Nonsense, Babs. You must come and wish!" He laughed. "Now don't protest. I'll carry you."

And suddenly stooping, he picked her up in his arms. She laughed and protested:

"Bill, put me down—don't be so silly."

"Little girls have got to come and wish." He carried her through the window and set her down on the balcony.

I bent closer over the paper. For I was remembering . . . A clear tropical night—frogs croaking . . . and a shooting star. I was standing there by the window, and I had turned and picked up Cinders and carried her out in my arms to see the stars and wish . . .

The lines of the crossword ran and blurred before my eyes.

A figure detached itself from the balcony and came into the room—Judith.

Judith must never catch me with tears in my eyes. It would never do. Hastily I swung round the bookcase and pretended to be looking for a book. I remembered having seen an old edition of Shakespeare there. Yes, here it was. I looked through *Othello*.

"What are you doing, Father?"

I mumbled something about the clue, my fingers turning over the pages. Yes, it was Iago.

"O, beware, my lord, of jealousy;
It is the green-eyed monster which doth mock
The meat it feeds on."

Judith went on with some other lines:

> "Not poppy, nor mandragora,
> Nor all the drowsy syrups of the world,
> Shall ever medicine thee to that sweet sleep
> Which thou owedst yesterday."

Her voice rang out, beautiful and deep.

The others were coming back, laughing and talking. Mrs. Franklin resumed her place on the chaise longue. Franklin came back to his seat and stirred his coffee. Norton and Elizabeth Cole finished drinking theirs and excused themselves, as they had promised to play bridge with the Luttrells.

Mrs. Franklin drank her coffee and then demanded her "drops." Judith got them for her from the bathroom, as Nurse Craven had just gone out.

Franklin was wandering aimlessly round the room. He stumbled over a small table. His wife said sharply:

"Don't be so clumsy, John."

"Sorry, Barbara. I was thinking of something."

Mrs. Franklin said rather affectedly:

"Such a great bear, aren't you, darling?"

He looked at her rather abstractedly. Then he said:

"Nice night; think I'll take a stroll."

He went out.

Mrs. Franklin said:

"He *is* a genius, you know. You can tell it from his manner. I really do admire him terrifically. Such a passion for his work."

"Yes, yes, clever fellow," said Boyd Carrington—rather perfunctorily.

Judith left the room abruptly, nearly colliding with Nurse Craven in the doorway.

Boyd Carrington said:

"What about a game of picquet, Babs?"

"Oh, lovely. Can you get hold of some cards, Nurse?"

Nurse Craven went to get cards, and I wished Mrs. Franklin good night and thanked her for the coffee.

Outside I overtook Franklin and Judith. They were standing looking out of the passage window. They were not speaking. Just standing side by side.

Franklin looked over his shoulder as I approached. He moved a step or two, hesitated and said:

"Coming out for a stroll, Judith?"

My daughter shook her head.

"Not tonight." She added abruptly, "I'm going to bed. Good night."

I went downstairs with Franklin. He was whistling softly to himself and smiling.

I remarked rather crossly, for I was feeling depressed myself:

"You seem pleased with yourself tonight."

He admitted it.

"Yes. I've done something that I've been meaning to do for a long time. Very satisfactory, that."

I parted from him downstairs and looked in on the bridge players for a minute. Norton winked at me when Mrs. Luttrell wasn't looking. The rubber seemed to be progressing with unusual harmony.

Allerton had still not come back. It seemed to me that the house was happier and less oppressive without him.

I went up to Poirot's room. I found Judith sitting with him. She smiled at me when I came in and did not speak.

"She has forgiven you, *mon ami*," said Poirot—an outrageous remark.

"Really," I spluttered. "I hardly think—"

Judith got up. She put an arm round my neck and kissed me. She said:

"Poor Father. Uncle Hercule shall *not* attack your dignity. *I* am the one to be forgiven. So forgive me and say good night."

I don't quite know why, but I said:

"I'm sorry, Judith. I'm very sorry. I didn't mean—"

She stopped me.

"That's all right. Let's forget it. Everything's all right now." She smiled a slow far-away smile. She said again: "Everything's all right now . . ." and quietly left the room.

When she had gone, Poirot looked at me.

"Well," he demanded, "what has been happening this evening?"

I spread out my hands.

"Nothing has happened or is likely to happen," I told him.

Actually I was very wide of the mark. For something did happen that night. Mrs. Franklin was taken violently ill. Two more doctors were sent for, but in vain. She died the following morning.

It was not until twenty-four hours later that we learned that her death was due to poisoning by physostigmine.

14

The inquest took place two days later. It was the second time I had attended an inquest in this part of the world.

The coroner was an able middle-aged man with a shrewd glance and a dry manner of speech.

The medical evidence was taken first. It established the fact that death was the result of poisoning by physostigmine, and that other alkaloids of the Calabar bean were also present. The poison must have been taken sometime on the preceding evening between seven o'clock and midnight. The police surgeon and his colleague refused to be more precise.

The next witness was Dr. Franklin. He created on the whole a good impression. His evidence was clear and simple. After his wife's death he had checked over his solutions in the laboratory. He had discovered that a certain bottle which should have contained a strong solution of alkaloids of the Calabar bean, with which he had been conducting experiments, had been filled up with ordinary water in which only a trace of the original contents was present. He could not say with certainty when this had been done, as he had not used that particular preparation for some days.

The question of access to the laboratory was then gone into. Dr. Franklin agreed that the laboratory was usually kept locked and that he usually had the key in his pocket. His assistant, Miss Hastings, had a duplicate key. Anyone who wished to go into the studio had to get the key from her or from himself. His wife had borrowed it occasionally, when she had left things belonging to her in the laboratory. He himself had never brought a solution of physostigmine into the house or into his wife's room and he thought that by no possibility could she have taken it accidentally.

Questioned further by the coroner, he said that his wife had for some time been in a low and nervous state of health. There was no organic disease. She suffered from depression and from a rapid alternation of moods.

Of late, he said, she had been cheerful and he had considered her improved in health and spirits. There had been no quarrel between them and they had been on good terms. On the last evening his wife had seemed in good spirits and not melancholy.

He said that his wife had occasionally spoken of ending her life but that he had not taken her remarks seriously. Asked the question definitely, he replied that in his opinion his wife had not been a suicidal type. That was his medical opinion as well as his personal one.

He was followed by Nurse Craven. She looked smart and efficient in her trim uniform, and her replies were crisp and professional. She had been in attendance on Mrs. Franklin for over two months. Mrs. Franklin suffered badly from depression. Witness had heard her say at least three times that she "wanted to end it all," that her life was useless and that she was a millstone round her husband's neck.

"Why did she say that? Had there been any altercation between them?"

"Oh no, but she was aware that her husband had recently been offered an appointment abroad. He had refused that in order not to leave her."

"And sometimes she felt morbidly about the fact?"

"Yes. She would blame her miserable health, and get all worked up."

"Did Dr. Franklin know about this?"

"I do not think she often said so to him."

"But she was subject to fits of depression?"

"Oh, definitely."

"Did she ever specifically mention committing suicide?"

"I think 'I want to end it all' was the phrase she used."

"She never suggested any particular method of taking her own life?"

"No. She was quite vague."

"Had there been anything especially to depress her of late?"

"No. She had been in reasonably good spirits."

"Do you agree with Dr. Franklin that she was in good spirits on the night of her death?"

Nurse Craven hesitated:

"Well—she was excited. She'd had a bad day—complained of pain and giddiness. She had seemed better in the evening—but her good spirits were a bit unnatural. She seemed feverish and rather artificial."

"Did you see anything of a bottle, or anything that might have contained the poison?"

"No."

"What did she eat and drink?"

"She had soup, a cutlet, green peas and mashed potatoes, and cherry tart. She had a glass of Burgundy with it."

"Where did the Burgundy come from?"

"There was a bottle in her room. There was some left afterwards, but I believe it was examined and found to be quite all right."

"Could she have put the drug in her glass without your seeing?"

"Oh yes, easily. I was to and fro in the room, tidying up and arranging things. I was not watching her. She had a little despatch case beside her and also a handbag. She could have put anything in the Burgundy, or later in the coffee, or in the hot milk she had last thing."

"Have you any idea as to what she could have done with the bottle or container if so?"

Nurse Craven considered.

"Well, I suppose she could have thrown it out of the window

later. Or put it in the wastepaper basket, or even have washed it out in the bathroom and put it back in the medicine cupboard. There are several empty bottles there. I save them because they come in handy."

"When did you last see Mrs. Franklin?"

"At ten-thirty. I settled her for the night. She had hot milk and she said she'd like an aspirin."

"How was she then?"

The witness considered a minute.

"Well, really, just as usual . . . No, I'd say she was perhaps just a bit overexcited."

"Not depressed?"

"Well, no, more strung-up, so to speak. But if it's suicide you're thinking of, it might make her that way. She might feel noble or exalted about it."

"Do you consider she was a likely person to take her own life?"

There was a pause. Nurse Craven seemed to be struggling to make up her mind.

"Well," she said at last, "I do and I don't. I—yes, on the whole I do. She was very unbalanced."

Sir William Boyd Carrington came next. He seemed genuinely upset, but gave his evidence clearly.

He had played picquet with the deceased on the night of her death. He had not noticed any signs of depression then, but in a conversation some days previously, Mrs. Franklin had mentioned the subject of taking her own life. She was a very unselfish woman, and deeply distressed at feeling that she was hampering her husband's career. She was devoted to her husband and very ambitious for him. She was sometimes very depressed about her own health.

Judith was called, but had little to say.

She knew nothing about the removal of the physostigmine from the laboratory. On the night of the tragedy Mrs. Franklin had seemed to her much as usual, though perhaps overexcited. She had never heard Mrs. Franklin mention suicide.

The last witness was Hercule Poirot. His evidence was given

with much emphasis and caused a considerable impression. He described a conversation he had had with Mrs. Franklin on the day previous to her decease. She had been very depressed and had expressed several times a wish to be out of it all. She was worried about her health and had confided in him that she had fits of deep melancholy when life did not seem worth living. She said that sometimes she felt it would be wonderful to go to sleep and never wake up.

His next reply caused an even greater sensation.

"On the morning of June tenth you were sitting outside the laboratory door?"

"Yes."

"Did you see Mrs. Franklin come out of the laboratory?"

"I did."

"Did she have anything in her hand?"

"She had a small bottle clasped in her right hand."

"You are quite sure of that?"

"Yes."

"Did she show any confusion at seeing you?"

"She looked startled, that is all."

The coroner proceeded to his summing-up. They must make up their minds, he said, how the deceased came to her death. They would have no difficulty in assigning the cause of death, the medical evidence had told them that. Deceased was poisoned by physostigmine sulphate. All they had to decide was whether she took it accidentally or by intent, or if it was administered to her by some other person. They had heard that deceased had fits of melancholy, that she was in poor health, and that while there was no organic disease, she was in a bad nervous condition. Mr. Hercule Poirot, a witness whose name must carry weight, had asserted positively that he had seen Mrs. Franklin come out of the laboratory with a small bottle in her hand and that she had seemed startled to see him. They might come to the conclusion that she had taken the poison from the laboratory with the intention of doing away with herself. She seemed to be suffering from an obsession that she was standing in her husband's light and obstructing his career. It was only fair to Dr. Franklin to say that he seemed to have been a kind and affectionate husband, and that he had never expressed annoyance at her delicacy, or complained that she hindered his career. The idea seemed to be entirely her own. Women in a certain condition of nervous collapse did get these persistent ideas. There was no evidence to show at what time, or in what vehicle the poison was taken. It was, perhaps, a little unusual that the bottle which originally contained the poison had not been found, but it was possible that, as Nurse Craven suggested, Mrs. Franklin had washed it and put it away in the bathroom cupboard from where she may have originally taken it. It was for the jury to make their own decision.

The verdict was arrived at after only a short delay.

The jury found that Mrs. Franklin took her own life while temporarily of unsound mind.

II

Half an hour later I was in Poirot's room. He was looking very exhausted. Curtiss had put him to bed and was reviving him with a stimulant.

I was dying to talk, but I had to contain myself until the valet had finished and left the room.

Then I burst out.

"Was that true, Poirot, what you said? That you saw a bottle in Mrs. Franklin's hand when she came out of the laboratory?"

A very faint smile crept over Poirot's bluish-tinged lips. He murmured:

"Did not *you* see it, my friend?"

"No, I did not."

"But you might not have noticed, *hein?*"

"No, perhaps not. I certainly can't swear she didn't have it." I looked at him doubtfully. "The question is, are you speaking the truth?"

"Do you think I would lie, my friend?"

"I wouldn't put it past you."

"Hastings, you shock and surprise me. Where is now your simple faith?"

"Well," I conceded, "I don't suppose you would really commit perjury."

Poirot said mildly:

"It would not be perjury. It was not on oath."

"Then it was a lie?"

Poirot waved his hand automatically.

"What I have said, *mon ami,* is said. It is unnecessary to discuss it."

"I simply don't understand you," I cried.

"What don't you understand?"

"Your evidence—all that about Mrs. Franklin's having talked about committing suicide—about her being depressed."

"*Enfin,* you heard her say such things yourself."

"Yes. But it was only one of many moods. You didn't make that clear."

"Perhaps I did not want to."

I stared at him.

"You *wanted* the verdict to be suicide?"

Poirot paused before replying. Then he said:

"I think, Hastings, that you do not appreciate the gravity of the situation. Yes, if you like, I wanted the verdict to be suicide . . ."

"But you don't think—yourself—that she did commit suicide?"

Slowly Poirot shook his head.

I said:

"You think—that she was murdered?"

"Yes, Hastings, she was murdered."

"Then why try to hush it up—to have it labelled and put aside as suicide? That stops all enquiry."

"Precisely."

"You want that?"

"Yes."

"But *why?*"

"Is it conceivable that you do not see? Never mind—let us not go into that. You must take my word for it that it *was* murder—deliberate, preconceived murder. I told you, Hastings, that a crime would be committed here, and that it was unlikely we should be able to prevent it—for the killer is both ruthless and determined."

I shivered. I said:

"And what happens next?"

Poirot smiled.

"The case is solved—labelled and put away as suicide. But you and I, Hastings, go on, working underground like moles. And, sooner or later, *we get X*."

I said:

"And supposing that—meanwhile—someone else is killed?"

Poirot shook his head.

"I do not think so. Unless, that is, somebody saw something or knows something—but if so, surely, they would have come forward to say so . . . ?"

15

My memory is a little vague about the events of the days immediately following the inquest on Mrs. Franklin. There was, of course, the funeral, which I may say was attended by a large number of the curious of Styles St. Mary. It was on that occasion that I was addressed by an old woman with rheumy eyes and an unpleasantly ghoulish manner.

She accosted me just as we were filing out of the cemetery.

"Remember you, sir, don't I?"

"Well—er, possibly—"

She went on, hardly listening to what I said.

"Twenty years ago and over. When the old lady died up at the Court. That was the first murder we had to Styles. Won't be the last, I say. Old Mrs. Inglethorp, her husband done her in, so we all said. Sure of it, we was." She leered at me cunningly. "Maybe it's the husband this time."

"What do you mean?" I said sharply. "Didn't you hear the verdict was suicide?"

"That's what the coroner said. But he might be wrong, don't you think?" She nudged me. "Doctors, they know how to do away with their wives. And she wasn't much good to him seemingly."

I turned on her angrily and she slunk away, murmuring she hadn't meant anything, only it seemed odd-like, didn't it, happening a second time? "And it's queer you should be there both times, sir, isn't it now?"

For one fantastic moment I wondered if she suspected me of having really committed both crimes. It was most disturbing. It certainly made me realize what a queer, haunting thing local suspicion is.

And it was not, after all, so far wrong. For somebody had killed Mrs. Franklin.

As I say, I remember very little of those days. Poirot's health, for one thing, was giving me grave concern. Curtiss came to me with his wooden face slightly disturbed and reported that Poirot had had a somewhat alarming heart attack.

"Seems to me, sir, he ought to see a doctor."

I went posthaste to Poirot, who negatived the suggestion most vigorously. It was, I thought, a little unlike him. He had always been, in my opinion, extremely fussy about his health. Distrusting draughts, wrapping up his neck in silk and wool, showing a horror of getting his feet damp, and taking his temperature and retiring to bed at the least suspicion of a chill—"for otherwise it may be for me a *fluxion de poitrine!*" In most little ailments, he had, I knew, always consulted a doctor immediately.

Now, when he was really ill, the position seemed reversed.

Yet perhaps that was the real reason. Those other ailments *had* been trifling. Now, when he was indeed a sick man, he feared, perhaps, admitting the reality of his illness. He made light of it because he was afraid.

He answered my protests with energy and bitterness.

"Ah, but I have consulted doctors—not one, but many! I have been to Blank and to Dash (he named two specialists) and they do what?—they send me to Egypt where immediately I am rendered much worse. I have been, too, to R."

R. was, I knew, a heart specialist. I asked quickly:

"What did he say?"

Poirot gave me a sudden quick sidelong glance—and my heart gave a sudden agonized leap.

He said quietly:

"He has done for me all that can be done. I have my treatments, my remedies, all close at hand. Beyond that—there is nothing. So you see, Hastings, to call in more doctors would be of no avail. The machine, *mon ami*, wears out. One cannot, alas, install the new engine and continue to run as before like a motor car."

"But look here, Poirot, surely there's something. Curtiss—"

Poirot said sharply: "Curtiss?"

"Yes, he came to me. He was worried— You had an attack—"

Poirot nodded gently.

"Yes, yes. They are, sometimes, these attacks, painful to witness. Curtiss, I think, is not used to these attacks of the heart."

"Won't you really see a doctor?"

"It is of no avail, my friend."

He spoke very gently but with finality. And again my heart felt a painful constriction. Poirot smiled at me. He said:

"This, Hastings, will be my last case. It will be, too, my most interesting case—and my most interesting criminal. For in X we have a technique superb, magnificent—that arouses admiration in spite of oneself. So far, *mon cher*, this X has operated with so much ability that he has defeated me—Hercule Poirot! He has developed the attack to which I can find no answer."

"If you had your health—" I began soothingly.

But apparently that was not the right thing to say. Hercule Poirot immediately flew into a rage.

"Ah! Have I got to tell you thirty-six times, and then again thirty-six, that there is no need of *physical* effort? One needs only —to think."

"Well—of course—yes, you can do that all right."

"All right? I can do it superlatively. My limbs they are paralyzed, my heart it plays me the tricks, but my brain, Hastings —my brain it functions without impairment of any kind. It is still of the first excellence, my brain."

"That," I said soothingly, "is splendid."

But as I went slowly downstairs, I thought to myself that Poirot's brain was not getting on with things as fast as it might do. First the narrow escape of Mrs. Luttrell and now the death of Mrs. Franklin. And what were we doing about it? Practically nothing.

II

It was the following day that Poirot said to me:

"You suggested, Hastings, that I should see a doctor."

"Yes," I said eagerly. "I'd feel much happier if you would."

"*Eh bien,* I will consent. I will see Franklin."

"Franklin?" I looked doubtful.

"Well, he is a doctor, is he not?"

"Yes, but—his main line is research, is it not?"

"Undoubtedly. He would not succeed, I fancy, as a general practitioner. He has not sufficiently what you call the 'side of the bed manner.' But he has the qualifications. In fact I should say that, as the films say, 'he knows his stuff better than most.'"

I was still not entirely satisfied. Although I did not doubt Franklin's ability, he had always struck me as a man who was impatient of and uninterested in human ailments. Possibly an admirable attitude for research work, but not so good for any sick persons he might attend.

However, for Poirot to go so far was a concession, and as Poirot had no local medical attendant, Franklin readily agreed to take a look at him. But he explained that if regular medical attendance was needed, a local practitioner must be called in. He could not attend the case.

Franklin spent a long time with him.

When he came out finally, I was waiting for him. I drew him into my room and shut the door.

"Well?" I demanded anxiously.

Franklin said thoughtfully:

"He's a very remarkable man."

"Oh! That, yes—" I brushed aside this self-evident fact. "But his health?"

"Oh! His health?" Franklin seemed quite surprised—as though I had mentioned something of no importance at all. "Oh! His health's rotten, of course."

It was not, I felt, at all a professional way of putting it. And yet I had heard—from Judith—that Franklin had been one of the most brilliant students of his time.

"How bad is he?" I demanded anxiously.

He shot me a look.

"D'you want to know?"

"Of course."

What did the fool think?

He almost immediately told me:

"Most people," he said, "don't want to know. They want soothing syrup. They want hope. They want reassurance ladled out in driblets. And of course amazing recoveries do occur. But they won't in Poirot's case."

"Do you mean—" Again that cold hand closed round my heart.

Franklin nodded.

"Oh yes, he's for it, all right. And pretty soon, I should say. I shouldn't tell you so if he hadn't authorized me to do so."

"Then—he knows."

Franklin said:

"He knows, all right. That heart of his may go out—phut—any moment. One can't say, of course, exactly *when*."

He paused, then he said slowly:

"From what he says, I gather he's worrying about getting something finished, something that—as he puts it—he's undertaken. D'you know about that?"

"Yes," I said. "I know."

Franklin shot me an interested glance.

"He wants to be sure of finishing off the job."

"I see."

I wondered if John Franklin had any idea of what that job was!

He said slowly:

"I hope he'll manage it. From what he said, it means a lot to him." He paused and added: "He's got a methodical mind."

I asked anxiously:

"Isn't there something that can be done—something in the way of treatment—"

He shook his head.

"Nothing doing. He's got ampoules of amyl nitrite to use when he feels an attack is coming on."

Then he said a rather curious thing.

"Got a very great respect for human life, hasn't he?"

"Yes—I suppose he has."

How often had I not heard Poirot say: "I do not approve of murder." That understatement, made so primly, had always tickled my fancy.

Franklin was going on:

"That's the difference between us. *I* haven't . . . !"

I looked at him curiously. He inclined his head with a faint smile.

"Quite true," he said. "Since death comes anyway, what does it matter if it comes early or late? There's so little difference."

"Then what on earth made you become a doctor if you feel like that?" I demanded with some indignation.

"Oh, my dear fellow—doctoring isn't just a matter of dodging the ultimate end—it's a lot more—it's improving *living*. If a healthy man dies, it doesn't matter—much. If an imbecile—a cretin—dies, it's a good thing—but if by the discovery of administering the correct gland you turn your cretin into a healthy, normal individual by correcting his thyroid deficiency, that, to my mind, matters a good deal."

I looked at him with more interest. I still felt that it would not be Dr. Franklin I should call in if I had the influenza, but I had to pay tribute to a kind of white-hot sincerity and a very real force in the man. I had noticed a change in him since his wife's death. He had displayed few of the conventional signs of mourning. On the contrary he seemed more alive, less absent-minded, and full of a new energy and fire.

He said abruptly, breaking into my thoughts:

"You and Judith aren't much alike, are you?"

"No, I suppose we're not."

"Is she like her mother?"

I reflected, then slowly shook my head.

"Not really. My wife was a merry, laughing creature. She wouldn't take anything seriously—and tried to make me the same, without much success, I'm afraid."

He smiled faintly.

"No, you're rather the heavy father, aren't you? So Judith says. Judith doesn't laugh much—serious young woman. Too much work, I expect. My fault."

He went into a brown study. I said conventionally:

"Your work must be very interesting."

"Eh?"

"I said your work must be interesting."

"Only to about half a dozen people. To everybody else it's darned dull—and they're probably right. Anyway"—he flung his head back, his shoulders squared themselves, he suddenly looked what he was, a powerful and virile man—"I've got my chance now! God, I could shout aloud. The Minister Institute people let me know today. The job's still open and I've got it. I start in ten days' time."

"For Africa?"

"Yes. It's grand."

"So soon." I felt slightly shocked.

He stared at me.

"What do you mean—*soon?* Oh." His brow cleared. "You mean after Barbara's death? Why on earth not? It's no good pretending, is it, that her death wasn't the greatest relief to me?"

He seemed amused by the expression on my face.

"I've not time, I'm afraid, for conventional attitudes. I fell in love with Barbara—she was a very pretty girl—married her and fell out of love with her again in about a year. I don't think it lasted even as long as that with her. I was a disappointment to her, of course. She thought she could influence me. She couldn't. I'm a selfish, pigheaded sort of brute, and I do what I want to do."

"But you did refuse this job in Africa on her account," I reminded him.

"Yes. That was purely financial, though, I'd undertaken to support Barbara in the way of life she was accustomed to. If I'd gone, it would have meant leaving her very short. But now"—he smiled a completely frank boyish smile—"it's turned out amazingly lucky for me."

I was revolted. It is true, I suppose, that many men whose

wives die are not precisely heartbroken and everyone more or less knows the fact. But this was so blatant.

He saw my face, but did not seem put out.

"Truth," he said, "is seldom appreciated. And yet it saves a lot of time and a lot of inaccurate speech."

I said sharply:

"And it doesn't worry you at all that your wife committed suicide?"

He said thoughtfully:

"I don't really believe she did commit suicide. Most unlikely—"

"But then, what do you think happened?"

He caught me up.

"I don't know. I don't think I—want to know. Understand?"

I stared at him. His eyes were hard and cold.

He said again:

"I don't want to know. I'm not—interested. See?"

I didn't see—but I didn't like it.

III

I don't know when it was that I noticed that Stephen Norton had something on his mind. He had been very silent after the inquest, and after that and the funeral were over, he still walked about, his eyes on the ground and his forehead puckered. He had a habit of running his hands through his short grey hair until it stuck up on end like Strumel Peter. It was comical but quite unconscious and denoted some perplexity of his mind. He returned absent-minded answers when you spoke to him, and it did at last dawn upon me that he was definitely worried about something. I asked him tentatively if he had had bad news of any kind, which he promptly negatived. That closed the subject for the time being.

But a little later he seemed to be trying to get an opinion from me on some matter in a clumsy, roundabout way.

Stammering a little, as he always did when he was serious about a thing, he embarked on an involved story centring on a point of ethics.

"You know, Hastings, it should be awfully simple to say when a thing's right or wrong—but really, when it comes to it, it isn't quite such plain sailing. I mean one may come across something—the kind of thing, you see, that isn't meant for you—it's all a kind of accident, and it's the sort of thing you couldn't take advantage of, and yet it might be most frightfully important. Do you see what I mean?"

"Not very well, I'm afraid," I confessed.

Norton's brow furrowed again. He ran his hands up through his hair again so that it stood upright in its usual comical manner.

"It's so hard to explain. What I mean is, suppose you just happened to see something in a private letter—one opened by mistake, that sort of thing—a letter meant for someone else and you began reading it because you thought it was written to you and so you actually read something you weren't meant to before you realized. That could happen, you know."

"Oh yes, of course it could."

"Well, I mean, what would one do?"

"Well—" I gave my mind to the problem. "I suppose you'd go to the person and say: 'I'm awfully sorry, but I opened this by mistake.'"

Norton sighed. He said it wasn't quite so simple as that.

"You see—you might have read something rather embarrassing, Hastings."

"That would embarrass the other person, you mean? I suppose you'd have to pretend you hadn't actually read anything—that you'd discovered your mistake in time."

"Yes." Norton said it after a moment's pause, and he did not seem to feel that he had yet arrived at a satisfactory solution.

He said rather wistfully:

"I wish I did know what I ought to do."

I said that I couldn't see that there was anything else he could do.

Norton said, the perplexed frown still on his forehead:

"You see, Hastings, there's rather more to it than that. Supposing that what you read was—well, rather important to someone else again, I mean."

I lost patience.

"Really, Norton, I don't see what you do mean. You can't go about reading other people's private letters, can you—"

"No, no, of course not. I didn't mean that. And anyway, it wasn't a letter at all. I only said that to try and explain the sort of thing. Naturally anything you saw or heard or read—by accident —you'd keep to yourself, unless—"

"Unless what?"

Norton said slowly:

"Unless it was something you *ought* to speak about."

I looked at him with suddenly awakened interest. He went on:

"Look here, think of it this way—supposing you saw something through a—a keyhole—"

Keyholes made me think of Poirot! Norton was stumbling on:

"What I mean is, you'd got a perfectly good reason for looking through the keyhole—the key might have stuck and you just looked to see if it was clear—or—or some quite good reason—and you never for one minute expected to see what you did see . . ."

For a moment or two I lost the thread of his stumbling sentences, for enlightenment had come to me. I remembered a day on a grassy knoll and Norton swinging up his glasses to see a speckled woodpecker. I remembered his immediate distress and embarrassment, his endeavours to prevent me from looking through the glasses in my turn. At the moment I had leaped to the conclusion that what he had seen was something to do with *me*—in fact that it was Allerton and Judith. But supposing that that was not the case? That he had seen something quite different? I had assumed that it was something to do with Allerton and Judith because I was so obsessed by them at that time that I could think of nothing else.

I said abruptly:

"Was it something you saw through those glasses of yours?"

Norton was both startled and relieved.

"I say, Hastings, how did you guess?"

"It was that day when you and I and Elizabeth Cole were up on that knoll, wasn't it?"

"Yes, that's right."

"And you didn't want me to see?"

"No. It wasn't—well, I mean it wasn't meant for any of us to see."

"What was it?"

Norton frowned again.

"That's just it. Ought I to say? I mean it was—well, it was spying. I saw something I wasn't meant to see. I wasn't looking for it —there really was a speckled woodpecker—a lovely fellow, and then I saw the other thing."

He stopped. I was curious, intensely curious, yet I respected his scruples.

I asked:

"Was it—something that mattered?"

He said slowly:

"It might matter. That's just it. I don't know."

I asked then:

"Has it something to do with Mrs. Franklin's death?"

He started.

"It's queer you should say that."

"Then it has?"

"No—no, not directly. But it might have." He said slowly: "It would throw a different light on certain things. It would mean that— Oh, damn it all, I don't know what to do!"

I was in a dilemma. I was agog with curiosity, yet I felt that Norton was very reluctant to say what he had seen. I could understand that. I should have felt the same myself. It is always unpleasant to come into possession of a piece of information that has been acquired in what the outside world would consider a dubious manner.

Then an idea struck me.

"Why not consult Poirot?"

"Poirot?" Norton seemed a little doubtful.

"Yes, ask his advice."

"Well," said Norton slowly, "it's an idea. Only, of course, he's a foreigner—" He stopped, rather embarrassed.

I knew what he meant. Poirot's scathing remarks on the subject of "playing the game" were only too familiar to me. I only wondered that Poirot had never thought of taking to bird glasses himself! He would have done if he had thought of it.

"He'd respect your confidence," I urged. "And you needn't act upon his advice if you don't like it."

"That's true," said Norton, his brow clearing. "You know, Hastings, I think that's just what I will do."

IV

I was astonished at Poirot's instant reaction to my piece of information.

"What is that you say, Hastings?"

He dropped the piece of thin toast he had been raising to his lips. He poked his head forward.

"Tell me. Tell me quickly."

I repeated the story.

"He saw something through the glasses that day," repeated Poirot thoughtfully. "Something that he will not tell you." His hand shot out and gripped my arm. "He has not told anyone else of this?"

"I don't think so. No, I'm sure he hasn't."

"Be very careful, Hastings. It is urgent that he should not tell anyone—he must not even hint. To do so might be dangerous."

"Dangerous?"

"Very dangerous."

Poirot's face was grave.

"Arrange with him, *mon ami*, to come up and see me this evening. Just an ordinary friendly little visit, you understand. Do not let anyone else suspect that there is any special reason for his coming. And be careful, Hastings; be very, very careful. Who else did you say was with you at the time?"

"Elizabeth Cole."

"Did she notice anything odd about his manner?"

I tried to recollect.

"I don't know. She may have. Shall I ask her if—"

"You will say nothing, Hastings—absolutely nothing."

16

I gave Norton Poirot's message.

"I'll go up and see him, certainly. I'd like to. But you know, Hastings, I'm rather sorry I mentioned that matter even to you."

"By the way," I said. "You haven't said anything to anyone else about it, have you?"

"No—at least—no, of course not."

"You're quite sure?"

"No, no, I haven't said anything."

"Well, don't. Not until after you've seen Poirot."

I had noticed the slight hesitation in his tone when he first answered, but his second assurance was quite firm. I was to remember that slight hesitation afterwards, though.

II

I went up again to the grassy knoll where we had been on that day. Someone else was there already. Elizabeth Cole. She turned her head as I came up the slope.

She said:

"You look very excited, Captain Hastings. Is anything the matter?"

I tried to calm myself.

"No, no, nothing at all. I'm just out of breath with walking fast." I added in an everyday commonplace voice:

"It's going to rain."

She looked up at the sky.

"Yes, I think it is."

We stood there silent for a minute or two. There was something about this woman that I found very sympathetic. Ever since she had told me who she really was, and the tragedy that had ruined her life, I had taken an interest in her. Two people who have suffered unhappiness have a great bond in common. Yet for her there was, or so I suspected, a second spring. I said now impulsively:

"Far from being excited, I'm depressed today. I've had bad news about my dear old friend."

"About M. Poirot?"

Her sympathetic interest led me to unburden myself.

When I had finished, she said softly:

"I see. So—the end might come any time?"

I nodded, unable to speak.

After a minute or two I said:

"When he's gone, I shall indeed be alone in the world."

"Oh no, you've got Judith—and your other children."

"They're scattered over the world, and Judith—well, she's got her work. She doesn't need me."

"I suspect that children don't ever need their parents until they are in trouble of some kind. You should make up your mind to that as to some fundamental law. I'm far more lonely than you are. My two sisters are far away—one in America and one in Italy."

"My dear girl," I said. "Your life's beginning."

"At thirty-five?"

"What's thirty-five? I wish I were thirty-five." I added maliciously: "I'm not quite blind, you know."

She turned an enquiring glance on me, then blushed.

"You don't think—oh! Stephen Norton and I are only friends. We've got a good deal in common—"

"All the better."

"He's—he's just awfully kind."

"Oh, my dear," I said. "Don't believe it's all kindness. We men aren't made that way."

But Elizabeth Cole had turned suddenly white. She said in a low, strained voice:

"You're cruel—blind! How can I ever think of—of marriage? With my history. With my sister a murderess—or if not that, insane. I don't know which is worse."

I said strongly:

"Don't let that prey on your mind. Remember, it may not be true."

"What do you mean? It is true."

"Don't you remember saying to me once: 'It wasn't Maggie'?"

She caught her breath.

"One feels like that."

"What one feels is often—true."

She stared at me.

"What do you mean?"

"Your sister," I said, "did not kill her father."

Her hand crept up to her mouth. Her eyes, wide and scared, looked into mine.

"You're mad," she said. "You must be mad. Who told you that?"

"Never mind," I said. "It's true. Someday I'll prove it to you."

III

Near the house I ran into Boyd Carrington.

"This is my last evening," he told me. "I move out tomorrow."

"To Knatton?"

"Yes."

"That's very exciting for you."

"Is it? I suppose it is." He gave a sigh. "Anyway, Hastings, I don't mind telling you, I shall be glad to leave here."

"The food is certainly pretty bad and the service isn't good."

"I don't mean that. After all, it's cheap, and you can't expect much from these paying guest places. No, Hastings, I mean more than discomfort. I don't like this house—there's some malign influence about it. Things happen here."

"They certainly do."

"I don't know what it is. Perhaps a house that has once had a murder in it is never quite the same afterwards . . . But I don't like it. First there was that accident to Mrs. Luttrell—a damned unlucky thing to happen. And then there was poor little Barbara."

He paused.

"The most unlikely person in the world to have committed suicide, *I* should have said."

I hesitated.

"Well, I don't know that I'd go as far as that—"

He interrupted me.

"Well, I would. Hang it all, I was with her most of the day before. She was in good spirits—enjoyed our outing. The only thing she was worrying about was whether John wasn't getting too much wrapped up in his experiments and might overdo things or try some of his messes upon himself. Do you know what I think, Hastings?"

"No."

"That husband of hers is the one who's responsible for her death. Nagged at her, I expect. She was always happy enough when she was with me. He let her see that she handicapped his precious career (I'd give him a career!) and it broke her up. Damned callous, that fellow, hasn't turned a hair. Told me as cool as anything he was off to Africa now. Really, you know, Hastings, I shouldn't be surprised if he'd actually murdered her."

"You don't mean that," I said sharply.

"No—no, I don't really. Though, mind you, mainly because I can see that if he murdered her, he wouldn't do it that way. I mean he was known to be working on this stuff—physostigmine—so it stands to reason if he'd done her in, he wouldn't have used that. But all the same, Hastings, I'm not the only one to think that Franklin's a suspicious character. I had the tip from someone who ought to know."

"Who was that?" I asked sharply.

Boyd Carrington lowered his voice.

"Nurse Craven."

"What?" I was intensely surprised.

"Hush. Don't shout. Yes, Nurse Craven put the idea into my

head. She's a smart girl, you know, got her wits about her. She doesn't like Franklin—hasn't liked him all along."

I wondered. I should have said that it was her own patient whom Nurse Craven had disliked. It occurred to me suddenly that Nurse Craven must know a good deal about the Franklin ménage.

"She's staying here tonight," said Boyd Carrington.

"What?" I was rather startled. Nurse Craven had left immediately after the funeral.

"Just for a night between cases," explained Boyd Carrington.

"I see."

I was vaguely disquieted by Nurse Craven's return, yet I could hardly have said why. Was there, I wondered, any reason for her coming back? She didn't like Franklin, Boyd Carrington had said . . .

Reassuring myself, I said with sudden vehemence:

"She's no right to hint things about Franklin. After all, it was her evidence that helped to establish suicide. That, and Poirot's seeing Mrs. Franklin coming out of the studio with a bottle in her hand."

Boyd Carrington snapped:

"What's a bottle? Women are always carrying bottles—scent bottles, hair lotion, nail polish. That wench of yours was running about with a bottle in her hand that evening—it doesn't mean *she* was thinking of suicide, does it? Nonsense!"

He broke off as Allerton came up to us. Most appropriately, in melodramatic fashion, there was a low rumble of thunder in the distance. I reflected, as I had reflected before, that Allerton was certainly cast for the part of the villain.

But he had been away from the house on the night of Barbara Franklin's death. And besides, what possible motive could he have had?

But then, I reflected, X never had a motive. That was the strength of his position. It was that, and that only, that was holding us up. And yet, at any minute, that tiny flash of illumination might come.

IV

I think that here and now I should like to place on record that I had never, all through, considered for one moment that Poirot might fail. In the conflict between Poirot and X, I had never contemplated the possibility that X might come out victor. In spite of Poirot's feebleness and ill health, I had faith in him as potentially the stronger of the two. I was used, you see, to Poirot's succeeding.

It was Poirot himself who first put a doubt into my head.

I went in to see him on my way down to dinner. I forget now exactly what led to it, but he suddenly used the phrase "if anything happens to me."

I protested immediately and loudly. Nothing would happen—nothing could happen.

"*Eh bien,* then you have not listened carefully to what Dr. Franklin told you."

"Franklin doesn't know. You're good for many a long year yet, Poirot."

"It is possible, my friend, though extremely unlikely. But I speak now in the particular and not the general sense. Though I may die very soon, it may still be not soon enough to suit our friend X."

"What?" My face showed my shocked reaction.

Poirot nodded.

"But yes, Hastings. X is, after all, intelligent. In fact, most intelligent. And X cannot fail to perceive that my elimination, even if it were only to precede natural decease by a few days, might be of inestimable advantage."

"But then—but then—what would happen?" I was bewildered.

"When the colonel falls, *mon ami,* the second in command takes over. You will continue."

"How can I? I'm entirely in the dark."

"I have arranged for that. If anything happens to me, my friend, you will find here"—he patted the locked dispatch case by his side—"all the clues you need. I have arranged, you see, for every eventuality."

"There is really no need to be clever. Just tell me now every-thing there is to know."

"No, my friend. The fact that you do not know what I know is a valuable asset."

"You have left me a clearly written account of things?"

"Certainly not. X might get hold of it."

"Then what have you left?"

"Indications in kind. They will mean nothing to X—be assured of that—but they will lead you to the discovery of the truth."

"I'm not so sure of that. Why must you have such a tortuous mind, Poirot? You always like making everything difficult. You always have!"

"And it is now with me a passion? Is that what you would say? Perhaps. But rest assured, my indications will lead you to the truth." He paused. Then he said: "And perhaps, then, you would wish that they had not led you so far. You would say in-stead: *'Ring down the curtain.'*"

Something in his voice started again that vague unformulated dread that I had once or twice felt spasms of already. It was as though somewhere, just out of sight, was a fact that I did not want to see—that I could not bear to acknowledge. Something that already, deep down, *I knew* . . .

I shook the feeling off and went down to dinner.

17

Dinner was a reasonably cheerful meal. Mrs. Luttrell was down again and in her best vein of artificial Irish gaiety. Franklin was more animated and cheerful than I had yet seen him. Nurse Craven I saw for the first time in mufti instead of her nurse's uniform. She was certainly a very attractive young woman now that she had cast off her professional reserve.

After dinner Mrs. Luttrell suggested bridge, but in the end some round games were started. About half-past nine Norton declared his intention of going up to see Poirot.

"Good idea," said Boyd Carrington. "Sorry he's been under the weather lately. I'll come up too."

I had to act quickly.

"Look here," I said, "do you mind—it really tires him too much to talk to more than one person at a time."

Norton took the cue and said quickly:

"I promised to lend him a book on birds."

Boyd Carrington said:

"All right. You coming back again, Hastings?"

"Yes."

I went up with Norton. Poirot was waiting. After a word or two I came down again. We began playing rummy.

Boyd Carrington, I think, resented the carefree atmosphere of Styles tonight. He thought, perhaps, that it was too soon after the tragedy for everyone to forget. He was absent-minded, forgot

frequently what he was doing, and at last excused himself from
further play.

He went to the window and opened it. The sound of thunder
could be heard in the distance. There was a storm about, although it had not yet reached us. He closed the window again
and came back. He stood for a minute or two watching us play.
Then he went out of the room.

I went up to bed at a quarter to eleven. I did not go in to
Poirot. He might be asleep. Moreover I felt a reluctance to think
any more about Styles and its problems. I wanted to sleep—to
sleep and forget.

I was just dropping off when a sound wakened me. I thought it
might have been a tap on my door. I called "Come in," but as
there was no response, I switched the light on and, getting up,
looked out into the corridor.

I saw Norton just coming from the bathroom and going into
his own room. He wore a checked dressing gown of particularly
hideous colouring and his hair was sticking up on end as usual.
He went into his room and shut the door, and immediately afterwards I heard him turn the key in the lock.

Overhead there was a low rumbling of thunder. The storm was
coming nearer.

I went back to bed with a slightly uneasy feeling induced by
the sound of that turning key.

It suggested, very faintly, sinister possibilities. Did Norton
usually lock his door at night? I wondered. Had Poirot warned
him to do so? I remembered with sudden uneasiness how Poirot's
door key had mysteriously disappeared.

I lay in bed and my uneasiness grew while the storm overhead
added to my feeling of nerviness. I got up at last and locked my
own door. Then I went back to bed and slept.

II

I went in to Poirot before going down to breakfast.

He was in bed and I was struck again by how ill he looked.
Deep lines of weariness and fatigue were on his face.

"How are you, old boy?"

He smiled patiently at me.

"I exist, my friend. I still exist."

"Not in pain?"

"No—just tired," he sighed, "very tired."

I nodded.

"What about last night? Did Norton tell you what he saw that day?"

"He told me, yes."

"What was it?"

Poirot looked at me long and thoughtfully before he replied:

"I am not sure, Hastings, that I had better tell you. You might misunderstand."

"What are you talking about?"

"Norton," said Poirot, "tells me he saw two people—"

"Judith and Allerton," I cried. "I thought so at the time."

"*Eh bien, non. Not* Judith and Allerton. Did I not tell you you would misunderstand? You are a man of one idea!"

"Sorry," I said, a little abashed. "Tell me."

"I will tell you tomorrow. I have much on which I wish to reflect."

"Does it—does it help with the case?"

Poirot nodded. He closed his eyes, leaning back in his pillows.

"The case is ended. Yes, it is ended. There are only some loose ends to be tied. Go down to breakfast, my friend. And as you go, send Curtiss to me."

I did so and went downstairs. I wanted to see Norton. I was deeply curious to know what it was that he had told Poirot.

Subconsciously I was still not happy. The lack of elation in Poirot's manner struck me disagreeably. Why this persistent secrecy? Why that deep inexplicable sadness? What was the *truth* of all this?

Norton was not at breakfast.

I strolled out into the garden afterwards. The air was fresh and cool after the storm. I noticed that it had rained heavily. Boyd Carrington was on the lawn. I felt pleased to see him and wished that I could take him into my confidence. I had wanted to all along. I was very tempted to do so now. Poirot was really unfit to carry on by himself.

This morning Boyd Carrington looked so vital, so sure of himself, that I felt a wave of warmth and reassurance.

"You're late up this morning," he said.

I nodded.

"I slept late."

"Bit of a thunderstorm last night. Hear it?"

I remembered now that I had been conscious of the rolling of thunder through my sleep.

"I felt a bit under the weather last night," said Boyd Carrington. "I feel a lot better today." He stretched his arms out and yawned.

"Where's Norton?" I asked.

"Don't think he's up yet. Lazy devil."

With common accord we raised our eyes. Where we were standing, the windows of Norton's room were just above us. I started. For alone in the façade of windows, Norton's were still shuttered.

I said: "That's odd. Do you think they've forgotten to call him?"

"Funny. Hope he's not ill. Let's go up and see."

We went up together. The housemaid, a rather stupid-looking girl, was in the passage. In answer to a question she replied that Mr. Norton hadn't answered when she knocked. She'd knocked once or twice but he hadn't seemed to hear. His door was locked.

A nasty foreboding swept over me. I rapped loudly on the door, calling as I did so:

"Norton—Norton. Wake up!"

And again with growing uneasiness:

"Wake up . . ."

III

When it was apparent that there was going to be no answer, we went and found Colonel Luttrell. He listened to us with a vague alarm showing in his faded blue eyes. He pulled uncertainly at his moustache.

Mrs. Luttrell, always the one for prompt decisions, made no bones about it.

"You'll have to get that door open somehow. There's nothing else for it."

For the second time in my life, I saw a door broken open at Styles. Behind that door was what had been behind a locked door on the first occasion. *Death by violence.*

Norton was lying on his bed in his dressing gown. The key of the door was in the pocket. In his hand was a small pistol, a mere toy, but capable of doing its work. There was a small hole in the exact centre of his forehead.

For a moment or two I could not think of what I was reminded. Something, surely very old . . .

I was too tired to remember.

IV

As I came into Poirot's room, he saw my face.

He said quickly:

"What has happened? Norton?"

"Dead!"

"How? When?"

Briefly I told him.

I ended wearily:

"They say it's suicide. What else can they say? The door was locked. The windows were shuttered. The key was in his pocket. Why! I actually saw him go in and heard him lock the door."

"You saw him, Hastings?"

"Yes, last night."

I explained:

"You're sure it was Norton?"

"Of course. I'd know that awful old dressing gown anywhere."

For a moment Poirot became his old self.

"Ah! But it is a *man* you are identifying, not a *dressing gown.* *Ma foi!* Anyone can wear a dressing gown."

"It's true," I said slowly, "that I didn't see his face. But it was his hair, all right, and that slight limp—"

"Anyone could limp, *mon Dieu!*"

I looked at him, startled.

"Do you mean to suggest, Poirot, that it *wasn't* Norton that I saw?"

"I am not suggesting anything of the kind. I am merely annoyed by the unscientific reasons you give for saying it was Norton. No, no, I do not for one minute suggest that it was *not* Norton. It would be difficult for it to be anyone else, for every man here is tall—very much taller than he was—and *enfin,* you cannot disguise height—that, no. Norton was only five foot five, I should say. *Tout de même,* it is like a conjuring trick, is it not? He goes into his room, locks the door, puts the key in his pocket, and is found shot with the pistol in his hand and the key still in his pocket."

"Then you don't believe," I said, "that he shot himself?"

Slowly Poirot shook his head.

"No," he said. "Norton did not shoot himself. He was deliberately killed."

V

I went downstairs in a maze. The thing was so inexplicable I may be forgiven, I hope, for not seeing the next inevitable step. I was dazed. My mind was not working properly.

And yet it was so logical. Norton had been killed—why? To prevent, or so I believed, his telling what he had seen.

But he had confided that knowledge to one other person.

So that person, too, was in danger . . .

And was not only in danger, but was helpless.

I *should* have known.

I *should* have foreseen . . .

"*Cher ami!*" Poirot had said to me as I left the room.

They were the last words I was ever to hear him say. For when Curtiss came to attend to his master, he found that master dead . . .

18

I don't want to write about it at all.

I want, you see, to think about it as little as possible. Hercule Poirot was dead—and with him died a good part of Arthur Hastings.

I will give you the bare facts without embroidery. It is all I can bear to do.

He died, they said, of natural causes. That is to say, he died of a heart attack. It was the way, so Franklin said, that he had expected him to go. Doubtless the shock of Norton's death brought one on. By some oversight, it seems, the amyl nitrite ampoules were not by his bed.

Was it an oversight? Did someone deliberately remove them? No, it must have been something more than that. X could not count on Poirot's having a heart attack.

For you see, I refuse to believe that Poirot's death was natural. He was killed, as Norton was killed, as Barbara Franklin was killed. And I don't know *why* they were killed—and I don't know who killed them!

There was an inquest on Norton and a verdict of suicide. The only point of doubt was raised by the surgeon, who said it was unusual for a man to shoot himself in the exact centre of his forehead. But that was the only shadow of a doubt. The whole thing was so plain. The door locked on the inside, the key in the dead man's pocket, the windows closely shuttered—the pistol in his hand. Norton had complained of headaches, it seemed, and some of his investments had been doing badly lately. Hardly reasons for suicide, but they had to put forward something.

The pistol was apparently his own. It had been seen lying on his dressing table twice by the housemaid during his stay at Styles. So that was that. Another crime beautifully stage-managed and as usual with no alternative solution.

In the duel between Poirot and X, X had won.

It was now up to me.

I went to Poirot's room and took away the dispatch box.

I knew that he had made me his executor, so I had a perfect right to do so. The key was round his neck.

In my own room I opened the box.

And at once I had a shock. *The dossiers of X's cases were gone.* I had seen them there only a day or two previously when Poirot unlocked it. That was proof, if I had been needing it, that X had been at work. Either Poirot had destroyed those papers himself (most unlikely) or else X had done so.

X. X. That damned fiend X.

But the case was not empty. I remembered Poirot's promise that I should find other indications which X would not know about.

Were these the indications?

There was a copy of one of Shakespeare's plays, *Othello,* in a small cheap edition. The other book was the play *John Ferguson* by St. John Ervine. There was a marker in it at the third act.

I stared at the two books blankly.

Here were the clues that Poirot had left for me—and they meant nothing to me at all!

What could they mean?

The only thing I could think of was a code of some kind. A word code based on the plays.

But if so, how was I to get at it?

There were no words, no letters, underlined anywhere. I tried gentle heat with no result.

I read the third act of *John Ferguson* carefully through. A most admirable and thrilling scene where the "wanting" Clutie John sits and talks and which ends with the younger Ferguson going out to seek for the man who has wronged his sister. Masterly character drawing—but I could hardly think that Poirot had left them to improve my taste in literature!

And then, as I turned the leaves of the book over, a slip of paper fell out. It bore a phrase in Poirot's handwriting: *"Talk to my valet Georges."*

Well, here was something. Possibly the key to the code, if code it was, had been left with Georges. I must get hold of his address and go to see him.

But first there was the sad business of burying my dear friend.

Here was the spot where he had lived when he first came to this country. He was to lie here at the last.

Judith was very kind to me in these days.

She spent a lot of time with me and helped to make all the arrangements. She was gentle and sympathetic. Elizabeth Cole and Boyd Carrington were very kind, too.

Elizabeth Cole was less affected by Norton's death than I should have thought. If she felt any deep grief, she kept it to herself.

And so it was all ended . . .

II

Yes, I must put it down.

It must be said.

The funeral was over. I was sitting with Judith, trying to make a few sketchy plans for the future.

She said then:

"But you see, dear, I shan't be here."

"Not here?"

"I shan't be in England."

I stared at her.

"I haven't liked to tell you before, Father. I didn't want to make things worse for you. But you've got to know now. I hope you won't mind too much. I'm going to Africa, you see, with Dr. Franklin."

I burst out at that. It was impossible. She couldn't do a thing

like that. Everyone would be bound to talk. To be an assistant to
him in England and especially when his wife was alive was one
thing, but to go abroad with him to Africa was another. It was
impossible and I was going to forbid it absolutely. Judith must
not do such a thing!

She didn't interrupt. She let me finish. She smiled very faintly.

"But, dearest," she said, "I'm not going as his assistant. I'm
going as his wife."

It hit me between the eyes.

I said—or rather stammered—"Al-Allerton?"

She looked faintly amused.

"There was never anything in that. I would have told you so if
you hadn't made me so angry. Besides, I wanted you to think,
well—what you did think. I didn't want you to know it was—
John."

"But I saw him kiss you one night—on the terrace."

She said impatiently:

"Oh, I daresay. I was miserable that night. These things happen. Surely you know that?"

I said:

"You can't marry Franklin yet—so soon."

"Yes, I can. I want to go out with him, and you've just said
yourself it's easier. We've nothing to wait for—now."

Judith and Franklin. Franklin and Judith.

Do you understand the thoughts that came into my mind—the
thoughts that had lain under the surface for some time?

Judith with a bottle in her hand, Judith with her young, passionate voice declaring that useless lives should go to make way
for useful ones. Judith whom I loved and whom Poirot also had
loved. Those two people that Norton had seen—had they been
Judith and *Franklin*? But if so—if so— No, that couldn't be true.
Not Judith. Franklin, perhaps—a strange man, a ruthless man, a
man who, if he made up his mind to murder, might murder again
and again.

Poirot had been willing to consult Franklin.

Why? What had he said to him that morning?

But not Judith. Not my lovely, grave young Judith.

And yet how strange Poirot had looked. How those words had rung out: "You may prefer to say: *'Ring down the curtain'* . . ."

And suddenly a fresh idea struck me. Monstrous! Impossible! Was the whole story of X a fabrication? Had Poirot come to Styles because he feared a tragedy in the Franklin ménage? Had he come to watch over Judith? Was *that* why he had resolutely told me nothing? Because the whole story of X was a fabrication, a smoke screen?

Was the whole heart of the tragedy Judith, my daughter?

Othello! It was *Othello* I had taken from the bookcase that night when Mrs. Franklin had died. Was that the clue?

Judith that night looking, so someone had said, like her namesake before she cut off the head of Holofernes. Judith—with death in her heart?

19

I am writing this in Eastbourne.

I came to Eastbourne to see Georges, formerly Poirot's valet.

Georges had been with Poirot many years. He was a competent, matter-of-fact man, with absolutely no imagination. He always stated things literally and took them at their face value.

Well, I went to see him. I told him about Poirot's death, and Georges reacted as Georges would react. He was distressed and grieved and managed very nearly to conceal the fact.

Then I said:

"He left with you, did he not, a message for me?"

Georges said at once:

"For you, sir? No, not that I am aware of."

I was surprised. I pressed him, but he was quite definite.

I said at last:

"My mistake, I suppose. Well, that's that. I wish you had been with him at the end."

"I wish so, too, sir."

"Still I suppose if your father was ill, you had to come to him."

Georges looked at me in a very curious manner. He said:

"I beg your pardon, sir. I don't quite understand you."

"You had to leave in order to look after your father, isn't that right?"

"I didn't wish to leave, sir. M. Poirot sent me away."

"Sent you away?" I stared.

"I don't mean, sir, that he discharged me. The understanding was that I was to return to his service later. But I left by his wish, and he arranged for suitable remuneration while I was here with my old father."

"But why, Georges, why?"

"I really couldn't say, sir."

"Didn't you ask?"

"No, sir. I didn't think it was my place to do so. M. Poirot always had his ideas, sir. A very clever gentleman, I always understood, sir, and very much respected."

"Yes, yes," I murmured abstractedly.

"Very particular about his clothes, he was—though given to having them rather foreign and fancy, if you know what I mean. But that, of course, is understandable, as he was a foreign gentleman. His hair, too, and his moustache."

"Ah! Those famous moustaches." I felt a twinge of pain as I remembered his pride in them.

"Very particular about his moustache, he was," went on Georges. "Not very fashionable the way he wore it, but it suited *him,* sir, if you know what I mean."

I said I did know. Then I murmured delicately:

"I suppose he dyed it as well as his hair?"

"He did—er—touch up his moustache a little—but not his hair —not of late years."

"Nonsense," I said. "It was as black as a raven—looked quite like a wig, it was so unnatural."

Georges coughed apologetically.

"Excuse me, sir, it was a wig. M. Poirot's hair came out a good deal lately, so he took to a wig."

I thought how odd it was that a valet knew more about a man than his closest friend did.

I went back to the question that puzzled me.

"But have you really no idea why M. Poirot sent you away as he did? Think, man, *think.*"

Georges endeavoured to do so, but he was clearly not very good at thinking.

"I can only suggest, sir," he said at last, "that he discharged me because he wanted to engage Curtiss."

"Curtiss? Why should he want to engage Curtiss?"

Georges coughed again.

"Well, sir, I really cannot say. He did not seem to me, when I saw him, as a—excuse me—particularly bright specimen, sir. He was strong physically, of course, but I should hardly have thought that he was quite the class M. Poirot would have liked. He'd been assistant in a mental home at one time, I believe."

I stared at Georges.

Curtiss!

Was that the reason why Poirot had insisted on telling me so little? Curtiss, the one man I had never considered! Yes, and Poirot was content to have it so, to have me combing the guests at Styles for the mysterious X. But X was *not* a guest.

Curtiss!

One-time assistant in a mental home. And hadn't I read somewhere that people who have been patients in mental homes and asylums sometimes remain or go back there as assistants?

A queer, dumb, stupid-looking man—a man who might kill for some strange warped reason of his own . . .

And if so—if so . . .

Why, then a great cloud would roll away from me!

Curtiss—?

POSTSCRIPT

(Note by Captain Arthur Hastings:
The following manuscript came into my possession four months after the death of my friend Hercule Poirot. I received a communication from a firm of lawyers asking me to call at their office. There, "in accordance with the instructions of their client, the late M. Hercule Poirot," they handed me a sealed packet. I reproduce its contents here.)

Manuscript written by Hercule Poirot:
Mon cher ami,

I shall have been dead four months when you read these words. I have debated long whether or not to write down what is written here, and I have decided that it is necessary for someone to know the truth about the second "Affaire Styles." Also I hazard a conjecture that by the time you read this you will have evolved the most preposterous theories—and possibly may be giving pain to yourself.

But let me say this: You should, *mon ami,* have easily been able to arrive at the truth. I saw to it that you had every indication. If you have not, it is because, as always, you have far too beautiful and trusting a nature. *A la fin comme au commencement.*

But you should know, at least, who killed Norton—even if you are still in the dark as to who killed Barbara Franklin. The latter may be a shock to you.

To begin with, as you know, I sent for you. I told you that I needed you. That was true. I told you that I wanted you to be my ears and my eyes. That again was true, very true—if not in the sense that you understood it! You were to see what I wanted you to see and hear what I wanted you to hear.

You complained, *cher ami,* that I was "unfair" in my presentation of this case. I withheld from you knowledge that I had myself. That is to say, I refused to tell you the identity of X. That is quite true. I had to do so—though not for the reasons that I advanced. You will see the reason presently.

And now let us examine this matter of X. I showed you the résumé of the various cases. I pointed out to you that in each separate case it seemed quite clear that the person accused, or suspected, had actually committed the crimes in question, that there was no *alternate* solution. And I then proceeded to the second important fact—that in each case X had been either on the scene or closely involved. You then jumped to a deduction that was, paradoxically, both true and false. You said that X had committed all the murders.

But, my friend, the circumstances were such that in each case (or very nearly) *only* the accused person could have done the crime. On the other hand, if so, how account for X? Apart from a person connected with the police force or with, say, a firm of criminal lawyers, it is not reasonable for any man or woman to be involved in five murder cases. It does not, you comprehend, happen! Never, never does it occur that someone says confidentially: "Well, as a matter of fact, I've actually known five murderers"! No, no, *mon ami,* it is not possible, that. So we get the curious result that we have here a case of catalysis—a reaction between two substances that takes place only in the presence of a third substance, that third substance apparently taking no part in the reaction and remaining unchanged. That is the position. It means that where X was present, crimes took place—but X did not actively take part in these crimes.

An extraordinary, an abnormal situation! And I saw that I

had come across at last, at the end of my career, the perfect criminal, the criminal who had invented such a technique that *he could never be convicted of crime.*

It was amazing. But it was not new. There were parallels. And here comes in the first of the "clues" I left you. The play of *Othello.* For there, magnificently delineated, we have the original of X. Iago is the perfect murderer. The deaths of Desdemona, of Cassio—indeed of Othello himself—are all Iago's crimes, planned by him, carried out by him. And *he* remains outside the circle, untouched by suspicion—or could have done so. For your great Shakespeare, my friend, had to deal with the dilemma that his own art had brought about. To unmask Iago, he had to resort to the clumsiest of devices—the handkerchief—a piece of work not at all in keeping with Iago's general technique and a blunder of which one feels certain he would not have been guilty.

Yes, there is there the perfection of the art of murder. Not even a word of *direct* suggestion. He is always holding back others from violence, refuting with horror suspicions that have not been entertained until he mentions them!

And the same technique is seen in the brilliant third act of *John Ferguson*—where the "half-witted" Clutie John induces others to kill the man that he himself hates. It is a wonderful piece of psychological suggestion.

Now you must realize this, Hastings. Everyone is a potential murderer—in everyone there arises from time to time the *wish* to kill—though not the *will* to kill. How often have you not felt or heard others say: "She made me so furious I felt I could have killed her!" "I could have killed B. for saying so-and-so!" "I was so angry I could have murdered him!" And all those statements are literally true. Your mind at such moments is quite clear. You would like to kill so-and-so. *But you do not do it.* Your will has to assent to your desire. In young children, the brake is as yet acting imperfectly. I have known a child, annoyed by its kitten, say: "Keep still or I'll hit you on the head and kill you" and actually do so—to be stunned and horrified a moment later when it realizes that the kitten's life will not return—because, you see, really the child loves that kitten dearly. So then, we are all potential murderers. And the art of X was this: not to suggest the *desire*, but to break down the normal decent resistance. It was an art perfected by long practice. X knew the exact word, the exact phrase, the intonation even to suggest and to bring cumulative pressure on a weak spot! It could be done. It was done without the victim ever suspecting. It was not hypnotism—hypnotism would not have been successful. It was something more insidious, more deadly. It was a marshalling of the forces of a human being to widen a breach instead of repairing it. It called on the best in a man and set it in alliance with the worst.

You should know, Hastings—for it happened to you . . .

So now, perhaps, you begin to see what some of my remarks that annoyed and confused you really meant. When I spoke of a crime to be committed, I was not always referring to the same crime. I told you that I was at Styles for a purpose. I was there, I said, because a crime was going to be committed. You were surprised at my certainty on that point. But I was able to be certain—for the crime, you see, was to be committed *by myself* . . .

Yes, my friend, it is odd—and laughable—and terrible! I, who do not approve of murder—I, who value human life—have ended my career by committing murder. Perhaps it is because I have been too self-righteous, too conscious of rectitude—that this terrible dilemma had to come to me. For you see, Hastings, there are two sides to it. It is my work in life to save the innocent—to *prevent* murder—and this—this is the only way I can do it! Make no mistake. X could not be touched by the law. He was safe. By no ingenuity that I could think of could he be defeated any other way.

And yet, my friend—I was reluctant. I saw what had to be done—but I could not bring myself to do it. I was like Hamlet—eternally putting off the evil day . . . And then the next attempt happened—the attempt on Mrs. Luttrell.

I had been curious, Hastings, to see if your well-known flair for the obvious would work. It did. Your very first reaction was a mild suspicion of Norton. And you were quite right. Norton was the man. You had no reason for your belief—except the perfectly sound if slightly half-hearted suggestion that he was insignificant. There, I think, you came very close to the truth.

I have considered his life history with some care. He was the only son of a masterful and bossy woman. He seems to have had at no time any gift for asserting himself or for impressing his personality on other people. He has always been slightly lame and was unable to take part in games at school.

One of the most significant things you told me was a remark about him having been laughed at at school for nearly being sick when seeing a dead rabbit. There, I think, was an incident that may have left a deep impression on him. He disliked blood and violence and his prestige suffered in consequence. Subconsciously, I should say, he has waited to redeem himself by being bold and ruthless.

I should imagine that he began to discover quite young his own power for influencing people. He is a good listener, he has a quiet, sympathetic personality. People liked him without, at the same time, noticing him very much. He resented this—and then made use of it. He discovered how ridiculously easy it was, by using the correct words and supplying the correct stimuli, to influence his fellow creatures. The only thing necessary was to understand them—to penetrate their thoughts, their secret reactions and wishes.

Can you realize, Hastings, that such a discovery might feed a sense of power? Here was he, Stephen Norton, whom everyone liked and despised—and he could make people do things they didn't want to do—or (mark this) thought they did not want to do.

I can visualize him developing this hobby of his . . . And little by little developing a morbid taste for violence at second hand. The violence for which he lacked physical stamina and for the lack of which he had been derided.

Yes, his hobby grows and grows until it comes to be a passion, a necessity! It was a drug, Hastings—a drug that induced craving as surely as opium or cocaine might have done.

Norton, the gentle-natured loving man, was a secret sadist. He was an addict of pain, of mental torture. There has been an epidemic of that in the world of late years—*L'appétit vient en mangeant.*

It fed two lusts—the lust of the sadist and the lust of power. He, Norton, had the keys of life and of death.

Like any other drug slave, he had to have his supply of the drug. He found victim after victim. I have no doubt there have been more cases than the five I actually tracked down. In each of those he played the same part. He knew Etherington, he stayed one summer in the village where Riggs lived and drank with Riggs in the local pub. On a cruise he met the girl Freda Clay and encouraged and played upon her half-formed conviction that if her old aunt died it would be really a good thing—a release for Auntie and a life of financial ease and pleasure for herself. He was a friend of the Litchfields and when talking to him, Margaret Litchfield saw herself in the light of a heroine delivering her sisters from their life sentence of imprisonment. But I do not believe, Hastings, that any of these people would have done what they did—but for Norton's influence.

And now we come to the events at Styles. I had been on Norton's track for some time. He became acquainted with the Franklins and at once I scented danger. You must understand that even Norton has to have a nucleus on which to work. You can only develop a thing of which the seed is already present. In *Othello*, for instance, I have always been of the belief that already present in Othello's mind was the conviction (possibly correct) that Desdemona's love for him was the passionate unbalanced hero worship of a young girl for a famous warrior and not the balanced love of a *woman* for Othello the *man*. He may have realized that Cassio was her true mate and that in time she would come to realize the fact.

The Franklins presented a most agreeable prospect to our Norton. All kinds of possibilities! You have doubtless realized by now, Hastings (what anyone of sense could have seen perfectly plainly all along), that Franklin was in love with Judith and she with him. His brusqueness, his habit of never looking at her, of forsaking any attempt at courtesy, ought to have told you that the man was head over ears in love with her. But Franklin is a man of great strength of character and also of great rectitude. His speech is brutally unsentimental, but he is a man of very definite standards. In his code a man sticks to the wife he has chosen.

Judith, as I should have thought even you could have seen, was deeply and unhappily in love with him. She thought you had grasped the fact that day you found her in the rose garden. Hence her furious outburst. Characters like hers cannot stand any expression of pity or sympathy. It was like touching a raw wound.

Then she discovered that you thought it was Allerton she cared for. She let you think so, thereby shielding herself from clumsy sympathy and from a further probing of the wound. She flirted with Allerton as a kind of desperate solace. She knew exactly the type of man he was. He amused her and distracted her, but she never had the least feeling for him.

Norton, of course, knew exactly how the wind lay. He saw possibilities in the Franklin trio. I may say that he started first on Franklin, but drew a complete blank. Franklin is the one type of man who is quite immune from Norton's kind of insidious suggestion. Franklin has a clear-cut, black and white mind, with an exact knowledge of his own feeling—and a complete disregard for outside pressure. Moreover, the great passion of his life is his work. His absorption in it makes him far less vulnerable.

With Judith, Norton was far more successful. He played very cleverly on the theme of useless lives. It was an article of faith with Judith—and the fact that her secret desires were in accordance with it was a fact that she ignored stridently while Norton knew it to be an ally. He was very clever about it—taking himself the opposite point of view, gently ridiculing the idea that she would ever have the nerve to do such a decisive action. "It is the kind of thing that all young people say—but never do!" Such an old cheap jibe—and how often it works, Hastings! So vulnerable they are, these children! So ready, though they do not recognize it that way, to take a dare!

And with the useless Barbara out of the way, then the road is clear for Franklin and Judith. That was never said—that was never allowed to come into the open. It was stressed that the *personal* angle had nothing to do with it—nothing at all. For if Judith once recognized that it had, she would have reacted violently. But with a murder addict so far advanced as Norton, one iron in the fire is not enough. He sees opportunities for pleasure everywhere. He found one in the Luttrells.

Cast your mind back, Hastings. Remember the very first evening you played bridge. Norton's remarks to you afterwards, uttered so loud that you were afraid Colonel Luttrell would hear. Of course! Norton meant him to hear! He never lost an opportunity of underlining it—rubbing it in. And finally his efforts culminated in success. It happened under your nose, Hastings, and you never saw how it was done. The foundations were already laid—the increasing sense of a burden borne, of shame at the figure he cut in front of other men, in a deep growing resentment against his wife.

Remember exactly what happened. Norton says he is thirsty. (Did he know Mrs. Luttrell is in the house and will come upon the scene?) The Colonel reacts immediately as the open-handed host which he is by nature. He offers drinks. He goes to get them. You are all sitting outside the window. His wife arrives—there is the inevitable scene—which he knows is being overheard. He comes out. It might have been glossed over by a good pretence—Boyd Carrington could have done it well. (He has a certain amount of worldly wisdom and a tactful manner—though otherwise he is one of the most pompous and boring individuals that I have ever come across! Just the sort of man you would admire!) You yourself could have acquitted yourself not too badly. But Norton rushes into speech, heavily, fatuously, underlining tact until it screams to heaven and makes things much worse. He babbles of bridge (more recalled humiliations), talks aimlessly of shooting accidents. And prompt on his cue, just as Norton intended, that old woolly-headed ass Boyd Carrington comes out with his story of an Irish batman who shot his brother—a story, Hastings, that *Norton told to Boyd Carrington,* knowing quite well that the old fool would bring it out as his own whenever suitably prompted. You see, the supreme suggestion will not come from Norton. *Mon Dieu, non!*

It is all set, then. The cumulative effect. The breaking point. Affronted in his instincts as a host—shamed before his fellow men, writhing under the knowledge that they are quite convinced he has not got the guts to do anything but submit meekly to bullying—and then the key words of escape. The rook rifle, accidents—man who shot his brother—and suddenly, bobbing up, his wife's head . . . "Quite safe—an accident . . . *I'll* show them . . . I'll show *her* . . . damn her! I wish she was dead . . . She *shall* be dead!"

He did not kill her, Hastings. Myself, I think that, even as he fired, instinctively he missed *because he wanted to miss*. And afterwards—afterwards the evil spell was broken. She was his wife, the woman he loved in spite of everything.

One of Norton's crimes that did not quite come off.

Ah, but his next attempt! Do you realize, Hastings, that it was *you* who came next? Throw your mind back—recall everything. *You*, my honest, kindly Hastings! He found every weak spot in your mind—yes, and every decent and conscientious one, too.

Allerton is the type of man you instinctively dislike and fear. He is the type of man that you think ought to be abolished. And everything you heard about him and thought about him was true. Norton tells you a certain story about him—an entirely true story as far as the facts go. (Though actually the girl concerned was a neurotic type and came of poor stock.)

It appeals to your conventional and somewhat old-fashioned instincts. This man is the villain, the seducer, the man who ruins girls and drives them to suicide! Norton induces Boyd Carrington to tackle you also. You are impelled to "speak to Judith." Judith, as could be predicted, immediately responds by saying she will do as she chooses with her life. That makes you believe the worst.

See now the different stops on which Norton plays. Your love for your child. The intense old-fashioned sense of responsibility that a man like you feels for his children. The slight self-importance of your nature. "*I* must do something. It all depends on *me*." Your feeling of helplessness owing to the lack of your wife's wise judgment. Your loyalty—I must not fail her. And, on the baser side, your vanity—through association with me you have learned all the tricks of the trade! And lastly, that inner feeling which most men have about their daughters—a father's unreasoning jealousy and dislike for the man who takes his daughter away from him. Norton played, Hastings, like a virtuoso on all these themes. And you responded.

You accept things too easily at their face value. You always have done. You accepted quite easily the fact that it was Judith to whom Allerton was talking in the summerhouse. Yet you did not see her, you did not even hear her speak. And incredibly, even the next morning, you still thought it was Judith. You rejoiced because she had "changed her mind."

But if you had taken the trouble to examine the facts, you would have discovered at once that there had never been any question of Judith going up to London that day! And you failed to make another most obvious inference. There was someone who was going off for the day—and who was furious at not being able to do so. Nurse Craven. Allerton is not a man who confines himself to the pursuit of one woman! His affair with Nurse Craven had progressed much further than the mere flirtation he was having with Judith.

No, stage management again by Norton.

You saw Allerton and Judith kiss. Then Norton shoves you back round the corner. He doubtless knows quite well that Allerton is going to meet Nurse Craven in the summerhouse. After a little argument he lets you go but still accompanies you. The sentence you overhear Allerton speaking is magnificent for his purpose and he swiftly drags you away before you have a chance to discover that the woman is not Judith!

Yes, the virtuoso! And your reaction is immediate, complete on all those themes! You responded. You made up your mind to do murder.

But fortunately, Hastings, you had a friend whose brain still functioned. And not only his brain!

I said at the beginning of this that if you have not arrived at the truth, it is because you have too trusting a nature. You believe what is said to you. You believed what *I* said to you . . .

Yet it was all very easy for you to discover the truth. I had sent Georges away—why? I had replaced him with a less experienced and clearly much less intelligent man—why? I was not being attended by a doctor—I, who have always been careful about my health—I would not hear of seeing one—why?

Do you see now why you were necessary to me at Styles? I had to have someone who accepted what I said without question. You accepted my statement that I came back from Egypt much worse than when I went. I did not. I came back very much better! You could have found out the fact if you had taken the trouble. But no, you believed. I sent away Georges because I could not have succeeded in making him think that I had suddenly lost all power in my limbs. Georges is extremely intelligent about what he sees. He would have known that I was shamming.

Do you understand, Hastings? All the time that I was pretending to be helpless and deceiving Curtiss, I was not helpless at all. I could walk—with a limp.

I heard you come up that evening. I heard you hesitate and then go into Allerton's room. And at once I was on the alert. I was already much exercised about your state of mind.

I did not delay. I was alone. Curtiss had gone down to supper. I slipped out of my room and across the passage. I heard you in Allerton's bathroom. And promptly, my friend, in the manner you so much deplore, I dropped to my knees and looked through the keyhole of the bathroom door. One could see through it, fortunately, as there is a bolt and not a key on the inside.

I perceived your manipulations with the sleeping tablets. I realized what your idea was.

And so, my friend, I acted. I went back to my room. I made my preparations. When Curtiss came up, I sent him to fetch you. You came, yawning and explaining that you had a headache. I made at once the big fuss—urged remedies on you. For the sake of peace you consented to drink a cup of chocolate. You gulped it down quickly so as to get away quicker. But I, too, my friend, have some sleeping tablets.

And so, you slept—slept until morning, when you awoke your own sane self and were horrified at what you had so nearly done.

You were safe now—one does not attempt these things twice—not when one has relapsed into sanity.

But it decided *me,* Hastings! For whatever I might not know about other people did not apply to you. *You* are not a murderer, Hastings! But you might have been hanged for one—for a murder committed by another man who in the eyes of the law would be guiltless.

You, my good, my honest, my oh-so-honourable Hastings—so kindly, so conscientious—so innocent!

Yes, I must act. I knew that my time was short—and for that I was glad. For the worst part of murder, Hastings, is its effect on the murderer. I, Hercule Poirot, might come to believe myself divinely appointed to deal out death to all and sundry . . . But mercifully, there would not be time for that to happen. The end would come soon. And I was afraid that Norton might succeed with someone who was unutterably dear to us both. I am talking of your daughter . . .

And now we come to the death of Barbara Franklin. Whatever your ideas may be on the subject, Hastings, I do not think you have once suspected the truth.

For you see, Hastings, *you* killed Barbara Franklin.

Mais oui, you did!

There was, you see, yet another angle to the triangle. One that I did not fully take into account. As it happened, Norton's tactics there were unseen and unheard by either of us. But I have no doubt that he employed them . . .

Did it ever enter your mind to wonder, Hastings, why Mrs. Franklin was willing to come to Styles? It is not, when you think of it, at all her line of country. She likes comfort, good food and above all social contacts. Styles is not gay—it is not well run—it is in the dead country. And yet it was Mrs. Franklin who insisted on spending the summer there.

Yes, there was a third angle—Boyd Carrington. Mrs. Franklin was a disappointed woman. That was at the root of her neurotic illness. She was ambitious both socially and financially. She married Franklin because she expected him to have a brilliant career.

He was brilliant, but not in her way. His brilliance would never bring him newspaper notoriety or a Harley Street reputation. He would be known to half a dozen men of his own profession and would publish articles in learned journals. The outside world would not hear of him—and he would certainly not make money.

And here is Boyd Carrington—home from the East—just come into a baronetcy and money, and Boyd Carrington has always felt tenderly sentimental towards the pretty seventeen-year-old girl he nearly asked to marry him. He is going to Styles, he suggests the Franklins come too—and Barbara comes.

How maddening it is for her! Obviously she has lost none of her old charm for this rich, attractive man—but he is old-fashioned—not the type of man to suggest divorce. And John Franklin, too, has no use for divorce. If John Franklin were to die —then she could be Lady Boyd Carrington—and oh, what a wonderful life that would be!

Norton, I think, found her only too ready a tool.

It was all too obvious, Hastings, when you come to think of it. Those first few tentative attempts at establishing how fond she was of her husband. She overdid it a little—murmuring about "ending it all" because she was a drag on him.

And then an entirely new line. Her fears that Franklin might experiment upon himself.

It ought to have been so obvious to us, Hastings! She was preparing us for John Franklin to die of physostigmine poisoning. No question, you see, of anyone trying to poison him—oh no—just pure scientific research. He takes the harmless alkaloid, and it turns out to be harmful after all.

The only thing was it was a little too swift. You told me that she was not pleased to find Boyd Carrington having his fortune told by Nurse Craven. Nurse Craven was an attractive young woman with a keen eye for men. She had had a try at Dr. Franklin and had not met with success. (Hence her dislike for

Judith.) She is carrying on with Allerton—but she knows quite well he is not serious. Inevitable that she should cast her eye on the rich and still attractive Sir William. And Sir William was, perhaps, only too ready to be attracted. He had already noticed Nurse Craven as a healthy, good-looking girl.

Barbara Franklin has a fright and decides to act quickly. The sooner she is a pathetic, charming and not inconsolable widow, the better.

And so, after a morning of nerves, she sets the scene.

Do you know, *mon ami*, I have some respect for the Calabar bean. This time, you see, it worked. It spared the innocent and slew the guilty.

Mrs. Franklin asks you all up to her room. She makes coffee with much fuss and display. As you tell me, her own coffee is beside her, her husband's on the other side of the bookcase table.

And then there are the shooting stars and everyone goes out and only you, my friend, are left—you and your crossword puzzle and your memories—and to hide emotion, you swing round the bookcase to find a quotation in Shakespeare.

And so they come back and Mrs. Franklin drinks the coffee full of the Calabar bean alkaloids that were meant for dear scientific John, and John Franklin drinks the nice plain cup of coffee that was meant for clever Mrs. Franklin.

But you will see, Hastings, if you think a minute, that although I realized what had happened, I saw that there was only one thing to be done. I could not *prove* what had happened. And if Mrs. Franklin's death was thought to be anything but suicide, suspicion would inevitably fall on either Franklin or Judith. On two people who were utterly and completely innocent. So I did what I had a perfect right to do—laid stress on, and put conviction into, my repetition of Mrs. Franklin's extremely unconvincing remarks on the subject of putting an end to herself.

I could do it—and I was probably the only person who could. For you see my statement carried weight. I am a man experienced in the matter of committing murder. If *I* am convinced it is suicide, well then, it will be accepted as suicide.

It puzzled you, I could see, and you were not pleased. But mercifully you did not suspect the true danger.

But will you think of it after I am gone? Will it come into your mind, lying there like some dark serpent that now and then raises its head and says: "Suppose Judith . . . ?"

It may do. And therefore I am writing this. You must know the truth.

There was one person whom the verdict of suicide did not satisfy. Norton. He was balked, you see, of his pound of flesh. As I say, he is a sadist. He wants the whole gamut of emotion, suspicion, fear, the coils of the law. He was deprived of all that. The murder he had arranged had gone awry.

But presently he saw what one may call a way of recouping himself. He began to throw out hints. Earlier on he had pretended to see something through his glasses. Actually he intended to convey the exact impression that he did convey—namely, that he saw Allerton and Judith in some compromising attitude. But not having said anything definite, he could use that incident in a different way.

Supposing, for instance, that he says he saw *Franklin* and Judith. That will open up an interesting new angle of the suicide case! It may, perhaps, throw doubts on whether it was suicide . . .

So, *mon ami,* I decided that what had to be done must be done at once. I arranged that you should bring him to my room that night . . .

I will tell you now exactly what happened. Norton, no doubt, would have been delighted to tell me his arranged story. I gave him no time. I told him, clearly and definitely, all that I knew about him.

He did not deny it. No, *mon ami,* he sat back in his chair and smirked. *Mais oui,* there is no other word for it—he smirked. He asked me what I thought I was going to do about this amusing idea of mine. I told him that I proposed to execute him.

"Ah," he said, "I see. The dagger or the cup of poison?"

We were about to have chocolate together at the time. He has a sweet tooth, M. Norton.

"The simplest," I said, "would be the cup of poison."

And I handed him the cup of chocolate I had just poured out.

"In that case," he said, "would you mind my drinking from your cup instead of from mine?"

I said: "Not at all." In effect, it was quite immaterial. As I have said, I, too, take the sleeping tablets. The only thing is that since I have been taking them every night for a considerable period, I have acquired a certain tolerance, and a dose that would send M. Norton to sleep would have very little effect upon me. The dose was in the chocolate itself. We both had the same. His portion took effect in due course, mine had little effect upon me, especially when counteracted with a dose of my strychnine tonic.

And so to the last chapter. When Norton was asleep, I got him into my wheelchair—fairly easy, it has many types of mechanism—and wheeled him back in it to its usual place in the window embrasure behind the curtains.

Curtiss then "put me to bed." When everything was quiet, I wheeled Norton to his room. It remained, then, to avail myself of the eyes and ears of my excellent friend Hastings.

You may not have realized it, but I wear a wig, Hastings. You will realize even less that I wear a false moustache. (Even Georges does not know that!) I pretended to burn it by accident soon after Curtiss came, and at once had my hairdresser make me a replica.

I put on Norton's dressing gown, ruffled up my grey hair on end, and came down the passage and rapped on your door. Presently you came and looked with sleepy eyes into the passage. You saw Norton leave the bathroom and limp across the passage into his own room. You heard him turn the key in the lock on the inside.

I then replaced the dressing gown on Norton, laid him on his bed, and shot him with a small pistol that I acquired abroad and which I have kept carefully locked up except for two occasions when (nobody being about) I have put it ostentatiously on Norton's dressing table, he himself being well away somewhere those mornings.

Then I left the room after putting the key in Norton's pocket. I myself locked the door from the outside with the duplicate key which I have possessed for some time. I wheeled the chair back to my room.

Since then I have been writing this explanation.

I am very tired—and the exertions I have been through have strained me a good deal. It will not, I think, be long before . . .

There are one or two things I would like to stress.

Norton's were the perfect crimes.

Mine was not. It was not intended to be.

The easiest way and the best way for me to have killed him was to have done so quite openly—to have had, shall we say, an accident with my little pistol. I should have professed dismay, regret—a most unfortunate accident. They would have said: "Old ga-ga didn't realize it was loaded—*ce pauvre vieux.*"

I did not choose to do that.

I will tell you why.

It is because, Hastings, I chose to be "sporting."

Mais oui, sporting! I am doing all the things that so often you have reproached me with not doing. I am playing fair with you. I am giving you a run for your money. I am playing the game. You have every chance to discover the truth.

In case you disbelieve me, let me enumerate all the clues.

The keys.

You know, for I have told you so, that Norton arrived here *after* I did. You know, for you have been told, that I changed my room after I got here. You know, for again it has been told to you, that since I have been at Styles, the key of my room disappeared and I had another made.

Therefore when you ask yourself: Who could have killed Norton? Who could have shot him and still have left the room (apparently) locked on the inside since the key is in Norton's pocket? The answer is: "Hercule Poirot, who since he has been here has possessed duplicate keys of one of the rooms."

The man you saw in the passage.

I myself asked you if you were sure the man you saw in the

passage was Norton. You were startled. You asked me if I intended to suggest it was *not* Norton. I replied, truthfully, that I did not at all intend to suggest it was not Norton. (Naturally, since I had taken a good deal of trouble to suggest it *was* Norton.) I then brought up the question of *height*. All the men, I said, were much taller than Norton. But there *was* a man who was shorter than Norton—Hercule Poirot. And it is comparatively easy with raised heels or elevators in the shoes to add to one's height.

You were under the impression that I was a helpless invalid. But why? Only because I *said so*. And I had sent away Georges. That was my last indication to you, "Go and talk to Georges."

Othello and Clutie John show you that X was Norton.

Then who could have killed Norton?

Only Hercule Poirot.

And once you suspected that, everything would have fallen into place—the things I had said and done, my inexplicable reticence. Evidence from the doctors in Egypt, from my own doctor in London, that I was not incapable of walking about. The evidence of Georges as to my wearing a wig. The fact which I was unable to disguise, and which you ought to have noticed, that I limp much more than Norton does.

And last of all, the pistol shot. My one weakness. I should, I am aware, have shot him through the temple. I could not bring myself to produce an effect so lopsided, so haphazard. No, I shot him symmetrically, in the exact centre of the forehead . . .

Oh, Hastings, Hastings! *That* should have told you the truth.

But perhaps, after all, you *have* suspected the truth? Perhaps when you read this, you already *know*.

But somehow I do not think so . . .

No, you are too trusting . . .

You have too beautiful a nature . . .

What shall I say more to you? Both Franklin and Judith, I think you will find, knew the truth although they will not have told it to you. They will be happy together, those two. They will be poor, and innumerable tropical insects will bite them and strange fevers will attack them—but we all have our own ideas of the perfect life, have we not?

And you, my poor lonely Hastings? Ah, my heart bleeds for you, dear friend. Will you, for the last time, take the advice of your old Poirot?

After you have read this, take a train or a car or a series of buses and go to find Elizabeth Cole, who is also Elizabeth Litchfield. Let her read this, or tell her what is in it. Tell her that you, too, might have done what her sister Margaret did—only for Margaret Litchfield there was no watchful Poirot at hand. Take the nightmare away from her, show her that her father was killed, not by his daughter, but by that kind sympathetic family friend, that "honest Iago," Stephen Norton.

For it is not right, my friend, that a woman like that, still young, still attractive, should refuse life because she believes herself to be tainted. No, it is not right. Tell her so, you, my friend, who are yourself still not unattractive to women . . .

Eh bien, I have no more now to say. I do not know, Hastings, if what I have done is justified or not justified. No—I do not know. I do not believe that a man should take the law into his own hands . . .

But on the other hand, I *am* the law! As a young man in the Belgian police force I shot down a desperate criminal who sat on a roof and fired at people below. In a state of emergency martial law is proclaimed.

By taking Norton's life, I have saved other lives—innocent lives. But still I do not know . . . It is perhaps right that I should not know. I have always been so sure—too sure . . .

But now I am very humble and I say like a little child: "I do not know . . ."

Good-bye, *cher ami.* I have moved the amyl nitrite ampoules away from beside my bed. I prefer to leave myself in the hands of the *bon Dieu.* May his punishment, or his mercy, be swift!

We shall not hunt together again, my friend. Our first hunt was here—and our last . . .

They were good days.

Yes, they have been good days. . . .

End of Hercule Poirot's manuscript

(Final note by Captain Arthur Hastings:

I have finished reading . . . I can't believe it all yet . . . But he is right. I should have known. I should have known when I saw the bullet hole so symmetrically in the middle of the forehead.

Queer—it's just come to me—the thought in the back of my mind that morning.

The mark on Norton's forehead—it was like the brand of Cain. . . .)

The Mysterious
Affair at Styles

CONTENTS

1

I Go to Styles

The intense interest aroused in the public by what was known at the time as "The Styles Case" has now somewhat subsided. Nevertheless, in view of the world-wide notoriety which attended it, I have been asked, both by my friend Poirot and the family themselves, to write an account of the whole story. This, we trust, will effectually silence the sensational rumours which still persist.

I will therefore briefly set down the circumstances which led to my being connected with the affair.

I had been invalided home from the Front; and, after spending some months in a rather depressing Convalescent Home, was given a month's sick leave. Having no near relations or friends, I was trying to make up my mind what to do, when I ran across John Cavendish. I had seen very little of him for some years. Indeed, I had never known him particularly well. He was a good fifteen years my senior, for one thing, though he hardly looked his forty-five years. As a boy, though, I had often stayed at Styles, his mother's place in Essex.

We had a good yarn about old times, and it ended in his inviting me down to Styles to spend my leave there.

"The mater will be delighted to see you again—after all those years," he added.

"Your mother keeps well?" I asked.

"Oh, yes. I suppose you know that she has married again?"

I am afraid I showed my surprise rather plainly. Mrs. Cavendish, who had married John's father when he was a widower with two sons, had been a handsome woman of middle-age as I remembered her. She certainly could not be a day less than seventy now. I recalled her as an energetic, autocratic personality, somewhat inclined to charitable and social notoriety, with a fondness for opening bazaars and playing the Lady Bountiful. She was a most generous woman, and possessed a considerable fortune of her own.

Their country-place, Styles Court, had been purchased by Mr. Cavendish early in their married life. He had been completely under his wife's ascendancy, so much so that, on dying, he left the place to her for her lifetime, as well as the larger part of his income; an arrangement that was distinctly unfair to his two sons. Their stepmother, however, had always been most generous to them; indeed, they were so young at the time of their father's remarriage that they always thought of her as their own mother.

Lawrence, the younger, had been a delicate youth. He had qualified as a doctor but early relinquished the profession of medicine, and lived at home while pursuing literary ambitions; though his verses never had any marked success.

John practised for some time as a barrister, but had finally settled down to the more congenial life of a country squire. He had married two years ago, and had taken his wife to live at Styles, though I entertained a shrewd suspicion that he would have preferred his mother to increase his allowance, which would have enabled him to have a home of his own. Mrs. Cavendish, however, was a lady who liked to make her own plans, and expected other people to fall in with them, and in this case she certainly had the whip hand, namely: the purse strings.

John noticed my surprise at the news of his mother's remarriage and smiled rather ruefully.

"Rotten little bounder too!" he said savagely. "I can tell you, Hastings, it's making life jolly difficult for us. As for Evie—you remember Evie?"

"No."

"Oh, I suppose she was after your time. She's the mater's factotum, companion, Jack of all trades! A great sport—old Evie! Not precisely young and beautiful, but as game as they make them."

"You were going to say——?"

"Oh, this fellow! He turned up from nowhere, on the pretext of being a second cousin or something of Evie's, though she didn't seem particularly keen to acknowledge the relationship. The fellow is an absolute outsider, anyone can see that. He's got a great black beard, and wears patent leather boots in all weathers! But the mater cottoned to him at once, took him on as secretary—you know how she's always running a hundred societies?"

I nodded.

"Well, of course the war has turned the hundreds into thousands. No doubt the fellow was very useful to her. But you could have knocked us all down with a feather when, three months ago, she suddenly announced that she and Alfred were engaged! The fellow must be at least twenty years younger than she is! It's simply bare-faced fortune hunting; but there you are—she is her own mistress, and she's married him."

"It must be a difficult situation for you all."

"Difficult! It's damnable!"

Thus it came about that, three days later, I descended from the train at Styles St. Mary, an absurd little station, with no apparent reason for existence, perched up in the midst of green fields and country lanes. John Cavendish was waiting on the platform, and piloted me out to the car.

"Got a drop or two of petrol still, you see," he remarked. "Mainly owing to the mater's activities."

The village of Styles St. Mary was situated about two miles from the little station, and Styles Court lay a mile the other side of it. It was a still, warm day in early July. As one looked out over the flat Essex country, lying so green and peaceful under the afternoon sun, it seemed almost impossible to believe that, not so very far away, a great war was running its appointed course. I felt I had suddenly strayed into another world. As we turned in at the lodge gates, John said:

"I'm afraid you'll find it very quiet down here, Hastings."

"My dear fellow, that's just what I want."

"Oh, it's pleasant enough if you want to lead the idle life. I drill with the volunteers twice a week, and lend a hand at the farms. My wife works regularly 'on the land'. She is up at five every morning to milk, and keeps at it steadily until lunch-time. It's a jolly good life taking it all round—if it weren't for that fellow Alfred Inglethorp!" He checked the car suddenly, and glanced at his watch. "I wonder if we've time to pick up Cynthia. No, she'll have started from the hospital by now."

"Cynthia! That's not your wife?"

"No, Cynthia is a protégée of my mother's, the daughter of an old schoolfellow of hers, who married a rascally solicitor. He came a cropper, and the girl was left an orphan and penniless. My mother came to the rescue, and Cynthia has been with us nearly two years now. She works in the Red Cross Hospital at Tadminster, seven miles away."

As he spoke the last words, we drew up in front of the fine old house. A lady in a stout tweed skirt, who was bending over a flower bed, straightened herself at our approach.

"Hullo, Evie, here's our wounded hero! Mr. Hastings—Miss Howard."

Miss Howard shook hands with a hearty, almost painful, grip. I had an impression of very blue eyes in a sunburnt face. She was a pleasant-looking woman of about forty, with a deep voice, almost manly in its stentorian tones, and had a large sensible square body, with feet to match—these last encased in good thick boots. Her conversation, I soon found, was couched in the telegraphic style.

"Weeds grow like house afire. Can't keep even with 'em. Shall press you in. Better be careful."

"I'm sure I shall be only too delighted to make myself useful," I responded.

"Don't say it. Never does. Wish you hadn't later."

"You're a cynic, Evie," said John, laughing. "Where's tea to-day—inside or out?"

"Out. Too fine a day to be cooped up in the house."

"Come on then, you've done enough gardening for to-day.

'The labourer is worthy of his hire', you know. Come and be refreshed."

"Well," said Miss Howard, drawing off her gardening gloves, "I'm inclined to agree with you."

She led the way round the house to where tea was spread under the shade of a large sycamore.

A figure rose from one of the basket chairs, and came a few steps to meet us.

"My wife, Hastings," said John.

I shall never forget my first sight of Mary Cavendish. Her tall, slender form, outlined against the bright light; the vivid sense of slumbering fire that seemed to find expression only in those wonderful tawny eyes of hers, remarkable eyes, different from any other woman's that I have ever known; the intense power of stillness she possessed, which nevertheless conveyed the impression of a wild untamed spirit in an exquisitely civilised body—all these things are burnt into my memory. I shall never forget them.

She greeted me with a few words of pleasant welcome in a low clear voice, and I sank into a basket chair feeling distinctly glad that I had accepted John's invitation. Mrs. Cavendish gave me some tea, and her few quiet remarks heightened my first impression of her as a thoroughly fascinating woman. An appreciative listener is always stimulating, and I described, in a humorous manner, certain incidents of my Convalescent Home, in a way which, I flatter myself, greatly amused my hostess. John, of course, good fellow though he is, could hardly be called a brilliant conversationalist.

At that moment a well remembered voice floated through the open French window near at hand:

"Then you'll write to the Princess after tea, Alfred? I'll write to Lady Tadminster for the second day, myself. Or shall we wait until we hear from the Princess? In case of a refusal, Lady Tadminster might open it the first day, and Mrs. Crosbie the second. Then there's the Duchess—about the school fête."

There was the murmur of a man's voice, and then Mrs. Inglethorp's rose in reply:

"Yes, certainly. After tea will do quite well. You are so thoughtful, Alfred dear."

The French window swung open a little wider, and a handsome white-haired old lady, with a somewhat masterful cast of features, stepped out of it on to the lawn. A man followed her, a suggestion of deference in his manner.

Mrs. Inglethorp greeted me with effusion.

"Why, if it isn't too delightful to see you again, Mr. Hastings, after all these years. Alfred, darling, Mr. Hastings—my husband."

I looked with some curiosity at "Alfred darling". He certainly struck a rather alien note. I did not wonder at John objecting to his beard. It was one of the longest and blackest I have ever seen. He wore gold rimmed pince-nez, and had a curious impassivity of feature. It struck me that he might look natural on a stage, but was strangely out of place in real life. His voice was rather deep and unctuous. He placed a wooden hand in mine and said:

"This is a pleasure, Mr. Hastings." Then, turning to his wife: "Emily dearest, I think that cushion is a little damp."

She beamed fondly on him, as he substituted another with every demonstration of the tenderest care. Strange infatuation of an otherwise sensible woman!

With the presence of Mr. Inglethorp, a sense of constraint and veiled hostility seemed to settle down upon the company. Miss Howard, in particular, took no pains to conceal her feelings. Mrs. Inglethorp, however, seemed to notice nothing unusual. Her volubility, which I remembered of old, had lost nothing in the intervening years, and she poured out a steady flood of conversation, mainly on the subject of the forthcoming bazaar which she was organizing and which was to take place shortly. Occasionally she referred to her husband over a question of days or dates. His watchful and attentive manner never varied. From the very first I took a firm and rooted dislike to him, and I flatter myself that my first judgments are usually fairly shrewd.

Presently Mrs. Inglethorp turned to give some instructions about letters to Evelyn Howard, and her husband addressed me in his painstaking voice:

"Is soldiering your regular profession, Mr. Hastings?"

"No, before the war I was in Lloyd's."

"And you will return there after it is over?"

"Perhaps. Either that or a fresh start altogether."

Mary Cavendish leant forward.

"What would you really choose as a profession, if you could just consult your inclination?"

"Well, that depends."

"No secret hobby?" she asked. "Tell me—you're drawn to something? Every one is—usually something absurd."

"You'll laugh at me."

She smiled.

"Perhaps."

"Well, I've always had a secret hankering to be a detective!"

"The real thing—Scotland Yard? Or Sherlock Holmes?"

"Oh, Sherlock Holmes by all means. But really, seriously, I am awfully drawn to it. I came across a man in Belgium once, a very famous detective, and he quite inflamed me. He was a marvellous little fellow. He used to say that all good detective work was a mere matter of method. My system is based on his—though of course I have progressed rather further. He was a funny little man, a great dandy, but wonderfully clever."

"Like a good detective story myself," remarked Miss Howard. "Lots of nonsense written, though. Criminal discovered in last chapter. Every one dumfounded. Real crime—you'd know at once."

"There have been a great number of undiscovered crimes," I argued.

"Don't mean the police, but the people that are right in it. The family. You couldn't really hoodwink them. They'd know."

"Then," I said, much amused, "you think that if you were mixed up in a crime, say a murder, you'd be able to spot the murderer right off?"

"Of course I should. Mightn't be able to prove it to a pack of lawyers. But I'm certain I'd know. I'd feel it in my finger-tips if he came near me."

"It might be a 'she,'" I suggested.

"Might. But murder's a violent crime. Associate it more with a man."

"Not in a case of poisoning." Mrs. Cavendish's clear voice startled me. "Dr. Bauerstein was saying yesterday that, owing to the general ignorance of the more uncommon poisons among the medical profession, there were probably countless cases of poisoning quite unsuspected."

"Why, Mary, what a gruesome conversation!" cried Mrs. Inglethorp. "It makes me feel as if a goose were walking over my grave. Oh, there's Cynthia!"

A young girl in V. A. D. uniform ran lightly across the lawn.

"Why, Cynthia, you are late to-day. This is Mr. Hastings—Miss Murdoch."

Cynthia Murdoch was a fresh-looking young creature, full of life and vigour. She tossed off her little V. A. D. cap, and I admired the great loose waves of her auburn hair, and the smallness and whiteness of the hand she held out to claim her tea. With dark eyes and eyelashes she would have been a beauty.

She flung herself down on the ground beside John, and as I handed her a plate of sandwiches she smiled up at me.

"Sit down here on the grass, do. It's ever so much nicer."

I dropped down obediently.

"You work at Tadminster, don't you, Miss Murdoch?"

She nodded.

"For my sins."

"Do they bully you, then?" I asked, smiling.

"I should like to see them!" cried Cynthia with dignity.

"I have got a cousin who is nursing," I remarked. "And she is terrified of 'Sisters'."

"I don't wonder. Sisters *are*, you know, Mr. Hastings. They simp-ly *are!* You've no idea! But I'm not a nurse, thank heaven, I work in the dispensary."

"How many people do you poison?" I asked, smiling.

Cynthia smiled too.

"Oh, hundreds!" she said.

"Cynthia," called Mrs. Inglethorp, "do you think you could write a few notes for me?"

"Certainly, Aunt Emily."

She jumped up promptly, and something in her manner reminded me that her position was a dependent one, and that Mrs. Inglethorp, kind as she might be in the main, did not allow her to forget it.

My hostess turned to me.

"John will show you your room. Supper is at half-past seven. We have given up late dinner for some time now. Lady Tadminster, our Member's wife—she was the late Lord Abbotsbury's daughter—does the same. She agrees with me that one must set an example of economy. We are quite a war household; nothing is wasted here—every scrap of waste paper, even, is saved and sent away in sacks."

I expressed my appreciation, and John took me into the house and up the broad staircase, which forked right and left half-way to different wings of the building. My room was in the left wing, and looked out over the park.

John left me, and a few minutes later I saw him from my window walking slowly across the grass arm in arm with Cynthia Murdoch. I heard Mrs. Inglethorp call "Cynthia" impatiently, and the girl started and ran back to the house. At the same moment, a man stepped out from the shadow of a tree and walked slowly in the same direction. He looked about forty, very dark with a melancholy clean-shaven face. Some violent emotion seemed to be mastering him. He looked up at my window as he passed, and I recognized him, though he had changed much in the fifteen years that had elapsed since we last met. It was John's younger brother, Lawrence Cavendish. I wondered what it was that had brought that singular expression to his face.

Then I dismissed him from my mind, and returned to the contemplation of my own affairs.

The evening passed pleasantly enough; and I dreamed that night of that enigmatical woman, Mary Cavendish.

The next morning dawned bright and sunny, and I was full of the anticipation of a delightful visit.

I did not see Mrs. Cavendish until lunch-time, when she volunteered to take me for a walk, and we spent a charming afternoon roaming in the woods, returning to the house about five.

As we entered the large hall, John beckoned us both into the smoking-room. I saw at once by his face that something disturbing had occurred. We followed him in, and he shut the door after us.

"Look here, Mary, there's the deuce of a mess. Evie's had a row with Alfred Inglethorp, and she's off."

"Evie? Off?"

John nodded gloomily.

"Yes; you see she went to the mater, and—Oh, here's Evie herself."

Miss Howard entered. Her lips were set grimly together, and she carried a small suit-case. She looked excited and determined, and slightly on the defensive.

"At any rate," she burst out, "I've spoken my mind!"

"My dear Evelyn," cried Mrs. Cavendish, "this can't be true!"

Miss Howard nodded grimly.

"True enough! Afraid I said some things to Emily she won't forget or forgive in a hurry. Don't mind if they've only sunk in a bit. Probably water off a duck's back, though. I said right out: 'You're an old woman, Emily, and there's no fool like an old fool. The man's twenty years younger than you, and don't you fool yourself as to what he married you for. Money! Well, don't let him have too much of it. Farmer Raikes has got a very pretty young wife. Just ask your Alfred how much time he spends over there.' She was very angry. Natural! I went on: 'I'm going to warn you, whether you like it or not. That man would as soon murder you in your bed as look at you. He's a bad lot. You can say what you like to me, but remember what I've told you. He's a bad lot!' "

"What did she say?"

Miss Howard made an extremely expressive grimace.

" 'Darling Alfred'—'dearest Alfred'—'wicked calumnies'—'wicked lies'—'wicked woman'—to accuse her 'dear husband'! The sooner I left her house the better. So I'm off."

"But not now?"

"This minute!"

For a moment we sat and stared at her. Finally John Cavendish, finding his persuasions of no avail, went off to look up the trains. His wife followed him, murmuring something about persuading Mrs. Inglethorp to think better of it.

As she left the room, Miss Howard's face changed. She leant towards me eagerly.

"Mr. Hastings, you're honest. I can trust you?"

I was a little startled. She laid her hand on my arm, and sank her voice to a whisper.

"Look after her, Mr. Hastings. My poor Emily. They're a lot of sharks—all of them. Oh, I know what I'm talking about. There isn't one of them that's not hard up and trying to get money out of her. I've protected her as much as I could. Now I'm out of the way, they'll impose upon her."

"Of course, Miss Howard," I said, "I'll do everything I can, but I'm sure you're excited and overwrought."

She interrupted me by slowly shaking her forefinger.

"Young man, trust me. I've lived in the world rather longer than you have. All I ask you is to keep your eyes open. You'll see what I mean."

The throb of the motor came through the open window, and Miss Howard rose and moved to the door. John's voice sounded outside. With her hand on the handle, she turned her head over her shoulder, and beckoned to me.

"Above all, Mr. Hastings, watch that devil—her husband!"

There was no time for more. Miss Howard was swallowed up in an eager chorus of protests and good-byes. The Inglethorps did not appear.

As the motor drove away, Mrs. Cavendish suddenly detached herself from the group, and moved across the drive to the lawn to meet a tall bearded man who had been evidently making for the house. The colour rose in her cheeks as she held out her hand to him.

"Who is that?" I asked sharply, for instinctively I distrusted the man.

"That's Dr. Bauerstein," said John shortly.

"And who is Dr. Bauerstein?"

"He's staying in the village doing a rest cure, after a bad nervous breakdown. He's a London specialist; a very clever man—one of the greatest living experts on poisons, I believe."

"And he's a great friend of Mary's," put in Cynthia, the irrepressible.

John Cavendish frowned and changed the subject.

"Come for a stroll, Hastings. This has been a most rotten business. She always had a rough tongue, but there is no stauncher friend in England than Evelyn Howard."

He took the path through the plantation, and we walked down to the village through the woods which bordered one side of the estate.

As we passed through one of the gates on our way home again, a pretty young woman of gipsy type coming in the opposite direction bowed and smiled.

"That's a pretty girl," I remarked appreciatively.

John's face hardened.

"That is Mrs. Raikes."

"The one that Miss Howard——"

"Exactly," said John, with rather unnecessary abruptness.

I thought of the white-haired old lady in the big house, and that vivid wicked little face that had just smiled into ours, and a vague chill of foreboding crept over me. I brushed it aside.

"Styles is really a glorious old place," I said to John.

He nodded rather gloomily.

"Yes, it's a fine property. It'll be mine some day—should be mine now by rights, if my father had only made a decent will. And then I shouldn't be so damned hard up as I am now."

"Hard up, are you?"

"My dear Hastings, I don't mind telling you that I'm at my wit's end for money."

"Couldn't your brother help you?"

"Lawrence? He's gone through every penny he ever had, publishing rotten verses in fancy bindings. No, we're an impecunious lot. My mother's always been awfully good to us, I must say. That is, up to now. Since her marriage, of course——" he broke off, frowning.

For the first time I felt that, with Evelyn Howard, something indefinable had gone from the atmosphere. Her presence had spelt security. Now that security was removed—and the air seemed rife with suspicion. The sinister face of Dr. Bauerstein recurred to me unpleasantly. A vague suspicion of every one and everything filled my mind. Just for a moment I had a premonition of approaching evil.

2

The 16th and 17th of July

I had arrived at Styles on the 5th of July. I come now to the
events of the 16th and 17th of that month. For the convenience
of the reader I will recapitulate the incidents of those days in as
exact a manner as possible. They were elicited subsequently at
the trial by a process of long and tedious cross-examinations.

I received a letter from Evelyn Howard a couple of days after
her departure, telling me she was working as a nurse at the big
hospital in Middlingham, a manufacturing town some fifteen
miles away, and begging me to let her know if Mrs. Inglethorp
should show any wish to be reconciled.

The only fly in the ointment of my peaceful days was Mrs.
Cavendish's extraordinary, and, for my part, unaccountable pref-
erence for the society of Dr. Bauerstein. What she saw in the
man I cannot imagine, but she was always asking him up to the
house, and often went off for long expeditions with him. I must
confess that I was quite unable to see his attraction.

The 16th of July fell on a Monday. It was a day of turmoil.
The famous bazaar had taken place on Saturday, and an entertainment, in connection with the same charity, at which Mrs.
Inglethorp was to recite a War poem, was to be held that night.
We were all busy during the morning arranging and decorating
the Hall in the village where it was to take place. We had a late
luncheon and spent the afternoon resting in the garden. I noticed

that John's manner was somewhat unusual. He seemed very excited and restless.

After tea, Mrs. Inglethorp went to lie down to rest before her efforts in the evening and I challenged Mary Cavendish to a single at tennis.

About a quarter to seven, Mrs. Inglethorp called to us that we should be late as supper was early that night. We had rather a scramble to get ready in time; and before the meal was over the motor was waiting at the door.

The entertainment was a great success, Mrs. Inglethorp's recitation receiving tremendous applause. There were also some tableaux in which Cynthia took part. She did not return with us, having been asked to a supper party, and to remain the night with some friends who had been acting with her in the tableaux.

The following morning, Mrs. Inglethorp stayed in bed to breakfast, as she was rather over-tired; but she appeared in her briskest mood about 12.30, and swept Lawrence and myself off to a luncheon party.

"Such a charming invitation from Mrs. Rolleston. Lady Tadminster's sister, you know. The Rollestons came over with the Conqueror—one of our oldest families."

Mary had excused herself on the plea of an engagement with Dr. Bauerstein.

We had a pleasant luncheon, and as we drove away Lawrence suggested that we should return by Tadminster, which was barely a mile out of our way, and pay a visit to Cynthia in her dispensary. Mrs. Inglethorp replied that this was an excellent idea, but as she had several letters to write she would drop us there, and we could come back with Cynthia in the pony-trap.

We were detained under suspicion by the hospital porter, until Cynthia appeared to vouch for us, looking very cool and sweet in her long white overall. She took us up to her sanctum, and introduced us to her fellow dispenser, a rather awe-inspiring individual, whom Cynthia cheerily addressed as "Nibs."

"What a lot of bottles!" I exclaimed, as my eye travelled round the small room. "Do you really know what's in them all?"

"Say something original," groaned Cynthia. "Every single person who comes up here says that. We are really thinking of bestowing a prize on the first individual who does *not* say: 'What a lot of bottles!' And I know the next thing you're going to say is: 'How many people have you poisoned?'"

I pleaded guilty with a laugh.

"If you people only knew how fatally easy it is to poison some one by mistake, you wouldn't joke about it. Come on, let's have tea. We've got all sorts of secret stores in that cupboard. No, Lawrence—that's the poison cupboard. The big cupboard—that's right."

We had a very cheery tea, and assisted Cynthia to wash up afterwards. We had just put away the last tea-spoon when a knock came at the door. The countenances of Cynthia and Nibs were suddenly petrified into a stern and forbidding expression.

"Come in," said Cynthia, in a sharp professional tone.

A young and rather scared looking nurse appeared with a bottle which she proffered to Nibs, who waved her towards Cynthia with the somewhat enigmatical remark:

"*I'm* not really here to-day."

Cynthia took the bottle and examined it with the severity of a judge.

"This should have been sent up this morning."

"Sister is very sorry. She forgot."

"Sister should read the rules outside the door."

I gathered from the little nurse's expression that there was not the least likelihood of her having the hardihood to retail this message to the dreaded "Sister".

"So now it can't be done until to-morrow," finished Cynthia.

"Don't you think you could possibly let us have it to-night?"

"Well," said Cynthia graciously, "we are very busy, but if we have time it shall be done."

The little nurse withdrew, and Cynthia promptly took a jar from the shelf, refilled the bottle, and placed it on the table outside the door.

I laughed.

"Discipline must be maintained?"

"Exactly. Come out on our little balcony. You can see all the outside wards there."

I followed Cynthia and her friend and they pointed out the different wards to me. Lawrence remained behind, but after a few moments Cynthia called to him over her shoulder to come and join us. Then she looked at her watch.

"Nothing more to do, Nibs?"

"No."

"All right. Then we can lock up and go."

I had seen Lawrence in quite a different light that afternoon. Compared to John, he was an astoundingly difficult person to get to know. He was the opposite of his brother in almost every respect, being unusually shy and reserved. Yet he had a certain charm of manner, and I fancied that, if one really knew him well, one could have a deep affection for him. I had always fancied that his manner to Cynthia was rather constrained, and that she on her side was inclined to be shy of him. But they were both gay enough this afternoon, and chatted together like a couple of children.

As we drove through the village, I remembered that I wanted some stamps, so accordingly we pulled up at the post office.

As I came out again, I cannoned into a little man who was just entering. I drew aside and apologised, when suddenly, with a loud exclamation, he clasped me in his arms and kissed me warmly.

"*Mon ami* Hastings!" he cried. "It is indeed *mon ami* Hastings!"

"Poirot!" I exclaimed.

I turned to the pony-trap.

"This is a very pleasant meeting for me, Miss Cynthia. This is my old friend, Monsieur Poirot, whom I have not seen for years."

"Oh, we know Monsieur Poirot," said Cynthia gaily. "But I had no idea he was a friend of yours."

"Yes, indeed," said Poirot seriously, "I know Mademoiselle Cynthia. It is by the charity of that good Mrs. Inglethorp that I am here." Then, as I looked at him inquiringly: "Yes, my friend, she had kindly extended hospitality to seven of my countrypeople who, alas, are refugees from their native land. We Belgians will always remember her with gratitude."

Poirot was an extraordinary looking little man. He was hardly more than five feet, four inches, but carried himself with great dignity. His head was exactly the shape of an egg, and he always perched it a little on one side. His moustache was very stiff and military. The neatness of his attire was almost incredible, I believe a speck of dust would have caused him more pain than a bullet wound. Yet this quaint dandyfied little man who, I was sorry to see, now limped badly, had been in his time one of the most celebrated members of the Belgian police. As a detective, his *flair* had been extraordinary, and he had achieved triumphs by unravelling some of the most baffling cases of the day.

He pointed out to me the little house inhabited by him and his fellow Belgians, and I promised to go and see him at an early date. Then he raised his hat with a flourish to Cynthia, and we drove away.

"He's a dear little man," said Cynthia. "I'd no idea you knew him."

"You've been entertaining a celebrity unawares," I replied.

And, for the rest of the way home, I recited to them the various exploits and triumphs of Hercule Poirot.

We arrived back in a very cheerful mood. As we entered the hall, Mrs. Inglethorp came out of her boudoir. She looked flushed and upset.

"Oh, it's you," she said.

"Is there anything the matter, Aunt Emily?" asked Cynthia.

"Certainly not," said Mrs. Inglethorp sharply. "What should there be?" Then catching sight of Dorcas, the parlourmaid, going into the dining-room, she called to her to bring some stamps into the boudoir.

"Yes, m'm." The old servant hesitated, then added diffidently: "Don't you think m'm, you'd better get to bed? You're looking very tired."

"Perhaps you're right, Dorcas—yes—no—not now. I've some letters I must finish by post-time. Have you lighted the fire in my room as I told you?"

"Yes, m'm."

"Then I'll go to bed directly after supper."

She went into the boudoir again, and Cynthia stared after her.

"Goodness gracious! I wonder what's up?" she said to Lawrence.

He did not seem to have heard her, for without a word he turned on his heel and went out of the house.

I suggested a quick game of tennis before supper and, Cynthia agreeing, I ran upstairs to fetch my racquet.

Mrs. Cavendish was coming down the stairs. It may have been my fancy, but she, too, was looking odd and disturbed.

"Had a good walk with Dr. Bauerstein?" I asked, trying to appear as indifferent as I could.

"I didn't go," she replied abruptly. "Where is Mrs. Inglethorp?"

"In the boudoir."

Her hand clenched itself on the banisters, then she seemed to nerve herself for some encounter, and went rapidly past me down the stairs across the hall to the boudoir, the door of which she shut behind her.

As I ran out to the tennis court a few moments later, I had to pass the open boudoir window, and was unable to help overhearing the following scrap of dialogue. Mary Cavendish was saying in the voice of a woman desperately controlling herself:

"Then you won't show it to me?"

To which Mrs. Inglethorp replied:

"My dear Mary, it has nothing to do with that matter."

"Then show it to me."

"I tell you it is not what you imagine. It does not concern you in the least."

To which Mary Cavendish replied, with a rising bitterness:

"Of course, I might have known you would shield him."

Cynthia was waiting for me, and greeted me eagerly with:

"I say! There's been the most awful row! I've got it all out of Dorcas."

"What kind of a row?"

"Between Aunt Emily and *him*. I do hope she's found him out at last!"

"Was Dorcas there, then?"

"Of course not. She 'happened to be near the door'. It was a real old bust-up. I do wish I knew what it was all about."

I thought of Mrs. Raikes's gipsy face, and Evelyn Howard's warnings, but wisely decided to hold my peace, whilst Cynthia exhausted every possible hypothesis, and cheerfully hoped, "Aunt Emily will send him away, and will never speak to him again."

I was anxious to get hold of John, but he was nowhere to be seen. Evidently something very momentous had occurred that afternoon. I tried to forget the few words I had overheard; but, do what I would, I could not dismiss them altogether from my mind. What was Mary Cavendish's concern in the matter?

Mr. Inglethorp was in the drawing-room when I came down to supper. His face was impassive as ever, and the strange unreality of the man struck me afresh.

Mrs. Inglethorp came down last. She still looked agitated, and during the meal there was a somewhat constrained silence. Inglethorp was unusually quiet. As a rule, he surrounded his wife with little attentions, placing a cushion at her back, and altogether playing the part of the devoted husband. Immediately after supper, Mrs. Inglethorp retired to her boudoir again.

"Send my coffee in here, Mary," she called. "I've just five minutes to catch the post."

Cynthia and I went and sat by the open window in the drawing-room. Mary Cavendish brought our coffee to us. She seemed excited.

"Do you young people want lights, or do you enjoy the twilight?" she asked. "Will you take Mrs. Inglethorp her coffee, Cynthia? I will pour it out."

"Do not trouble, Mary," said Inglethorp. "I will take it to Emily." He poured it out, and went out of the room carrying it carefully.

Lawrence followed him, and Mrs. Cavendish sat down by us.

We three sat for some time in silence. It was a glorious night, hot and still. Mrs. Cavendish fanned herself gently with a palm leaf.

"It's almost too hot," she murmured. "We shall have a thunderstorm."

Alas, that these harmonious moments can never endure! My paradise was rudely shattered by the sound of a well known, and heartily disliked, voice in the hall.

"Dr. Bauerstein!" exclaimed Cynthia. "What a funny time to come."

I glanced jealously at Mary Cavendish, but she seemed quite undisturbed, the delicate pallor of her cheeks did not vary.

In a few moments, Alfred Inglethorp had ushered the doctor in, the latter laughing, and protesting that he was in no fit state for a drawing-room. In truth, he presented a sorry spectacle, being literally plastered with mud.

"What have you been doing, doctor?" cried Mrs. Cavendish.

"I must make my apologies," said the doctor. "I did not really mean to come in, but Mr. Inglethorp insisted."

"Well, Bauerstein, you are in a plight," said John, strolling in from the hall. "Have some coffee, and tell us what you have been up to."

"Thank you, I will." He laughed rather ruefully, as he described how he had discovered a very rare species of fern in an inaccessible place, and in his efforts to obtain it had lost his footing, and slipped ignominiously into a neighbouring pond.

"The sun soon dried me off," he added, "but I'm afraid my appearance is very disreputable."

At this juncture, Mrs. Inglethorp called to Cynthia from the hall, and the girl ran out.

"Just carry up my despatch-case, will you, dear? I'm going to bed."

The door into the hall was a wide one. I had risen when Cynthia did, John was close by me. There were therefore three witnesses who could swear that Mrs. Inglethorp was carrying her coffee, as yet untasted, in her hand.

My evening was utterly and entirely spoilt by the presence of

Dr. Bauerstein. It seemed to me the man would never go. He rose at last, however, and I breathed a sigh of relief.

"I'll walk down to the village with you," said Mr. Inglethorp. "I must see our agent over those estate accounts." He turned to John. "No one need sit up. I will take the latch-key."

3

The Night of the Tragedy

To make this part of my story clear, I append the following plan of the first floor of Styles. The servants' rooms are reached

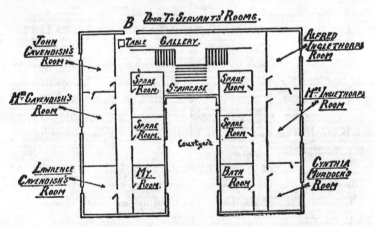

through the door B. They have no communication with the right wing, where the Inglethorps' rooms were situated.

It seemed to be the middle of the night when I was awakened by Lawrence Cavendish. He had a candle in his hand, and the agitation of his face told me at once that something was seriously wrong.

"What's the matter?" I asked, sitting up in bed, and trying to collect my scattered thoughts.

"We are afraid my mother is very ill. She seems to be having some kind of fit. Unfortunately she has locked herself in."

"I'll come at once."

I sprang out of bed; and, pulling on a dressing-gown, followed Lawrence along the passage and the gallery to the right wing of the house.

John Cavendish joined us, and one or two of the servants were standing round in a state of awe-stricken excitement. Lawrence turned to his brother.

"What do you think we had better do?"

Never, I thought, had his indecision of character been more apparent.

John rattled the handle of Mrs. Inglethorp's door violently, but with no effect. It was obviously locked or bolted on the inside. The whole household was aroused by now. The most alarming sounds were audible from the interior of the room. Clearly something must be done.

"Try going through Mr. Inglethorp's room, sir," cried Dorcas. "Oh, the poor mistress!"

Suddenly I realized that Alfred Inglethorp was not with us—that he alone had given no sign of his presence. John opened the door of his room. It was pitch dark, but Lawrence was following with the candle, and by its feeble light we saw that the bed had not been slept in, and that there was no sign of the room having been occupied.

We went straight to the connecting door. That, too, was locked or bolted on the inside. What was to be done?

"Oh, dear, sir," cried Dorcas, wringing her hands, "what ever shall we do?"

"We must try and break the door in, I suppose. It'll be a tough job, though. Here, let one of the maids go down and wake Baily and tell him to go for Dr. Wilkins at once. Now then, we'll have a try at the door. Half a moment, though, isn't there a door into Miss Cynthia's rooms?"

"Yes, sir, but that's always bolted. It's never been undone."

"Well, we might just see."

He ran rapidly down the corridor to Cynthia's room. Mary

Cavendish was there, shaking the girl—who must have been an unusually sound sleeper—and trying to wake her.

In a moment or two he was back.

"No good. That's bolted too. We must break in the door. I think this one is a shade less solid than the one in the passage."

We strained and heaved together. The framework of the door was solid, and for a long time it resisted our efforts, but at last we felt it give beneath our weight, and finally, with a resounding crash, it was burst open.

We stumbled in together, Lawrence still holding his candle. Mrs. Inglethorp was lying on the bed, her whole form agitated by violent convulsions, in one of which she must have overturned the table beside her. As we entered, however, her limbs relaxed, and she fell back upon the pillows.

John strode across the room, and lit the gas. Turning to Annie, one of the housemaids, he sent her downstairs to the dining-room for brandy. Then he went across to his mother whilst I unbolted the door that gave on the corridor.

I turned to Lawrence, to suggest that I had better leave them now that there was no further need of my services, but the words were frozen on my lips. Never have I seen such a ghastly look on any man's face. He was white as chalk, the candle he held in his shaking hand was sputtering onto the carpet, and his eyes, petrified with terror, or some such kindred emotion, stared fixedly over my head at a point on the further wall. It was as though he had seen something that turned him to stone. I instinctively followed the direction of his eyes, but I could see nothing unusual. The still feebly flickering ashes in the grate, and the row of prim ornaments on the mantelpiece, were surely harmless enough.

The violence of Mrs. Inglethorp's attack seemed to be passing. She was able to speak in short gasps.

"Better now—very sudden—stupid of me—to lock myself in."

A shadow fell on the bed and, looking up, I saw Mary Cavendish standing near the door with her arm around Cynthia. She seemed to be supporting the girl, who looked utterly dazed and unlike herself. Her face was heavily flushed, and she yawned repeatedly.

"Poor Cynthia is quite frightened," said Mrs. Cavendish in a low clear voice. She herself, I noticed, was dressed in her white land smock. Then it must be later than I thought. I saw that a faint streak of daylight was showing through the curtains of the windows, and that the clock on the mantelpiece pointed to close upon five o'clock.

A strangled cry from the bed startled me. A fresh access of pain seized the unfortunate old lady. The convulsions were of a violence terrible to behold. Everything was confusion. We thronged round her, powerless to help or alleviate. A final convulsion lifted her from the bed, until she appeared to rest upon her head and her heels, with her body arched in an extraordinary manner. In vain Mary and John tried to administer more brandy. The moments flew. Again the body arched itself in that peculiar fashion.

At that moment, Dr. Bauerstein pushed his way authoritatively into the room. For one instant he stopped dead, staring at the figure on the bed, and, at the same instant, Mrs. Inglethorp cried out in a strangled voice, her eyes fixed on the doctor:

"Alfred—Alfred——" Then she fell back motionless on the pillows.

With a stride, the doctor reached the bed, and seizing her arms worked them energetically, applying what I knew to be artificial respiration. He issued a few short sharp orders to the servants. An imperious wave of his hand drove us all to the door. We watched him, fascinated, though I think we all knew in our hearts that it was too late, and that nothing could be done now. I could see by the expression on his face that he himself had little hope.

Finally he abandoned his task, shaking his head gravely. At that moment, we heard footsteps outside, and Dr. Wilkins, Mrs. Inglethorp's own doctor, a portly, fussy little man, came bustling in.

In a few words Dr. Bauerstein explained how he had happened to be passing the lodge gates as the car came out, and had run up to the house as fast as he could, whilst the car went on to fetch Dr. Wilkins. With a faint gesture of the hand, he indicated the figure on the bed.

"Ve—ry sad. Ve—ry sad," murmured Dr. Wilkins. "Poor dear lady. Always did far too much—far too much—against my advice. I warned her. Her heart was far from strong. 'Take it easy,' I said to her, 'Take—it—easy'. But no—her zeal for good works was too great. Nature rebelled. Na—ture—re—belled."

Dr. Bauerstein, I noticed, was watching the local doctor narrowly. He still kept his eyes fixed on him as he spoke.

"The convulsions were of a peculiar violence, Dr. Wilkins. I am sorry you were not here in time to witness them. They were quite—tetanic in character."

"Ah!" said Dr. Wilkins wisely.

"I should like to speak to you in private," said Dr. Bauerstein. He turned to John. "You do not object?"

"Certainly not."

We all trooped out into the corridor, leaving the two doctors alone, and I heard the key turned in the lock behind us.

We went slowly down the stairs. I was violently excited. I have a certain talent for deduction, and Dr. Bauerstein's manner had started a flock of wild surmises in my mind. Mary Cavendish laid her hand upon my arm.

"What is it? Why did Dr. Bauerstein seem so—peculiar?"

I looked at her.

"Do you know what I think?"

"What?"

"Listen!" I looked round, the others were out of earshot. I lowered my voice to a whisper. "I believe she has been poisoned! I'm certain Dr. Bauerstein suspects it."

"*What?*" She shrank against the wall, the pupils of her eyes dilating wildly. Then, with a sudden cry that startled me, she cried out: "No, no—not that—not that!" And breaking from me, fled up the stairs. I followed her, afraid that she was going to faint. I found her leaning against the banisters, deadly pale. She waved me away impatiently.

"No, no—leave me. I'd rather be alone. Let me just be quiet for a minute or two. Go down to the others."

I obeyed her reluctantly. John and Lawrence were in the dining-room. I joined them. We were all silent, but I suppose I voiced the thoughts of us all when I at last broke it by saying:

"Where is Mr. Inglethorp?"

John shook his head.

"He's not in the house."

Our eyes met. Where *was* Alfred Inglethorp? His absence was strange and inexplicable. I remembered Mrs. Inglethorp's dying words. What lay beneath them? What more could she have told us, if she had had time?

At last we heard the doctors descending the stairs. Dr. Wilkins was looking important and excited, and trying to conceal an inward exultation under a manner of decorous calm. Dr. Bauerstein remained in the background, his grave bearded face unchanged. Dr. Wilkins was the spokesman for the two. He addressed himself to John:

"Mr. Cavendish, I should like your consent to a post-mortem."

"Is that necessary?" asked John gravely. A spasm of pain crossed his face.

"Absolutely," said Dr. Bauerstein.

"You mean by that——?"

"That neither Dr. Wilkins nor myself could give a death certificate under the circumstances."

John bent his head.

"In that case, I have no alternative but to agree."

"Thank you," said Dr. Wilkins briskly. "We propose that it should take place to-morrow night—or rather to-night." And he glanced at the daylight. "Under the circumstances, I am afraid an inquest can hardly be avoided—these formalities are necessary, but I beg that you won't distress yourselves."

There was a pause, and then Dr. Bauerstein drew two keys from his pocket, and handed them to John.

"These are the keys of the two rooms. I have locked them and, in my opinion, they would be better kept locked for the present."

The doctors then departed.

I had been turning over an idea in my head, and I felt that the moment had now come to broach it. Yet I was a little chary of doing so. John, I knew, had a horror of any kind of publicity, and was an easy going optimist, who preferred never to meet trouble half-way. It might be difficult to convince him of the soundness of my plan. Lawrence, on the other hand, being less conventional, and having more imagination, I felt I might count upon as an ally. There was no doubt that the moment had come for me to take the lead.

"John," I said, "I am going to ask you something."

"Well?"

"You remember my speaking of my friend Poirot? The Belgian who is here? He has been a most famous detective."

"Yes."

"I want you to let me call him in—to investigate this matter."

"What—now? Before the post-mortem?"

"Yes, time is an advantage if—if—there has been foul play."

"Rubbish!" cried Lawrence angrily. "In my opinion the whole thing is a mare's nest of Bauerstein's! Wilkins hadn't an idea of such a thing, until Bauerstein put it into his head. But, like all specialists, Bauerstein's got a bee in his bonnet. Poisons are his hobby, so of course he sees them everywhere."

I confess that I was surprised by Lawrence's attitude. He was so seldom vehement about anything.

John hesitated.

"I can't feel as you do, Lawrence," he said at last, "I'm inclined to give Hastings a free hand, though I should prefer to wait a bit. We don't want any unnecessary scandal."

"No, no," I cried eagerly, "you need have no fear of that. Poirot is discretion itself."

"Very well, then, have it your own way. I leave it in your hands. Though, if it is as we suspect, it seems a clear enough case. God forgive me if I am wronging him!"

I looked at my watch. It was six o'clock. I determined to lose no time.

Five minutes' delay, however, I allowed myself. I spent it in ransacking the library until I discovered a medical book which gave a description of strychnine poisoning.

4

Poirot Investigates

The house which the Belgians occupied in the village was quite close to the park gates. One could save time by taking a narrow path through the long grass, which cut off the detours of the winding drive. So I, accordingly, went that way. I had nearly reached the lodge, when my attention was arrested by the running figure of a man approaching me. It was Mr. Inglethorp. Where had he been? How did he intend to explain his absence?

He accosted me eagerly.

"My God! This is terrible! My poor wife! I have only just heard."

"Where have you been?" I asked.

"Denby kept me late last night. It was one o'clock before we'd finished. Then I found that I'd forgotten the latch-key after all. I didn't want to arouse the household, so Denby gave me a bed."

"How did you hear the news?" I asked.

"Wilkins knocked Denby up to tell him. My poor Emily! She was so self-sacrificing—such a noble character. She overtaxed her strength."

A wave of revulsion swept over me. What a consummate hypocrite the man was!

"I must hurry on," I said, thankful that he did not ask me whither I was bound.

In a few minutes I was knocking at the door of Leastways Cottage.

Getting no answer, I repeated my summons impatiently. A window above me was cautiously opened, and Poirot himself looked out.

He gave an exclamation of surprise at seeing me. In a few brief words, I explained the tragedy that had occurred, and that I wanted his help.

"Wait, my friend, I will let you in, and you shall recount to me the affair whilst I dress."

In a few moments he had unbarred the door, and I followed him up to his room. There he installed me in a chair, and I related the whole story, keeping back nothing, and omitting no circumstance, however insignificant, whilst he himself made a careful and deliberate toilet.

I told him of my awakening, of Mrs. Inglethorp's dying words, of her husband's absence, of the quarrel the day before, of the scrap of conversation between Mary and her mother-in-law that I had overheard, of the former quarrel between Mrs. Inglethorp and Evelyn Howard, and of the latter's inuendoes.

I was hardly as clear as I could wish. I repeated myself several times, and occasionally had to go back to some detail that I had forgotten. Poirot smiled kindly on me.

"The mind is confused? Is it not so? Take time, *mon ami*. You are agitated; you are excited—it is but natural. Presently, when we are calmer, we will arrange the facts, neatly, each in his proper place. We will examine—and reject. Those of importance we will put on one side; those of no importance, pouf!"—he screwed up his cherub-like face, and puffed comically enough—"blow them away!"

"That's all very well," I objected, "but how are you going to decide what is important, and what isn't. That always seems the difficulty to me."

Poirot shook his head energetically. He was now arranging his moustache with exquisite care.

"Not so. *Voyons!* One fact leads to another—so we continue. Does the next fit in with that? *A merveille!* Good! We can proceed. This next little fact—no! Ah, that is curious! There is something missing—a link in the chain that is not there. We examine. We search. And that little curious fact, that possibly paltry little detail that will not tally, we put it here!" He made an extravagant gesture with his hand. "It is significant! It is tremendous!"

"Y—es—"

"Ah!" Poirot shook his forefinger so fiercely at me that I quailed before it. "Beware! Peril to the detective who says: 'It is so small—it does not matter. It will not agree. I will forget it.' That way lies confusion! Everything matters."

"I know. You always told me that. That's why I have gone into all the details of this thing whether they seemed to me relevant or not."

"And I am pleased with you. You have a good memory, and you have given me the facts faithfully. Of the order in which you present them, I say nothing—truly, it is deplorable! But I make allowances—you are upset. To that I attribute the circumstance that you have omitted one fact of paramount importance."

"What is that?" I asked.

"You have not told me if Mrs. Inglethorp ate well last night."

I stared at him. Surely the war had affected the little man's brain. He was carefully engaged in brushing his coat before putting it on, and seemed wholly engrossed in the task.

"I don't remember," I said. "And, anyway, I don't see——"

"You do not see? But it is of the first importance."

"I can't see why," I said, rather nettled. "As far as I can remember, she didn't eat much. She was obviously upset, and it had taken her appetite away. That was only natural."

"Yes," said Poirot thoughtfully, "it was only natural."

He opened a drawer, and took out a small despatch-case, then turned to me.

"Now I am ready. We will proceed to the château, and study matters on the spot. Excuse me, *mon ami*, you dressed in haste, and your tie is on one side. Permit me." With a deft gesture, he rearranged it.

"*Ça y est!* Now, shall we start?"

We hurried up the village, and turned in at the lodge gates.

Poirot stopped for a moment, and gazed sorrowfully over the beautiful expanse of park, still glittering with morning dew.

"So beautiful, so beautiful, and yet, the poor family, plunged in sorrow, prostrated with grief."

He looked at me keenly as he spoke, and I was aware that I reddened under his prolonged gaze.

Was the family prostrated by grief? Was the sorrow at Mrs. Inglethorp's death so great? I realized that there was an emotional lack in the atmosphere. The dead woman had not the gift of commanding love. Her death was a shock and a distress, but she would not be passionately regretted.

Poirot seemed to follow my thoughts. He nodded his head gravely.

"No, you are right," he said, "it is not as though there was a blood tie. She has been kind and generous to these Cavendishes, but she was not their own mother. Blood tells—always remember that—blood tells."

"Poirot," I said, "I wish you would tell me why you wanted to know if Mrs. Inglethorp ate well last night? I have been turning it over in my mind, but I can't see how it has anything to do with the matter."

He was silent for a minute or two as we walked along, but finally he said:

"I do not mind telling you—though, as you know, it is not my habit to explain until the end is reached. The present contention is that Mrs. Inglethorp died of strychnine poisoning, presumably administered in her coffee."

"Yes?"

"Well, what time was the coffee served?"

"About eight o'clock."

"Therefore she drank it between then and half-past eight—certainly not much later. Well, strychnine is a fairly rapid poison. Its effects would be felt very soon, probably in about an hour. Yet, in Mrs. Inglethorp's case, the symptoms do not manifest themselves until five o'clock the next morning: nine hours! But a heavy meal, taken at about the same time as the poison, might retard its effects, though hardly to that extent. Still, it is a possibility to be taken into account. But, according to you, she ate very little for supper, and yet the symptoms do not develop until early the next morning! Now that is a curious circumstance, my friend. Something may arise at the autopsy to explain it. In the meantime, remember it."

As we neared the house, John came out and met us. His face looked weary and haggard.

"This is a very dreadful business, Monsieur Poirot," he said. "Hastings has explained to you that we are anxious for no publicity?"

"I comprehend perfectly."

"You see, it is only suspicion so far. We have nothing to go upon."

"Precisely. It is a matter of precaution only."

John turned to me, taking out his cigarette-case, and lighting a cigarette as he did so.

"You know that fellow Inglethorp is back?"

"Yes. I met him."

John flung the match into an adjacent flower bed, a proceeding which was too much for Poirot's feelings. He retrieved it, and buried it neatly.

"It's jolly difficult to know how to treat him."

"That difficulty will not exist long," pronounced Poirot quietly.

John looked puzzled, not quite understanding the portent of this cryptic saying. He handed the two keys which Dr. Bauerstein had given him to me.

"Show Monsieur Poirot everything he wants to see."

"The rooms are locked?" asked Poirot.

"Dr. Bauerstein considered it advisable."

Poirot nodded thoughtfully.

"Then he is very sure. Well, that simplifies matters for us."

We went up together to the room of the tragedy. For convenience I append a plan of the room and the principal articles of furniture in it.

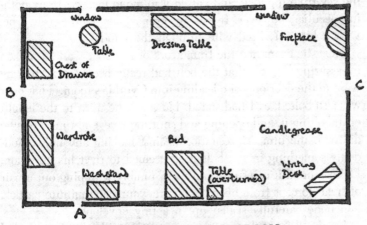

MRS. INGLETHORP'S BEDROOM
A.—Door into Passage
B.—Door into Mr. Inglethorp's Room.
C.—Door into Cynthia's Room

Poirot locked the door on the inside, and proceeded to a minute inspection of the room. He darted from one object to the other with the agility of a grasshopper. I remained by the door, fearing to obliterate any clues. Poirot, however, did not seem grateful to me for my forbearance.

"What have you, my friend?" he cried, "that you remain there like—how do you say it?—ah, yes, the stuck pig?"

I explained that I was afraid of obliterating any foot-marks.

"Foot-marks? But what an idea! There has already been practically an army in the room! What foot-marks are we likely to find? No, come here and aid me in my search. I will put down my little case until I need it."

He did so, on the round table by the window, but it was an ill-advised proceeding; for, the top of it being loose, it tilted up, and precipitated the despatch-case on to the floor.

"*En voilà une table!*" cried Poirot. "Ah, my friend, one may live in a big house and yet have no comfort."

After which piece of moralizing, he resumed his search.

A small purple despatch-case, with a key in the lock, on the writing-table, engaged his attention for some time. He took out the key from the lock, and passed it to me to inspect. I saw nothing peculiar, however. It was an ordinary key of the Yale type, with a bit of twisted wire through the handle.

Next, he examined the framework of the door we had broken in, assuring himself that the bolt had really been shot. Then he went to the door opposite leading into Cynthia's room. That door was also bolted, as I had stated. However, he went to the length of unbolting it, and opening and shutting it several times; this he did with the utmost precaution against making any noise. Suddenly something in the bolt itself seemed to rivet his attention. He examined it carefully, and then, nimbly whipping out a pair of small forceps from his case, he drew out some minute particle which he carefully sealed up in a tiny envelope.

On the chest of drawers there was a tray with a spirit lamp and a small saucepan on it. A small quantity of a dark fluid remained in the saucepan, and an empty cup and saucer that had been drunk out of stood near it.

I wondered how I could have been so unobservant as to overlook this. Here was a clue worth having. Poirot delicately dipped his finger into the liquid, and tasted it gingerly. He made a grimace.

"Coco—with—I think—rum in it."

He passed on to the debris on the floor, where the table by the bed had been overturned. A reading-lamp, some books, matches, a bunch of keys, and the crushed fragments of a coffee-cup lay scattered about.

"Ah, this is curious," said Poirot.

"I must confess that I see nothing particularly curious about it."

"You do not? Observe the lamp—the chimney is broken in two places; they lie there as they fell. But see, the coffee-cup is absolutely smashed to powder."

"Well," I said wearily, "I suppose some one must have stepped on it."

"Exactly," said Poirot, in an odd voice. "Some one stepped on it."

He rose from his knees, and walked slowly across to the mantelpiece, where he stood abstractedly fingering the ornaments, and straightening them—a trick of his when he was agitated.

"*Mon ami*," he said, turning to me, "somebody stepped on that cup, grinding it to powder, and the reason they did so was either because it contained strychnine or—which is far more serious— because it did not contain strychnine!"

I made no reply. I was bewildered, but I knew that it was no good asking him to explain. In a moment or two he roused himself, and went on with his investigations. He picked up the bunch of keys from the floor, and twirling them round in his fingers finally selected one, very bright and shining, which he tried in the lock of the purple despatch-case. It fitted, and he opened the box, but after a moment's hesitation, closed and relocked it, and slipped the bunch of keys, as well as the key that had originally stood in the lock, into his own pocket.

"I have no authority to go through these papers. But it should be done—at once!"

He then made a very careful examination of the drawers of the wash-stand. Crossing the room to the left-hand window, a round stain, hardly visible on the dark brown carpet, seemed to interest him particularly. He went down on his knees, examining it minutely—even going so far as to smell it.

Finally, he poured a few drops of the coco into a test tube, sealing it up carefully. His next proceeding was to take out a little notebook.

"We have found in this room," he said, writing busily, "six points of interest. Shall I enumerate them, or will you?"

"Oh, you," I replied hastily.

"Very well, then. One, a coffee-cup that has been ground into powder; two, a despatch-case with a key in the lock; three, a stain on the floor."

"That may have been done some time ago," I interrupted.

"No, for it is still perceptibly damp and smells of coffee. Four, a fragment of some dark green fabric—only a thread or two, but recognizable."

"Ah!" I cried. "That was what you sealed up in the envelope."

"Yes. It may turn out to be a piece of one of Mrs. Inglethorp's own dresses, and quite unimportant. We shall see. Five, *this!*" With a dramatic gesture, he pointed to a large splash of candle grease on the floor by the writing-table. "It must have been done since yesterday, otherwise a good housemaid would have at once removed it with blotting-paper and a hot iron. One of my best hats once—but that is not to the point."

"It was very likely done last night. We were very agitated. Or perhaps Mrs. Inglethorp herself dropped her candle."

"You brought only one candle into the room?"

"Yes. Lawrence Cavendish was carrying it. But he was very upset. He seemed to see something over here"—I indicated the mantelpiece—"that absolutely paralysed him."

"That is interesting," said Poirot quickly. "Yes, it is suggestive" —his eye sweeping the whole length of the wall—"but it was not his candle that made this great patch, for you perceive that this is white grease; whereas Monsieur Lawrence's candle, which is still on the dressing-table, is pink. On the other hand, Mrs. Inglethorp had no candlestick in the room, only a reading-lamp."

"Then," I said, "what do you deduce?"

To which my friend only made a rather irritating reply, urging me to use my own natural faculties.

"And the sixth point?" I asked. "I suppose it is the sample of coco."

"No," said Poirot thoughtfully, "I might have included that in the six, but I did not. No, the sixth point I will keep to myself for the present."

He looked quickly round the room. "There is nothing more to be done here, I think, unless"—he stared earnestly and long at the dead ashes in the grate. "The fire burns—and it destroys. But by chance—there might be—let us see!"

Deftly, on hands and knees, he began to sort the ashes from the grate into the fender, handling them with the greatest caution. Suddenly, he gave a faint exclamation.

"The forceps, Hastings!"

I quickly handed them to him, and with skill he extracted a small piece of half charred paper.

"There, *mon ami!*" he cried. "What do you think of that?"

I scrutinized the fragment. This is an exact reproduction of it:—

I was puzzled. It was unusually thick, quite unlike ordinary notepaper. Suddenly an idea struck me.

"Poirot!" I cried. "This is a fragment of a will!"

"Exactly."

I looked up at him sharply.

"You are not surprised?"

"No," he said gravely, "I expected it."

I relinquished the piece of paper, and watched him put it away in his case, with the same methodical care that he bestowed on everything. My brain was in a whirl. What was this complication of a will? Who had destroyed it? The person who had left the candle grease on the floor? Obviously. But how had anyone gained admission? All the doors had been bolted on the inside.

"Now, my friend," said Poirot briskly, "we will go. I should like to ask a few questions of the parlourmaid—Dorcas, her name is, is it not?"

We passed through Alfred Inglethorp's room, and Poirot delayed long enough to make a brief but fairly comprehensive examination of it. We went out through that door, locking both it and that of Mrs. Inglethorp's room as before.

I took him down to the boudoir which he had expressed a wish to see, and went myself in search of Dorcas.

When I returned with her, however, the boudoir was empty.

"Poirot," I cried, "where are you?"

"I am here, my friend."

He had stepped outside the French window, and was standing,

apparently, lost in admiration, before the various shaped flower beds.

"Admirable!" he murmured. "Admirable! What symmetry! Observe that crescent; and those diamonds—their neatness rejoices the eye. The spacing of the plans, also, is perfect. It has been recently done; is it not so?"

"Yes, I believe they were at it yesterday afternoon. But come in —Dorcas is here."

"*Eh bien, eh bien!* Do not grudge me a moment's satisfaction of the eye."

"Yes, but this affair is more important."

"And how do you know that these fine begonias are not of equal importance?"

I shrugged my shoulders. There was really no arguing with him if he chose to take that line.

"You do not agree? But such things have been. Well, we will come in and interview the brave Dorcas."

Dorcas was standing in the boudoir, her hands folded in front of her, and her grey hair rose in stiff waves under her white cap. She was the very model and picture of a good old-fashioned servant.

In her attitude towards Poirot, she was inclined to be suspicious, but he soon broke down her defences. He drew forward a chair.

"Pray be seated, mademoiselle."

"Thank you, sir."

"You have been with your mistress many years, is it not so?"

"Ten years, sir."

"That is a long time, and very faithful service. You were much attached to her, were you not?"

"She was a very good mistress to me, sir."

"Then you will not object to answering a few questions. I put them to you with Mr. Cavendish's full approval."

"Oh, certainly, sir."

"Then I will begin by asking you about the events of yesterday afternoon. Your mistress had a quarrel?"

"Yes, sir. But I don't know that I ought——" Dorcas hesitated.

Poirot looked at her keenly.

"My good Dorcas, it is necessary that I should know every detail of that quarrel as fully as possible. Do not think that you are betraying your mistress's secrets. Your mistress lies dead, and it is necessary that we should know all—if we are to avenge her. Nothing can bring her back to life, but we do hope, if there has been foul play, to bring the murderer to justice."

"Amen to that," said Dorcas fiercely. "And, naming no names, there's *one* in this house that none of us could ever abide! And an ill day it was when first *he* darkened the threshold."

Poirot waited for her indignation to subside, and then, resuming his business-like tone, he asked:

"Now, as to this quarrel? What is the first you heard of it?"

"Well, sir, I happened to be going along the hall outside yesterday——"

"What time was that?"

"I couldn't say exactly, sir, but it wasn't teatime by a long way. Perhaps four o'clock—or it may have been a bit later. Well, sir, as I said, I happened to be passing along, when I heard voices very loud and angry in here. I didn't exactly mean to listen, but—well, there it is. I stopped. The door was shut, but the mistress was speaking very sharp and clear, and I heard what she said quite plainly. 'You have lied to me, and deceived me,' she said. I didn't hear what Mr. Inglethorp replied. He spoke a good bit lower than she did—but she answered: 'How dare you? I have kept you and clothed you and fed you! You owe everything to me! And this is how you repay me! By bringing disgrace upon our name!' Again I didn't hear what he said, but she went on: 'Nothing that you can say will make any difference. I see my duty clearly. My mind is made up. You need not think that any fear of publicity, or scandal between husband and wife will deter me.' Then I thought I heard them coming out, so I went off quickly."

"You are sure it was Mr. Inglethorp's voice you heard?"

"Oh, yes, sir, whose else's could it be?"

"Well, what happened next?"

"Later, I came back to the hall; but it was all quiet. At five o'clock, Mrs. Inglethorp rang the bell and told me to bring her a cup of tea—nothing to eat—to the boudoir. She was looking dreadful—so white and upset. 'Dorcas,' she says, 'I've had a great shock.' 'I'm sorry for that, m'm,' I says. 'You'll feel better after a nice hot cup of tea, m'm.' She had something in her hand. I don't know if it was a letter, or just a piece of paper, but it had writing on it, and she kept staring at it, almost as if she couldn't believe what was written there. She whispered to herself, as though she had forgotten I was there: 'These few words—and everything's changed.' And then she says to me: 'Never trust a man, Dorcas, they're not worth it!' I hurried off, and got her a good strong cup of tea, and she thanked me, and said she'd feel better when she'd drunk it. 'I don't know what to do,' she says. 'Scandal between husband and wife is a dreadful thing, Dorcas. I'd rather hush it up if I could.' Mrs. Cavendish came in just then, so she didn't say any more."

"She still had the letter, or whatever it was, in her hand?"

"Yes, sir."

"What would she be likely to do with it afterwards?"

"Well, I don't know, sir, I expect she would lock it up in that purple case of hers."

"Is that where she usually kept important papers?"

"Yes, sir. She brought it down with her every morning, and took it up every night."

"When did she lose the key of it?"

"She missed it yesterday at lunch-time, sir, and told me to look carefully for it. She was very much put out about it."

"But she had a duplicate key?"

"Oh, yes, sir."

Dorcas was looking very curiously at him and, to tell the truth, so was I. What was all this about a lost key? Poirot smiled.

"Never mind, Dorcas, it is my business to know things. Is this the key that was lost?" He drew from his pocket the key that he had found in the lock of the despatch-case upstairs.

"Dorcas's eyes looked as though they would pop out of her head.

"That's it, sir, right enough. But where did you find it? I looked everywhere for it."

"Ah, but you see it was not in the same place yesterday as it was today. Now, to pass to another subject, had your mistress a dark green dress in her wardrobe?"

Dorcas was rather startled by the unexpected question.

"No, sir."

"Are you quite sure?"

"Oh, yes, sir."

"Has anyone else in the house got a green dress?"

Dorcas reflected.

"Miss Cynthia has a green evening dress."

"Light or dark green?"

"A light green, sir; a sort of chiffong, they call it."

"Ah, that is not what I want. And nobody else has anything green?"

"No, sir—not that I know of."

Poirot's face did not betray a trace of whether he was disappointed or otherwise. He merely remarked:

"Good, we will leave that and pass on. Have you any reason to believe that your mistress was likely to take a sleeping powder last night?"

"Not *last* night, sir, I know she didn't."

"Why do you know so positively?"

"Because the box was empty. She took the last one two days ago, and she didn't have any more made up."

"You are quite sure of that?"

"Positive, sir."

"Then that is cleared up! By the way, your mistress didn't ask you to sign any paper yesterday?"

"To sign a paper? No, sir."

"When Mr. Hastings and Mr. Lawrence came in yesterday evening, they found your mistress busy writing letters. I suppose you can give me no idea to whom these letters were addressed?"

"I'm afraid I couldn't, sir. I was out in the evening. Perhaps Annie could tell you, though she's a careless girl. Never cleared the coffee-cups away last night. That's what happens when I'm not here to look after things."

Poirot lifted his hand.

"Since they have been left, Dorcas, leave them a little longer, I pray you. I should like to examine them."

"Very well, sir."

"What time did you go out last evening?"

"About six o'clock, sir."

"Thank you, Dorcas, that is all I have to ask you." He rose and strolled to the window. "I have been admiring these flower beds. How many gardeners are employed here, by the way?"

"Only three now, sir. Five, we had, before the war, when it was kept as a gentleman's place should be. I wish you could have seen it then, sir. A fair sight it was. But now there's only old Manning, and young William, and a new-fashioned woman gardener in breeches and such-like. Ah, these are dreadful times!"

"The good times will come again, Dorcas. At least, we hope so. Now, will you send Annie to me here?"

"Yes, sir. Thank you, sir."

"How did you know that Mrs. Inglethorp took sleeping powders?" I asked, in lively curiosity, as Dorcas left the room. "And about the lost key and the duplicate?"

"One thing at a time. As to the sleeping powders, I knew by this." He suddenly produced a small cardboard box, such as chemists use for powders.

"Where did you find it?"

"In the wash-stand drawer in Mrs. Inglethorp's bedroom. It was Number Six of my catalogue."

"But I suppose, as the last powder was taken two days ago, it is not of much importance?"

"Probably not, but do you notice anything that strikes you as peculiar about this box?"

I examined it closely.

"No, I can't say that I do."

"Look at the label."

I read the label carefully: " 'One powder to be taken at bedtime, if required. Mrs. Inglethorp.' No, I see nothing unusual."

"Not the fact that there is no chemist's name?"

"Ah!" I exclaimed. "To be sure, that is odd!"

"Have you ever known a chemist to send out a box like that, without his printed name?"

"No, I can't say that I have."

I was becoming quite excited, but Poirot damped my ardour by remarking:

"Yet the explanation is quite simple. So do not intrigue yourself, my friend."

An audible creaking proclaimed the approach of Annie, so I had no time to reply.

Annie was a fine, strapping girl, and was evidently labouring under intense excitement, mingled with a certain ghoulish enjoyment of the tragedy.

Poirot came to the point at once, with a business-like briskness.

"I sent for you, Annie, because I thought you might be able to tell me something about the letters Mrs. Inglethorp wrote last night. How many were there? And can you tell me any of the names and addresses?"

Annie considered.

"There were four letters, sir. One was to Miss Howard, and one was to Mr. Wells, the lawyer, and the other two I don't think I remember, sir—oh, yes, one was to Ross's, the caterers in Tadminster. The other one, I don't remember."

"Think," urged Poirot.

Annie racked her brains in vain.

"I'm sorry, sir, but it's clean gone. I don't think I can have noticed it."

"It does not matter," said Poirot, not betraying any sign of disappointment. "Now I want to ask you about something else. There is a saucepan in Mrs. Inglethorp's room with some coco in it. Did she have that every night?"

"Yes, sir, it was put in her room every evening, and she warmed it up in the night—whenever she fancied it."

"What was it? Plain coco?"

"Yes, sir, made with milk, with a teaspoonful of sugar, and two teaspoonfuls of rum in it."

"Who took it to her room?"

"I did, sir."

"Always?"

"Yes, sir."

"At what time?"

"When I went to draw the curtains, as a rule, sir."

"Did you bring it straight up from the kitchen then?"

"No, sir, you see there's not much room on the gas stove, so Cook used to make it early, before putting the vegetables on for supper. Then I used to bring it up, and put it on the table by the swing door, and take it into her room later."

"The swing door is in the left wing, is it not?"

"Yes, sir."

"And the table, is it on this side of the door, or on the farther—servants' side?"

"It's this side, sir."

"What time did you bring it up last night?"

"About quarter-past seven, I should say, sir."

"And when did you take it into Mrs. Inglethorp's room?"

"When I went to shut up, sir. About eight o'clock. Mrs. Inglethorp came up to bed before I'd finished."

"Then, between 7.15 and 8 o'clock, the coco was standing on the table in the left wing?"

"Yes, sir." Annie had been growing redder and redder in the face, and now she blurted out unexpectedly:

"And if there *was* salt in it, sir, it wasn't me. I never took the salt near it."

"What makes you think there was salt in it?" asked Poirot.

"Seeing it on the tray, sir."

"You saw some salt on the tray?"

"Yes. Coarse kitchen salt, it looked. I never noticed it when I took the tray up, but when I came to take it into the mistress's room I saw it at once, and I suppose I ought to have taken it down again, and asked Cook to make some fresh. But I was in a hurry, because Dorcas was out, and I thought maybe the coco itself was all right, and the salt had only gone on the tray. So I dusted it off with my apron, and took it in."

I had the utmost difficulty in controlling my excitement. Unknown to herself, Annie had provided us with an important piece of evidence. How she would have gaped if she had realized that her "coarse kitchen salt" was strychnine, one of the most deadly poisons known to mankind. I marvelled at Poirot's calm. His self-control was astonishing. I awaited his next question with impatience, but it disappointed me.

"When you went into Mrs. Inglethorp's room, was the door leading into Miss Cynthia's room bolted?"

"Oh! Yes, sir; it always was. It had never been opened."

"And the door into Mr. Inglethorp's room? Did you notice if that was bolted too?"

Annie hesitated.

"I couldn't rightly say, sir; it was shut but I couldn't say whether it was bolted or not."

"When you finally left the room, did Mrs. Inglethorp bolt the door after you?"

"No, sir, not then, but I expect she did later. She usually did lock it at night. The door into the passage, that is."

"Did you notice any candle grease on the floor when you did the room yesterday?"

"Candle grease? Oh, no, sir. Mrs. Inglethorp didn't have a candle, only a reading-lamp."

"Then, if there had been a large patch of candle grease on the floor, you think you would have been sure to have seen it?"

"Yes, sir, and I would have taken it out with a piece of blotting-paper and a hot iron."

Then Poirot repeated the question he had put to Dorcas:

"Did your mistress ever have a green dress?"

"No, sir."

"Nor a mantle, nor a cape, nor a—how do you call it?—a sports coat?"

"Not green sir."

"Nor anyone else in the house?"

Annie reflected.

"No, sir."

"You are sure of that?"

"Quite sure."

"*Bien!* That is all I want to know. Thank you very much."

With a nervous giggle, Annie took herself creakingly out of the room. My pent up excitement burst forth.

"Poirot," I cried, "I congratulate you! This is a great discovery."

"What is a great discovery?"

"Why, that it was the coco and not the coffee that was poisoned. That explains everything! Of course it did not take effect until the early morning, since the coco was only drunk in the middle of the night."

"So you think that the coco—mark well what I say, Hastings, the *coco*—contained strychnine?"

"Of course! That salt on the tray, what else could it have been?"

"It might have been salt," replied Poirot placidly.

I shrugged my shoulders. If he was going to take the matter that way, it was no good arguing with him. The idea crossed my mind, not for the first time, that poor old Poirot was growing old. Privately I thought it lucky that he had associated with him some one of a more receptive type of mind.

Poirot was surveying me with quietly twinkling eyes.

"You are not pleased with me, *mon ami?*"

"My dear Poirot," I said coldly, "it is not for me to dictate to you. You have a right to your own opinion, just as I have to mine."

"A most admirable sentiment," remarked Poirot, rising briskly to his feet. "Now I have finished with this room. By the way, whose is the smaller desk in the corner?"

"Mr. Inglethorp's."

"Ah!" He tried the roll top tentatively. "Locked. But perhaps one of Mrs. Inglethorp's keys would open it." He tried several, twisting and turning them with a practised hand, and finally uttering an ejaculation of satisfaction. "*Voilà!* It is not the key, but it will open it at a pinch." He slid back the roll top, and ran a rapid eye over the neatly filed papers. To my surprise, he did not examine them, merely remarking approvingly as he relocked the desk: "Decidedly, he is a man of method, this Mr. Inglethorp!"

A "man of method" was, in Poirot's estimation, the highest praise that could be bestowed on any individual.

I felt that my friend was not what he had been as he rambled on disconnectedly:

"There were no stamps in his desk, but there might have been eh, *mon ami*? There might have been? Yes"—his eyes wandered round the room—"this boudoir has nothing more to tell us. It did not yield much. Only this."

He pulled a crumpled envelope out of his pocket, and tossed it over to me. It was rather a curious document. A plain, dirty looking old envelope with a few words scrawled across it, apparently at random. The following is a facsimile of it:

possessed

I am possessed

He is possessed

I am possessed

possessed

5

"It isn't Strychnine, is it?"

"Where did you find this?" I asked Poirot, in lively curiosity.

"In the waste-paper basket. You recognise the handwriting?"

"Yes, it is Mrs. Inglethorp's. But what does it mean?"

Poirot shrugged his shoulders.

"I cannot say—but it is suggestive."

A wild idea flashed across me. Was it possible that Mrs. Inglethorp's mind was deranged? Had she some fantastic idea of demoniacal possession? And, if that were so, was it not also possible that she might have taken her own life?

I was about to expound these theories to Poirot, when his own words distracted me.

"Come," he said, "now to examine the coffee-cups!"

"My dear Poirot! What on earth is the good of that, now that we know about the coco?"

"Oh, *là là!* That miserable coco!" cried Poirot flippantly.

He laughed with apparent enjoyment, raising his arms to heaven in mock despair, in what I could not but consider the worst possible taste.

"And, anyway," I said, with increasing coldness, "as Mrs. Inglethorp took her coffee upstairs with her, I do not see what you expect to find, unless you consider it likely that we shall discover a packet of strychnine on the coffee tray!"

Poirot was sobered at once.

"Come, come, my friend," he said, slipping his arm through mine. *"Ne vous fâchez pas!* Allow me to interest myself in my coffee-cups, and I will respect your coco. There! Is it a bargain?"

He was so quaintly humorous that I was forced to laugh; and we went together to the drawing-room, where the coffee-cups and tray remained undisturbed as we had left them.

Poirot made me recapitulate the scene of the night before, listening very carefully, and verifying the position of the various cups.

"So Mrs. Cavendish stood by the tray—and poured out. Yes. Then she came across to the window where you sat with Mademoiselle Cynthia. Yes. Here are the three cups. And the cup on the mantelpiece, half drunk, that would be Mr. Lawrence Cavendish's. And the one on the tray?"

"John Cavendish's. I saw him put it down there."

"Good. One, two, three, four, five—but where, then, is the cup of Mr. Inglethorp?"

"He does not take coffee."

"Then all are accounted for. One moment, my friend."

With infinite care, he took a drop or two from the grounds in each cup, sealing them up in separate test tubes, tasting each in turn as he did so. His physiognomy underwent a curious change. An expression gathered there that I can only describe as half puzzled, and half relieved.

"Bien!" he said at last. "It is evident! I had an idea—but clearly I was mistaken. Yes, altogether I was mistaken. Yet it is strange. But no matter!"

And, with a characteristic shrug, he dismissed whatever it was that was worrying him from his mind. I could have told him from the beginning that this obsession of his over the coffee was bound to end in a blind alley, but I restrained my tongue. After all, though he was old, Poirot had been a great man in his day.

"Breakfast is ready," said John Cavendish, coming in from the hall. "You will breakfast with us, Monsieur Poirot?"

Poirot acquiesced. I observed John. Already he was almost restored to his normal self. The shock of the events of the last night had upset him temporarily, but his equable poise soon swung back to the normal. He was a man of very little imagination, in sharp contrast with his brother, who had, perhaps, too much.

Ever since the early hours of the morning, John had been hard at work, sending telegrams—one of the first had gone to Evelyn Howard—writing notices for the papers, and generally occupying himself with the melancholy duties that a death entails.

"May I ask how things are proceeding?" he said. "Do your investigations point to my mother having died a natural death—or —or must we prepare ourselves for the worst?"

"I think, Mr. Cavendish," said Poirot gravely, "that you would do well not to buoy yourself up with any false hopes. Can you tell me the views of the other members of the family?"

"My brother Lawrence is convinced that we are making a fuss over nothing. He says that everything points to its being a simple case of heart failure."

"He does, does he? That is very interesting—very interesting," murmured Poirot softly. "And Mrs. Cavendish?"

A faint cloud passed over John's face.

"I have not the least idea what my wife's views on the subject are."

The answer brought a momentary stiffness in its train. John broke the rather awkward silence by saying with a slight effort:

"I told you, didn't I, that Mr. Inglethorp has returned?"

Poirot bent his head.

"It's an awkward position for all of us. Of course one has to treat him as usual—but, hang it all, one's gorge does rise at sitting down to eat with a possible murderer!"

Poirot nodded sympathetically.

"I quite understand. It is a very difficult situation for you, Mr. Cavendish. I would like to ask you one question. Mr. Inglethorp's reason for not returning last night was, I believe, that he had forgotten the latch-key. Is not that so?"

"Yes."

"I suppose you are quite sure that the latch-key *was* forgotten— that he did not take it after all?"

"I have no idea. I never thought of looking. We always keep it in the hall drawer. I'll go and see if it's there now."

Poirot held up his hand with a faint smile.

"No, no, Mr. Cavendish, it is too late now. I am certain that you would find it. If Mr. Inglethorp did take it, he has had ample time to replace it by now."

"But do you think——"

"I think nothing. If anyone had chanced to look this morning before his return, and seen it there, it would have been a valuable point in his favour. That is all."

John looked perplexed.

"Do not worry," said Poirot smoothly. "I assure you that you need not let it trouble you. Since you are so kind, let us go and have some breakfast."

Every one was assembled in the dining-room. Under the circumstances, we were naturally not a cheerful party. The reaction after a shock is always trying, and I think we were all suffering from it. Decorum and good breeding naturally enjoined that our demeanour should be much as usual, yet I could not help wondering if this self-control were really a matter of great difficulty. There were no red eyes, no signs of secretly indulged grief. I felt that I was right in my opinion that Dorcas was the person most affected by the personal side of the tragedy.

I pass over Alfred Inglethorp, who acted the bereaved widower in a manner that I felt to be disgusting in its hypocrisy. Did he know that we suspected him, I wondered. Surely he could not be unaware of the fact, conceal it as we would. Did he feel some secret stirring of fear, or was he confident that his crime would go unpunished? Surely the suspicion in the atmosphere must warn him that he was already a marked man.

But did every one suspect him? What about Mrs. Cavendish? I watched her as she sat at the head of the table, graceful, composed, enigmatic. In her soft grey frock, with white ruffles at the wrists falling over her slender hands, she looked very beautiful. When she chose, however, her face could be sphinx-like in its inscrutability. She was very silent, hardly opening her lips, and yet in some queer way I felt that the great strength of her personality was dominating us all.

And little Cynthia? Did she suspect? She looked very tired and ill, I thought. The heaviness and languor of her manner were very marked. I asked her if she were feeling ill, and she answered frankly:

"Yes, I've got the most beastly headache."

"Have another cup of coffee, mademoiselle?" said Poirot solicitously. "It will revive you. It is unparalleled for the *mal de tête*." He jumped up and took her cup.

"No sugar," said Cynthia, watching him, as he picked up the sugar-tongs.

"No sugar? You abandon it in the war-time, eh?"

"No, I never take it in coffee."

"*Sacré!*" murmured Poirot to himself, as he brought back the replenished cup.

Only I heard him, and glancing up curiously at the little man I saw that his face was working with suppressed excitement, and his eyes were as green as a cat's. He had heard or seen something that had affected him strongly—but what was it? I do not usually label myself as dense, but I must confess that nothing out of the ordinary had attracted *my* attention.

In another moment, the door opened and Dorcas appeared.

"Mr. Wells to see you, sir," she said to John.

I remembered the name as being that of the lawyer to whom Mrs. Inglethorp had written the night before.

John rose immediately.

"Show him into my study." Then he turned to us. "My mother's lawyer," he explained. And in a lower voice: "He is also Coroner—you understand. Perhaps you would like to come with me?"

We acquiesced and followed him out of the room. John strode on ahead and I took the opportunity of whispering to Poirot:

"There will be an inquest then?"

Poirot nodded absently. He seemed absorbed in thought; so much so that my curiosity was aroused.

"What is it? You are not attending to what I say."

"It is true, my friend. I am much worried."

"Why?"

"Because Mademoiselle Cynthia does not take sugar in her coffee."

"What? You cannot be serious?"

"But I am most serious. Ah, there is something there that I do not understand. My instinct was right."

"What instinct?"

"The instinct that led me to insist on examining those coffee-cups. *Chut!* no more now!"

We followed John into his study, and he closed the door behind us.

Mr. Wells was a pleasant man of middle-age, with keen eyes, and the typical lawyer's mouth. John introduced us both, and explained the reason of our presence.

"You will understand, Wells," he added, "that this is all strictly private. We are still hoping that there will turn out to be no need for investigation of any kind."

"Quite so, quite so," said Mr. Wells soothingly. "I wish we could have spared you the pain and publicity of an inquest, but of course it's quite unavoidable in the absence of a doctor's certificate."

"Yes, I suppose so."

"Clever man, Bauerstein. Great authority on toxicology, I believe."

"Indeed," said John with a certain stiffness in his manner. Then he added rather hesitatingly: "Shall we have to appear as witnesses—all of us, I mean?"

"You, of course—and ah—er—Mr.—er—Inglethorp."

A slight pause ensued before the lawyer went on in his soothing manner:

"Any other evidence will be simply confirmatory, a mere matter of form."

"I see."

A faint expression of relief swept over John's face. It puzzled me, for I saw no occasion for it.

"If you know of nothing to the contrary," pursued Mr. Wells, "I had thought of Friday. That will give us plenty of time for the doctor's report. The post-mortem is to take place to-night, I believe?"

"Yes."

"Then that arrangement will suit you?"

"Perfectly."

"I need not tell you, my dear Cavendish, how distressed I am at this most tragic affair."

"Can you give us no help in solving it, monsieur?" interposed Poirot, speaking for the first time since we had entered the room.

"I?"

"Yes, we heard that Mrs. Inglethorp wrote to you last night. You should have received the letter this morning."

"I did, but it contains no information. It is merely a note asking me to call upon her this morning, as she wanted my advice on a matter of great importance."

"She gave you no hint as to what that matter might be?"

"Unfortunately, no."

"That is a pity," said John.

"A great pity," agreed Poirot gravely.

There was silence. Poirot remained lost in thought for a few minutes. Finally he turned to the lawyer again.

"Mr. Wells, there is one thing I should like to ask you—that is, if it is not against professional etiquette. In the event of Mrs. Inglethorp's death, who would inherit her money?"

The lawyer hesitated a moment, and then replied:

"The knowledge will be public property very soon, so if Mr. Cavendish does not object——"

"Not at all," interpolated John.

"I do not see any reason why I should not answer your question. By her last will, dated August of last year, after various unimportant legacies to servants, etc., she gave her entire fortune to her stepson, Mr. John Cavendish."

"Was not that—pardon the question, Mr. Cavendish—rather unfair to her other stepson, Mr. Lawrence Cavendish?"

"No, I do not think so. You see, under the terms of their father's will, while John inherited the property, Lawrence, at his stepmother's death, would come into a considerable sum of money. Mrs. Inglethorp left her money to her elder stepson, knowing that he would have to keep up Styles. It was, to my mind, a very fair and equitable distribution."

Poirot nodded thoughtfully.

"I see. But I am right in saying, am I not, that by your English law that will was automatically revoked when Mrs. Inglethorp remarried?"

Mr. Wells bowed his head.

"As I was about to proceed, Monsieur Poirot, that document is now null and void."

"*Hein!*" said Poirot. He reflected for a moment, and then asked: "Was Mrs. Inglethorp herself aware of that fact?"

"I do not know. She may have been."

"She was," said John unexpectedly. "We were discussing the matter of wills being revoked by marriage only yesterday."

"Ah! One more question, Mr. Wells. You say 'her last will.' Had Mrs. Inglethorp, then, made several former wills?"

"On an average, she made a new will at least once a year," said Mr. Wells imperturbably. "She was given to changing her mind as to her testamentary dispositions, now benefiting one, now another member of her family."

"Suppose," suggested Poirot, "that, unknown to you, she had made a new will in favour of some one who was not, in any sense of the word, a member of the family—we will say Miss Howard, for instance—would you be surprised?"

"Not in the least."

"Ah!" Poirot seemed to have exhausted his questions.

I drew close to him, while John and the lawyer were debating the question of going through Mrs. Inglethorp's papers.

"Do you think Mrs. Inglethorp made a will leaving all her money to Miss Howard?" I asked in a low voice, with some curiosity.

Poirot smiled.

"No."

"Then why did you ask?"

"Hush!"

John Cavendish had turned to Poirot.

"Will you come with us, Monsieur Poirot? We are going through my mother's papers. Mr. Inglethorp is quite willing to leave it entirely to Mr. Wells and myself."

"Which simplifies matters very much," murmured the lawyer. "As technically, of course, he was entitled——" He did not finish the sentence.

"We will look through the desk in the boudoir first," explained John, "and go up to her bedroom afterwards. She kept her most important papers in a purple despatch-case, which we must look through carefully."

"Yes," said the lawyer, "it is quite possible that there may be a later will than the one in my possession."

"There *is* a later will." It was Poirot who spoke.

"What?" John and the lawyer looked at him startled.

"Or, rather," pursued my friend imperturbably, "there *was* one."

"What do you mean—there was one? Where is it now?"

"Burnt!"

"Burnt?"

"Yes. See here." He took out the charred fragment we had found in the grate in Mrs. Inglethorp's room, and handed it to the lawyer with a brief explanation of when and where he had found it.

"But possibly this is an old will?"

"I do not think so. In fact I am almost certain that it was made no earlier than yesterday afternoon."

"What?" "Impossible!" broke simultaneously from both men. Poirot turned to John.

"If you will allow me to send for your gardener, I will prove it to you."

"Oh, of course—but I don't see——"

Poirot raised his hand.

"Do as I ask you. Afterwards you shall question as much as you please."

"Very well." He rang the bell.

Dorcas answered it in due course.

"Dorcas, will you tell Manning to come round and speak to me here."

"Yes, sir."

Dorcas withdrew.

We waited in a tense silence. Poirot alone seemed perfectly at his ease, and dusted a forgotten corner of the bookcase.

The clumping of hobnailed boots on the gravel outside proclaimed the approach of Manning. John looked questioningly at Poirot. The latter nodded.

"Come inside, Manning," said John, "I want to speak to you."

Manning came slowly and hesitatingly through the French window, and stood as near it as he could. He held his cap in his hands, twisting it very carefully round and round. His back was much bent, though he was probably not as old as he looked, but his eyes were sharp and intelligent, and belied his slow and rather cautious speech.

"Manning," said John, "this gentleman will put some questions to you which I want you to answer."

"Yessir," mumbled Manning.

Poirot stepped forward briskly. Manning's eye swept over him with a faint contempt.

"You were planting a bed of begonias round by the south side of the house yesterday afternoon, were you not, Manning?"

"Yes, sir, me and Willum."

"And Mrs. Inglethorp came to the window and called you, did she not?"

"Yes, sir, she did."

"Tell me in your own words exactly what happened after that."

"Well, sir, nothing much. She just told Willum to go on his bicycle down to the village, and bring back a form of will, or such-like—I don't know what exactly—she wrote it down for him."

"Well?"

"Well, he did, sir."

"And what happened next?"

"We went on with the begonias, sir."

"Did not Mrs. Inglethorp call you again?"

"Yes, sir, both me and Willum, she called."

"And then?"

"She made us come right in, and sign our names at the bottom of a long paper—under where she'd signed."

"Did you see anything of what was written above her signature?" asked Poirot sharply.

"No, sir, there was a bit of blotting-paper over that part."

"And you signed where she told you?"

"Yes, sir, first me and then Willum."

"What did she do with it afterwards?"

"Well, sir, she slipped it into a long envelope, and put it inside a sort of purple box that was standing on the desk."

"What time was it when she first called you?"

"About four, I should say, sir."

"Not earlier? Couldn't it have been about half-past three?"

"No, I shouldn't say so, sir. It would be more likely to be a bit after four—not before it."

"Thank you, Manning, that will do," said Poirot pleasantly.

The gardener glanced at his master, who nodded, whereupon Manning lifted a finger to his forehead with a low mumble, and backed cautiously out of the window.

We all looked at each other.

"Good heavens!" murmured John. "What an extraordinary coincidence."

"How—a coincidence?"

"That my mother should have made a will on the very day of her death!"

Mr. Wells cleared his throat and remarked drily:

"Are you so sure it is a coincidence, Cavendish?"

"What do you mean?"

"Your mother, you tell me, had a violent quarrel with—some one yesterday afternoon——"

"What do you mean?" cried John again. There was a tremor in his voice, and he had gone very pale.

"In consequence of that quarrel, your mother very suddenly and hurriedly makes a new will. The contents of that will we shall never know. She told no one of its provisions. This morning, no doubt, she would have consulted me on the subject—but she had no chance. The will disappears, and she takes its secret with her to her grave. Cavendish, I much fear there is no coincidence there. Monsieur Poirot, I am sure you agree with me that the facts are very suggestive."

"Suggestive, or not," interrupted John, "we are most grateful to Monsieur Poirot for elucidating the matter. But for him, we should never have known of this will. I suppose, I may not ask you, monsieur, what first led you to suspect the fact?"

Poirot smiled and answered:

"A scribbled over old envelope, and a freshly planted bed of begonias."

John, I think, would have pressed his questions further, but at that moment the loud purr of a motor was audible, and we all turned to the window as it swept past.

"Evie!" cried John. "Excuse me, Wells." He went hurriedly out into the hall.

Poirot looked inquiringly at me.

"Miss Howard," I explained.

"Ah, I am glad she has come. There is a woman with a head and a heart too, Hastings. Though the good God gave her no beauty!"

I followed John's example, and went out into the hall, where Miss Howard was endeavouring to extricate herself from the voluminous mass of veils that enveloped her head. As her eyes fell on me, a sudden pang of guilt shot through me. This was the woman who had warned me so earnestly, and to whose warning I had, alas, paid no heed! How soon, and how contemptuously, I had dismissed it from my mind. Now that she had been proved justified in so tragic a manner, I felt ashamed. She had known Alfred Inglethorp only too well. I wondered whether, if she had remained at Styles, the tragedy would have taken place, or would the man have feared her watchful eyes?

I was relieved when she shook me by the hand, with her well remembered painful grip. The eyes that met mine were sad, but not reproachful; that she had been crying bitterly, I could tell by the redness of her eyelids, but her manner was unchanged from its old blunt gruffness.

"Started the moment I got the wire. Just come off night duty. Hired car. Quickest way to get here."

"Have you had anything to eat this morning, Evie?" asked John.

"No."

"I thought not. Come along, breakfast's not cleared away yet, and they'll make you some fresh tea." He turned to me. "Look after her, Hastings, will you? Wells is waiting for me. Oh, here's Monsieur Poirot. He's helping us, you know, Evie."

Miss Howard shook hands with Poirot, but glanced suspiciously over her shoulder at John.

"What do you mean—helping us?"

"Helping us to investigate."

"Nothing to investigate. Have they taken him to prison yet?"

"Taken who to prison?"

"Who? Alfred Inglethorp, of course!"

"My dear Evie, do be careful. Lawrence is of the opinion that my mother died from heart seizure."

"More fool, Lawrence!" retorted Miss Howard. "Of course Alfred Inglethorp murdered poor Emily—as I always told you he would."

"My dear Evie, don't shout so. Whatever we may think or suspect, it is better to say as little as possible for the present. The inquest isn't until Friday."

"Not until fiddlesticks!" The snort Miss Howard gave was truly magnificent. "You're all off your heads. The man will be out of the country by then. If he's any sense, he won't stay here tamely and wait to be hanged."

John Cavendish looked at her helplessly.

"I know what it is," she accused him, "you've been listening to the doctors. Never should. What do they know? Nothing at all—or just enough to make them dangerous. I ought to know—my own father was a doctor. That little Wilkins is about the greatest fool that even I have ever seen. Heart seizure! Sort of thing he would say. Anyone with any sense could see at once that her husband had poisoned her. I always said he'd murder her in her bed, poor soul. Now he's done it. And all you can do is to murmur silly things about 'heart seizure' and 'inquest on Friday.' You ought to be ashamed of yourself, John Cavendish."

"What do you want me to do?" asked John, unable to help a faint smile. "Dash it all, Evie, I can't haul him down to the local police station by the scruff of his neck."

"Well, you might do something. Find out how he did it. He's a crafty beggar. Dare say he soaked fly papers. Ask Cook if she's missed any."

It occurred to me very forcibly at that moment that to harbour Miss Howard and Alfred Inglethorp under the same roof, and keep the peace between them, was likely to prove a Herculean task, and I did not envy John. I could see by the expression of his face that he fully appreciated the difficulty of the position. For the moment, he sought refuge in retreat, and left the room precipitately.

Dorcas brought in fresh tea. As she left the room, Poirot came over from the window where he had been standing, and sat down facing Miss Howard.

"Mademoiselle," he said gravely, "I want to ask you something."

"Ask away," said the lady, eyeing him with some disfavour.

"I want to be able to count upon your help."

"I'll help you to hang Alfred with pleasure," she replied gruffly. "Hanging's too good for him. Ought to be drawn and quartered, like in good old times."

"We are at one then," said Poirot, "for I, too, want to hang the criminal."

"Alfred Inglethorp?"

"Him, or another."

"No question of another. Poor Emily was never murdered until *he* came along. I don't say she wasn't surrounded by sharks —she was. But it was only her purse they were after. Her life was safe enough. But along comes Mr. Alfred Inglethorp—and within two months—hey presto!"

"Believe me, Miss Howard," said Poirot very earnestly, "if Mr.

Inglethorp is the man, he shall not escape me. On my honour, I will hang him as high as Haman!"

"That's better," said Miss Howard more enthusiastically.

"But I must ask you to trust me. Now your help may be very valuable to me. I will tell you why. Because, in all this house of mourning, yours are the only eyes that have wept."

Miss Howard blinked, and a new note crept into the gruffness of her voice.

"If you mean that I was fond of her—yes, I was. You know, Emily was a selfish old woman in her way. She was very generous, but she always wanted a return. She never let people forget what she had done for them—and, that way, she missed love. Don't think she ever realized it, though, or felt the lack of it. Hope not, anyway. I was on a different footing. I took my stand from the first. 'So many pounds a year I'm worth to you. Well and good. But not a penny piece besides—not a pair of gloves, nor a theatre ticket.' She didn't understand—was very offended sometimes. Said I was foolishly proud. It wasn't that—but I couldn't explain. Anyway, I kept my self-respect. And so, out of the whole bunch, I was the only one who could allow myself to be fond of her. I watched over her. I guarded her from the lot of them. And then a glib-tongued scoundrel comes along, and pooh! all my years of devotion go for nothing."

Poirot nodded sympathetically.

"I understand, mademoiselle, I understand all you feel. It is most natural. You think that we are lukewarm—that we lack fire and energy—but trust me, it is not so."

John stuck his head in at this juncture, and invited us both to come up to Mrs. Inglethorp's room, as he and Mr. Wells had finished looking through the desk in the boudoir."

As we went up the stairs, John looked back to the dining-room door, and lowered his voice confidentially:

"Look here, what's going to happen when these two meet?"

I shook my head helplessly.

"I've told Mary to keep them apart if she can."

"Will she be able to do so?"

"The Lord only knows. There's one thing, Inglethorp himself won't be too keen on meeting her."

"You've got the keys still, haven't you, Poirot?" I asked, as we reached the door of the locked room.

Taking the keys from Poirot, John unlocked it, and we all passed in. The lawyer went straight to the desk, and John followed him.

"My mother kept most of her important papers in this despatch-case, I believe," he said.

Poirot drew out the small bunch of keys.

"Permit me. I locked it, out of precaution, this morning."

"But it's not locked now."

"Impossible!"

"See." And John lifted the lid as he spoke.

"*Milles tonnerres!*" cried Poirot, dumbfounded. "And I—who have both the keys in my pocket!" He flung himself upon the case. Suddenly he stiffened. "*En voilà une affaire!* This lock has been forced!"

"What?"

Poirot laid down the case again.

"But who forced it? Why should they? When? But the door was locked?" These exclamations burst from us disjointedly.

Poirot answered them categorically—almost mechanically.

"Who? That is the question. Why? Ah, if I only knew. When? Since I was here an hour ago. As to the door being locked, it is a very ordinary lock. Probably any other of the doorkeys in this passage would fit it."

We stared at one another blankly. Poirot had walked over to the mantelpiece. He was outwardly calm, but I noticed his hands, which from long force of habit were mechanically straightening the spill vases on the mantelpiece, were shaking violently.

"See here, it was like this," he said at last. "There was something in that case—some piece of evidence, slight in itself perhaps, but still enough of a clue to connect the murderer with the crime. It was vital to him that it should be destroyed before it was discovered and its significance appreciated. Therefore, he took the risk, the great risk, of coming in here. Finding the case locked, he was obliged to force it, thus betraying his presence. For him to take that risk, it must have been something of great importance."

"But what was it?"

"Ah!" cried Poirot, with a gesture of anger. "That, I do not know! A document of some kind, without doubt, possibly the scrap of paper Dorcas saw in her hand yesterday afternoon. And I—" his anger burst forth freely—"miserable animal that I am! I guessed nothing! I have behaved like an imbecile! I should never have left that case here. I should have carried it away with me. Ah, triple pig! And now it is gone. It is destroyed—but is it destroyed? Is there not yet a chance—we must leave no stone unturned—"

He rushed like a madman from the room, and I followed him as soon as I had sufficiently recovered my wits. But, by the time I had reached the top of the stairs, he was out of sight.

Mary Cavendish was standing where the staircase branched, staring down into the hall in the direction in which he had disappeared.

"What has happened to your extraordinary little friend, Mr. Hastings? He has just rushed past me like a mad bull."

"He's rather upset about something," I remarked feebly. I really did not know how much Poirot would wish me to disclose. As I saw a faint smile gather on Mrs. Cavendish's expressive mouth, I endeavoured to try and turn the conversation by saying: "They haven't met yet, have they?"

"Who?"

"Mr. Inglethorp and Miss Howard."

She looked at me in rather a disconcerting manner.

"Do you think it would be such a disaster if they did meet?"

"Well, don't you?" I said, rather taken aback.

"No." She was smiling in her quiet way. "I should like to see a good flare up. It would clear the air. At present we are all thinking so much, and saying so little."

"John doesn't think so," I remarked. "He's anxious to keep them apart."

"Oh, John!"

Something in her tone fired me, and I blurted out:

"Old John's an awfully good sort."

She studied me curiously for a minute or two, and then said, to my great surprise:

"You are loyal to your friend. I like you for that."

"Aren't you my friend too?"

"I am a very bad friend."

"Why do you say that?"

"Because it is true. I am charming to my friends one day, and forget all about them the next."

I don't know what impelled me, but I was nettled, and I said foolishly and not in the best of taste:

"Yet you seem to be invariably charming to Dr. Bauerstein!"

Instantly I regretted my words. Her face stiffened. I had the impression of a steel curtain coming down and blotting out the real woman. Without a word, she turned and went swiftly up the stairs, whilst I stood like an idiot gaping after her.

I was recalled to other matters by a frightful row going on below. I could hear Poirot shouting and expounding. I was vexed to think that my diplomacy had been in vain. The little man appeared to be taking the whole house into his confidence, a proceeding of which I, for one, doubted the wisdom. Once again I could not help regretting that my friend was so prone to lose his head in moments of excitement. I stepped briskly down the stairs. The sight of me calmed Poirot almost immediately. I drew him aside.

"My dear fellow," I said, "is this wise? Surely you don't want the whole house to know of this occurrence? You are actually playing into the criminal's hands."

"You think so, Hastings?"

"I am sure of it."

"Well, well, my friend, I will be guided by you."

"Good. Although, unfortunately, it is a little too late now."

"True."

He looked so crestfallen and abashed that I felt quite sorry, though I still thought my rebuke a just and wise one.

"Well," he said at last, "let us go, *mon ami.*"

"You have finished here?"

"For the moment, yes. You will walk back with me to the village?"

"Willingly."

He picked up his little suit-case, and we went out through the open window in the drawing-room. Cynthia Murdoch was just coming in, and Poirot stood aside to let her pass.

"Excuse me, mademoiselle, one minute."

"Yes?" she turned inquiringly.

"Did you ever make up Mrs. Inglethorp's medicines?"

A slight flush rose in her face, as she answered rather constrainedly:

"No."

"Only her powders?"

The flush deepened as Cynthia replied:

"Oh, yes, I did make up some sleeping powders for her once."

"These?"

Poirot produced the empty box which had contained powders. She nodded.

"Can you tell me what they were? Sulphonal? Veronal?"

"No, they were bromide powders."

"Ah! Thank you, mademoiselle; good morning."

As we walked briskly away from the house, I glanced at him more than once. I had often before noticed that, if anything excited him, his eyes turned green like a cat's. They were shining like emeralds now.

"My friend," he broke out at last, "I have a little idea, a very strange, and probably utterly impossible idea. And yet—it fits in."

I shrugged my shoulders. I privately thought that Poirot was rather too much given to these fantastic ideas. In this case, surely, the truth was only too plain and apparent.

"So that is the explanation of the blank label on the box," I remarked. "Very simple, as you said. I really wonder that I did not think of it myself."

Poirot did not appear to be listening to me.

"They have made one more discovery, là-bas," he observed, jerking his thumb over his shoulder in the direction of Styles. "Mr. Wells told me as we were going upstairs."

"What was it?"

"Locked up in the desk in the boudoir, they found a will of Mrs. Inglethorp's, dated before her marriage, leaving her fortune to Alfred Inglethorp. It must have been made just at the time they were engaged. It came quite as a surprise to Wells—and to John Cavendish also. It was written on one of those printed will forms, and witnessed by two of the servants—not Dorcas."

"Did Mr. Inglethorp know of it?"

"He says not."

"One might take that with a grain of salt," I remarked sceptically. "All these wills are very confusing. Tell me, how did those scribbled words on the envelope help you to discover that a will was made yesterday afternoon?"

Poirot smiled.

"*Mon ami,* have you ever, when writing a letter, been arrested by the fact that you did not know how to spell a certain word?"

"Yes, often. I suppose every one has."

"Exactly. And have you not, in such a case, tried the word once or twice on the edge of the blotting-paper, or a spare scrap of paper, to see if it looked right? Well, that is what Mrs. Inglethorp did. You will notice that the word 'possessed' is spelt first with one 's' and subsequently with two—correctly. To make sure, she had further tried it in a sentence, thus: 'I am possessed.' Now, what did that tell me? It told me that Mrs. Inglethorp had been writing the word 'possessed' that afternoon, and, having the fragment of paper found in the grate fresh in my mind, the possibility of a will—(a document almost certain to contain that word) —occurred to me at once. This possibility was confirmed by a further circumstance. In the general confusion, the boudoir had not been swept that morning, and near the desk were several traces of brown mould and earth. The weather had been perfectly fine for some days, and no ordinary boots would have left such a heavy deposit.

"I strolled to the window, and saw at once that the begonia beds had been newly planted. The mould in the beds was exactly similar to that on the floor of the boudoir, and also I learnt from you that they *had* been planted yesterday afternoon. I was now sure that one, or possibly both of the gardeners—for there were two sets of footprints in the bed—had entered the boudoir, for if Mrs. Inglethorp had merely wished to speak to them she would in all probability have stood at the window, and they would not have come into the room at all. I was now quite convinced that she had made a fresh will, and had called the two gardeners in to witness her signature. Events proved that I was right in my supposition."

"That was very ingenious," I could not help admitting. "I must confess that the conclusions I drew from those few scribbled words were quite erroneous."

He smiled.

"You gave too much rein to your imagination. Imagination is a good servant, and a bad master. The simplest explanation is always the most likely."

"Another point—how did you know that the key of the despatch-case had been lost?"

"I did not know it. It was a guess that turned out to be correct. You observed that it had a piece of twisted wire through the handle. That suggested to me at once that it had possibly been wrenched off a flimsy key-ring. Now, if it had been lost and recovered, Mrs. Inglethorp would at once have replaced it on her bunch; but on her bunch I found what was obviously the duplicate key, very new and bright, which led me to the hypothesis that somebody else had inserted the original key in the lock of the despatch-case."

"Yes," I said, "Alfred Inglethorp, without doubt."

Poirot looked at me curiously.

"You are very sure of his guilt?"

"Well, naturally. Every fresh circumstance seems to establish it more clearly."

"On the contrary," said Poirot quietly, "there are several points in his favour."

"Oh, come now!"

"Yes."

"I see only one."

"And that?"

"That he was not in the house last night."

"'Bad shot!' as you English say! You have chosen the one point that to my mind tells against him."

"How is that?"

"Because if Mr. Inglethorp knew that his wife would be poisoned last night, he would certainly have arranged to be away from the house. His excuse was an obviously trumped up one. That leaves us two possibilities: either he knew what was going to happen or he had a reason of his own for his absence."

"And that reason?" I asked sceptically.

Poirot shrugged his shoulders.

"How should I know? Discreditable, without doubt. This Mr. Inglethorp, I should say, is somewhat of a scoundrel—but that does not of necessity make him a murderer."

I shook my head, unconvinced.

"We do not agree, eh?" said Poirot. "Well, let us leave it. Time will show which of us is right. Now let us turn to other aspects of the case. What do you make of the fact that all the doors of the bedroom were bolted on the inside?"

"Well——" I considered. "One must look at it logically."

"True."

"I should put it this way. The doors *were* bolted—our own eyes have told us that—yet the presence of the candle grease on the floor, and the destruction of the will, prove that during the night some one entered the room. You agree so far?"

"Perfectly. Put with admirable clearness. Proceed."

"Well," I said, encouraged, "as the person who entered did not do so by the window, nor by miraculous means, it follows that the door must have been opened from inside by Mrs. Inglethorp herself. That strengthens the conviction that the person in question was her husband. She would naturally open the door to her own husband."

Poirot shook his head.

"Why should she? She had bolted the door leading into his room—a most unusual proceeding on her part—she had had a most violent quarrel with him that very afternoon. No, he was the last person she would admit."

"But you agree with me that the door must have been opened by Mrs. Inglethorp herself?"

"There is another possibility. She may have forgotten to bolt the door into the passage when she went to bed, and have got up later, towards morning, and bolted it then."

"Poirot, is that seriously your opinion?"

"No, I do not say it is so, but it might be. Now, to turn to another feature, what do you make of the scrap of conversation you overheard between Mrs. Cavendish and her mother-in-law?"

"I had forgotten that," I said thoughtfully. "That is as enigmatical as ever. It seems incredible that a woman like Mrs. Cavendish, proud and reticent to the last degree, should interfere so violently in what was certainly not her affair."

"Precisely. It was an astonishing thing for a woman of her breeding to do."

"It is certainly curious," I agreed. "Still, it is unimportant, and need not be taken into account."

A groan burst from Poirot.

"What have I always told you? Everything must be taken into account. If the fact will not fit the theory—let the theory go."

"Well, we shall see," I said, nettled.

"Yes, we shall see."

We had reached Leastways Cottage, and Poirot ushered me upstairs to his own room. He offered me one of the tiny Russian cigarettes he himself occasionally smoked. I was amused to notice that he stowed away the used matches most carefully in a little china pot. My momentary annoyance vanished.

Poirot had placed our two chairs in front of the open window which commanded a view of the village street. The fresh air blew in warm and pleasant. It was going to be a hot day.

Suddenly my attention was arrested by a weedy looking young man rushing down the street at a great pace. It was the expression on his face that was extraordinary—a curious mingling of terror and agitation.

"Look, Poirot!" I said.

He leant forward.

"Tiens!" he said. "It is Mr. Mace, from the chemist's shop. He is coming here."

The young man came to a halt before Leastways Cottage, and, after hesitating a moment, pounded vigorously at the door.

"A little minute," cried Poirot from the window. "I come."

Motioning to me to follow him, he ran swiftly down the stairs and opened the door. Mr. Mace began at once.

"Oh, Mr. Poirot, I'm sorry for the inconvenience, but I heard that you'd just come back from the Hall?"

"Yes, we have."

The young man moistened his dry lips. His face was working curiously.

"It's all over the village about old Mrs. Inglethorp dying so suddenly. They do say——" he lowered his voice cautiously—"that it's poison?"

Poirot's face remained quite impassive.

"Only the doctors can tell us that, Mr. Mace."

"Yes, exactly—of course——" The young man hesitated, and then his agitation was too much for him. He clutched Poirot by the arm, and sank his voice to a whisper: "Just tell me this, Mr. Poirot, it isn't—it isn't strychnine, is it?"

I hardly heard what Poirot replied. Something evidently of a non-committal nature. The young man departed, and as he closed the door Poirot's eyes met mine.

"Yes," he said nodding gravely. "He will have evidence to give at the inquest."

We went slowly upstairs again. I was opening my lips, when Poirot stopped me with a gesture of his hand.

"Not now, not now, *mon ami*. I have need of reflection. My mind is in some disorder—which is not well."

For about ten minutes he sat in dead silence, perfectly still, except for several expressive motions of his eyebrows, and all the time his eyes grew steadily greener. At last he heaved a deep sigh.

"It is well. The bad moment has passed. Now all is arranged and classified. One must never permit confusion. The case is not clear yet—no. For it is of the most complicated! It puzzles *me*. *Me*, Hercule Poirot! There are two facts of significance."

"And what are they?"

"The first is the state of the weather yesterday. That is very important."

"But it was a glorious day!" I interrupted. "Poirot, you're pulling my leg!"

"Not at all. The thermometer registered 80° in the shade. Do not forget that, my friend. It is the key to the whole riddle!"

"And the second point?" I asked.

"The important fact that Monsieur Inglethorp wears very peculiar clothes, has a black beard, and uses glasses."

"Poirot, I cannot believe you are serious."

"I am absolutely serious, my friend."

"But this is childish!"

"No, it is very momentous."

"And supposing the Coroner's jury returns a verdict of Wilful Murder against Alfred Inglethorp. What becomes of your theories, then?"

"They would not be shaken because twelve stupid men had happened to make a mistake! But that will not occur. For one thing, a country jury is not anxious to take responsibility upon itself, and Mr. Inglethorp stands practically in the position of local squire. Also," he added placidly, "*I* should not allow it!"

"*You* would not allow it?"

"No."

I looked at the extraordinary little man, divided between annoyance and amusement. He was so tremendously sure of himself. As though he read my thoughts, he nodded gently.

"Oh, yes, *mon ami*, I would do what I say." He got up and laid his hand on my shoulder. His physiognomy underwent a complete change. Tears came into his eyes. "In all this, you see, I think of that poor Mrs. Inglethorp who is dead. She was not extravagantly loved—no. But she was very good to us Belgians—I owe her a debt."

I endeavoured to interrupt, but Poirot swept on.

"Let me tell you this, Hastings. She would never forgive me if I let Alfred Inglethorp, her husband, be arrested *now*—when a word from me could save him!"

6

The Inquest

In the interval before the inquest, Poirot was unfailing in his activity. Twice he was closeted with Mr. Wells. He also took long walks into the country. I rather resented his not taking me into his confidence, the more so as I could not in the least guess what he was driving at.

It occurred to me that he might have been making inquiries at Raikes's farm; so, finding him out when I called at Leastways Cottage on Wednesday evening, I walked over there by the fields, hoping to meet him. But there was no sign of him, and I hesitated to go right up to the farm itself. As I walked away, I met an aged rustic, who leered at me cunningly.

"You'm from the Hall, bain't you?" he asked.

"Yes. I'm looking for a friend of mine whom I thought might have walked this way."

"A little chap? As waves his hands when he talks? One of them Belgies from the village?"

"Yes," I said eagerly. "He has been here, then?"

"Oh, ay, he's been here, right enough. More'n once too. Friend of yours, is he? Ah, you gentlemen from the Hall—you'n a pretty lot!" And he leered more jocosely than ever.

"Why, do the gentlemen from the Hall come here often?" I asked, as carelessly as I could.

He winked at me knowingly.

"*One* does, mister. Naming no names, mind. And a very liberal gentleman too! Oh, thank you, sir, I'm sure."

I walked on sharply. Evelyn Howard had been right then, and I experienced a sharp twinge of disgust, as I thought of Alfred Inglethorp's liberality with another woman's money. Had that piquant gipsy face been at the bottom of the crime, or was it the baser mainspring of money? Probably a judicious mixture of both.

On one point, Poirot seemed to have a curious obsession. He once or twice observed to me that he thought Dorcas must have made an error in fixing the time of the quarrel. He suggested to her repeatedly that it was 4.30, and not 4 o'clock when she had heard the voices.

But Dorcas was unshaken. Quite an hour, or even more, had elapsed between the time when she had heard the voices and 5 o'clock, when she had taken tea to her mistress.

The inquest was held on Friday at the Stylites Arms in the village. Poirot and I sat together, not being required to give evidence.

The preliminaries were gone through. The jury viewed the body, and John Cavendish gave evidence of identification.

Further questioned, he described his awakening in the early hours of the morning, and the circumstances of his mother's death.

The medical evidence was next taken. There was a breathless hush, and every eye was fixed on the famous London specialist, who was known to be one of the greatest authorities of the day on the subject of toxicology.

In a few brief words, he summed up the result of the post-mortem. Shorn of its medical phraseology and technicalities, it amounted to the fact that Mrs. Inglethorp had met her death as the result of strychnine poisoning. Judging from the quantity recovered, she must have taken not less than three-quarters of a grain of strychnine, but probably one grain or slightly over.

"Is it possible, that she could have swallowed the poison by accident?" asked the Coroner.

"I should consider it very unlikely. Strychnine is not used for domestic purposes, as some poisons are, and there are restrictions placed on its sale."

"Does anything in your examination lead you to determine how the poison was administered?"

"No."

"You arrived at Styles before Dr. Wilkins, I believe?"

"That is so. The motor met me just outside the lodge gates, and I hurried there as fast as I could."

"Will you relate to us exactly what happened next?"

"I entered Mrs. Inglethorp's room. She was at that moment in a typical tetanic convulsion. She turned towards me, and gasped out: 'Alfred—Alfred——'"

"Could the strychnine have been administered in Mrs. Inglethorp's after-dinner coffee which was taken to her by her husband?"

"Possibly, but strychnine is a fairly rapid drug in its action. The symptoms appear from one to two hours after it has been swallowed. It is retarded under certain conditions, none of which, however, appear to have been present in this case. I presume Mrs. Inglethorp took the coffee after dinner about eight o'clock, whereas the symptoms did not manifest themselves until the early hours of the morning, which, on the face of it, points to the drug having been taken much later in the evening."

"Mrs. Inglethorp was in the habit of drinking a cup of coco in the middle of the night. Could the strychnine have been administered in that?"

"No, I myself took a sample of the coco remaining in the saucepan and had it analysed. There was no strychnine present."

I heard Poirot chuckle softly beside me.

"How did you know?" I whispered.

"Listen."

"I should say"—the doctor was continuing—"that I would have been considerably surprised at any other result."

"Why?"

"Simply because strychnine has an unusually bitter taste. It can be detected in a solution of 1 in 70,000, and can only be disguised by some strongly flavoured substance. Coco would be quite powerless to mask it."

One of the jury wanted to know if the same objection applied to coffee.

"No. Coffee has a bitter taste of its own which would probably cover the taste of the strychnine."

"Then you consider it more likely that the drug was administered in the coffee, but that for some unknown reason its action was delayed."

"Yes, but, the cup being completely smashed, there is no possibility of analyzing its contents."

This concluded Dr. Bauerstein's evidence. Dr. Wilkins corroborated it on all points. Sounded as to the possibility of suicide, he repudiated it utterly. The deceased, he said, suffered from a weak heart, but otherwise enjoyed perfect health, and was of a cheerful and well balanced disposition. She would be one of the last people to take her own life.

Lawrence Cavendish was next called. His evidence was quite unimportant, being a mere repetition of that of his brother. Just as he was about to step down, he paused, and said rather hesitatingly:

"I should like to make a suggestion if I may?"

He glanced deprecatingly at the Coroner, who replied briskly:

"Certainly, Mr. Cavendish, we are here to arrive at the truth of this matter, and welcome anything that may lead to further elucidation."

"It is just an idea of mine," explained Lawrence. "Of course I may be quite wrong, but it still seems to me that my mother's death might be accounted for by natural means."

"How do you make that out, Mr. Cavendish?"

"My mother, at the time of her death, and for some time before it, was taking a tonic containing strychnine."

"Ah!" said the Coroner.

The jury looked up, interested.

"I believe," continued Lawrence, "that there have been cases where the cumulative effect of a drug, administered for some time, has ended by causing death. Also, is it not possible that she may have taken an overdose of her medicine by accident?"

"This is the first we have heard of the deceased taking strychnine at the time of her death. We are much obliged to you, Mr. Cavendish."

Dr. Wilkins was recalled and ridiculed the idea.

"What Mr. Cavendish suggests is quite impossible. Any doctor would tell you the same. Strychnine is, in a certain sense, a cumulative poison, but it would be quite impossible for it to result in sudden death in this way. There would have to be a long period of chronic symptoms which would at once have attracted my attention. The whole thing is absurd."

"And the second suggestion? That Mrs. Inglethorp may have inadvertently taken an overdose?"

"Three, or even four doses, would not have resulted in death. Mrs. Inglethorp always had an extra large amount of medicine made up at a time, as she dealt with Coot's, the Cash Chemists in Tadminster. She would have had to take very nearly the whole bottle to account for the amount of strychnine found at the post-mortem."

"Then you consider that we may dismiss the tonic as not being in any way instrumental in causing her death?"

"Certainly. The supposition is ridiculous."

The same juryman who had interrupted before here suggested that the chemist who made up the medicine might have committed an error.

"That, of course, is always possible," replied the doctor.

But Dorcas, who was the next witness called, dispelled even that possibility. The medicine had not been newly made up. On the contrary, Mrs. Inglethorp had taken the last dose on the day of her death.

So the question of the tonic was finally abandoned, and the Coroner proceeded with his task. Having elicited from Dorcas how she had been awakened by the violent ringing of her mistress's bell, and had subsequently roused the household, he passed to the subject of the quarrel on the preceding afternoon.

Dorcas's evidence on this point was substantially what Poirot and I had already heard, so I will not repeat it here.

The next witness was Mary Cavendish. She stood very upright, and spoke in a low, clear, and perfectly composed voice. In answer to the Coroner's question, she told how, her alarm clock having aroused her at 4.30 as usual, she was dressing, when she was startled by the sound of something heavy falling.

"That would have been the table by the bed?" commented the Coroner.

"I opened my door," continued Mary, "and listened. In a few minutes a bell rang violently. Dorcas came running down and woke my husband, and we all went to my mother-in-law's room, but it was locked——"

The Coroner interrupted her.

"I really do not think we need trouble you further on that point. We know all that can be known of the subsequent happenings. But I should be obliged if you would tell us all you overheard of the quarrel the day before."

"I?"

There was a faint insolence in her voice. She raised her hand and adjusted the ruffle of lace at her neck, turning her head a little as she did so. And quite spontaneously the thought flashed across my mind: "She is gaining time!"

"Yes. I understand," continued the Coroner deliberately, "that you were sitting reading on the bench just outside the long window of the boudoir. That is so, is it not?"

This was news to me and glancing sideways at Poirot, I fancied that it was news to him as well.

There was the faintest pause, the mere hesitation of a moment, before she answered:

"Yes, that is so."

"And the boudoir window was open, was it not?"

Surely her face grew a little paler as she answered:

"Yes."

"Then you cannot have failed to hear the voices inside, especially as they were raised in anger. In fact, they would be more audible where you were than in the hall."

"Possibly."

"Will you repeat to us what you overheard of the quarrel?"

"I really do not remember hearing anything."

"Do you mean to say you did not hear voices?"

"Oh, yes, I heard the voices, but I did not hear what they said." A faint spot of colour came into her cheek. "I am not in the habit of listening to private conversations."

The Coroner persisted.

"And you remember nothing at all? *Nothing,* Mrs. Cavendish? Not one stray word or phrase to make you realize that it *was* a private conversation?"

She paused, and seemed to reflect, still outwardly as calm as ever.

"Yes; I remember, Mrs. Inglethorp said something—I do not remember exactly what—about causing scandal between husband and wife."

"Ah!" the Coroner leant back satisfied. "That corresponds with what Dorcas heard. But excuse me, Mrs. Cavendish, although you realized it was a private conversation, you did not move away? You remained where you were?"

I caught the momentary gleam of her tawny eyes as she raised them. I felt certain that at that moment she would willingly have torn the little lawyer, with his insinuations, into pieces, but she replied quietly enough:

"No. I was very comfortable where I was. I fixed my mind on my book."

"And that is all you can tell us?"

"That is all."

The examination was over, though I doubted if the Coroner was entirely satisfied with it. I think he suspected that Mary Cavendish could tell more if she chose.

Amy Hill, shop assistant, was next called, and deposed to having sold a will form on the afternoon of the 17th to William Earl, under-gardener at Styles.

William Earl and Manning succeeded her, and testified to witnessing a document. Manning fixed the time at about 4.30, William was of the opinion that it was rather earlier.

Cynthia Murdoch came next. She had, however, little to tell. She had known nothing of the tragedy, until awakened by Mrs. Cavendish.

"You did not hear the table fall?"

"No. I was fast asleep."

The Coroner smiled.

"A good conscience makes a sound sleeper," he observed. "Thank you, Miss Murdoch, that is all."

"Miss Howard."

Miss Howard produced the letter written to her by Mrs. Inglethorp on the evening of the 17th. Poirot and I had, of course, already seen it. It added nothing to our knowledge of the tragedy. The following is a facsimile:

July 17th   Styles Court
                                Essex

My dear Evelyn

Can we not bury the hatchet? I have found it hard to forgive the things you said against my dear husband but I am an old woman & very fond of you

Yours affectionately

Emily Inglethorp

It was handed to the jury who scrutinized it attentively.

"I fear it does not help us much," said the Coroner, with a sigh. "There is no mention of any of the events of that afternoon."

"Plain as a pikestaff to me," said Miss Howard shortly. "It shows clearly enough that my poor old friend had just found out she'd been made a fool of!"

"It says nothing of the kind in the letter," the Coroner pointed out.

"No, because Emily never could bear to put herself in the wrong. But I know her. She wanted me back. But she wasn't going to own that I'd been right. She went round about. Most people do. Don't believe in it myself."

Mr. Wells smiled faintly. So, I noticed, did several of the jury. Miss Howard was obviously quite a public character.

"Anyway, all this tomfoolery is a great waste of time," continued the lady, glancing up and down the jury disparagingly. "Talk—talk—talk! When all the time we know perfectly well——"

The Coroner interrupted her in an agony of apprehension: "Thank you, Miss Howard, that is all."

I fancy he breathed a sigh of relief when she complied.

Then came the sensation of the day. The Coroner called Albert Mace, chemist's assistant.

It was our agitated young man of the pale face. In answer to the Coroner's questions, he explained that he was a qualified pharmacist, but had only recently come to this particular shop, as the assistant formerly there had just been called up for the army.

These preliminaries completed, the Coroner proceeded to business.

"Mr. Mace, have you lately sold strychnine to any unauthorized person?"

"Yes, sir."

"When was this?"

"Last Monday night."

"Monday? Not Tuesday?"

"No, sir, Monday, the 16th."

"Will you tell us to whom you sold it?"

You could have heard a pin drop.

"Yes, sir. It was to Mr. Inglethorp."

Every eye turned simultaneously to where Alfred Inglethorp was sitting, impassive and wooden. He started slightly, as the damning words fell from the young man's lips. I half thought he was going to rise from his chair, but he remained seated, although a remarkably well acted expression of astonishment rose on his face.

"You are sure of what you say?" asked the Coroner sternly.

"Quite sure, sir."

"Are you in the habit of selling strychnine indiscriminately over the counter?"

The wretched young man wilted visibly under the Coroner's frown.

"Oh, no, sir—of course not. But, seeing it was Mr. Inglethorp of the Hall, I thought there was no harm in it. He said it was to poison a dog."

Inwardly I sympathized. It was only human nature to endeavour to please "The Hall"—especially when it might result in custom being transferred from Coot's to the local establishment.

"Is it not customary for anyone purchasing poison to sign a book?"

"Yes, sir, Mr. Inglethorp did so."

"Have you got the book here?"

"Yes, sir."

It was produced; and, with a few words of stern censure, the Coroner dismissed the wretched Mr. Mace.

Then, amidst a breathless silence, Alfred Inglethorp was called. Did he realize, I wondered, how closely the halter was being drawn around his neck?

The Coroner went straight to the point.

"On Monday evening last, did you purchase strychnine for the purpose of poisoning a dog?"

Inglethorp replied with perfect calmness:

"No, I did not. There is no dog at Styles, except an outdoor sheepdog, which is in perfect health."

"You deny absolutely having purchased strychnine from Albert Mace on Monday last?"

"I do."

"Do you also deny *this?*"

The Coroner handed him the register in which his signature was inscribed.

"Certainly I do. The hand-writing is quite different from mine. I will show you."

He took an old envelope out of his pocket, and wrote his name on it, handing it to the jury. It was certainly utterly dissimilar.

"Then what is your explanation of Mr. Mace's statement?"

Alfred Inglethorp replied imperturbably:

"Mr. Mace must have been mistaken."

The Coroner hesitated for a moment, and then said:

"Mr. Inglethorp, as a mere matter of form, would you mind telling us where you were on the evening of Monday, July 16th?"

"Really—I cannot remember."

"That is absurd, Mr. Inglethorp," said the Coroner sharply. "Think again."

Inglethorp shook his head.

"I cannot tell you. I have an idea that I was out walking."

"In what direction?"

"I really can't remember."

The Coroner's face grew graver.

"Were you in company with anyone?"

"No."

"Did you meet anyone on your walk?"

"No."

"That is a pity," said the Coroner dryly. "I am to take it then that you decline to say where you were at the time that Mr. Mace positively recognized you as entering the shop to purchase strychnine?"

"If you like to take it that way, yes."

"Be careful, Mr. Inglethorp."

Poirot was fidgeting nervously.

"*Sacré!*" he murmured. "Does this imbecile of a man *want* to be arrested?"

Inglethorp was indeed creating a bad impression. His futile denials would not have convinced a child. The Coroner, however, passed briskly to the next point, and Poirot drew a deep breath of relief.

"You had a discussion with your wife on Tuesday afternoon?"

"Pardon me," interrupted Alfred Inglethorp, "you have been misinformed. I had no quarrel with my dear wife. The whole story is absolutely untrue. I was absent from the house the entire afternoon."

"Have you anyone who can testify to that?"

"You have my word," said Inglethorp haughtily.

The Coroner did not trouble to reply.

"There are two witnesses who will swear to having heard your disagreement with Mrs. Inglethorp."

"Those witnesses were mistaken."

I was puzzled. The man spoke with such quiet assurance that I was staggered. I looked at Poirot. There was an expression of exultation on his face which I could not understand. Was he at last convinced of Alfred Inglethorp's guilt?

"Mr. Inglethorp," said the Coroner, "you have heard your wife's dying words repeated here. Can you explain them in any way?"

"Certainly I can."

"You can?"

"It seems to me very simple. The room was dimly lighted. Dr. Bauerstein is much of my height and build, and, like me, wears a beard. In the dim light, and suffering as she was, my poor wife mistook him for me."

"Ah!" murmured Poirot to himself. "But it is an idea, that!"

"You think it is true?" I whispered.

"I do not say that. But it is truly an ingenious supposition."

"You read my wife's last words as an accusation"—Inglethorp was continuing—"they were, on the contrary, an appeal to me."

The Coroner reflected a moment, then he said:

"I believe, Mr. Inglethorp, that you yourself poured out the coffee, and took it to your wife that evening?"

"I poured it out, yes. But I did not take it to her. I meant to do so, but I was told that a friend was at the hall door, so I laid down the coffee on the hall table. When I came through the hall again a few minutes later, it was gone."

This statement might, or might not, be true, but it did not seem to me to improve matters much for Inglethorp. In any case, he had had ample time to introduce the poison.

At that point, Poirot nudged me gently, indicating two men who were sitting together near the door. One was a little, sharp, dark, ferret faced man, the other was tall and fair.

I questioned Poirot mutely. He put his lips to my ear.

"Do you know who that little man is?"

I shook my head.

"That is Detective Inspector James Japp of Scotland Yard—Jimmy Japp. The other man is from Scotland Yard too. Things are moving quickly, my friend."

I stared at the two men intently. There was certainly nothing of the policeman about them. I should never have suspected them of being official personages.

I was still staring, when I was startled and recalled by the verdict being given:

"Wilful Murder against some person or persons unknown."

7

Poirot Pays His Debts

As we came out of the Stylites Arms, Poirot drew me aside by a gentle pressure of the arm. I understood his object. He was waiting for the Scotland Yard men.

In a few moments, they emerged, and Poirot at once stepped forward, and accosted the shorter of the two.

"I fear you do not remember me, Inspector Japp."

"Why, if it isn't Mr. Poirot!" cried the Inspector. He turned to the other man. "You've heard me speak of Mr. Poirot? It was in 1904 he and I worked together—the Abercrombie forgery case—you remember, he was run down in Brussels. Ah, those were great days, moosier. Then, do you remember 'Baron' Altara? There was a pretty rogue for you! He eluded the clutches of half the police in Europe. But we nailed him in Antwerp—thanks to Mr. Poirot here."

As these friendly reminiscences were being indulged in, I drew nearer, and was introduced to Detective Inspector Japp, who in his turn, introduced us both to his companion, Superintendent Summerhaye.

"I need hardly ask what you are doing here, gentlemen," remarked Poirot.

Japp closed one eye knowingly.

"No, indeed. Pretty clear case I should say."

But Poirot answered gravely:

"There I differ from you."

"Oh, come!" said Summerhaye, opening his lips for the first time. "Surely the whole thing is clear as daylight. The man's caught red-handed. How he could be such a fool beats me!"

But Japp was looking attentively at Poirot.

"Hold your fire, Summerhaye," he remarked jocularly. "Me and Moosier here have met before—and there's no man's judgment I'd sooner take than his. If I'm not greatly mistaken, he's got something up his sleeve. Isn't that so, moosier?"

Poirot smiled.

"I have drawn certain conclusions—yes."

Summerhaye was still looking rather sceptical, but Japp continued his scrutiny of Poirot.

"It's this way," he said, "so far, we've only seen the case from the outside. That's where the Yard's at a disadvantage in a case of this kind, where the murder's only out, so to speak, after the inquest. A lot depends on being on the spot first thing, and that's where Mr. Poirot's had the start of us. We shouldn't have been here as soon as this even, if it hadn't been for the fact that there was a smart doctor on the spot, who gave us the tip through the Coroner. But you've been on the spot from the first, and you may have picked up some little hints. From the evidence at the inquest, Mr. Inglethorp murdered his wife as sure as I stand here, and if anyone but you hinted the contrary I'd laugh in his face. I must say I was surprised the jury didn't bring it in Wilful Murder against him right off. I think they would have, if it hadn't been for the Coroner—he seemed to be holding them back."

"Perhaps, though, you have a warrant for his arrest in your pocket now," suggested Poirot.

A kind of wooden shutter of officialdom came down from Japp's expressive countenance.

"Perhaps I have, and perhaps I haven't," he remarked dryly. Poirot looked at him thoughtfully.

"I am very anxious, Messieurs, that he should not be arrested."

"I dare say," observed Summerhaye sarcastically.

Japp was regarding Poirot with comical perplexity.

"Can't you go a little further, Mr. Poirot? A wink's as good as a nod—from you. You've been on the spot—and the Yard doesn't want to make any mistakes, you know."

Poirot nodded gravely.

"That is exactly what I thought. Well, I will tell you this. Use your warrant: Arrest Mr. Inglethorp. But it will bring you no kudos—the case against him will be dismissed at once! *Comme ça!*" And he snapped his fingers expressively.

Japp's face grew grave, though Summerhaye gave an incredulous snort.

As for me, I was literally dumb with astonishment. I could only conclude that Poirot was mad.

Japp had taken out a handkerchief, and was gently dabbing his brow.

"I daren't do it, Mr. Poirot. I'd take your word, but there's others over me who'll be asking what the devil I mean by it. Can't you give me a little more to go on?"

Poirot reflected a moment.

"It can be done," he said at last. "I admit I do not wish it. It forces my hand. I would have preferred to work in the dark just for the present, but what you say is very just—the word of a Belgian policeman, whose day is past, is not enough! And Alfred Inglethorp must not be arrested. That I have sworn, as my friend Hastings here knows. See, then, my good Japp, you go at once to Styles?"

"Well, in about half an hour. We're seeing the Coroner and the doctor first."

"Good. Call for me in passing—the last house in the village. I will go with you. At Styles, Mr. Inglethorp will give you, or if he refuses—as is probable—I will give you such proofs that shall satisfy you that the case against him could not possibly be sustained. Is that a bargain?"

"That's a bargain," said Japp heartily. "And, on behalf of the Yard, I'm much obliged to you, though I'm bound to confess I can't at present see the faintest possible loop-hole in the evidence, but you always were a marvel! So long, then, moosier."

The two detectives strode away, Summerhaye with an incredulous grin on his face.

"Well, my friend," cried Poirot, before I could get in a word, "what do you think? *Mon Dieu!* I had some warm moments in that court; I did not figure to myself that the man would be so pig-headed as to refuse to say anything at all. Decidedly, it was the policy of an imbecile."

"H'm! There are other explanations besides that of imbecility," I remarked. "For, if the case against him is true, how could he defend himself except by silence?"

"Why, in a thousand ingenious ways," cried Poirot. "See; say that it is I who have committed this murder, I can think of seven most plausible stories! Far more convincing than Mr. Inglethorp's stony denials!"

I could not help laughing.

"My dear Poirot, I am sure you are capable of thinking of seventy! But, seriously, in spite of what I heard you say to the detectives, you surely cannot still believe in the possibility of Alfred Inglethorp's innocence?"

"Why not now as much as before? Nothing has changed."

"But the evidence is so conclusive."

"Yes, too conclusive."

We turned in at the gate of Leastways Cottage, and proceeded up the now familiar stairs.

"Yes, yes, too conclusive," continued Poirot, almost to himself. "Real evidence is usually vague and unsatisfactory. It has to be examined—sifted. But here the whole thing is cut and dried. No, my friend, this evidence has been very cleverly manufactured—so cleverly that it has defeated its own ends."

"How do you make that out?"

"Because, so long as the evidence against him was vague and intangible, it was very hard to disprove. But, in his anxiety, the criminal has drawn the net so closely that one cut will set Inglethorp free."

I was silent. And in a minute or two, Poirot continued:

"Let us look at the matter like this. Here is a man, let us say, who sets out to poison his wife. He has lived by his wits as the saying goes. Presumably, therefore, he has some wits. He is not altogether a fool. Well, how does he set about it? He goes boldly to the village chemist's and purchases strychnine under his own name, with a trumped up story about a dog which is bound to be proved absurd. He does not employ the poison that night. No, he waits until he has had a violent quarrel with her, of which the whole household is cognisant, and which naturally directs their suspicions upon him. He prepares no defence—no shadow of an alibi, yet he knows the chemist's assistant must necessarily come forward with the facts. Bah! do not ask me to believe that any man could be so idiotic! Only a lunatic, who wished to commit suicide by causing himself to be hanged, would act so!"

"Still—I do not see—" I began.

"Neither do I see. I tell you, *mon ami*, it puzzles me. Me—Hercule Poirot!"

"But if you believe him innocent, how do you explain his buying the strychnine?"

"Very simply. He did *not* buy it."

"But Mace recognized him!"

"I beg your pardon, he saw a man with a black beard like Mr. Inglethorp's, and wearing glasses like Mr. Inglethorp, and dressed in Mr. Inglethorp's rather noticeable clothes. He could not recognize a man whom he had probably only seen in the distance, since, you remember, he himself had only been in the village a fortnight, and Mrs. Inglethorp dealt principally with Coot's in Tadminster."

"Then you think——"

"*Mon ami*, do you remember the two points I laid stress upon? Leave the first one for the moment, what was the second?"

"The important fact that Alfred Inglethorp wears peculiar clothes, has a black beard and uses glasses," I quoted.

"Exactly. Now suppose anyone wished to pass himself off as John or Lawrence Cavendish. Would it be easy?"

"No," I said thoughtfully. "Of course an actor——"

But Poirot cut me short ruthlessly.

"And why would it not be easy? I will tell you, my friend: Because they are both clean-shaven men. To make up successfully as one of these two in broad daylight, it would need an actor of genius, and a certain initial facial resemblance. But in the case of Alfred Inglethorp, all that is changed. His clothes, his beard, the glasses which hide his eyes—those are the salient points about his personal appearance. Now, what is the first instinct of the criminal? To divert suspicion from himself, is it not so? And how can he best do that? By throwing it on some one else. In this instance, there was a man ready to his hand. Everybody was predisposed to believe in Mr. Inglethorp's guilt. It was a foregone conclusion that he would be suspected; but, to make it a sure thing there must be tangible proof—such as the actual buying of the poison, and that, with a man of the peculiar appearance of Mr. Inglethorp, was not difficult. Remember, this young Mace had never actually spoken to Mr. Inglethorp. How should he doubt that the man in his clothes, with his beard and his glasses, was not Alfred Inglethorp?"

"It may be so," I said, fascinated by Poirot's eloquence. "But, if that was the case, why does he not say where he was at six o'clock on Monday evening?"

"Ah, why indeed?" said Poirot, calming down. "If he were arrested, he probably would speak, but I do not want it to come to that. I must make him see the gravity of his position. There is, of course, something discreditable behind his silence. If he did not murder his wife, he is, nevertheless, a scoundrel, and has something of his own to conceal, quite apart from the murder."

"What can it be?" I mused, won over to Poirot's views for the moment, although still retaining a faint conviction that the obvious deduction was the correct one.

"Can you not guess?" asked Poirot, smiling.

"No, can you?"

"Oh, yes, I had a little idea sometime ago—and it has turned out to be correct."

"You never told me," I said reproachfully.

Poirot spread out his hands apologetically.

"Pardon me, *mon ami*, you were not precisely *sympathique*." He turned to me earnestly. "Tell me—you see now that he must not be arrested?"

"Perhaps," I said doubtfully, for I was really quite indifferent to the fate of Alfred Inglethorp, and thought that a good fright would do him no harm.

Poirot, who was watching me intently, gave a sigh.

"Come, my friend," he said, changing the subject, "apart from Mr. Inglethorp, how did the evidence at the inquest strike you?"

"Oh, pretty much what I expected."

"Did nothing strike you as peculiar about it?"

My thoughts flew to Mary Cavendish, and I hedged:

"In what way?"

"Well Mr. Lawrence Cavendish's evidence for instance?"

I was relieved.

"Oh, Lawrence! No, I don't think so. He's always a nervous chap."

"His suggestion that his mother might have been poisoned accidentally by means of the tonic she was taking, that did not strike you as strange—*hein?*"

"No, I can't say it did. The doctors ridiculed it of course. But it was quite a natural suggestion for a layman to make."

"But Monsieur Lawrence is not a layman. You told me yourself that he had started by studying medicine, and that he had taken his degree."

"Yes, that's true. I never thought of that." I was rather startled. "It *is* odd."

Poirot nodded.

"From the first, his behaviour has been peculiar. Of all the household, he alone would be likely to recognize the symptoms of strychnine poisoning, and yet we find him the only member of the family to uphold strenuously the theory of death from natural causes. If it had been Monsieur John, I could have understood it. He has no technical knowledge, and is by nature unimaginative. But Monsieur Lawrence—no! And now, to-day, he puts forward a suggestion that he himself must have known was ridiculous. There is food for thought in this, *mon ami!*"

"It's very confusing," I agreed.

"Then there is Mrs. Cavendish," continued Poirot. "That's another who is not telling all she knows! What do you make of her attitude?"

"I don't know what to make of it. It seems inconceivable that she should be shielding Alfred Inglethorp. Yet that is what it looks like."

Poirot nodded reflectively.

"Yes, it is queer. One thing is certain, she overheard a good deal more of that 'private conversation' than she was willing to admit."

"And yet she is the last person one would accuse of stooping to eavesdrop!"

"Exactly. One thing her evidence *has* shown me. I made a mistake. Dorcas was quite right. The quarrel did take place earlier in the afternoon, about four o'clock, as she said."

I looked at him curiously. I had never understood his insistence on that point.

"Yes, a good deal that was peculiar came out to-day," continued Poirot. "Dr. Bauerstein, now, what was *he* doing up and dressed at that hour in the morning? It is astonishing to me that no one commented on the fact."

"He has insomnia, I believe," I said doubtfully.

"Which is a very good, or a very bad explanation," remarked Poirot. "It covers everything, and explains nothing. I shall keep my eye on our clever Dr. Bauerstein."

"Any more faults to find with the evidence?" I inquired satirically.

"*Mon ami,*" replied Poirot gravely, "when you find that people are not telling you the truth—look out! Now, unless I am much mistaken, at this inquest to-day only one—at most, two persons were speaking the truth without reservation or subterfuge."

"Oh, come now, Poirot! I won't cite Lawrence, or Mrs. Cavendish. But there's John—and Miss Howard, surely they were speaking the truth?"

"Both of them, my friend? One, I grant you, but both——!"

His words gave me an unpleasant shock. Miss Howard's evidence, unimportant as it was, had been given in such a downright straightforward manner that it had never occurred to me to doubt her sincerity. Still, I had a great respect for Poirot's sagacity —except on the occasions when he was what I described to myself as "foolishly pig-headed."

"Do you really think so?" I asked. "Miss Howard had always seemed to me so essentially honest—almost uncomfortably so."

Poirot gave me a curious look, which I could not quite fathom. He seemed to speak, and then checked himself.

"Miss Murdoch too," I continued, "there's nothing untruthful about *her*."

"No. But it was strange that she never heard a sound, sleeping next door; whereas Mrs. Cavendish, in the other wing of the building, distinctly heard the table fall."

"Well, she's young. And she sleeps soundly."

"Ah, yes, indeed! She must be a famous sleeper, that one!"

I did not quite like the tone of his voice, but at that moment a smart knock reached our ears, and looking out of the window we perceived the two detectives waiting for us below.

Poirot seized his hat, gave a ferocious twist to his moustache, and, carefully brushing an imaginary speck of dust from his sleeve, motioned me to precede him down the stairs; there we joined the detectives and set out for Styles.

I think the appearance of the two Scotland Yard men was rather a shock—especially to John, though of course, after the verdict, he had realized that it was only a matter of time. Still, the presence of the detectives brought the truth home to him more than anything else could have done.

Poirot had conferred with Japp in a low tone on the way up, and it was the latter functionary who requested that the household, with the exception of the servants, should be assembled together in the drawing-room. I realized the significance of this. It was up to Poirot to make his boast good.

Personally, I was not sanguine. Poirot might have excellent reasons for his belief in Inglethorp's innocence, but a man of the type of Summerhaye would require tangible proofs, and these I doubted if Poirot could supply.

Before very long we had all trooped into the drawing-room, the door of which Japp closed. Poirot politely set chairs for every one. The Scotland Yard men were the cynosure of all eyes. I think that for the first time we realized that the thing was not a bad dream, but a tangible reality. We had read of such things—now we ourselves were actors in the drama. To-morrow the daily papers, all over England, would blazon out the news in staring headlines:

"MYSTERIOUS TRAGEDY IN ESSEX"
"WEALTHY LADY POISONED"

There would be pictures of Styles, snap-shots of "The family leaving the Inquest"—the village photographer had not been idle! All the things that one had read a hundred times—things that happen to other people, not to oneself. And now, in this house, a murder had been committed. In front of us were "the detectives in charge of the case." The well known glib phraseology passed rapidly through my mind in the interval before Poirot opened the proceedings.

I think every one was a little surprised that it should be he and not one of the official detectives who took the initiative.

"*Mesdames* and *messieurs*," said Poirot, bowing as though he were a celebrity about to deliver a lecture, "I have asked you to come here all together, for a certain object. That object, it concerns Mr. Alfred Inglethorp."

Inglethorp was sitting a little by himself—I think, unconsciously, every one had drawn his chair slightly away from him— and he gave a faint start as Poirot pronounced his name.

"Mr. Inglethorp," said Poirot, addressing him directly, "a very dark shadow is resting on this house—the shadow of murder."

Inglethorp shook his head sadly.

"My poor wife," he murmured. "Poor Emily! It is terrible."

"I do not think, monsieur," said Poirot pointedly, "that you quite realize how terrible it may be—for you." And as Inglethorp did not appear to understand, he added: "Mr. Inglethorp, you are standing in very grave danger."

The two detectives fidgeted. I saw the official caution "Anything you say will be used in evidence against you," actually hovering on Summerhaye's lips. Poirot went on.

"Do you understand now, monsieur?"

"No. What do you mean?"

"I mean," said Poirot deliberately, "that you are suspected of poisoning your wife."

A little gasp ran round the circle at this plain speaking.

"Good heavens!" cried Inglethorp, starting up. "What a monstrous idea! I—poison my dearest Emily!"

"I do not think"—Poirot watched him narrowly—"that you quite realize the unfavourable nature of your evidence at the inquest. Mr. Inglethorp, knowing what I have now told you, do you still refuse to say where you were at six o'clock on Monday afternoon?"

With a groan, Alfred Inglethorp sank down again and buried his face in his hands. Poirot approached and stood over him.

"Speak!" he cried menacingly.

With an effort, Inglethorp raised his face from his hands. Then, slowly and deliberately, he shook his head.

"You will not speak?"

"No. I do not believe that anyone could be so monstrous as to accuse me of what you say."

Poirot nodded thoughtfully, like a man whose mind is made up.

"*Soit!*" he said. "Then I must speak for you."

Alfred Inglethorp sprang up again.

"You? How can you speak? You do not know——" he broke off abruptly.

Poirot turned to face us. "*Mesdames* and *messieurs!* I speak! Listen! I, Hercule Poirot, affirm that the man who entered the chemist's shop, and purchased strychnine at six o'clock on Monday last was not Mr. Inglethorp, for at six o'clock on that day Mr. Inglethorp was escorting Mrs. Raikes back to her home from a neighbouring farm. I can produce no less than five witnesses to swear to having seen them together, either at six or just after and, as you may know, the Abbey Farm, Mrs. Raikes's home, is at least two and a half miles distant from the village. There is absolutely no question as to the alibi!"

8

Fresh Suspicions

There was a moment's stupefied silence. Japp, who was the least surprised of any of us, was the first to speak.

"My word," he cried, "you're the goods! And no mistake, Mr. Poirot! These witnesses of yours are all right, I suppose?"

"*Voilà!* I have prepared a list of them—names and addresses. You must see them, of course. But you will find it all right."

"I'm sure of that." Japp lowered his voice. "I'm much obliged to you. A pretty mare's nest arresting him would have been." He turned to Inglethorp. "But, if you'll excuse me, sir, why couldn't you say all this at the inquest?"

"I will tell you why," interrupted Poirot. "There was a certain rumour——"

"A most malicious and utterly untrue one," interrupted Alfred Inglethorp in an agitated voice.

"And Mr. Inglethorp was anxious to have no scandal revived just at present. Am I right?"

"Quite right." Inglethorp nodded. "With my poor Emily not yet buried, can you wonder I was anxious that no more lying rumours should be started."

"Between you and me, sir," remarked Japp, "I'd sooner have any amount of rumours than be arrested for murder. And I venture to think your poor lady would have felt the same. And, if it hadn't been for Mr. Poirot here, arrested you would have been, as sure as eggs is eggs!"

"I was foolish, no doubt," murmured Inglethorp. "But you do not know, Inspector, how I have been persecuted and maligned." And he shot a baleful glance at Evelyn Howard.

"Now, sir," said Japp, turning briskly to John, "I should like to see the lady's bedroom, please, and after that I'll have a little chat with the servants. Don't you bother about anything. Mr. Poirot, here, will show me the way."

As they all went out of the room, Poirot turned and made me a sign to follow him upstairs. There he caught me by the arm, and drew me aside.

"Quick, go to the other wing. Stand there—just this side of the baize door. Do not move till I come." Then, turning rapidly, he rejoined the two detectives.

I followed his instructions, taking up my position by the baize door, and wondering what on earth lay behind the request. Why was I to stand in this particular spot on guard? I looked thoughtfully down the corridor in front of me. An idea struck me. With the exception of Cynthia Murdoch's, every one's room was in this left wing. Had that anything to do with it? Was I to report who came or went? I stood faithfully at my post. The minutes passed. Nobody came. Nothing happened.

It must have been quite twenty minutes before Poirot rejoined me.

"You have not stirred?"

"No, I've stuck here like a rock. Nothing's happened."

"Ah!" Was he pleased, or disappointed? "You've seen nothing at all?"

"No."

"But you have probably heard something? A big bump—eh, *mon ami?*"

"No."

"Is it possible? Ah, but I am vexed with myself! I am not usually clumsy. I made but a slight gesture"—I know Poirot's gestures—"with the left hand, and over went the table by the bed!"

He looked so childishly vexed and crest-fallen that I hastened to console him.

"Never mind, old chap. What does it matter? Your triumph

downstairs excited you. I can tell you, that was a surprise to us all. There must be more in this affair of Inglethorp's with Mrs. Raikes than we thought, to make him hold his tongue so persistently. What are you going to do now? Where are the Scotland Yard fellows?"

"Gone down to interview the servants. I showed them all our exhibits. I am disappointed in Japp. He has no method!"

"Hullo!" I said, looking out of the window. "Here's Dr. Bauerstein. I believe you're right about that man, Poirot. I don't like him."

"He is clever," observed Poirot meditatively.

"Oh, clever as the devil! I must say I was overjoyed to see him in the plight he was in on Tuesday. You never saw such a spectacle!" And I described the doctor's adventure. "He looked a regular scarecrow! Plastered with mud from head to foot."

"You saw him, then?"

"Yes. Of course, he didn't want to come in—it was just after dinner—but Mr. Inglethorp insisted."

"What?" Poirot caught me violently by the shoulders. "Was Dr. Bauerstein here on Tuesday evening? Here? And you never told me? Why did you not tell me? Why? Why?"

He appeared to be in an absolute frenzy.

"My dear Poirot," I expostulated, "I never thought it would interest you. I didn't know it was of any importance."

"Importance? It is of the first importance! So Dr. Bauerstein was here on Tuesday night—the night of the murder. Hastings, do you not see? That alters everything—everything!"

I had never seen him so upset. Loosening his hold of me, he mechanically straightened a pair of candlesticks, still murmuring to himself: "Yes, that alters everything—everything."

Suddenly he seemed to come to a decision.

"*Allons!*" he said. "We must act at once. Where is Mr. Cavendish?"

John was in the smoking-room. Poirot went straight to him.

"Mr. Cavendish, I have some important business in Tadminster. A new clue. May I take your motor?"

"Why, of course. Do you mean at once?"

"If you please."

John rang the bell, and ordered round the car. In another ten minutes, we were racing down the park and along the high road to Tadminster.

"Now, Poirot," I remarked resignedly, "perhaps you will tell me what all this is about?"

"Well, *mon ami*, a good deal you can guess for yourself. Of course you realize that, now Mr. Inglethorp is out of it, the whole position is greatly changed. We are face to face with an entirely new problem. We know now that there is one person who did not buy the poison. We have cleared away the manufactured clues. Now for the real ones. I have ascertained that anyone in the household, with the exception of Mrs. Cavendish, who was playing tennis with you, could have personated Mr. Inglethorp on Monday evening. In the same way, we have his statement that he put the coffee down in the hall. No one took much notice of that at the inquest—but now it has a very different significance. We must find out who did take that coffee to Mrs. Inglethorp eventually, or who passed through the hall whilst it was standing there. From your account, there are only two people whom we can positively say did not go near the coffee—Mrs. Cavendish, and Mademoiselle Cynthia."

"Yes, that is so." I felt an inexpressible lightening of the heart. Mary Cavendish could certainly not rest under suspicion.

"In clearing Alfred Inglethorp," continued Poirot, "I have been obliged to show my hand sooner than I intended. As long as I might be thought to be pursuing him, the criminal would be off his guard. Now, he will be doubly careful. Yes—doubly careful." He turned to me abruptly. "Tell me, Hastings, you yourself— have you no suspicions of anybody?"

I hesitated. To tell the truth, an idea, wild and extravagant in itself, had once or twice that morning flashed through my brain. I had rejected it as absurd, nevertheless it persisted.

"You couldn't call it a suspicion," I murmured. "It's so utterly foolish."

"Come now," urged Poirot encouragingly. "Do not fear. Speak your mind. You should always pay attention to your instincts."

"Well then," I blurted out, "it's absurd—but I suspect Miss Howard of not telling all she knows!"

"Miss Howard?"

"Yes—you'll laugh at me——"

"Not at all. Why should I?"

"I can't help feeling," I continued blunderingly; "that we've rather left her out of the possible suspects, simply on the strength of her having been away from the place. But, after all, she was only fifteen miles away. A car would do it in half an hour. Can we say positively that she was away from Styles on the night of the murder?"

"Yes, my friend," said Poirot unexpectedly, "we can. One of my first actions was to ring up the hospital where she was working."

"Well?"

"Well, I learnt that Miss Howard had been on afternoon duty on Tuesday, and that—a convoy coming in unexpectedly—she had kindly offered to remain on night duty, which offer was gratefully accepted. That disposes of that."

"Oh!" I said, rather nonplussed. "Really," I continued, "it's her extraordinary vehemence against Inglethorp that started me off suspecting her. I can't help feeling she'd do anything against him. And I had an idea she might know something about the destroying of the will. She might have burnt the new one, mistaking it for the earlier one in his favour. She is so terribly bitter against him."

"You consider her vehemence unnatural?"

"Y—es. She is so very violent. I wonder really whether she is quite sane on that point."

Poirot shook his head energetically.

"No, no, you are on a wrong tack there. There is nothing weak-minded or degenerate about Miss Howard. She is an excellent specimen of well balanced English beef and brawn. She is sanity itself."

"Yet her hatred of Inglethorp seems almost a mania. My idea was—a very ridiculous one, no doubt—that she had intended to poison him—and that, in some way, Mrs. Inglethorp got hold of it by mistake. But I don't at all see how it could have been done. The whole thing is absurd and ridiculous to the last degree."

"Still you are right in one thing. It is always wise to suspect everybody until you can prove logically, and to your own satisfaction, that they are innocent. Now, what reasons are there against Miss Howard's having deliberately poisoned Mrs. Inglethorp?"

"Why, she was devoted to her!" I exclaimed.

"Tcha! Tcha!" cried Poirot irritably. "You argue like a child. If Miss Howard were capable of poisoning the old lady, she would be quite equally capable of simulating devotion. No, we must look elsewhere. You are perfectly correct in your assumption that her vehemence against Alfred Inglethorp is too violent to be natural; but you are quite wrong in the deduction you draw from it. I have drawn my own deductions, which I believe to be correct, but I will not speak of them at present." He paused a minute, then went on. "Now, to my way of thinking, there is one insuperable objection to Miss Howard's being the murderess."

"And that is?"

"That in no possible way could Mrs. Inglethorp's death benefit Miss Howard. Now there is no murder without a motive."

I reflected.

"Could not Mrs. Inglethorp have made a will in her favour?" Poirot shook his head.

"But you yourself suggested that possibility to Mr. Wells?" Poirot smiled.

"That was for a reason. I did not want to mention the name of the person who was actually in my mind. Miss Howard occupied very much the same position, so I used her name instead."

"Still, Mrs. Inglethorp might have done so. Why, that will, made on the afternoon of her death may——"

But Poirot's shake of the head was so energetic that I stopped.

"No, my friend. I have certain little ideas of my own about that will. But I can tell you this much—it was not in Miss Howard's favour."

I accepted his assurance, though I did not really see how he could be so positive about the matter.

"Well," I said, with a sigh, "we will acquit Miss Howard, then. It is partly your fault that I ever came to suspect her. It was what you said about her evidence at the inquest that set me off."

Poirot looked puzzled.

"What did I say about her evidence at the inquest?"

"Don't you remember? When I cited her and John Cavendish as being above suspicion?"

"Oh—ah—yes." He seemed a little confused, but recovered himself. "By the way, Hastings, there is something I want you to do for me."

"Certainly. What is it?"

"Next time you happen to be alone with Lawrence Cavendish, I want you to say this to him. 'I have a message for you, from Poirot. He says: "Find the extra coffee-cup, and you can rest in peace!"' Nothing more. Nothing less."

"'Find the extra coffee-cup, and you can rest in peace.' Is that right?" I asked, much mystified.

"Excellent."

"But what does it mean?"

"Ah, that I will leave you to find out. You have access to the facts. Just say that to him, and see what he says."

"Very well—but it's all extremely mysterious."

We were running into Tadminster now, and Poirot directed the car to the "Analytical Chemist."

Poirot hopped down briskly, and went inside. In a few minutes he was back again.

"There," he said. "That is all my business."

"What were you doing there?" I asked, in lively curiosity.

"I left something to be analysed."

"Yes, but what?"

"The sample of coco I took from the saucepan in the bed-room."

"But that has already been tested!" I cried, stupefied. "Dr. Bauerstein had it tested, and you yourself laughed at the possibility of there being strychnine in it."

"I know Dr. Bauerstein had it tested," replied Poirot quietly.

"Well, then?"

"Well, I have a fancy for having it analysed again, that is all."

And not another word on the subject could I drag out of him. This proceeding of Poirot's, in respect of the coco, puzzled me intensely. I could see neither rhyme nor reason in it. However, my confidence in him, which at one time had rather waned, was fully restored since his belief in Alfred Inglethorp's innocence had been so triumphantly vindicated.

The funeral of Mrs. Inglethorp took place the following day, and on Monday, as I came down to a late breakfast, John drew me aside, and informed me that Mr. Inglethorp was leaving that morning, to take up his quarters at the Stylites Arms until he should have completed his plans.

"And really it's a great relief to think he's going, Hastings," continued my honest friend. "It was bad enough before, when we thought he'd done it, but I'm hanged if it isn't worse now, when we all feel guilty for having been so down on the fellow. The fact is, we've treated him abominably. Of course, things did look black against him. I don't see how anyone could blame us for jumping to the conclusions we did. Still, there it is, we were in the wrong, and now there's a beastly feeling that one ought to make amends; which is difficult, when one doesn't like the fellow a bit better than one did before. The whole thing's damned awkward! And I'm thankful he's had the tact to take himself off. It's a good thing Styles wasn't the mater's to leave to him. Couldn't bear to think of the fellow lording it here. He's welcome to her money."

"You'll be able to keep up the place all right?" I asked.

"Oh, yes. There are the death duties, of course, but half my father's money goes with the place, and Lawrence will stay with us for the present, so there is his share as well. We shall be pinched at first, of course, because, as I once told you, I am in a bit of a hole financially myself. Still, the Johnnies will wait now."

In the general relief at Inglethorp's approaching departure, we had the most genial breakfast we had experienced since the tragedy. Cynthia, whose young spirits were naturally buoyant, was looking quite her pretty self again, and we all, with the exception of Lawrence, who seemed unalterably gloomy and nervous, were quietly cheerful, at the opening of a new and hopeful future.

The papers, of course, had been full of the tragedy. Glaring headlines, sandwiched biographies of every member of the household, subtle inuendoes, the usual familiar tag about the police having a clue. Nothing was spared us. It was a slack time. The war was momentarily inactive, and the newspapers seized with avidity on this crime in fashionable life: "The Mysterious Affair at Styles" was the topic of the moment.

Naturally it was very annoying for the Cavendishes. The house was constantly besieged by reporters, who were consistently denied admission, but who continued to haunt the village and the grounds, where they lay in wait with cameras, for any unwary members of the household. We all lived in a blast of publicity. The Scotland Yard men came and went, examining, questioning, lynx-eyed and reserved of tongue. Towards what end they were working, we did not know. Had they any clue, or would the whole thing remain in the category of undiscovered crimes?

After breakfast, Dorcas came up to me rather mysteriously, and asked if she might have a few words with me.

"Certainly. What is it, Dorcas?"

"Well, it's just this, sir. You'll be seeing the Belgian gentleman to-day perhaps?" I nodded. "Well, sir, you know how he asked me so particular if the mistress, or anyone else, had a green dress?"

"Yes, yes. You have found one?" My interest was aroused.

"No, not that, sir. But since then I've remembered what the young gentlemen"—John and Lawrence were still the "young gentlemen" to Dorcas—"call the 'dressing-up box.' It's up in the front attic, sir. A great chest, full of old clothes and fancy dresses, and what not. And it came to me sudden like that there might be a green dress amongst them. So, if you'd tell the Belgian gentleman——"

"I will tell him, Dorcas," I promised.

"Thank you very much, sir. A very nice gentleman he is, sir. And quite a different class from them two detectives from London, what goes prying about, and asking questions. I don't hold with foreigners as a rule, but from what the newspapers says I make out as how these brave Belges isn't the ordinary run of foreigners, and certainly he's a most polite spoken gentleman."

Dear old Dorcas! As she stood there, with her honest face upturned to mine, I thought what a fine specimen she was of the old-fashioned servant that is so fast dying out.

I thought I might as well go down to the village at once, and look up Poirot; but I met him half-way, coming up to the house, and at once gave him Dorcas's message.

"Ah, the brave Dorcas! We will look at the chest, although— but no matter—we will examine it all the same."

We entered the house by one of the windows. There was no one in the hall, and we went straight up to the attic.

Sure enough, there was the chest, a fine old piece, all studded with brass nails, and full to overflowing with every imaginable type of garment.

Poirot bundled everything out on the floor with scant ceremony. There were one or two green fabrics of varying shades; but Poirot shook his head over them all. He seemed somewhat apathetic in the search, as though he expected no great results from it. Suddenly he gave an exclamation.

"What is it?"

"Look!"

The chest was nearly empty, and there, reposing right at the bottom, was a magnificent black beard.

"*Ohó!*" said Poirot. "*Ohó!*" He turned it over in his hands, examining it closely. "New," he remarked. "Yes, quite new."

After a moment's hesitation, he replaced it in the chest, heaped all the other things on top of it as before, and made his way briskly downstairs. He went straight to the pantry, where we found Dorcas busily polishing her silver.

Poirot wished her good morning with Gallic politeness, and went on:

"We have been looking through that chest, Dorcas. I am much obliged to you for mentioning it. There is, indeed, a fine collection there. Are they often used, may I ask?"

"Well, sir, not very often nowadays, though from time to time we do have what the young gentlemen call 'a dress-up night.' And very funny it is sometimes, sir. Mr. Lawrence, he's wonderful. Most comic! I shall never forget the night he came down as the Char of Persia, I think he called it—a sort of Eastern King it was. He had the big paper knife in his hand, and 'Mind, Dorcas,' he says, 'you'll have to be very respectful. This is my specially sharpened scimitar, and it's off with your head if I'm at all displeased with you!' Miss Cynthia, she was what they call an Apache, or some such name—a Frenchified sort of cut-throat, I take it to be. A real sight she looked. You'd never have believed a pretty young lady like that could have made herself into such a ruffian. Nobody would have known her."

"These evenings must have been great fun," said Poirot genially. "I suppose Mr. Lawrence wore that fine black beard in the chest upstairs, when he was Shah of Persia?"

"He did have a beard, sir," replied Dorcas, smiling. "And well I know it, for he borrowed two skeins of my black wool to make it with! And I'm sure it looked wonderfully natural at a distance. I didn't know as there was a beard up there at all. It must have been got quite lately, I think. There was a red wig, I know, but nothing else in the way of hair. Burnt corks they use mostly—though 'tis messy getting it off again. Miss Cynthia was a nigger once, and, oh, the trouble she had."

"So Dorcas knows nothing about that black beard," said Poirot thoughtfully, as we walked out into the hall again.

"Do you think it is *the* one?" I whispered eagerly.

Poirot nodded.

"I do. You noticed it had been trimmed?"

"No."

"Yes. It was cut exactly the shape of Mr. Inglethorp's, and I found one or two snipped hairs. Hastings, this affair is very deep."

"Who put it in the chest, I wonder?"

"Some one with a good deal of intelligence," remarked Poirot drily. "You realize that he chose the one place in the house to hide it where its presence would not be remarked? Yes, he is intelligent. But we must be more intelligent. We must be so intelligent that he does not suspect us of being intelligent at all."

I acquiesced.

"There, *mon ami,* you will be of great assistance to me."

I was pleased with the compliment. There had been times when I hardly thought that Poirot appreciated me at my true worth.

"Yes," he continued, staring at me thoughtfully, "you will be invaluable."

This was naturally gratifying, but Poirot's next words were not so welcome.

"I must have an ally in the house," he observed reflectively.

"You have me," I protested.

"True, but you are not sufficient."

I was hurt, and showed it. Poirot hurried to explain himself.

"You do not quite take my meaning. You are known to be working with me. I want somebody who is not associated with us in any way."

"Oh, I see. How about John?"

"No, I think not."

"The dear fellow isn't perhaps very bright," I said thoughtfully.

"Here comes Miss Howard," said Poirot suddenly. "She is the very person. But I am in her black books, since I cleared Mr. Inglethorp. Still, we can but try."

With a nod that was barely civil, Miss Howard assented to Poirot's request for a few minutes' conversation.

We went into the little morning-room, and Poirot closed the door.

"Well, Monsieur Poirot," said Miss Howard impatiently, "what is it? Out with it. I'm busy."

"Do you remember, mademoiselle, that I once asked you to help me?"

"Yes, I do." The lady nodded. "And I told you I'd help you with pleasure—to hang Alfred Inglethorp."

"Ah!" Poirot studied her seriously. "Miss Howard, I will ask you one question. I beg of you to reply to it truthfully."

"Never tell lies," replied Miss Howard.

"It is this. Do you still believe that Mrs. Inglethorp was poisoned by her husband?"

"What do you mean?" she asked sharply. "You needn't think your pretty explanations influence me in the slightest. I'll admit that it wasn't he who bought strychnine at the chemist's shop. What of that? I dare say he soaked fly paper, as I told you at the beginning."

"That is arsenic—not strychnine," said Poirot mildly.

"What does that matter? Arsenic would put poor Emily out of the way just as well as strychnine. If I'm convinced he did it, it doesn't matter a jot to me *how* he did it."

"Exactly. *If* you are convinced he did it," said Poirot quietly. "I will put my question in another form. Did you ever in your heart of hearts believe that Mrs. Inglethorp was poisoned by her husband?"

"Good heavens!" cried Miss Howard. "Haven't I always told you the man is a villain? Haven't I always told you he would murder her in her bed? Haven't I always hated him like poison?"

"Exactly," said Poirot. "That bears out my little idea entirely."

"What little idea?"

"Miss Howard, do you remember a conversation that took place on the day of my friend's arrival here? He repeated it to me, and there is a sentence of yours that has impressed me very much. Do you remember affirming that if a crime had been committed, and anyone you loved had been murdered, you felt certain that you would know by instinct who the criminal was, even if you were quite unable to prove it?"

"Yes, I remember saying that. I believe it too. I suppose you think it nonsense?"

"Not at all."

"And yet you will pay no attention to my instinct against Alfred Inglethorp?"

"No," said Poirot curtly. "Because your instinct is not against Mr. Inglethorp."

"What?"

"No. You wish to believe he committed the crime. You believe him capable of committing it. But your instinct tells you he did not commit it. It tells you more—shall I go on?"

She was staring at him, fascinated, and made a slight affirmative movement of the hand.

"Shall I tell you why you have been so vehement against Mr. Inglethorp? It is because you have been trying to believe what you wish to believe. It is because you are trying to drown and stifle your instinct, which tells you another name——"

"No, no, no!" cried Miss Howard wildly, flinging up her hands. "Don't say it! Oh, don't say it! It isn't true! It can't be true. I don't know what put such a wild—such a dreadful—idea into my head!"

"I am right, am I not?" asked Poirot.

"Yes, yes; you must be a wizard to have guessed. But it can't be so—it's too monstrous, too impossible. It *must* be Alfred Inglethorp."

Poirot shook his head gravely.

"Don't ask me about it," continued Miss Howard, "because I shan't tell you. I won't admit it even to myself. I must be mad to think of such a thing."

Poirot nodded, as if satisfied.

"I will ask you nothing. It is enough for me that it is as I thought. And I—I, too, have an instinct. We are working together towards a common end."

"Don't ask me to help you, because I won't. I wouldn't lift a finger to—to——" She faltered.

"You will help me in spite of yourself. I ask you nothing—but you will be my ally. You will not be able to help yourself. You will do the only thing that I want of you."

"And that is?"

"You will watch!"

Evelyn Howard bowed her head.

"Yes, I can't help doing that. I am always watching—always hoping I shall be proved wrong."

"If we are wrong, well and good," said Poirot. "No one will be more pleased than I shall. But, if we are right? If we are right, Miss Howard, on whose side are you then?"

"I don't know, I don't know——"

"Come now."

"It could be hushed up."

"There must be no hushing up."

"But Emily herself——" She broke off.

"Miss Howard," said Poirot gravely, "this is unworthy of you."

Suddenly she took her face from her hands.

"Yes," she said quietly, "that was not Evelyn Howard who spoke!" She flung her head up proudly. "*This* is Evelyn Howard! And she is on the side of Justice! Let the cost be what it may." And with these words, she walked firmly out of the room.

"There," said Poirot, looking after her, "goes a very valuable ally. That woman, Hastings, has got brains as well as a heart."

I did not reply.

"Instinct is a marvellous thing," mused Poirot. "It can neither be explained nor ignored."

"You and Miss Howard seem to know what you are talking about," I observed coldly. "Perhaps you don't realize that I am still in the dark."

"Really? Is that so, *mon ami?*"

"Yes. Enlighten me, will you?"

Poirot studied me attentively for a moment or two. Then, to my intense surprise, he shook his head decidedly.

"No, my friend."

"Oh, look here, why not?"

"Two is enough for a secret."

"Well, I think it is very unfair to keep back facts from me."

"I am not keeping back facts. Every fact that I know is in your possession. You can draw your own deductions from them. This time it is a question of ideas."

"Still, it would be interesting to know."

Poirot looked at me very earnestly, and again shook his head.

"You see," he said sadly, "*you* have no instincts."

"It was intelligence you were requiring just now," I pointed out.

"The two often go together," said Poirot enigmatically.

The remark seemed so utterly irrelevant that I did not even

take the trouble to answer it. But I decided that if I made any interesting and important discoveries—as no doubt I should—I would keep them to myself, and surprise Poirot with the ultimate result.

There are times when it is one's duty to assert oneself.

9

Dr. Bauerstein

I had had no opportunity as yet of passing on Poirot's message to Lawrence. But now, as I strolled out on the lawn, still nursing a grudge against my friend's high-handedness, I saw Lawrence on the croquet lawn, aimlessly knocking a couple of very ancient balls about, with a still more ancient mallet.

It struck me that it would be a good opportunity to deliver my message. Otherwise, Poirot himself might relieve me of it. It was true that I did not quite gather its purport, but I flattered myself that by Lawrence's reply, and perhaps a little skillful cross-examination on my part, I should soon perceive its significance. Accordingly I accosted him.

"I've been looking for you," I remarked untruthfully.

"Have you?"

"Yes. The truth is, I've got a message for you—from Poirot."

"Yes?"

"He told me to wait until I was alone with you," I said, dropping my voice significantly, and watching him intently out of the corner of my eye. I have always been rather good at what is called, I believe, creating an atmosphere.

"Well?"

There was no change of expression in the dark melancholic face. Had he any idea of what I was about to say?

"This is the message." I dropped my voice still lower. "'Find the extra coffee-cup, and you can rest in peace.'"

"What on earth does he mean?" Lawrence stared at me in quite unaffected astonishment.

"Don't you know?"

"Not in the least. Do you?"

I was compelled to shake my head.

"What extra coffee-cup?"

"I don't know."

"He'd better ask Dorcas, or one of the maids, if he wants to know about coffee-cups. It's their business, not mine. I don't know anything about the coffee-cups, except that we've got some that are never used, which are a perfect dream! Old Worcester. You're not a connoisseur, are you, Hastings?"

I shook my head.

"You miss a lot. A really perfect bit of old china—it's pure delight to handle it, or even to look at it."

"Well, what am I to tell Poirot?"

"Tell him I don't know what he's talking about. It's double Dutch to me."

"All right."

I was moving off towards the house again when he suddenly called me back.

"I say, what was the end of that message? Say it over again, will you?"

"'Find the extra coffee-cup, and you can rest in peace.' Are you sure you don't know what it means?" I asked him earnestly.

He shook his head.

"No," he said musingly, "I don't. I—I wish I did."

The boom of the gong sounded from the house, and we went in together. Poirot had been asked by John to remain to lunch, and was already seated at the table.

By tacit consent, all mention of the tragedy was barred. We conversed on the war, and other outside topics. But after the cheese and biscuits had been handed round, and Dorcas had left the room, Poirot suddenly leant forward to Mrs. Cavendish.

"Pardon me, madame, for recalling unpleasant memories, but

I have a little idea"—Poirot's "little ideas" were becoming a perfect byword—"and would like to ask one or two questions."

"Of me? Certainly."

"You are too amiable, madame. What I want to ask is this: the door leading into Mrs. Inglethorp's room from that of Mademoiselle Cynthia, it was bolted, you say?"

"Certainly it was bolted," replied Mary Cavendish, rather surprised. "I said so at the inquest."

"Bolted?"

"Yes." She looked perplexed.

"I mean," explained Poirot, "you are sure it was bolted, and not merely locked?"

"Oh, I see what you mean. No, I don't know. I said bolted, meaning that it was fastened, and I could not open it, but I believe all the doors were found bolted on the inside."

"Still, as far as you are concerned, the door might equally well have been locked?"

"Oh, yes."

"You yourself did not happen to notice, madame, when you entered Mrs. Inglethorp's room, whether that door was bolted or not?"

"I—I believe it was."

"But you did not see it?"

"No. I—never looked."

"But *I* did," interrupted Lawrence suddenly. "I happened to notice that it *was* bolted."

"Ah, that settles it." And Poirot looked crestfallen.

I could not help rejoicing that, for once, one of his "little ideas" had come to naught.

After lunch Poirot begged me to accompany him home. I consented rather stiffly.

"You are annoyed, is it not so?" he asked anxiously, as we walked through the park.

"Not at all," I said coldly.

"That is well. That lifts a great load from my mind."

This was not quite what I had intended. I had hoped that he would have observed the stiffness of my manner. Still, the fervour of his words went towards the appeasing of my just displeasure. I thawed.

"I gave Lawrence your message," I said.

"And what did he say? He was entirely puzzled?"

"Yes. I am quite sure he had no idea of what you meant."

I had expected Poirot to be disappointed; but, to my surprise, he replied that that was as he had thought, and that he was very glad. My pride forbade me to ask any questions.

Poirot switched off on another tack.

"Mademoiselle Cynthia was not at lunch today? How was that?"

"She is at the hospital again. She resumed work to-day."

"Ah, she is an industrious little demoiselle. And pretty too. She is like pictures I have seen in Italy. I would rather like to see that dispensary of hers. Do you think she would show it to me?"

"I am sure she would be delighted. It's an interesting little place."

"Does she go there every day?"

"She has all Wednesdays off, and comes back to lunch on Saturdays. Those are her only times off."

"I will remember. Women are doing great work nowadays, and Mademoiselle Cynthia is clever—oh, yes, she has brains, that little one."

"Yes. I believe she has passed quite a stiff exam."

"Without doubt. After all, it is very responsible work. I suppose they have very strong poisons there?"

"Yes, she showed them to us. They are kept locked up in a little cupboard. I believe they have to be very careful. They always take out the key before leaving the room."

"Indeed. It is near the window, this cupboard?"

"No, right the other side of the room. Why?"

Poirot shrugged his shoulders.

"I wondered. That is all. Will you come in?"

We had reached the cottage.

"No. I think I'll be getting back. I shall go round the long way through the woods."

The woods round Styles were very beautiful. After the walk

across the open park, it was pleasant to saunter lazily through the cool glades. There was hardly a breath of wind, the very chirp of the birds was faint and subdued. I strolled on a little way, and finally flung myself down at the foot of a grand old beech-tree. My thoughts of mankind were kindly and charitable. I even forgave Poirot for his absurd secrecy. In fact, I was at peace with the world. Then I yawned.

I thought about the crime, and it struck me as being very unreal and far off.

I yawned again.

Probably, I thought, it really never happened. Of course, it was all a bad dream. The truth of the matter was that it was Lawrence who had murdered Alfred Inglethorp with a croquet mallet. But it was absurd of John to make such a fuss about it, and to go shouting out: "I tell you I won't have it!"

I woke up with a start.

At once I realized that I was in a very awkward predicament. For, about twelve feet away from me John and Mary Cavendish were standing facing each other, and they were evidently quarrelling. And, quite as evidently, they were unaware of my vicinity, for before I could move or speak John repeated the words which had aroused me from my dream.

"I tell you, Mary, I won't have it."

Mary's voice came, cool and liquid:

"Have *you* any right to criticize my actions?"

"It will be the talk of the village! My mother was only buried on Saturday, and here you are gadding about with the fellow."

"Oh," she shrugged her shoulders, "if it is only village gossip that you mind!"

"But it isn't. I've had enough of the fellow hanging about. He's a Polish Jew, anyway."

"A tinge of Jewish blood is not a bad thing. It leavens the"— she looked at him—"stolid stupidity of the ordinary Englishman."

Fire in her eyes, ice in her voice. I did not wonder that the blood rose to John's face in a crimson tide.

"Mary!"

"Well?" Her tone did not change.

The pleading died out of his voice.

"Am I to understand that you will continue to see Bauerstein against my express wishes?"

"If I choose."

"You defy me?"

"No, but I deny your right to criticize my actions. Have *you* no friends of whom I should disapprove?"

John fell back a pace. The colour ebbed slowly from his face.

"What do you mean?" he said, in an unsteady voice.

"You see!" said Mary quietly. "You *do* see, don't you, that *you* have no right to dictate to *me* as to the choice of my friends?"

John glanced at her pleadingly, a stricken look in his face.

"No right? Have I *no* right, Mary?" he said unsteadily. He stretched out his hands. "Mary——"

For a moment, I thought she wavered. A softer expression came over her face, then suddenly she turned almost fiercely away.

"None!"

She was walking away when John sprang after her, and caught her by the arm.

"Mary"—his voice was very quiet now—"are you in love with this fellow Bauerstein?"

She hesitated, and suddenly there swept across her face a strange expression, old as the hills, yet with something eternally young about it. So might some Egyptian sphinx have smiled.

She freed herself quietly from his arm, and spoke over her shoulder.

"Perhaps," she said; and then swiftly passed out of the little glade, leaving John standing there as though he had been turned to stone.

Rather ostentatiously, I stepped forward, crackling some dead branches with my feet as I did so. John turned. Luckily, he took it for granted that I had only just come upon the scene.

"Hullo, Hastings. Have you seen the little fellow safely back to his cottage? Quaint little chap! Is he any good, though, really?"

"He was considered one of the finest detectives of his day."

"Oh, well, I suppose there must be something in it, then. What a rotten world it is, though!"

"You find it so?" I asked.

"Good Lord, yes! There's this terrible business to start with. Scotland Yard men in and out of the house like a jack-in-the-box! Never know where they won't turn up next. Screaming headlines in every paper in the country—damn all journalists, I say! Do you know there was a whole crowd staring in at the lodge gates this morning. Sort of Madame Tussaud's chamber of horrors business that can be seen for nothing. Pretty thick, isn't it?"

"Cheer up, John!" I said soothingly. "It can't last for ever."

"Can't it, though? It can last long enough for us never to be able to hold up our heads again."

"No, no, you're getting morbid on the subject."

"Enough to make a man morbid, to be stalked by beastly journalists and stared at by gaping moon-faced idiots, wherever he goes! But there's worse than that."

"What?"

John lowered his voice:

"Have you ever thought, Hastings—it's a nightmare to me—who did it? I can't help feeling sometimes it must have been an accident. Because—because—who could have done it? Now Inglethorp's out of the way, there's no one else; no one, I mean, except—one of us."

Yes, indeed, that was nightmare enough for any man! One of us? Yes, surely it must be so, unless——

A new idea suggested itself to my mind. Rapidly, I considered it. The light increased. Poirot's mysterious doings, his hints—they all fitted in. Fool that I was not to have thought of this possibility before, and what a relief for us all.

"No, John," I said, "it isn't one of us. How could it be?"

"I know, but, still, who else is there?"

"Can't you guess?"

"No."

I looked cautiously round, and lowered my voice.

"Dr. Bauerstein!" I whispered.

"Impossible!"

"Not at all."

"But what earthly interest could he have in my mother's death?"

"That I don't see," I confessed, "but I'll tell you this: Poirot thinks so."

"Poirot? Does he? How do you know?"

I told him of Poirot's intense excitement on hearing that Dr. Bauerstein had been at Styles on the fatal night, and added:

"He said twice: 'That alters everything.' And I've been thinking. You know Inglethorp said he had put down the coffee in the hall? Well, it was just then that Bauerstein arrived. Isn't it possible that, as Inglethorp brought him through the hall, the doctor dropped something into the coffee in passing?"

"H'm," said John. "It would have been very risky."

"Yes, but it was possible."

"And then, how could he know it was her coffee? No, old fellow, I don't think that will wash."

But I had remembered something else.

"You're quite right. That wasn't how it was done. Listen." And I then told him of the coco sample which Poirot had taken to be analysed.

John interrupted just as I had done.

"But, look here, Bauerstein had had it analysed already?"

"Yes yes, that's the point. I didn't see it either until now. Don't you understand? Bauerstein had it analysed—that's just it! If Bauerstein's the murderer, nothing could be simpler than for him to substitute some ordinary coco for his sample, and send that to be tested. And of course they would find no strychnine! But no one would dream of suspecting Bauerstein, or think of taking another sample—except Poirot," I added, with belated recognition.

"Yes, but what about the bitter taste that coco won't disguise?"

"Well, we've only his word for that. And there are other possibilities. He's admittedly one of the world's greatest toxicologists——"

"One of the world's greatest what? Say it again."

"He knows more about poisons than almost anybody," I explained. "Well, my idea is, that perhaps he's found some way of making strychnine tasteless. Or it may not have been strychnine at all, but some obscure drug no one has ever heard of, which produces much the same symptoms."

"H'm, yes, that might be," said John. "But look here, how could he have got at the coco? That wasn't downstairs?"

"No, it wasn't," I admitted reluctantly.

And then, suddenly, a dreadful possibility flashed through my mind. I hoped and prayed it would not occur to John also. I glanced sideways at him. He was frowning perplexedly, and I drew a deep breath of relief, for the terrible thought that had flashed across my mind was this: that Dr. Bauerstein might have had an accomplice.

Yet surely it could not be! Surely no woman as beautiful as Mary Cavendish could be a murderess. Yet beautiful women had been known to poison.

And suddenly I remembered that first conversation at tea on the day of my arrival, and the gleam in her eyes as she had said that poison was a woman's weapon. How agitated she had been on that fatal Tuesday evening! Had Mrs. Inglethorp discovered something between her and Bauerstein, and threatened to tell her husband? Was it to stop that denunciation that the crime had been committed?

Then I remembered that enigmatical conversation between Poirot and Evelyn Howard. Was this what they had meant? Was this the monstrous possibility that Evelyn had tried not to believe?

Yes, it all fitted in.

No wonder Miss Howard had suggested "hushing it up." Now I understood that unfinished sentence of hers: "Emily herself——" And in my heart I agreed with her. Would not Mrs. Inglethorp have preferred to go unavenged rather than have such terrible dishonour fall upon the name of Cavendish.

"There's another thing," said John suddenly, and the unexpected sound of his voice made me start guiltily. "Something which makes me doubt if what you say can be true."

"What's that?" I asked, thankful that he had gone away from the subject of how the poison could have been introduced into the coco.

"Why, the fact that Bauerstein demanded a post-mortem. He needn't have done so. Little Wilkins would have been quite content to let it go at heart disease."

"Yes," I said doubtfully. "But we don't know. Perhaps he thought it safer in the long run. Some one might have talked afterwards. Then the Home Office might have ordered exhumation. The whole thing would have come out, then, and he would have been in an awkward position, for no one would have believed that a man of his reputation could have been deceived into calling it heart disease."

"Yes, that's possible," admitted John. "Still," he added, "I'm blest if I can see what his motive could have been."

I trembled.

"Look here," I said, "I may be altogether wrong. And, remember, all this is in confidence."

"Oh, of course—that goes without saying."

We had walked, as we talked, and now we passed through the little gate into the garden. Voices rose near at hand, for tea was spread out under the sycamore-tree, as it had been on the day of my arrival.

Cynthia was back from the hospital, and I placed my chair beside her, and told her of Poirot's wish to visit the dispensary.

"Of course! I'd love him to see it. He'd better come to tea there one day. I must fix it up with him. He's such a dear little man! But he *is* funny. He made me take the brooch out of my tie the other day, and put it in again, because he said it wasn't straight."

I laughed.

"It's quite a mania with him."

"Yes, isn't it?"

We were silent for a minute or two, and then, glancing in the direction of Mary Cavendish, and dropping her voice, Cynthia said:

"Mr. Hastings."

"Yes?"

"After tea, I want to talk to you."

Her glance at Mary had set me thinking. I fancied that between these two there existed very little sympathy. For the first time, it occurred to me to wonder about the girl's future. Mrs. Inglethorp had made no provision of any kind for her, but I imagined that John and Mary would probably insist on her making her home with them—at any rate until the end of the war. John, I knew, was very fond of her, and would be sorry to let her go.

John, who had gone into the house, now reappeared. His good-natured face wore an unaccustomed frown of anger.

"Confound those detectives! I can't think what they're after! They've been in every room in the house—turning things inside out, and upside down. It really is too bad! I suppose they took advantage of our all being out. I shall go for that fellow Japp, when I next see him!"

"Lot of Paul Prys," grunted Miss Howard.

Lawrence opined that they had to make a show of doing something.

Mary Cavendish said nothing.

After tea, I invited Cynthia to come for a walk, and we sauntered off into the woods together.

"Well?" I inquired, as soon as we were protected from prying eyes by the leafy screen.

With a sigh, Cynthia flung herself down, and tossed off her hat. The sunlight, piercing through the branches, turned the auburn of her hair to quivering gold.

"Mr. Hastings—you are always so kind, and you know such a lot."

It struck me at this moment that Cynthia was really a very charming girl! Much more charming than Mary, who never said things of that kind.

"Well?" I asked benignantly, as she hesitated.

"I want to ask your advice. What shall I do?"

"Do?"

"Yes. You see, Aunt Emily always told me I should be provided for. I suppose she forgot, or didn't think she was likely to die—anyway, I am *not* provided for! And I don't know what to do. Do you think I ought to go away from here at once?"

"Good heavens, no! They don't want to part with you, I'm sure."

Cynthia hesitated a moment, plucking up the grass with her tiny hands. Then she said: "Mrs. Cavendish does. She hates me."

"Hates you?" I cried, astonished.

Cynthia nodded.

"Yes. I don't know why, but she can't bear me; and *he* can't, either."

"There I know you're wrong," I said warmly. "On the contrary, John is very fond of you."

"Oh, yes—*John*. I meant Lawrence. Not, of course, that I care whether Lawrence hates me or not. Still, it's rather horrid when no one loves you, isn't it?"

"But they do, Cynthia dear," I said earnestly. "I'm sure you are mistaken. Look, there is John—and Miss Howard—"

Cynthia nodded rather gloomily. "Yes, John likes me, I think, and of course Evie, for all her gruff ways, wouldn't be unkind to a fly. But Lawrence never speaks to me if he can help it, and Mary can hardly bring herself to be civil to me. She wants Evie to stay on, is begging her to, but she doesn't want me, and—and—I don't know what to do." Suddenly the poor child burst out crying.

I don't know what possessed me. Her beauty, perhaps, as she sat there, with the sunlight glinting down on her head; perhaps the sense of relief at encountering someone who so obviously could have no connection with the tragedy; perhaps honest pity for her youth and loneliness. Anyway, I leant forward, and taking her little hand, I said awkwardly:

"Marry me, Cynthia."

Unwittingly, I had hit upon a sovereign remedy for her tears. She sat up at once, drew her hand away, and said, with some asperity:

"Don't be silly!"

I was a little annoyed.

"I'm not being silly. I am asking you to do me the honour of becoming my wife."

To my intense surprise, Cynthia burst out laughing, and called me a "funny dear".

"It's perfectly sweet of you," she said, "but you know you don't want to!"

"Yes, I do. I've got—"

"Never mind what you've got. You don't really want to—and I don't either."

"Well, of course, that settles it," I said stiffly. "But I don't see anything to laugh at. There's nothing funny about a proposal."

"No, indeed," said Cynthia. "Somebody might accept you next time. Good-bye, you've cheered me up *very* much."

And, with a final uncontrollable burst of merriment, she vanished through the trees.

Thinking over the interview, it struck me as being profoundly unsatisfactory.

It occurred to me suddenly that I would go down to the village, and look up Bauerstein. Somebody ought to be keeping an eye on the fellow. At the same time, it would be wise to allay any suspicions he might have as to his being suspected. I remembered how Poirot had relied on my diplomacy. Accordingly, I went to the little house with the "Apartments" card inserted in the window, where I knew he lodged, and tapped on the door.

An old woman came and opened it.

"Good afternoon," I said pleasantly. "Is Dr. Bauerstein in?"

She stared at me.

"Haven't you heard?"

"Heard what?"

"About him."

"What about him?"

"He's took."

"Took? Dead?"

"No, took by the perlice."

"By the police!" I gasped. "Do you mean they've arrested him?"

"Yes, that's it, and—"

I waited to hear no more, but tore up the village to find Poirot.

10

The Arrest

To my extreme annoyance, Poirot was not in, and the old Belgian who answered my knock informed me that he believed he had gone to London.

I was dumbfounded. What on earth could Poirot be doing in London! Was it a sudden decision on his part, or had he already made up his mind when he parted from me a few hours earlier?

I retraced my steps to Styles in some annoyance. With Poirot away, I was uncertain how to act. Had he foreseen this arrest? Had he not, in all probability, been the cause of it? Those questions I could not resolve. But in the meantime what was I to do? Should I announce the arrest openly at Styles, or not? Though I did not acknowledge it to myself, the thought of Mary Cavendish was weighing on me. Would it not be a terrible shock to her? For the moment, I set aside utterly any suspicions of her. She could not be implicated—otherwise I should have heard some hint of it.

Of course, there was no possibility of being able permanently to conceal Dr. Bauerstein's arrest from her. It would be announced in every newspaper on the morrow. Still, I shrank from blurting it out. If only Poirot had been accessible, I could have asked his advice. What possessed him to go posting off to London in this unaccountable way?

In spite of myself, my opinion of his sagacity was immeasurably heightened. I would never have dreamt of suspecting the doctor, had not Poirot put it into my head. Yes, decidedly, the little man was clever.

After some reflecting, I decided to take John into my confidence, and leave him to make the matter public or not, as he thought fit.

He gave vent to a prodigious whistle, as I imparted the news.

"Great Scot! You *were* right, then. I couldn't believe it at the time."

"No, it is astonishing until you get used to the idea, and see how it makes everything fit in. Now, what are we to do? Of course, it will be generally known to-morrow."

John reflected.

"Never mind," he said at last, "we won't say anything at present. There is no need. As you say, it will be known soon enough."

But to my intense surprise, on getting down early the next morning, and eagerly opening the newspapers, there was not a word about the arrest! There was a column of mere padding about "The Styles Poisoning Case", but nothing further. It was rather inexplicable, but I supposed that, for some reason or other, Japp wished to keep it out of the papers. It worried me just a little, for it suggested the possibility that there might be further arrests to come.

After breakfast, I decided to go down to the village, and see if Poirot had returned yet; but, before I could start, a well known face blocked one of the windows, and the well known voice said:

"*Bon jour, mon ami!*"

"Poirot," I exclaimed, with relief, and seizing him by both hands, I dragged him into the room. "I was never so glad to see anyone. Listen, I have said nothing to anybody but John. Is that right?"

"My friend," replied Poirot, "I do not know what you are talking about."

"Dr. Bauerstein's arrest, of course," I answered impatiently.

"Is Bauerstein arrested, then?"

"Did you not know it?"

"Not the least in the world." But, pausing a moment, he

added: "Still, it does not surprise me. After all, we are only four miles from the coast."

"The coast?" I asked, puzzled. "What has that got to do with it?"

Poirot shrugged his shoulders.

"Surely, it is obvious!"

"Not to me. No doubt I am very dense, but I cannot see what the proximity of the coast has got to do with the murder of Mrs. Inglethorp."

"Nothing at all, of course," replied Poirot, smiling. "But we were speaking of the arrest of Dr. Bauerstein."

"Well, he is arrested for the murder of Mrs. Inglethorp——"

"What?" cried Poirot, in apparently lively astonishment. "Dr. Bauerstein arrested for the murder of Mrs. Inglethorp?"

"Yes."

"Impossible! That would be too good a farce! Who told you that, my friend?"

"Well, no one exactly told me," I confessed. "But he is arrested."

"Oh, yes, very likely. But for espionage, *mon ami.*"

"Espionage?" I gasped.

"Precisely."

"Not for poisoning Mrs. Inglethorp?"

"Not unless our friend Japp has taken leave of his senses," replied Poirot placidly.

"But—but I thought you thought so too?"

Poirot gave me one look, which conveyed a wondering pity, and his full sense of the utter absurdity of such an idea.

"Do you mean to say," I asked, slowly adapting myself to the new idea, "that Dr. Bauerstein is a spy?"

Poirot nodded.

"Have you never suspected it?"

"It never entered my head."

"It did not strike you as peculiar that a famous London doctor should bury himself in a little village like this, and should be in the habit of walking about at all hours of the night, fully dressed?"

"No," I confessed, "I never thought of such a thing."

"He is, of course, a German by birth," said Poirot thoughtfully, "though he has practised so long in this country that nobody thinks of him as anything but an Englishman. He was naturalized about fifteen years ago. A very clever man."

"The blackguard!" I cried indignantly.

"Not at all. He is, on the contrary, a patriot. Think what he stands to lose. I admire the man myself."

But I could not look at it in Poirot's philosophical way.

"And this is the man with whom Mrs. Cavendish has been wandering about all over the country!" I cried indignantly.

"Yes. I should fancy he had found her very useful," remarked Poirot. "So long as gossip busied itself in coupling their names together, any other vagaries of the doctor's passed unobserved."

"Then you think he never really cared for her?" I asked eagerly—rather too eagerly, perhaps, under the circumstances.

"That, of course, I cannot say, but—shall I tell you my own private opinion, Hastings?"

"Yes."

"Well, it is this: that Mrs. Cavendish does not care, and never has cared one little jot about Dr. Bauerstein!"

"Do you really think so?" I could not disguise my pleasure.

"I am quite sure of it. And I will tell you why."

"Yes?"

"Because she cares for some one else, *mon ami*."

"Oh!" What did he mean? In spite of myself, an agreeable warmth spread over me. I am not a vain man where women are concerned, but I remembered certain evidences, too lightly thought of at the time, perhaps, but which certainly seemed to indicate——

My pleasing thoughts were interrupted by the sudden entrance of Miss Howard. She glanced round hastily to make sure there was no one else in the room, and quickly produced an old sheet of brown paper. This she handed to Poirot, murmuring as she did so the cryptic words:

"On top of the wardrobe." Then she hurriedly left the room.

Poirot unfolded the sheet of paper eagerly, and uttered an exclamation of satisfaction. He spread it out on the table.

"Come here, Hastings. Now tell me, what is that initial—J. or L.?"

It was a medium sized sheet of paper, rather dusty, as though it had lain by for some time. But it was the label that was attracting Poirot's attention. At the top, it bore the printed stamp of Messrs. Parkson's, the well known theatrical costumiers, and it was addressed to "—(the debatable initial) Cavendish, Esq., Styles Court, Styles St. Mary, Essex."

"It might be T., or it might be L.," I said, after studying the thing for a minute or two. "It certainly isn't a J."

"Good," replied Poirot, folding up the paper again. "I, also, am of your way of thinking. It is an L., depend upon it!"

"Where did it come from?" I asked curiously. "Is it important?"

"Moderately so. It confirms a surmise of mine. Having deduced its existence, I set Miss Howard to search for it, and, as you see, she has been successful."

"What did she mean by 'On the top of the wardrobe'?"

"She meant," replied Poirot promptly, "that she found it on top of a wardrobe."

"A funny place for a piece of brown paper," I mused.

"Not at all. The top of a wardrobe is an excellent place for brown paper and cardboard boxes. I have kept them there myself. Neatly arranged, there is nothing to offend the eye."

"Poirot," I asked earnestly, "have you made up your mind about this crime?"

"Yes—that is to say, I believe I know how it was committed."

"Ah!"

"Unfortunately, I have no proof beyond my surmise, unless——" With sudden energy, he caught me by the arm, and whirled me down the hall, calling out in French in his excitement: "Mademoiselle Dorcas, Mademoiselle Dorcas, *un moment, s'il vous plait!*"

Dorcas, quite flurried by the noise, came hurrying out of the pantry.

"My good Dorcas, I have an idea—a little idea—if it should prove justified, what magnificent chance! Tell me, on Monday, not Tuesday, Dorcas, but Monday, the day before the tragedy, did anything go wrong with Mrs. Inglethorp's bell?"

Dorcas looked very surprised.

"Yes, sir, now you mention it, it did; though I don't know how you came to hear of it. A mouse, or some such, must have nibbled the wire through. The man came and put it right on Tuesday morning."

With a long drawn exclamation of ecstasy, Poirot led the way back to the morning-room.

"See you, one should not ask for outside proof—no, reason should be enough. But the flesh is weak, it is consolation to find that one is on the right track. Ah, my friend, I am like a giant refreshed. I run! I leap!"

And, in very truth, run and leap he did, gambolling wildly down the stretch of lawn outside the long window.

"What is your remarkable little friend doing?" asked a voice behind me, and I turned to find Mary Cavendish at my elbow. She smiled, and so did I. "What is it all about?"

"Really, I can't tell you. He asked Dorcas some question about a bell, and appeared so delighted with her answer that he is capering about as you see!"

Mary laughed.

"How ridiculous! He's going out of the gate. Isn't he coming back today?"

"I don't know. I've given up trying to guess what he'll do next."

"Is he quite mad, Mr. Hastings?"

"I honestly don't know. Sometimes, I feel sure he is as mad as a hatter; and then, just as he is at his maddest, I find there is method in his madness."

"I see."

In spite of her laugh, Mary was looking thoughtful this morning. She seemed grave, almost sad.

It occurred to me that it would be a good opportunity to tackle her on the subject of Cynthia. I began rather tactfully, I thought, but I had not gone far before she stopped me authoritatively.

"You are an excellent advocate, I have no doubt, Mr. Hastings, but in this case your talents are quite thrown away. Cynthia will run no risk of encountering any unkindness from me."

I began to stammer feebly that I hoped she hadn't thought— But again she stopped me, and her words were so unexpected that they quite drove Cynthia, and her troubles out of my mind.

"Mr. Hastings," she said, "do you think I and my husband are happy together?"

I was considerably taken aback, and murmured something about it's not being my business to think anything of the sort.

"Well," she said quietly, "whether it is your business or not, I will tell you that we are *not* happy."

I said nothing, for I saw that she had not finished.

She began slowly, walking up and down the room, her head a little bent, and that slim, supple figure of hers swaying gently as she walked. She stopped suddenly, and looked up at me.

"You don't know anything about me, do you?" she asked. "Where I come from, who I was before I married John—anything, in fact? Well, I will tell you. I will make a father confessor of you. You are kind, I think—yes, I am sure you are kind."

Somehow, I was not quite as elated as I might have been. I remembered that Cynthia had begun her confidences in much the same way. Besides, a father confessor should be elderly, it is not at all the rôle for a young man.

"My father was English," said Mrs. Cavendish, "but my mother was a Russian."

"Ah," I said, "now I understand—"

"Understand what?"

"A hint of something foreign—different—that there has always been about you."

"My mother was very beautiful, I believe. I don't know, because I never saw her. She died when I was quite a little child. I believe there was some tragedy connected with her death—she took an overdose of some sleeping draught by mistake. However that may be, my father was broken-hearted. Shortly afterwards, he went into the Consular Service. Everywhere he went, I went with him. When I was twenty-three, I had been nearly all over the world. It was a splendid life—I loved it."

There was a smile on her face, and her head was thrown back. She seemed living in the memory of those old glad days.

"Then my father died. He left me very badly off. I had to go and live with some old aunts in Yorkshire." She shuddered. "You will understand me when I say that it was a deadly life for a girl brought up as I had been. The narrowness, the deadly monotony of it, almost drove me mad." She paused a minute, and added in a different tone: "And then I met John Cavendish."

"Yes?"

"You can imagine that, from my aunts' point of view, it was a very good match for me. But I can honestly say it was not this fact which weighed with me. No, he was simply a way of escape from the insufferable monotony of my life."

I said nothing, and after a moment, she went on:

"Don't misunderstand me. I was quite honest with him. I told him, what was true, that I liked him very much, that I hoped to come to like him more, but that I was not in any way what the world calls 'in love' with him. He declared that that satisfied him, and so—we were married."

She waited a long time, a little frown had gathered on her forehead. She seemed to be looking back earnestly into those past days.

"I think—I am sure—he cared for me at first. But I suppose we were not well matched. Almost at once, we drifted apart. He—it is not a pleasing thing for my pride, but it is the truth—tired of me very soon." I must have made some murmur of dissent, for she went on quickly: "Oh, yes, he did! Not that it matters now—now that we've come to the parting of the ways."

"What do you mean?"

She answered quietly:

"I mean that I am not going to remain at Styles."

"You and John are not going to live here?"

"John may live here, but I shall not."

"You are going to leave him?"

"Yes."

"But why?"

She paused a long time, and said at last:

"Perhaps—because I want to be—free!"

And, as she spoke, I had a sudden vision of broad spaces, virgin tracts of forests, untrodden lands—and a realization of what freedom would mean to such a nature as Mary Cavendish. I seemed to see her for a moment as she was, a proud wild creature, as untamed by civilization as some shy bird of the hills. A little cry broke from her lips:

"You don't know, you don't know, how this hateful place has been prison to me!"

"I understand," I said, "but—but don't do anything rash."

"Oh, rash!" Her voice mocked at my prudence.

Then suddenly I said a thing I could have bitten out my tongue for:

"You know that Dr. Bauerstein has been arrested?"

An instant coldness passed like a mask over her face, blotting out all expression.

"John was so kind as to break that to me this morning."

"Well, what do you think?" I asked feebly.

"Of what?"

"Of the arrest?"

"What should I think? Apparently he is a German spy; so the gardener had told John."

Her face and voice were absolutely cold and expressionless. Did she care, or did she not?

She moved away a step or two, and fingered one of the flower vases.

"These are quite dead. I must do them again. Would you mind moving—thank you, Mr. Hastings." And she walked quietly past me out of the window, with a cool little nod of dismissal.

No, surely she could not care for Bauerstein. No woman could act her part with that icy unconcern.

Poirot did not make his appearance the following morning, and there was no sign of the Scotland Yard men.

But, at lunch-time, there arrived a new piece of evidence—or rather lack of evidence. We had vainly tried to trace the fourth letter, which Mrs. Inglethorp had written on the evening preceding her death. Our efforts having been in vain, we had abandoned the matter, hoping that it might turn up of itself one day. And this is just what did happen, in the shape of a communication, which arrived by the second post from a firm of French music publishers, acknowledging Mrs. Inglethorp's cheque, and regretting they had been unable to trace a certain series of Russian folk-songs. So the last hope of solving the mystery, by means of Mrs. Inglethorp's correspondence on the fatal evening, had to be abandoned.

Just before tea, I strolled down to tell Poirot of the new disappointment, but found, to my annoyance, that he was once more out.

"Gone to London again?"

"Oh, no, monsieur, he has but taken the train to Tadminster. 'To see a young lady's dispensary,' he said."

"Silly ass!" I ejaculated. "I told him Wednesday was the one day she wasn't there! Well, tell him to look us up tomorrow morning, will you?"

"Certainly, monsieur."

But, on the following day, no sign of Poirot. I was getting angry. He was really treating us in the most cavalier fashion.

After lunch, Lawrence drew me aside, and asked if I was going down to see him.

"No, I don't think I shall. He can come up here if he wants to see us."

"Oh!" Lawrence looked indeterminate. Something unusually nervous and excited in his manner roused my curiosity.

"What is it?" I asked. "I could go if there's anything special."

"It's nothing much, but—well, if you are going, will you tell him—" he dropped his voice to a whisper—"I think I've found the extra coffee-cup!"

I had almost forgotten that enigmatical message of Poirot's, but now my curiosity was aroused afresh.

Lawrence would say no more, so I decided that I would descend from my high horse, and once more seek out Poirot at Leastways Cottage.

This time I was received with a smile. Monsieur Poirot was within. Would I mount? I mounted accordingly.

Poirot was sitting by the table, his head buried in his hands. He sprang up at my entrance.

"What is it?" I asked solicitously. "You are not ill, I trust?"

"No, no, not ill. But I decide an affair of great moment."

"Whether to catch the criminal or not?" I asked facetiously.

But, to my great surprise, Poirot nodded gravely.

" 'To speak or not to speak,' as your so great Shakespeare says, 'that is the question.' "

I did not trouble to correct the quotation.

"You are not serious, Poirot?"

"I am of the most serious. For the most serious of all things hangs in the balance."

"And that is?"

"A woman's happiness, *mon ami*," he said gravely.

I did not quite know what to say.

"The moment has come," said Poirot thoughtfully, "and I do not know what to do. For, see you, it is a big stake for which I play. No one but I, Hercule Poirot, would attempt it!" And he tapped himself proudly on the breast.

After pausing a few minutes respectfully, so as not to spoil his effect, I gave him Lawrence's message.

"Aha!" he cried. "So he has found the extra coffee-cup. That is good. He has more intelligence than would appear, this long-faced Monsieur Lawrence of yours!"

I did not myself think very highly of Lawrence's intelligence; but I forebore to contradict Poirot, and gently took him to task for forgetting my instructions as to which were Cynthia's days off.

"It is true. I have the head of a sieve. However, the other young lady was most kind. She was sorry for my disappointment, and showed me everything in the kindest way."

"Oh, well, that's all right, then, and you must go to tea with Cynthia another day."

I told him about the letter.

"I am sorry for that," he said. "I always had hopes of that letter. But no, it was not to be. This affair must all be unravelled from within." He tapped his forehead. "These little grey cells. It is 'up to them'—as you say over here." Then, suddenly, he asked: "Are you a judge of finger-marks, my friend?"

"No," I said, rather surprised, "I know that there are no two finger-marks alike, but that's as far as my science goes."

"Exactly."

He unlocked a little drawer, and took out some photographs which he laid on the table.

"I have numbered them, 1, 2, 3. Will you describe them to me?"

I studied the proofs attentively.

"All greatly magnified, I see. No. 1, I should say, are a man's finger-prints; thumb and first finger. No. 2 are a lady's; they are much smaller, and quite different in every way. No. 3"—I paused for some time—"there seem to be a lot of confused finger-marks, but here, very distinctly, are No. 1's."

"Overlapping the others?"

"Yes."

"You recognize them beyond fail?"

"Oh, yes; they are identical."

Poirot nodded, and gently taking the photographs from me locked them up again.

"I suppose," I said, "that as usual, you are not going to explain?"

"On the contrary. No. 1 were the finger-prints of Monsieur Lawrence. No. 2 were those of Mademoiselle Cynthia. They are not important. I merely obtained them for comparison. No. 3 is a little more complicated."

"Yes?"

"It is, as you see, highly magnified. You may have noticed a sort of blur extending all across the picture. I will not describe to you the special apparatus, dusting powder, etc., which I used. It is a well known process to the police, and by means of it you can obtain a photograph of the finger-prints on any object in a very short space of time. Well, my friend, you have seen the finger-marks—it remains to tell you the particular object on which they had been left."

"Go on—I am really excited."

"*Eh bien!* Photo No. 3 represents the highly magnified surface of a tiny bottle in the top poison cupboard of the dispensary in the Red Cross Hospital at Tadminster—which sounds like the house that Jack built!"

"Good heavens!" I exclaimed. "But what were Lawrence Cavendish's finger-marks doing on it? He never went near the poison cupboard the day we were there?"

"Oh, yes, he did!"

"Impossible! We were all together the whole time."

Poirot shook his head.

"No, my friend, there was a moment when you were not all together. There was a moment when you could not have been all together, or it would not have been necessary to call to Monsieur Lawrence to come and join you on the balcony."

"I'd forgotten that," I admitted. "But it was only for a moment."

"Long enough."

"Long enough for what?"

Poirot's smile became rather enigmatical.

"Long enough for a gentleman who had once studied medicine to gratify a very natural interest and curiosity."

Our eyes met. Poirot's were pleasantly vague. He got up and hummed a little tune. I watched him suspiciously.

"Poirot," I said, "what was in this particular little bottle?"

Poirot looked out of the window.

"Hydro-chloride of strychnine," he said, over his shoulder, continuing to hum.

"Good heavens!" I said it quite quietly. I was not surprised. I had expected that answer.

"They use the pure hydro-chloride of strychnine very little—only occasionally for pills. It is the official solution, Liq. Strychnine Hydro-clor. that is used in most medicines. That is why the finger-marks have remained undisturbed since then."

"How did you manage to take this photograph?"

"I dropped my hat from the balcony," explained Poirot simply. "Visitors were not permitted below at that hour, so, in spite of my many apologies, Mademoiselle Cynthia's colleague had to go down and fetch it for me."

"Then you knew what you were going to find?"

"No, not at all. I merely realized that it was possible, from your story, for Monsieur Lawrence to go to the poison cupboard. The possibility had to be confirmed, or eliminated."

"Poirot," I said, "your gaiety does not deceive me. This is a very important discovery."

"I do not know," said Poirot. "But one thing does strike me. No doubt it has struck you too."

"What is that?"

"Why, that there is altogether too much strychnine about this case. This is the third time we run up against it. There was strychnine in Mrs. Inglethorp's tonic. There is the strychnine sold across the counter at Styles St. Mary by Mace. Now we have more strychnine, handled by one of the household. It is confusing; and, as you know, I do not like confusion."

Before I could reply, one of the other Belgians opened the door and stuck his head in.

"There is a lady below, asking for Mr. Hastings."

"A lady?"

I jumped up. Poirot followed me down the narrow stairs. Mary Cavendish was standing in the doorway.

"I have been visiting an old woman in the village," she explained, "and as Lawrence told me you were with Monsieur Poirot I thought I would call for you."

"Alas, madame," said Poirot, "I thought you had come to honour me with a visit!"

"I will some day, if you ask me," she promised him, smiling.

"That is well. If you should need a father confessor, madame" —she started ever so slightly—"remember, Papa Poirot is always at your service."

She stared at him for a few minutes, as though seeking to read some deeper meaning into his words. Then she turned abruptly away.

"Come, will you not walk back with us too, Monsieur Poirot?"

"Enchanted, madame."

All the way to Styles, Mary talked fast and feverishly. It struck me that in some way she was nervous of Poirot's eyes.

The weather had broken, and the sharp wind was almost autumnal in its shrewishness. Mary shivered a little, and buttoned her black sports coat closer. The wind through the trees made a mournful noise, like some great giant sighing.

We walked up to the great door of Styles, and at once the knowledge came to us that something was wrong.

Dorcas came running out to meet us. She was crying and wringing her hands. I was aware of other servants huddled together in the background, all eyes and ears.

"Oh, m'am; oh, m'am! I don't know how to tell you—"

"What is it, Dorcas?" I asked impatiently. "Tell us at once."

"It's those wicked detectives. They've arrested him—they've arrested Mr. Cavendish!"

"Arrested Lawrence?" I gasped.

I saw a strange look come into Dorcas's eyes.

"No, sir. Not Mr. Lawrence—Mr. John."

Behind me, with a wild cry, Mary Cavendish fell heavily against me, and as I turned to catch her I met the quiet triumph in Poirot's eyes.

11

The Case for the Prosecution

The trial of John Cavendish for the murder of his stepmother took place two months later.

Of the intervening weeks I will say little, but my admiration and sympathy went out unfeignedly to Mary Cavendish. She ranged herself passionately on her husband's side, scorning the mere idea of his guilt, and fought for him tooth and nail.

I expressed my admiration to Poirot, and he nodded thoughtfully.

"Yes, she is of those women who show at their best in adversity. It brings out all that is sweetest and truest in them. Her pride and her jealousy have—"

"Jealousy?" I queried.

"Yes. Have you not realized that she is an unusually jealous woman? As I was saying, her pride and jealousy have been laid aside. She thinks of nothing but her husband, and the terrible fate that is hanging over him."

He spoke very feelingly, and I looked at him earnestly, remembering that last afternoon, when he had been deliberating whether or no to speak. With his tenderness for "a woman's happiness," I felt glad that the decision had been taken out of his hands.

"Even now," I said, "I can hardly believe it. You see, up to the very last minute, I thought it was Lawrence!"

Poirot grinned.

"I know you did."

"But John! My old friend John!"

"Every murderer is probably somebody's old friend," observed Poirot philosophically. "You cannot mix up sentiment and reason."

"I must say I think you might have given me a hint."

"Perhaps, *mon ami*, I did not do so, just because he *was* your old friend."

I was rather disconcerted by this, remembering how I had busily passed on to John what I believed to be Poirot's views concerning Bauerstein. He, by the way, had been acquitted of the charge brought against him. Nevertheless, although he had been too clever for them this time, and the charge of espionage could not be brought home to him, his wings were pretty well clipped for the future.

I asked Poirot whether he thought John would be condemned. To my intense surprise, he replied that, on the contrary, he was extremely likely to be acquitted.

"But, Poirot—" I protested.

"Oh, my friend, have I not said to you all along that I have no proofs. It is one thing to know that a man is guilty, it is quite another matter to prove him so. And, in this case, there is terribly little evidence. That is the whole trouble. I, Hercule Poirot, know, but I lack the last link in my chain. And unless I can find that missing link—" He shook his head gravely.

"When did you first suspect John Cavendish?" I asked, after a minute or two.

"Did you not suspect him at all?"

"No, indeed."

"Not after that fragment of conversation you overheard between Mrs. Cavendish and her mother-in-law, and her subsequent lack of frankness at the inquest?"

"No."

"Did you not put two and two together, and reflect that if it was not Alfred Inglethorp who was quarrelling with his wife—and you remember, he strenuously denied it at the inquest—it must be either Lawrence or John. Now, if it was Lawrence, Mary Cavendish's conduct was just as inexplicable. But if, on the other hand, it was John, the whole thing was explained quite naturally."

"So," I cried, a light breaking in upon me, "it was John who quarrelled with his mother that afternoon?"

"Exactly."

"And you have known this all along?"

"Certainly. Mrs. Cavendish's behaviour could only be explained that way."

"And yet you say he may be acquitted?"

Poirot shrugged his shoulders.

"Certainly I do. At the police court proceedings, we shall hear the case for the prosecution, but in all probability his solicitors will advise him to reserve his defence. That will be sprung upon us at the trial. And—ah, by the way, I have a word of caution to give you, my friend. I must not appear in the case."

"What?"

"No. Officially, I have nothing to do with it. Until I have found that last link in my chain, I must remain behind the scenes. Mrs. Cavendish must think I am working for her husband, not against him."

"I say, that's playing it a bit low down," I protested.

"Not at all. We have to deal with a most clever and unscrupulous man, and we must use any means in our power—otherwise he will slip through our fingers. That is why I have been careful to remain in the background. All the discoveries have been made by Japp, and Japp will take all the credit. If I am called upon to give evidence at all"—he smiled broadly—"it will probably be as a witness for the defence."

I could hardly believe my ears.

"It is quite *en règle*," continued Poirot. "Strangely enough, I can give evidence that will demolish one contention of the prosecution."

"Which one?"

"The one that relates to the destruction of the will. John Cavendish did not destroy that will."

Poirot was a true prophet. I will not go into the details of the police court proceedings, as it involves many tiresome repetitions. I will merely state baldly that John Cavendish reserved his defence, and was duly committed for trial.

September found us all in London. Mary took a house in Kensington, Poirot being included in the family party.

I myself had been given a job at the War Office, so was able to see them continually.

As the weeks went by, the state of Poirot's nerves grew worse and worse. That "last link" he talked about was still lacking. Privately, I hoped it might remain so, for what happiness could there be for Mary, if John were not acquitted?

On September 15th John Cavendish appeared in the dock at the Old Bailey, charged with "The Wilful Murder of Emily Agnes Inglethorp," and pleaded "Not Guilty."

Sir Ernest Heavywether, the famous K. C., had been engaged to defend him.

Mr. Philips, K. C., opened the case for the Crown.

The murder, he said, was a most premeditated and cold-blooded one. It was neither more nor less than the deliberate poisoning of a fond and trusting woman by the stepson to whom she had been more than a mother. Ever since his boyhood, she had supported him. He and his wife had lived at Styles Court in every luxury, surrounded by her care and attention. She had been their kind and generous benefactress.

He proposed to call witnesses to show how the prisoner, a profligate and spendthrift, had been at the end of his financial tether, and had also been carrying on an intrigue with a certain Mrs. Raikes, a neighbouring farmer's wife. This having come to his stepmother's ears, she taxed him with it on the afternoon before her death, and a quarrel ensued, part of which was overheard. On the previous day, the prisoner had purchased strychnine at the village chemist's shop, wearing a disguise by means of which he hoped to throw the onus of the crime upon another man—to wit, Mrs. Inglethorp's husband, of whom he had been bitterly jealous. Luckily for Mr. Inglethorp, he had been able to produce an unimpeachable alibi.

On the afternoon of July 17th, continued Counsel, immediately after the quarrel with her son, Mrs. Inglethorp made a new will. This will was found destroyed in the grate of her bedroom the following morning, but evidence had come to light which showed that it had been drawn up in favour of her husband. Deceased had already made a will in his favour before her marriage, but—and Mr. Philips wagged an expressive forefinger—the prisoner was not aware of that. What had induced the deceased to make a fresh will, with the old one still extant, he could not say. She was an old lady, and might possibly have forgotten the former one; or—this seemed to him more likely—she may have had an idea that it was revoked by her marriage, as there had been some conversation on the subject. Ladies were not always very well versed in legal knowledge. She had, about a year before, executed a will in favour of the prisoner. He would call evidence to show that it was the prisoner who ultimately handed his stepmother her coffee on the fatal night. Later in the evening, he had sought admission to her room, on which occasion, no doubt, he found an opportunity of destroying the will which, as far as he knew, would render the one in his favour valid.

The prisoner had been arrested in consequence of the discovery, in his room, by Detective Inspector Japp—a most brilliant officer—of the identical phial of strychnine which had been sold at the village chemist's to the supposed Mr. Inglethorp on the day before the murder. It would be for the jury to decide whether or no these damning facts constituted an overwhelming proof of the prisoner's guilt.

And, subtly implying that a jury which did not so decide, was quite unthinkable, Mr. Philips sat down and wiped his forehead.

The first witnesses for the prosecution were mostly those who had been called at the inquest, the medical evidence being again taken first.

Sir Ernest Heavywether, who was famous all over England for the unscrupulous manner in which he bullied witnesses, only asked two questions.

"I take it, Dr. Bauerstein, that strychnine, as a drug, acts quickly?"

"Yes."

"And that you are unable to account for the delay in this case?"

"Yes."

"Thank you."

Mr. Mace identified the phial handed him by Counsel as that sold by him to "Mr. Inglethorp." Pressed, he admitted that he only knew Mr. Inglethorp by sight. He had never spoken to him. The witness was not cross-examined.

Alfred Inglethorp was called, and denied having purchased the poison. He also denied having quarrelled with his wife. Various witnesses testified to the accuracy of these statements.

The gardeners' evidence, as to the witnessing of the will was taken, and then Dorcas was called.

Dorcas, faithful to her "young gentlemen," denied strenuously that it could have been John's voice she heard, and resolutely declared, in the teeth of everything, that it was Mr. Inglethorp who had been in the boudoir with her mistress. A rather wistful smile passed across the face of the prisoner in the dock. He knew only too well how useless her gallant defiance was, since it was not the object of the defence to deny this point. Mrs. Cavendish, of course, could not be called upon to give evidence against her husband.

After various questions on other matters, Mr. Philips asked:

"In the month of June last, do you remember a parcel arriving for Mr. Lawrence Cavendish from Parkson's?"

Dorcas shook her head.

"I don't remember, sir. It may have done, but Mr. Lawrence was away from home part of June."

"In the event of a parcel arriving for him whilst he was away, what would be done with it?"

"It would either be put in his room or sent on after him."

"By you?"

"No, sir, I should leave it on the hall table. It would be Miss Howard who would attend to anything like that."

Evelyn Howard was called and, after being examined on other points, was questioned as to the parcel.

"Don't remember. Lots of parcels come. Can't remember one special one."

"You do not know if it was sent after Mr. Lawrence Cavendish to Wales, or whether it was put in his room?"

"Don't think it was sent after him. Should have remembered it if it was."

"Supposing a parcel arrived addressed to Mr. Lawrence Cavendish, and afterwards it disappeared, should you remark its absence?"

"No, don't think so. I should think some one had taken charge of it."

"I believe, Miss Howard, that it was you who found this sheet of brown paper?" He held up the same dusty piece which Poirot and I had examined in the morning-room at Styles.

"Yes, I did."

"How did you come to look for it?"

"The Belgian detective who was employed on the case asked me to search for it."

"Where did you eventually discover it?"

"On the top of—of—a wardrobe."

"On top of the prisoner's wardrobe?"

"I—I believe so."

"Did you not find it yourself?"

"Yes."

"Then you must know where you found it?"

"Yes, it was on the prisoner's wardrobe."

"That is better."

An assistant from Parkson's, Theatrical Costumiers, testified that on June 29th, they had supplied a black beard to Mr. L. Cavendish, as requested. It was ordered by letter, and a postal order was enclosed. No, they had not kept the letter. All transactions were entered in their books. They had sent the beard, as directed, to "L. Cavendish, Esq., Styles Court."

Sir Ernest Heavywether rose ponderously.

"Where was the letter written from?"

"From Styles Court."

"The same address to which you sent the parcel?"

"Yes."

"And the letter came from there?"

"Yes."

Like a beast of prey, Heavywether fell upon him:

"How do you know?"

"I—I don't understand."

"How do you know that letter came from Styles? Did you notice the postmark?"

"No—but—"

"Ah, you did *not* notice the postmark! And yet you affirm so confidently that it came from Styles. It might, in fact, have been any postmark?"

"Y—es."

"In fact, the letter, though written on stamped notepaper, might have been posted from anywhere? From Wales, for instance?"

The witness admitted that such might be the case, and Sir Ernest signified that he was satisfied.

Elizabeth Wells, second housemaid at Styles, stated that after she had gone to bed she remembered that she had bolted the front door, instead of leaving it on the latch as Mr. Inglethorp had requested. She had accordingly gone downstairs again to rectify her error. Hearing a slight noise in the West wing, she had peeped along the passage, and had seen Mr. John Cavendish knocking at Mrs. Inglethorp's door.

Sir Ernest Heavywether made short work of her, and under his unmerciful bullying she contradicted herself hopelessly, and Sir Ernest sat down again with a satisfied smile on his face.

With the evidence of Annie, as to the candle grease on the floor, and as to seeing the prisoner take the coffee into the boudoir, the proceedings were adjourned until the following day.

As we went home, Mary Cavendish spoke bitterly against the prosecuting counsel.

"That hateful man! What a net he has drawn around my poor John! How he twisted every little fact until he made it seem what it wasn't!"

"Well," I said consolingly, "it will be the other way about to-morrow."

"Yes," she said meditatively; then suddenly dropped her voice. "Mr. Hastings, you do not think—surely it could not have been Lawrence— Oh, no, that could not be!"

But I myself was puzzled, and as soon as I was alone with Poirot I asked him what he thought Sir Ernest was driving at.

"Ah!" said Poirot appreciatively. "He is a clever man, that Sir Ernest."

"Do you think he believes Lawrence guilty?"

"I do not think he believes or cares anything! No, what he is trying for is to create such confusion in the minds of the jury that they are divided in their opinion as to which brother did it. He is endeavouring to make out that there is quite as much evidence against Lawrence as against John—and I am not at all sure that he will not succeed."

Detective Inspector Japp was the first witness called when the trial was reopened, and gave his evidence succinctly and briefly. After relating the earlier events, he proceeded:

"Acting on information received, Superintendent Summerhaye and myself searched the prisoner's room, during his temporary absence from the house. In his chest of drawers, hidden beneath some underclothing, we found: first, a pair of gold-rimmed pince-nez similar to those worn by Mr. Inglethorp"—these were exhibited—"secondly, this phial."

The phial was that already recognized by the chemist's assistant, a tiny bottle of blue glass, containing a few grains of a white crystalline powder, and labelled: "Strychnine Hydro-chloride. POISON."

A fresh piece of evidence discovered by the detectives since the police court proceedings was a long, almost new piece of blotting-paper. It had been found in Mrs. Inglethorp's cheque book, and on being reversed at a mirror, showed clearly the words: ". . . erything of which I die possessed I leave to my beloved husband Alfred Ing . . .". This placed beyond question the fact that the destroyed will had been in favour of the deceased lady's husband. Japp then produced the charred fragment of paper recovered from the grate, and this, with the discovery of the beard in the attic, completed his evidence.

But Sir Ernest's cross-examination was yet to come.

"What day was it when you searched the prisoner's room?"

"Tuesday, the 24th of July."

"Exactly a week after the tragedy?"

"Yes."

"You found these two objects, you say in the chest of drawers. Was the drawer unlocked?"

"Yes."

"Does it not strike you as unlikely that a man who had committed a crime should keep the evidence of it in an unlocked drawer for anyone to find?"

"He might have stowed them there in a hurry."

"But you have just said it was a whole week since the crime. He would have had ample time to remove them and destroy them."

"Perhaps."

"There is no perhaps about it. Would he, or would he not have had plenty of time to remove and destroy them?"

"Yes."

"Was the pile of underclothes under which the things were hidden heavy or light?"

"Heavyish."

"In other words, it was winter underclothing. Obviously, the prisoner would not be likely to go to that drawer?"

"Perhaps not."

"Kindly answer my question. Would the prisoner, in the hottest week of a hot summer, be likely to go to a drawer containing winter underclothing. Yes, or no?"

"No."

"In that case, is it not possible that the articles in question might have been put there by a third person, and that the prisoner was quite unaware of their presence?"

"I should not think it likely."

"But it is possible?"

"Yes."

"That is all."

More evidence followed. Evidence as to the financial difficulties in which the prisoner had found himself at the end of July. Evidence as to his intrigue with Mrs. Raikes—poor Mary, that must have been bitter hearing for a woman of her pride. Evelyn Howard had been right in her facts, though her animosity against Alfred Inglethorp had caused her to jump to the conclusion that he was the person concerned.

Lawrence Cavendish was then put into the box. In a low voice, in answer to Mr. Philips's questions, he denied having ordered anything from Parkson's in June. In fact, on June 29th, he had been staying away, in Wales.

Instantly, Sir Ernest's chin was shooting pugnaciously forward.

"You deny having ordered a black beard from Parkson's on June 29th?"

"I do."

"Ah! In the event of anything happening to your brother, who will inherit Styles Court?"

The brutality of the question called a flush to Lawrence's pale face. The judge gave vent to a faint murmur of disapprobation, and the prisoner in the dock leant forward angrily.

Heavywether cared nothing for his client's anger.

"Answer my question, if you please."

"I suppose," said Lawrence quietly, "that I should."

"What do you mean by you 'suppose'? Your brother has no children. You *would* inherit it, wouldn't you?"

"Yes."

"Ah, that's better," said Heavywether, with ferocious geniality. "And you'd inherit a good slice of money too, wouldn't you?"

"Really, Sir Ernest," protested the Judge, "these questions are not relevant."

Sir Ernest bowed, and having shot his arrow proceeded.

"On Tuesday, the 17th July, you went, I believe, with another guest, to visit the dispensary at the Red Cross Hospital in Tadminster?"

"Yes."

"Did you—while you happened to be alone for a few seconds—unlock the poison cupboard, and examine some of the bottles?"

"I—I—may have done so."

"I put it to you that you did do so?"

"Yes."

Sir Ernest fairly shot the next question at him.

"Did you examine one bottle in particular?"

"No, I do not think so."

"Be careful, Mr. Cavendish. I am referring to a little bottle of Hydro-chloride of Strychnine."

Lawrence was turning a sickly greenish colour.

"N—o—I am sure I didn't."

"Then how do you account for the fact that you left the unmistakable impress of your finger-prints on it?"

The bullying manner was highly efficacious with a nervous disposition.

"I—I suppose I must have taken up the bottle."

"I suppose so too! Did you abstract any of the contents of the bottle?"

"Certainly not."

"Then why did you take it up?"

"I once studied to be a doctor. Such things naturally interest me."

"Ah! So poisons 'naturally interest' you, do they? Still, you waited to be alone before gratifying that 'interest' of yours?"

"That was pure chance. If the others had been there, I should have done just the same."

"Still, as it happens, the others were not there?"

"No, but——"

"In fact, during the whole afternoon, you were only alone for a couple of minutes, and it happened—I say, it happened—to be during those two minutes that you displayed your 'natural interest' in Hydro-chloride of Strychnine?"

Lawrence stammered pitiably.

"I—I——"

With a satisfied and expressive countenance, Sir Ernest observed:

"I have nothing more to ask you, Mr. Cavendish."

This bit of cross-examination had caused great excitement in court. The heads of the many fashionably attired women present were busily laid together, and their whispers became so loud that the judge angrily threatened to have the court cleared if there was not immediate silence.

There was little more evidence. The hand-writing experts were called upon for their opinion of the signature of "Alfred Inglethorp" in the chemist's poison register. They all declared unanimously that it was certainly not his hand-writing, and gave it as their view that it might be that of the prisoner disguised. Cross-examined, they admitted that it might be the prisoner's hand-writing cleverly counterfeited.

Sir Ernest Heavywether's speech in opening the case for the defence was not a long one, but it was backed by the full force of his emphatic manner. Never, he said, in the course of his long experience, had he known a charge of murder rest on slighter evidence. Not only was it entirely circumstantial, but the greater part of it was practically unproved. Let them take the testimony they had heard and sift it impartially. The strychnine had been found in a drawer in the prisoner's room. That drawer was an unlocked one, as he had pointed out, and he submitted that there was no evidence to prove that it was the prisoner who had concealed the poison there. It was, in fact, a wicked and malicious attempt on the part of some third person to fix the crime on the prisoner. The prosecution had been unable to produce a shred of evidence in support of their contention that it was the prisoner who ordered the black beard from Parkson's. The quarrel which had taken place between prisoner and his stepmother was freely admitted, but both it and his financial embarrassments had been grossly exaggerated.

His learned friend—Sir Ernest nodded carelessly at Mr. Philips —had stated that if prisoner were an innocent man, he would have come forward at the inquest to explain that it was he, and not Mr. Inglethorp, who had been the participator in the quarrel. He thought the facts had been misrepresented. What had actually occurred was this. The prisoner, returning to the house on

Tuesday evening, had been authoritatively told that there had been a violent quarrel between Mr. and Mrs. Inglethorp. No suspicion had entered the prisoner's head that anyone could possibly have mistaken his voice for that of Mr. Inglethorp. He naturally concluded that his stepmother had had two quarrels.

The prosecution averred that on Monday, July 16th, the prisoner had entered the chemist's shop in the village, disguised as Mr. Inglethorp. The prisoner, on the contrary, was at that time at a lonely spot called Marston's Spinney, where he had been summoned by an anonymous note, couched in blackmailing terms, and threatening to reveal certain matters to his wife unless he complied with its demands. The prisoner had, accordingly, gone to the appointed spot, and after waiting there vainly for half an hour had returned home. Unfortunately, he had met with no one on the way there or back who could vouch for the truth of his story, but luckily he had kept the note, and it would be produced as evidence.

As for the statement relating to the destruction of the will, the prisoner had formerly practised at the Bar, and was perfectly well aware that the will made in his favour a year before was automatically revoked by his stepmother's remarriage. He would call evidence to show who did destroy the will, and it was possible that that might open up quite a new view of the case.

Finally, he would point out to the jury that there was evidence against other people besides John Cavendish. He would direct their attention to the fact that the evidence against Mr. Lawrence Cavendish was quite as strong, if not stronger than that against his brother.

He would now call the prisoner.

John acquitted himself well in the witness-box. Under Sir Ernest's skilful handling, he told his tale credibly and well. The anonymous note received by him was produced, and handed to the jury to examine. The readiness with which he admitted his financial difficulties, and the disagreement with his stepmother, lent value to his denials.

At the close of his examination, he paused, and said:

"I should like to make one thing clear. I utterly reject and disapprove of Sir Ernest Heavywether's insinuations against my brother. My brother, I am convinced, had no more to do with the crime than I have."

Sir Ernest merely smiled, and noted with a sharp eye that John's protest had produced a very favourable impression on the jury.

Then the cross-examination began.

"I understand you to say that it never entered your head that the witnesses at the inquest could possibly have mistaken your voice for that of Mr. Inglethorp. Is not that very surprising?"

"No, I don't think so. I was told there had been a quarrel between my mother and Mr. Inglethorp, and it never occurred to me that such was not really the case."

"Not when the servant Dorcas repeated certain fragments of the conversation—fragments which you must have recognized?"

"I did not recognize them."

"Your memory must be unusually short!"

"No, but we were both angry, and, I think, said more than we meant. I paid very little attention to my mother's actual words."

Mr. Philips's incredulous sniff was a triumph of forensic skill. He passed on to the subject of the note.

"You have produced this note very opportunely. Tell me, is there nothing familiar about the hand-writing of it?"

"Not that I know of."

"Do you not think that it bears a marked resemblance to your own hand-writing—carelessly disguised?"

"No, I do not think so."

"I put it to you that it is your own hand-writing!"

"No."

"I put it to you that, anxious to prove an alibi, you conceived the idea of a fictitious and rather incredible appointment, and wrote this note yourself in order to bear out your statement!"

"No."

"Is it not a fact that, at the time you claim to have been waiting about at a solitary and unfrequented spot, you were really in the chemist's shop in Styles St. Mary, where you purchased strychnine in the name of Alfred Inglethorp?"

"No, that is a lie."

"I put it to you that, wearing a suit of Mr. Inglethorp's clothes, with a black beard trimmed to resemble his, you were there—and signed the register in his name!"

"That is absolutely untrue."

"Then I will leave the remarkable similarity of hand-writing between the note, the register, and your own, to the consideration of the jury," said Mr. Philips, and sat down with the air of a man who has done his duty, but who was nevertheless horrified by such deliberate perjury.

After this, as it was growing late, the case was adjourned till Monday.

Poirot, I noticed, was looking profoundly discouraged. He had that little frown between the eyes that I knew so well.

"What is it, Poirot?" I inquired.

"Ah, *mon ami*, things are going badly, badly."

In spite of myself, my heart gave a leap of relief. Evidently there was a likelihood of John Cavendish being acquitted.

When we reached the house, my little friend waved aside Mary's offer of tea.

"No, I thank you, madame. I will mount to my room."

I followed him. Still frowning, he went across to the desk and took out a small pack of patience cards. Then he drew up a chair to the table, and, to my utter amazement, began solemnly to build card houses!

My jaw dropped involuntarily, and he said at once:

"No, *mon ami*, I am not in my second childhood! I steady my nerves, that is all. This employment requires precision of the fingers. With precision of the fingers goes precision of the brain. And never have I needed that more than now!"

"What is the trouble?" I asked.

With a great thump on the table, Poirot demolished his carefully built up edifice.

"It is this, *mon ami!* That I can build card houses seven stories high, but I cannot"—thump—"find"—thump—"that last link of which I spoke to you."

I could not quite tell what to say, so I held my peace, and he began slowly building up the cards again, speaking in jerks as he did so.

"It is done—so! By placing—one card—on another—with mathematical—precision!"

I watched the card house rising under his hands, story by story. He never hesitated or faltered. It was really almost like a conjuring trick.

"What a steady hand you've got," I remarked. "I believe I've only seen your hand shake once."

"On an occasion when I was enraged, without doubt," observed Poirot, with great placidity.

"Yes indeed! You were in a towering rage. Do you remember? It was when you discovered that the lock of the despatch-case in Mrs. Inglethorp's bedroom had been forced. You stood by the mantelpiece, twiddling the things on it in your usual fashion, and your hand shook like a leaf! I must say——"

But I stopped suddenly. For Poirot, uttering a hoarse and inarticulate cry, again annihilated his masterpiece of cards, and putting his hands over his eyes swayed backwards and forwards, apparently suffering the keenest agony.

"Good heavens, Poirot!" I cried. "What is the matter? Are you taken ill?"

"No, no," he gasped. "It is—it is—that I have an idea!"

"Oh!" I exclaimed, much relieved. "One of your 'little ideas'?"

"Ah, *ma foi*, no!" replied Poirot frankly. "This time it is an idea gigantic! Stupendous! And you—*you*, my friend, have given it to me!"

Suddenly clasping me in his arms, he kissed me warmly on both cheeks, and before I had recovered from my surprise ran headlong from the room.

Mary Cavendish entered at that moment.

"What *is* the matter with Monsieur Poirot? He rushed past me crying out: 'A garage! For the love of Heaven, direct me to a garage, madame!' And, before I could answer, he had dashed out into the street."

I hurried to the window. True enough, there he was, tearing

down the street, hatless, and gesticulating as he went. I turned to Mary with a gesture of despair.

"He'll be stopped by a policeman in another minute. There he goes, round the corner!"

Our eyes met, and we stared helplessly at one another.

"What can be the matter?"

I shook my head.

"I don't know. He was building card houses, when suddenly he said he had an idea, and rushed off as you saw."

"Well," said Mary, "I expect he will be back before dinner." But night fell, and Poirot had not returned.

12

The Last Link

Poirot's abrupt departure had intrigued us all greatly. Sunday morning wore away, and still he did not reappear. But about three o'clock a ferocious and prolonged hooting outside drove us to the window, to see Poirot alighting from a car, accompanied by Japp and Summerhaye. The little man was transformed. He radiated an absurd complacency. He bowed with exaggerated respect to Mary Cavendish.

"Madame, I have your permission to hold a little *réunion* in the *salon?* It is necessary for every one to attend."

Mary smiled sadly.

"You know, Monsieur Poirot, that you have *carte blanche* in every way."

"You are too amiable, madame."

Still beaming, Poirot marshalled us all into the drawing-room, bringing forward chairs as he did so.

"Miss Howard—here. Mademoiselle Cynthia. Monsieur Lawrence. The good Dorcas. And Annie. *Bien!* We must delay our proceedings a few minutes until Mr. Inglethorp arrives. I have sent him a note."

Miss Howard rose immediately from her seat.

"If that man comes into the house, I leave it!"

"No, no!" Poirot went up to her and pleaded in a low voice.

Finally Miss Howard consented to return to her chair. A few minutes later Alfred Inglethorp entered the room.

The company once assembled, Poirot rose from his seat with the air of a popular lecturer, and bowed politely to his audience.

"*Messieurs, mesdames,* as you all know, I was called in by Monsieur John Cavendish to investigate this case. I at once examined the bedroom of the deceased which, by the advice of the doctors, had been kept locked, and was consequently exactly as it had been when the tragedy occurred. I found: first, a fragment of green material; secondly, a stain on the carpet near the window, still damp; thirdly, an empty box of bromide powders.

"To take the fragment of green material first, I found it caught in the bolt of the communicating door between that room and the adjoining one occupied by Mademoiselle Cynthia. I handed the fragment over to the police who did not consider it of much importance. Nor did they recognize it for what it was—a piece torn from a green land armlet."

There was a little stir of excitement.

"Now there was only one person at Styles who worked on the land—Mrs. Cavendish. Therefore it must have been Mrs. Cavendish who entered deceased's room through the door communicating with Mademoiselle Cynthia's room."

"But that door was bolted on the inside!" I cried.

"When I examined the room, yes. But in the first place we have only her word for it, since it was she who tried that particular door and reported it fastened. In the ensuing confusion she would have had ample opportunity to shoot the bolt across. I took an early opportunity of verifying my conjectures. To begin with, the fragment corresponds exactly with a tear in Mrs. Cavendish's armlet. Also, at the inquest, Mrs. Cavendish declared that she had heard, from her own room, the fall of the table by the bed. I took an early opportunity of testing that statement, by stationing my friend Monsieur Hastings, in the left wing of the building, just outside Mrs. Cavendish's door. I myself, in company with the police, went to the deceased's room, and whilst there I, apparently accidentally, knocked over the table in question, but found that, as I had expected, Monsieur Hastings had heard no sound at all. This confirmed my belief that Mrs. Cavendish was not speaking the truth when she declared that she had been dressing in her room at the time of the tragedy. In fact, I was convinced that, far from having been in her own room, Mrs. Cavendish was actually in the deceased's room when the alarm was given."

I shot a quick glance at Mary. She was very pale, but smiling.

"I proceeded to reason on that assumption. Mrs. Cavendish is in her mother-in-law's room. We will say that she is seeking for something and has not yet found it. Suddenly Mrs. Inglethorp awakens and is seized with an alarming paroxysm. She flings out her arm, overturning the bed table, and then pulls desperately at the bell. Mrs. Cavendish, startled, drops her candle, scattering the grease on the carpet. She picks it up, and retreats quickly to Mademoiselle Cynthia's room, closing the door behind her. She hurries out into the passage, for the servants must not find her where she is. But it is too late! Already footsteps are echoing along the gallery which connects the two wings. What can she do? Quick as thought, she hurries back to the young girl's room, and starts shaking her awake. The hastily aroused household come trooping down the passage. They are all busily battering at Mrs. Inglethorp's door. It occurs to nobody that Mrs. Cavendish has not arrived with the rest, but—and this is significant—I can find no one who saw her come from the other wing." He looked at Mary Cavendish. "Am I right, madame?"

She bowed her head.

"Quite right, monsieur. You understand that, if I had thought I would do my husband any good by revealing these facts, I would have done so. But it did not seem to me to bear upon the question of his guilt or innocence."

"In a sense, that is correct, madame. But it cleared my mind of many misconceptions, and left me free to see other facts in their true significance."

"The will!" cried Lawrence. "Then it was you, Mary, who destroyed the will?"

She shook her head, and Poirot shook his also.

"No," he said quietly. "There is only one person who could possibly have destroyed that will—Mrs. Inglethorp herself!"

"Impossible!" I exclaimed. "She had only made it out that very afternoon!"

"Nevertheless, *mon ami*, it was Mrs. Inglethorp. Because, in no other way can you account for the fact that, on one of the hottest days of the year, Mrs. Inglethorp ordered a fire to be lighted in her room."

I gave a gasp. What idiots we had been never to think of that fire as being incongruous! Poirot was continuing:

"The temperature on that day, messieurs, was 80° in the shade. Yet Mrs. Inglethorp ordered a fire! Why? Because she wished to destroy something, and could think of no other way. You will remember that, in consequence of the War economies practised at Styles, no waste paper was thrown away. There was therefore no means of destroying a thick document such as a will. The moment I heard of a fire being lighted in Mrs. Inglethorp's room, I leaped to the conclusion that it was to destroy some important document—possibly a will. So the discovery of the charred fragment in the grate was no surprise to me. I did not, of course, know at the time that the will in question had only been made that afternoon, and I will admit that, when I learnt that fact, I fell into a grievous error. I came to the conclusion that Mrs. Inglethorp's determination to destroy her will arose as a direct consequence of the quarrel she had that afternoon, and that therefore the quarrel took place after, and not before the making of the will.

"Here, as we know, I was wrong, and I was forced to abandon that idea. I faced the problem from a new standpoint. Now, at 4 o'clock, Dorcas overheard her mistress saying angrily: 'You need not think that any fear of publicity, or scandal between husband and wife will deter me.' I conjectured, and conjectured rightly, that these words were addressed, not to her husband, but to Mr. John Cavendish. At 5 o'clock, an hour later, she uses almost the same words, but the standpoint is different. She admits to Dorcas, 'I don't know what to do; scandal between husband and wife is a dreadful thing.' At 4 o'clock she has been angry, but completely mistress of herself. At 5 o'clock she is in violent distress, and speaks of having had 'a great shock.'

"Looking at the matter psychologically, I drew one deduction which I was convinced was correct. The second 'scandal' she spoke of was not the same as the first—and it concerned herself!

"Let us reconstruct. At 4 o'clock, Mrs. Inglethorp quarrels with her son, and threatens to denounce him to his wife—who, by the way, overheard the greater part of the conversation. At 4.30, Mrs. Inglethorp, in consequence of a conversation on the validity of wills, makes a will in favour of her husband, which the two gardeners witness. At 5 o'clock, Dorcas finds her mistress in a state of considerable agitation, with a slip of paper—'a letter,' Dorcas thinks—in her hand, and it is then that she orders the fire in her room to be lighted. Presumably, then, between 4.30 and 5 o'clock, something has occurred to occasion a complete revolution of feeling, since she is now as anxious to destroy the will, as she was before to make it. What was that something?

"As far as we know, she was quite alone during that half-hour. Nobody entered or left that boudoir. What then occasioned this sudden change of sentiment?

"One can only guess, but I believe my guess to be correct. Mrs. Inglethorp had no stamps in her desk. We know this, because later she asked Dorcas to bring her some. Now in the opposite corner of the room stood her husband's desk—locked. She was anxious to find some stamps, and, according to my theory, she tried her own keys in the desk. That one of them fitted I know. She therefore opened the desk, and in searching for the stamps she came across something else—that slip of paper which Dorcas saw in her hand, and which assuredly was never meant for Mrs. Inglethorp's eyes. On the other hand, Mrs. Cavendish believed that the slip of paper to which her mother-in-law clung so tenaciously was a written proof of her own husband's infidelity. She demanded it from Mrs. Inglethorp who assured her, quite truly, that it had nothing to do with that matter. Mrs. Cavendish did not believe her. She thought that Mrs. Inglethorp was shielding her stepson. Now Mrs. Cavendish is a very resolute woman, and, behind her mask of reserve, she was madly jealous of her husband. She determined to get hold of that paper at all costs, and in this resolution chance came to her aid. She happened to pick up the key of Mrs. Inglethorp's despatch-case, which had been lost that morning. She knew that her mother-in-law invariably kept all important papers in this particular case.

"Mrs. Cavendish, therefore, made her plans as only a woman driven desperate through jealousy could have done. Some time in the evening she unbolted the door leading into Mademoiselle Cynthia's room. Possibly she applied oil to the hinges, for I found that it opened quite noiselessly when I tried it. She put off her project until the early hours of the morning as being safer, since the servants were accustomed to hearing her move about her room at that time. She dressed completely in her land kit, and made her way quietly through Mademoiselle Cynthia's room into that of Mrs. Inglethorp."

He paused a moment, and Cynthia interrupted:

"But I should have woken up if anyone had come through my room?"

"Not if you were drugged, mademoiselle."

"Drugged?"

"*Mais, oui!*"

"You remember"—he addressed us collectively again—"that through all the tumult and noise next door Mademoiselle Cynthia slept. That admitted of two possibilities. Either her sleep was feigned—which I did not believe—or her unconsciousness was induced by artificial means.

"With this latter idea in my mind, I examined all the coffee-cups most carefully, remembering that it was Mrs. Cavendish who had brought Mademoiselle Cynthia her coffee the night before. I took a sample from each cup, and had them analysed—with no result. I had counted the cups carefully, in the event of one having been removed. Six persons had taken coffee, and six cups were duly found. I had to confess myself mistaken.

"Then I discovered that I had been guilty of a very grave oversight. Coffee had been brought in for seven persons, not six, for Dr. Bauerstein had been there that evening. This changed the face of the whole affair, for there was now one cup missing. The servants noticed nothing, since Annie, the housemaid, who took in the coffee, brought in seven cups, not knowing that Mr. Inglethorp never drank it, whereas Dorcas, who cleared them away the following morning, found six as usual—or strictly speaking she found five, the sixth being the one found broken in Mrs. Inglethorp's room.

"I was confident that the missing cup was that of Mademoiselle Cynthia. I had an additional reason for that belief in the fact that all the cups found contained sugar, which Mademoiselle Cynthia never took in her coffee. My attention was attracted by the story of Annie about some 'salt' on the tray of coco which she took every night to Mrs. Inglethorp's room. I accordingly secured a sample of that coco, and sent it to be analysed."

"But that had already been done by Dr. Bauerstein," said Lawrence quickly.

"Not exactly. The analyst was asked by him to report whether strychnine was, or was not, present. He did not have it tested, as I did, for a narcotic."

"For a narcotic?"

"Yes. Here is the analyst's report. Mrs. Cavendish administered a safe, but effectual, narcotic to both Mrs. Inglethorp and Mademoiselle Cynthia. And it is possible that she had a *mauvais quart d'heure* in consequence! Imagine her feelings when her mother-in-law is suddenly taken ill and dies, and immediately after she hears the word 'Poison'! She has believed that the sleeping draught she administered was perfectly harmless, but there is no doubt that for one terrible moment she must have feared that Mrs. Inglethorp's death lay at her door. She is seized with panic, and under its influence she hurries downstairs, and quickly drops the coffee-cup and saucer used by Mademoiselle Cynthia into a large brass vase, where it is discovered later by Monsieur Lawrence. The remains of the coco she dare not touch. Too many eyes are upon her. Guess at her relief when strychnine is mentioned, and she discovers that after all the tragedy is not her doing.

"We are now able to account for the symptoms of strychnine poisoning being so long in making their appearance. A narcotic taken with strychnine will delay the action of the poison for some hours."

Poirot paused. Mary looked up at him, the colour slowly rising in her face.

"All you have said is quite true, Monsieur Poirot. It was the most awful hour of my life. I shall never forget it. But you are wonderful. I understand now——"

"What I meant when I told you that you could safely confess to Papa Poirot, eh? But you would not trust me."

"I see everything now," said Lawrence. "The drugged coco, taken on top of the poisoned coffee, amply accounts for the delay."

"Exactly. But was the coffee poisoned, or was it not? We come to a little difficulty here, since Mrs. Inglethorp never drank it."

"What?" The cry of surprise was universal.

"No. You will remember my speaking of a stain on the carpet in Mrs. Inglethorp's room? There were some peculiar points about that stain. It was still damp, it exhaled a strong odour of coffee, and imbedded in the nap of the carpet I found some little splinters of china. What had happened was plain to me, for not two minutes before I had placed my little case on the table near the window, and the table, tilting up, had deposited it upon the floor on precisely the identical spot. In exactly the same way, Mrs. Inglethorp had laid down her cup of coffee on reaching her room the night before, and the treacherous table had played her the same trick.

"What happened next is mere guess work on my part, but I should say that Mrs. Inglethorp picked up the broken cup and placed it on the table by the bed. Feeling in need of a stimulant of some kind, she heated up her coco, and drank it off then and there. Now we are faced with a new problem. We know the coco contained no strychnine. The coffee was never drunk. Yet the strychnine must have been administered between seven and nine o'clock that evening. What third medium was there—a medium so suitable for disguising the taste of strychnine that it is extraordinary no one has thought of it?" Poirot looked round the room, and then answered himself impressively. "Her medicine!"

"Do you mean that the murderer introduced the strychnine into her tonic?" I cried.

"There was no need to introduce it. It was already there—in the mixture. The strychnine that killed Mrs. Inglethorp was the identical strychnine prescribed by Dr. Wilkins. To make that clear to you, I will read you an extract from a book on dispensing which I found in the Dispensary of the Red Cross Hospital at Tadminster:

"The following prescription has become famous in text books:

> Strychninae Sulph.......gr. 1
> Potass Bromide...........zvi
> Aqua ad...............zviii
> Fiat Mistura

This solution deposits in a few hours the greater part of the strychnine salt as an insoluble bromide in transparent crystals. A lady in England lost her life by taking a similar mixture: the precipitated strychnine collected at the bottom, and in taking the last dose she swallowed nearly all of it!

"Now there was, of course, no bromide in Dr. Wilkins's prescription, but you will remember that I mentioned an empty box of bromide powders. One or two of those powders introduced into the full bottle of medicine would effectually precipitate the strychnine, as the book describes, and cause it to be taken in the last dose. You will learn later that the person who usually poured out Mrs. Inglethorp's medicine was always extremely careful not to shake the bottle, but to leave the sediment at the bottom of it undisturbed.

"Throughout the case, there have been evidences that the tragedy was intended to take place on Monday evening. On that day, Mrs. Inglethorp's bell wire was neatly cut, and on Monday evening Mademoiselle Cynthia was spending the night with friends, so that Mrs. Inglethorp would have been quite alone in the right wing, completely shut off from help of any kind, and would have died, in all probability, before medical aid could have been summoned. But in her hurry to be in time for the village entertainment Mrs. Inglethorp forgot to take her medicine, and the next day she lunched away from home, so that the last—and fatal—dose was actually taken twenty-four hours later than had been anticipated by the murderer; and it is owing to that delay that the final proof—the last link of the chain—is now in my hands."

Amid breathless excitement, he held out three thin strips of paper.

"A letter in the murderer's own handwriting, *mes amis!* Had it been a little clearer in its terms, it is possible that Mrs. Inglethorp, warned in time, would have escaped. As it was, she realized her danger, but not the manner of it."

In the deathly silence, Poirot pieced together the slips of paper and, clearing his throat, read:

'Dearest Evelyn:

'You will be anxious at hearing nothing. It is all right—only it will be to-night instead of last night. You understand. There's a good time coming once the old woman is dead and out of the way. No one can possibly bring home the crime to me. That idea of yours about the bromides was a stroke of genius! But we must be very circumspect. A false step——'

"Here, my friends, the letter breaks off. Doubtless the writer was interrupted; but there can be no question as to his identity. We all know this hand-writing and——"

A howl that was almost a scream broke the silence.

"You devil! How did you get it?"

A chair was overturned. Poirot skipped nimbly aside. A quick movement on his part, and his assailant fell with a crash.

"*Messieurs, mesdames,*" said Poirot, with a flourish, "let me introduce you to the murderer, Mr. Alfred Inglethorp!"

13

Poirot Explains

"Poirot, you old villain," I said, "I've half a mind to strangle you! What do you mean by deceiving me as you have done?"

We were sitting in the library. Several hectic days lay behind us. In the room below, John and Mary were together once more, while Alfred Inglethorp and Miss Howard were in custody. Now at last, I had Poirot to myself, and could relieve my still burning curiosity.

Poirot did not answer me for a moment, but at last he said:

"I did not deceive you, *mon ami*. At most, I permitted you to deceive yourself."

"Yes, but why?"

"Well, it is difficult to explain. You see, my friend, you have a nature so honest, and a countenance so transparent, that—*enfin*, to conceal your feelings is impossible! If I had told you my ideas, the very first time you saw Mr. Alfred Inglethorp that astute gentleman would have—in your so expressive idiom—'smelt a rat'! And then, *bon jour* to our chances of catching him!"

"I think that I have more diplomacy than you give me credit for."

"My friend," besought Poirot, "I implore you, do not enrage yourself! Your help has been of the most invaluable. It is but the extremely beautiful nature that you have, which made me pause."

"Well," I grumbled, a little mollified. "I still think you might have given me a hint."

"But I did, my friend. Several hints. You would not take them. Think now, did I ever say to you that I believed John Cavendish guilty? Did I not, on the contrary, tell you that he would almost certainly be acquitted?"

"Yes, but——"

"And did I not immediately afterwards speak of the difficulty of bringing the murderer to justice? Was it not plain to you that I was speaking of two entirely different persons?"

"No," I said, "it was not plain to me!"

"Then again," continued Poirot, "at the beginning, did I not repeat to you several times that I didn't want Mr. Inglethorp arrested *now*? That should have conveyed something to you."

"Do you mean to say you suspected him as long ago as that?"

"Yes. To begin with, whoever else might benefit by Mrs. Inglethorp's death, her husband would benefit the most. There was no getting away from that. When I went up to Styles with you that first day, I had no idea as to how the crime had been committed, but from what I knew of Mr. Inglethorp I fancied that it would be very hard to find anything to connect him with it. When I arrived at the château, I realized at once that it was Mrs. Inglethorp who had burnt the will; and there, by the way, you cannot complain, my friend, for I tried my best to force on you the significance of that bedroom fire in midsummer."

"Yes, yes," I said impatiently. "Go on."

"Well, my friend, as I say, my views as to Mr. Inglethorp's guilt were very much shaken. There was, in fact, so much evidence against him that I was inclined to believe that he had not done it."

"When did you change your mind?"

"When I found that the more efforts I made to clear him, the more efforts he made to get himself arrested. Then, when I discovered that Inglethorp had nothing to do with Mrs. Raikes, and that in fact it was John Cavendish who was interested in that quarter, I was quite sure."

"But why?"

"Simply this. If it had been Inglethorp who was carrying on an intrigue with Mrs. Raikes, his silence was perfectly comprehensible. But, when I discovered that it was known all over the village that it was John who was attracted by the farmer's pretty wife, his silence bore quite a different interpretation. It was nonsense to pretend that he was afraid of the scandal, as no possible scandal could attach to him. This attitude of his gave me furiously to think, and I was slowly forced to the conclusion that Alfred Inglethorp wanted to be arrested. *Eh bien!* from that moment, I was equally determined that he should not be arrested."

"Wait a moment. I don't see why he wished to be arrested?"

"Because, *mon ami,* it is the law of your country that a man once acquitted can never be tried again for the same offence. Aha! but it was clever—his idea! Assuredly, he is a man of method. See here, he knew that in his position he was bound to be suspected, so he conceived the exceedingly clever idea of preparing a lot of manufactured evidence against himself. He wished to be suspected. He wished to be arrested. He would then produce his irreproachable alibi—and, hey presto, he was safe for life!"

"But I still don't see how he managed to prove his alibi, and yet go to the chemist's shop?"

Poirot stared at me in surprise.

"Is it possible? My poor friend! You have not yet realized that it was Miss Howard who went to the chemist's shop?"

"Miss Howard?"

"But, certainly. Who else? It was most easy for her. She is of a good height, her voice is deep and manly; moreover, remember, she and Inglethorp are cousins, and there is a distinct resemblance between them, especially in their gait and bearing. It was simplicity itself. They are a clever pair!"

"I am still a little fogged as to how exactly the bromide business was done," I remarked.

"*Bon!* I will reconstruct for you as far as possible. I am inclined to think that Miss Howard was the master mind in that affair. You remember her once mentioning that her father was a doctor? Possibly she dispensed his medicines for him, or she may have taken the idea from one of the many books lying about when Mademoiselle Cynthia was studying for her exam. Anyway, she was familiar with the fact that the addition of a bromide to a mixture containing strychnine would cause the precipitation of the latter. Probably the idea came to her quite suddenly. Mrs. Inglethorp had a box of bromide powders, which she occasionally took at night. What could be easier quietly than to dissolve one or more of those powders in Mrs. Inglethorp's large sized bottle of medicine when it came from Coot's? The risk is practically nil. The tragedy will not take place until nearly a fortnight later. If anyone has seen either of them touching the medicine, they will have forgotten it by that time. Miss Howard will have engineered her quarrel, and departed from the house. The lapse of time, and her absence, will defeat all suspicion. Yes, it was a clever idea! If they had left it alone, it is possible the crime might never have been brought home to them. But they were not satisfied. They tried to be too clever—and that was their undoing."

Poirot puffed at his tiny cigarette, his eyes fixed on the ceiling.

"They arranged a plan to throw suspicion on John Cavendish, by buying strychnine at the village chemist's, and signing the register in his hand-writing.

"On Monday Mrs. Inglethorp will take the last dose of her medicine. On Monday, therefore, at six o'clock, Alfred Inglethorp arranges to be seen by a number of people at a spot far removed from the village. Miss Howard has previously made up a cock and bull story about him and Mrs. Raikes to account for his holding his tongue afterwards. At six o'clock, Miss Howard, disguised as Alfred Inglethorp, enters the chemist's shop, with her story about a dog, obtains the strychnine, and writes the name of Alfred Inglethorp in John's hand-writing, which she had previously studied carefully.

"But, as it will never do if John, too, can prove an alibi, she writes him an anonymous note—still copying his hand-writing— which takes him to a remote spot where it is exceedingly unlikely that anyone will see him.

"So far, all goes well. Miss Howard goes back to Middlingham. Alfred Inglethorp returns to Styles. There is nothing that can compromise him in any way, since it is Miss Howard who has the strychnine, which, after all, is only wanted as a blind to throw suspicion on John Cavendish.

"But now a hitch occurs. Mrs. Inglethorp does not take her medicine that night. The broken bell, Cynthia's absence—arranged by Inglethorp through his wife—all these are wasted. And then—he makes his slip.

"Mrs. Inglethorp is out, and he sits down to write to his accomplice, who, he fears, may be in a panic at the non-success of their plan. It is probable that Mrs. Inglethorp returned earlier than he expected. Caught in the act, and somewhat flurried he hastily shuts and locks his desk. He fears that if he remains in the room he may have to open it again, and that Mrs. Inglethorp might catch sight of the letter before he could snatch it up. So he goes out and walks in the woods, little dreaming that Mrs. Inglethorp will open his desk, and discover the incriminating document.

"But this, as we know, is what happened. Mrs. Inglethorp reads it, and becomes aware of the perfidy of her husband and Evelyn Howard, though, unfortunately, the sentence about the bromides conveys no warning to her mind. She knows that she is in danger—but is ignorant of where the danger lies. She decides to say nothing to her husband, but sits down and writes to her solicitor, asking him to come on the morrow, and she also determines to destroy immediately the will which she has just made. She keeps the fatal letter."

"It was to discover that letter, then, that her husband forced the lock of the despatch-case?"

"Yes, and from the enormous risk he ran we can see how fully he realized its importance. That letter excepted, there was absolutely nothing to connect him with the crime."

"There's only one thing I can't make out, why didn't he destroy it at once when he got hold of it?"

"Because he did not dare take the biggest risk of all—that of keeping it on his own person."

"I don't understand."

"Look at it from his point of view. I have discovered that there were only five short minutes in which he could have taken it—the five minutes immediately before our own arrival on the scene, for before that time Annie was brushing the stairs, and would have seen anyone who passed going to the right wing. Figure to yourself the scene! He enters the room, unlocking the door by means of one of the other doorkeys—they were all much alike. He hurries to the despatch-case—it is locked, and the keys are nowhere to be seen. That is a terrible blow to him, for it means that his presence in the room cannot be concealed as he had hoped. But he sees clearly that everything must be risked for the sake of that damning piece of evidence. Quickly, he forces the lock with a penknife, and turns over the papers until he finds what he is looking for.

"But now a fresh dilemma arises: he dare not keep that piece of paper on him. He may be seen leaving the room—he may be searched. If the paper is found on him, it is certain doom. Probably, at this minute, too, he hears the sounds below of Mr. Wells and John leaving the boudoir. He must act quickly. Where can he hide this terrible slip of paper? The contents of the waste-paper-basket are kept and in any case, are sure to be examined. There are no means of destroying it; and he dare not keep it. He looks round, and he sees—what do you think, *mon ami?*"

I shook my head.

"In a moment, he has torn the letter into long thin strips, and rolling them up into spills he thrusts them hurriedly in amongst the other spills in the vase on the mantelpiece."

I uttered an exclamation.

"No one would think of looking there," Poirot continued. "And he will be able, at his leisure, to come back and destroy this solitary piece of evidence against him."

"Then, all the time, it was in the spill vase in Mrs. Inglethorp's bedroom, under our very noses?" I cried.

Poirot nodded.

"Yes, my friend. That is where I discovered my 'last link,' and I owe that very fortunate discovery to you."

"To me?"

"Yes. Do you remember telling me that my hand shook as I was straightening the ornaments on the mantelpiece?"

"Yes, but I don't see——"

"No, but I saw. Do you know, my friend, I remembered that earlier in the morning, when we had been there together, I had straightened all the objects on the mantelpiece. And, if they were already straightened, there would be no need to straighten them again, unless, in the meantime, some one else had touched them."

"Dear me," I murmured, "so that is the explanation of your extraordinary behaviour. You rushed down to Styles, and found it still there?"

"Yes, and it was a race for time."

"But I still can't understand why Inglethorp was such a fool as to leave it there when he had plenty of opportunity to destroy it."

"Ah, but he had no opportunity. *I* saw to that."

"You?"

"Yes. Do you remember reproving me for taking the household into my confidence on the subject?"

"Yes."

"Well, my friend, I saw there was just one chance. I was not sure then if Inglethorp was the criminal or not, but if he was I reasoned that he would not have the paper on him, but would have hidden it somewhere, and by enlisting the sympathy of the household I could effectually prevent his destroying it. He was already under suspicion, and by making the matter public I secured the services of about ten amateur detectives, who would be watching him unceasingly, and being himself aware of their watchfulness he would not dare seek further to destroy the document. He was therefore forced to depart from the house, leaving it in the spill vase."

"But surely Miss Howard had ample opportunities of aiding him."

"Yes, but Miss Howard did not know of the paper's existence. In accordance with their prearranged plan, she never spoke to Alfred Inglethorp. They were supposed to be deadly enemies, and until John Cavendish was safely convicted they neither of them dared risk a meeting. Of course I had a watch kept on Mr.

Inglethorp, hoping that sooner or later he would lead me to the hiding-place. But he was too clever to take any chances. The paper was safe where it was; since no one had thought of looking there in the first week, it was not likely they would do so afterwards. But for your lucky remark, we might never have been able to bring him to justice."

"I understand that now; but when did you first begin to suspect Miss Howard?"

"When I discovered that she had told a lie at the inquest about the letter she had received from Mrs. Inglethorp."

"Why, what was there to lie about?"

"You saw that letter? Do you recall its general appearance?"

"Yes—more or less."

"You will recollect, then, that Mrs. Inglethorp wrote a very distinctive hand, and left large clear spaces between her words. But if you look at the date at the top of the letter you will notice that 'July 17th' is quite different in this respect. Do you see what I mean?"

"No," I confessed, "I don't."

"You do not see that that letter was not written on the 17th, but on the 7th—the day after Miss Howard's departure? The '1' was written in before the '7' to turn it into the '17th'."

"But why?"

"That is exactly what I asked myself. Why does Miss Howard suppress the letter written on the 17th, and produce this faked one instead? Because she did not wish to show the letter of the 17th. Why, again? And at once a suspicion dawned in my mind. You will remember my saying that it was wise to beware of people who were not telling you the truth."

"And yet," I cried indignantly, "after that, you gave me two reasons why Miss Howard could not have committed the crime!"

"And very good reasons too," replied Poirot. "For a long time they were a stumbling-block to me until I remembered a very significant fact: that she and Alfred Inglethorp were cousins. She could not have committed the crime single-handed, but the reasons against that did not debar her from being an accomplice. And, then, there was that rather over-vehement hatred of hers! It concealed a very opposite emotion. There was, undoubtedly, a tie of passion between them long before he came to Styles. They had already arranged their infamous plot—that he should marry this rich, but rather foolish old lady, induce her to make a will leaving her money to him, and then gain their ends by a very cleverly conceived crime. If all had gone as they planned, they would probably have left England, and lived together on their poor victim's money.

"They are a very astute and unscrupulous pair. While suspicion was to be directed against him, she would be making quiet preparations for a very different *dénouement*. She arrives from Middlingham with all the compromising items in her possession. No suspicion attaches to her. No notice is paid to her coming and going in the house. She hides the strychnine and glasses in John's room. She puts the beard in the attic. She will see to it that sooner or later they are duly discovered."

"I don't quite see why they tried to fix the blame on John," I remarked. "It would have been much easier for them to bring the crime home to Lawrence."

"Yes, but that was mere chance. All the evidence against him arose out of pure accident. It must, in fact, have been distinctly annoying to the pair of schemers."

"His manner was unfortunate," I observed thoughtfully.

"Yes. You realize, of course, what was at the back of that?"

"No."

"You did not understand that he believed Mademoiselle Cynthia guilty of the crime?"

"No," I exclaimed, astonished. "Impossible!"

"Not at all. I myself nearly had the same idea. It was in my mind when I asked Mr. Wells that first question about the will. Then there were the bromide powders which she had made up, and her clever male impersonations, as Dorcas recounted them to us. There was really more evidence against her than anyone else."

"You are joking, Poirot!"

"No. Shall I tell you what made Monsieur Lawrence turn so pale when he first entered his mother's room on the fatal night? It was because, whilst his mother lay there, obviously poisoned, he

saw, over your shoulder, that the door into Mademoiselle
Cynthia's room was unbolted."

"But he declared that he saw it bolted?" I cried.

"Exactly," said Poirot dryly. "And that was just what
confirmed my suspicion that it was not. He was shielding Mademoiselle Cynthia."

"But why should he shield her?"

"Because he is in love with her."

I laughed.

"There, Poirot, you are quite wrong! I happen to know for a
fact that, far from being in love with her, he positively dislikes
her."

"Who told you that, *mon ami?*"

"Cynthia herself."

"*La pauvre petite!* And she was concerned?"

"She said that she did not mind at all."

"Then she certainly did mind very much," remarked Poirot.
"They are like that—*les femmes!*"

"What you say about Lawrence is a great surprise to me," I
said.

"But why? It was most obvious. Did not Monsieur Lawrence
make the sour face every time Mademoiselle Cynthia spoke and
laughed with his brother? He had taken it into his long head that
Mademoiselle Cynthia was in love with Monsieur John. When
he entered his mother's room, and saw her obviously poisoned, he
jumped to the conclusion that Mademoiselle Cynthia knew
something about the matter. He was nearly driven desperate.
First he crushed the coffee-cup to powder under his feet, remembering that *she* had gone up with his mother the night before,
and he determined that there should be no chance of testing its
contents. Thenceforward, he strenuously, and quite uselessly,
upheld the theory of 'Death from natural causes.'"

"And what about the 'extra coffee-cup?'"

"I was fairly certain that it was Mrs. Cavendish who had hidden it, but I had to make sure. Monsieur Lawrence did not know
at all what I meant; but, on reflection, he came to the conclusion

that if he could find an extra coffee-cup anywhere his lady love would be cleared of suspicion. And he was perfectly right."

"One thing more. What did Mrs. Inglethorp mean by her dying words?"

"They were, of course, an accusation against her husband."

"Dear me, Poirot," I said with a sigh, "I think you have explained everything. I am glad it has all ended so happily. Even John and his wife are reconciled."

"Thanks to me."

"How do you mean—thanks to you?"

"My dear friend, do you not realize that it was simply and solely the trial which has brought them together again? That John Cavendish still loved his wife, I was convinced. Also, that she was equally in love with him. But they had drifted very far apart. It all arose from a misunderstanding. She married him without love. He knew it. He is a sensitive man in his way, he would not force himself upon her if she did not want him. And, as he withdrew, her love awoke. But they are both unusually proud, and their pride held them inexorably apart. He drifted into an entanglement with Mrs. Raikes, and she deliberately cultivated the friendship of Dr. Bauerstein. Do you remember the day of John Cavendish's arrest, when you found me deliberating over a big decision?"

"Yes, I quite understood your distress."

"Pardon me, *mon ami*, but you did not understand it in the least. I was trying to decide whether or not I would clear John Cavendish at once. I could have cleared him—though it might have meant a failure to convict the real criminals. They were entirely in the dark as to my real attitude up to the very last moment —which partly accounts for my success."

"Do you mean that you could have saved John Cavendish from being brought to trial?"

"Yes, my friend. But I eventually decided in favour of 'a woman's happiness.' Nothing but the great danger through which they have passed could have brought these two proud souls together again."

I looked at Poirot in silent amazement. The colossal cheek of the little man! Who on earth but Poirot would have thought of a trial for murder as a restorer of conjugal happiness!

"I perceive your thoughts, *mon ami,*" said Poirot, smiling at me. "No one but Hercule Poirot would have attempted such a thing! And you are wrong in condemning it. The happiness of one man and one woman is the greatest thing in all the world."

His words took me back to earlier events. I remembered Mary as she lay white and exhausted on the sofa, listening, listening. There had come the sound of the bell below. She had started up. Poirot had opened the door, and meeting her agonized eyes had nodded gently. "Yes, madame," he said. "I have brought him back to you." He had stood aside, and as I went out I had seen the look in Mary's eyes, as John Cavendish had caught his wife in his arms.

"Perhaps you are right, Poirot," I said gently. "Yes, it is the greatest thing in the world."

Suddenly, there was a tap at the door, and Cynthia peeped in.

"I—I—only——"

"Come in," I said, springing up.

She came in, but did not sit down.

"I—only wanted to tell you something——"

"Yes?"

Cynthia fidgeted with a little tassel for some moments, then, suddenly exclaiming: "You dears!," kissed first me and then Poirot, and rushed out of the room again.

"What on earth does this mean?" I asked, surprised.

It was very nice to be kissed by Cynthia, but the publicity of the salute rather impaired the pleasure.

"It means that she has discovered Monsieur Lawrence does not dislike her as much as she thought," replied Poirot philosophically.

"But——"

"Here he is."

Lawrence at that moment passed the door.

"Eh! Monsieur Lawrence," called Poirot. "We must congratulate you, is it not so?"

Lawrence blushed, and then smiled awkwardly. A man in love is a sorry spectacle. Now Cynthia had looked charming.

I sighed.

"What is it, *mon ami?*"

"Nothing," I said sadly. "They are two delightful women!"

"And neither of them is for you?" finished Poirot. "Never mind. Console yourself, my friend. We may hunt together again, who knows? And then——"

THE END